The Sapphire Ghost

Books by EM Templin

Seraphine Ghosts
Book 1: The Sapphire Ghost

Coming Soon!
Book 2: The Sapphire Ghost Reprisal
Book 3: Purple Sapphire Ghost Apparitions
Book 4: The Legacies Warfare
Book 5: The Original and Legacies – Collective Chaos

For more information
visit: SpeakingVolumes.us

The Sapphire Ghost

EM Templin

SPEAKING VOLUMES, LLC
NAPLES, FLORIDA
2025

The Sapphire Ghost

Copyright © 2024 by EM Templin

All rights reserved. No part of this book may be reproduced or transmitted in any form or by any means without written permission.

ISBN 979-8-89022-224-4

To all the real-life heroes who work tirelessly
to help those affected by human trafficking.

Acknowledgments

To Ray and Cole who put up with me hiding away to complete this book.
To my agent Al Longden for helping me make this dream a reality.
A special thank you: Matthew Doty who was always available when I called with strange questions. Diane Padgett and Mary Tamburello for believing in this story.

Chapter One

April 28, 2014

Apprehension hung rancid in the air like stale garbage on a hot summer day.

Congressman Phillip Ashman toyed with the gray invitation with the gift of malevolence that had brought him to this address. He wondered about *the Ghost,* the man who made the request. This mysterious person was reputed to be an undiluted form of justice. Stories of him were shared around dark lodges with nervous laughter whenever a colleague came tumbling down. The Ghost had become a legend, almost mythic, over two decades.

The congressman felt the hair prickle the back of his thick neck. He tugged at the collar of his white dress shirt. Ashman's ordinarily pale face was now blotched red, accentuating what was left of his blond hair. He took a paper napkin from the stainless-steel double-sided dispenser on the table, wiped it across his light brows, and contemplated what he might have done to be brought to the attention of such an individual. The Ghost, a name he had heard in gossip and rumor, was a man whose reputation was synonymous with dread and cloaked in fear. Luckily, he felt he did not fit the Ghost's standard victim. If he were meant to be a victim, surely he would not have been given an invitation to his own execution? The neatly handwritten note inside the envelope simply said: *Your presence is requested at 124 North Street, Satsuma, Alabama on April 28th at 2:00 p.m.* That did not sound like a threat; however, it was not something the congressman felt he could ignore.

The red vinyl creaked under Ashman's weight as he watched out the large street-side windows of the vacant diner. Then he turned to observe the interior. A long mirror stretched behind the entire length of the counter. This allowed him to see the whole space, every corner, even the old, exposed pipes across the ceiling painted in a gunmetal gray. The smell of pine-scented cleaning products permeated the restaurant but did little to mask the aroma of recently fried foods, particularly hamburgers. His stomach grumbled. After all, he had taken no time to grab a bite to eat because he was too nervous.

Ashman looked again at his watch, wondering when the Ghost would arrive. Just then, the door to the kitchen pivoted open. A smart-looking, huge, dark-skinned man of around fifty walked through. He wore a charcoal gray Armani suit, neatly trimmed short hair, and a black anchor beard. The man, over six feet tall, stopped observed the setting.

The gentleman noted the congressman sitting in the back booth while he stood inside the door for a few long moments. Then, he tapped something into the smartphone in his right hand. This man walked to the front of the counter, took a seat at one of the red and chrome bar stools, and looked out the front window.

The congressman heard other footsteps behind the kitchen door within a few minutes. Another man entered, this one of average height, olive skin, and brown curly hair. The second gentleman wore a light blue-gray pinstriped suit with a plain white button-down shirt, no tie, and a dark gray felt fedora. Then, a third, a much younger man, came in behind the second one. The third man was dressed identically to the first. He looked Latino, the congressman noted, shorter than the others, and walked with a notable limp. This one went to the drinks cooler next to the ice cream freezer.

The Latino, possibly Colombian, slid the lid to the side of the old-fashioned red and white cooler. Taking out four small glass bottles, the smaller fellow popped the cap off the first and handed it to his acquaintance at the counter. In rapid succession, he opened two more. Pushing the last bottle against the opener on the cooler, he removed the cap, strolled over to the booth, and set a bottle in front of the congressman. He then placed the other soda opposite the congressman. Without a word, he returned to perch on a stool beside the first man. The second guy with the fedora stood behind the counter, watching something outside the window. He stared as though looking far away. "Few places like this left," the Ghost said to no one in particular.

Turning his attention to Congressman Ashman, the Ghost approached the back booth. He removed a small Sig 9 mm from underneath his coat and placed it on the table. Then he removed his hat, laid it on top of the gun, and slid into the banquette across from the congressman. Nerves fluttered in the pit of Ashman's stomach at the sight of the weapon.

The Sapphire Ghost

The Ghost, taking his first sip from the small glass bottle, said, "Ahh, now that is good; would you not agree, congressman?"

The congressman did not respond. Ashman had not touched the bottle but noticed the water droplets pooling at the bottom. The bottle was still hissing slightly from the bubbles. The congressman was unable to respond. Ashman tugged nervously on his shirt sleeves, playing with the blue opal cufflinks. He was screaming inside, begging for his nerve to return. Eventually, Ashman willed the muteness away and recovered his voice. He lifted the cold bottle and took several long swallows to squelch the heat inside his throat and cool the lava in his stomach.

"Yes, delicious. Can't get these very many places," Congressman Ashman managed to say, his voice now entirely under control.

"You may relax; I have no intentions of harming you. You, congressman, are a man of great fortitude and morality, qualities I admire," the Ghost said. "I am sure you wonder why I have asked you here," his voice quaked in a deep baritone.

"I have sat here speculating why you sent me an invitation. I know your reputation, so I can't for the life of me understand why."

"Phillip—may I call you Phillip? Let me tell you a story. A carpenter toils away, creating beautiful hand-crafted furniture pieces to display, tables, chairs, and a couple of bookcases. He toils long hours sanding and waxing each piece, so the woodgrains exhibit their color. The next week, he carefully loaded the furniture onto the bed of his truck and delivered it to a local shop. Along the way, a deer runs in front of the carpenter's truck, forcing him to stop abruptly. Those fine pieces of handmade art scatter and fall from the truck's bed. The question is, how does the carpenter deal with the loss of hours of labor and love poured into each piece?" The Ghost said, studying the congressman before he continued.

"This is more of a social call, and I am sure you will understand once you see what directed my attention to you." The Ghost then motioned to the Latino.

The younger man approached. He pulled a large gray envelope from the inside of his suit jacket and handed it to the Ghost. *Military* thought Ashman.

On the lapel of his charcoal suit was a single gold bar with two square blue sapphires. The man, who appeared to be a bodyguard, had no other jewelry or visible tattoos.

"I do not know; how does the carpenter cope with all that work being lost?" Ashman asked, curiosity urging him to ask.

"The carpenter picks up each piece and grieves over the lost beauty, but the furniture could still be of some use with some sanding and modifications. He takes it back to his workshop, knocks down the course bumps, smooths some rough edges, and cuts the legs to shorten a table. The next day, the carpenter takes them to a music school on the other side of the county. He offers to donate the damaged furniture to the dean, who gratefully accepts the gifts and asks for his card. The carpenter receives many phone calls for orders for the distressed furniture the following week. The dean gave the carpenter's number to those who admired his donated crafted pieces.

"You see, the carpenter took something broken and seemingly tragic and began to design unusual pieces that kept him busy for years. Had he decided that his only way to leave his mark on the world was by perfection, safe and comfortable, he would have missed a bountiful possibility. It is all about how you decide to see unexpected opportunities."

The congressman considered the story and its meaning. Was the Ghost giving him an unplanned opportunity? While he wondered, the Ghost removed the contents from the envelope and spread them on the table.

"Your bodyguards?" Ashman motioned to the two in the gray suits.

Looking over his staff, the Ghost responded. "They are much more than bodyguards. They are my prevention team. In my business, I need trust without question. They prevent me from being seen and becoming an actual ghost. I guess you could call them my shields to the modern world."

When the Ghost spoke again, Ashman realized there were no cameras inside the diner, but the Ghost continued before he could think about it.

"Do you recall close to a dozen donations to your campaign you received in intervals over six months, totaling three million dollars? I am sure you would remember donations of that size," The Ghost said, laying out the contents of the envelope in front of his audience of one.

The Sapphire Ghost

Ashman noticed the intense set of his jaw, the brown eyes, and the heavy dark brows with two vertical furrows like an eleven creased in between. The dark brown curly hair on his head seemed unnatural. Honestly, he was not someone you would take great notice of except for his gray-blue, tailored, well-cut suit, which was most definitely bespoke.

On Ghost's lapel was a pin as those of his bodyguards. It had a single princess-cut sapphire surrounded by eight small diamonds, discreet and barely noticeable against the color of his clothes. His gaze dropped to Ghost's left hand, where he noted a nasty scar on the back like a knife wound.

Ashman's thoughts wrenched back to the table when he saw something repulsive on the 8x10 photograph the Ghost laid directly in front of him. There were naked bodies of dead children, gray and dirty, tossed across one another like euthanized dogs. Ashman quickly looked up from the photograph. The Ghost gazed deep into the congressman's light blue eyes and watched Ashman's facial expression. The Ghost saw what he needed to see in them: eyes widened with genuine surprise. It was clear to the Ghost that the congressman had no knowledge of his most abundant benefactor.

"This is what Herbert Enterprises is into," the Ghost remarked.

"Herbert Enterprises sells boats off the Port of Mobile!" Ashman exclaimed.

Ashman's face seemed to want to run away as it grew red, and the lines began to fade around his eyes. He looked down at the picture again and swallowed the bile coming up.

"It is a shell company for something larger. As far as I have researched, the head is Jack or Byron King." The Ghost leaned back against the red vinyl as the seat creaked in protest. He gestured for the congressman to look through the rest of the papers.

Ashman turned the photograph face down, squeezing his eyes shut as if he could erase the image from his mind. The light in the diner seemed to dim while the room became claustrophobic, closing in on him. After a deep breath, he began filtering through the material before him. His usually steady hand trembled slightly, and Ashman could feel perspiration trickle down his chest.

Ashman read over the ledger, which showed mountains of cash flow in and out of Herbert Enterprises. Another entity, Camden Harbor Quest, apparently out of Australia, had the same corporate address.

"No such company in Australia," the Ghost said, reading his thoughts. "Camden Harbor Quest is a front for the world's largest online child pornography network."

The Ghost leaned onto the table, overlapping his fingers on the envelope, and softly spoke as he turned the harsh photograph back over. "Those children, mostly American, were used up and sent out to be dumped into the sea when one of my *friends* intersected the freight."

"Holy sh . . . oot!" the congressman uttered. "I'll get an investigation started, return the money. I don't want any part of this."

The Ghost noted the congressman's lack of color on his face. His voice quivered as he spoke, and his hands shook relentlessly. The Ghost motioned for the younger man to bring another soda. The Ghost watched as Luca placed a second bottle in front of Ashman.

"Have another cola. I think your blood sugar is low," the Ghost remarked.

Ashman took the bottle with an unsteady hand, nearly letting it slip as spots danced in his vision. He drained the entire bottle without taking a breath. With a casual bluntness, the Ghost got to the point of the meeting.

"Now listen carefully. You will not indicate that you know any more than you did fifteen minutes ago," The Ghost said. "You will, however, invite them to your next fundraiser. If anyone from Herbert Enterprises accepts the invitation, I need you to call that number," he added, sliding a gray card over to him. "That is all I want from you."

Ashman took the shiny card, holding it between his thumb and index finger, and studied it. Only a single phone number was neatly written on one side under a red G. After hearing other politicians malign the Ghost for his illegal and deadly missions, Ashman wanted to see another gray envelope making its way to the FBI's backroom.

"That's all you want?" Ashman's voice was higher pitched than usual.

"A deer has run out in front of your truck, and you've hit the brakes. What you do with the broken furniture is up to you," the Ghost said.

The Sapphire Ghost

The congressman stared at the Ghost, who seemed to be in a quiet state of reflection.

"What about . . . that *money*?" Ashman nearly slurred the word like it tasted terrible.

"Do with that what you will. Use it for your campaign, Phillip. I would really appreciate you being reelected. Then maybe you can promote a bill you believe in and join Congressman Ashley Jeffries on H.R B47345." The Ghost smiled, but it was a sad one. "You will not speak to anyone about this meeting. There is no need to collect anything for fingerprints as I do not have any," the Ghost said. He held up his fingers to show his smooth finger pads.

The Ghost slid out and stood up, replacing the hat and tucking the gun in the holster at his back under his jacket. "I am hoping for a long, productive relationship, Phillip. I think you are a rare man of integrity. As with the carpenter, sometimes we can see what is possible even if it is not what we anticipated." He looked directly at the congressman, still holding the card with all that information on the table.

Chapter Two

As soon as the three men left the diner, Luca Medina, the Colombian, changed the car's plates from Georgia to Texas. Luca was the youngest member of the Sapphire Order and had served the Ghost for seven years. Gavin Garrison sat in the sedan's back, gently removed the latex from his face and left hand and carefully placed it in the protective cases. He removed the brown contact lenses, dropped them back in their case, and added eyedrops to his gray eyes. Sliding the wig off, Gavin scratched at his short salt-and-pepper hair.

He took his tan leather satchel from the floorboard and pulled out a heavy brown expanding cardboard folder. He was studying the papers and photographs inside yet again. The King was invisible; nothing led directly to him. The cargo he was into was kids. Ages did not matter; Gavin Garrison's people had intercepted children from three to nineteen. Most of these children had been abducted from malls and backyards or bought from drug-addicted parents. Others were from impoverished countries where families were so destitute that parents sold their children into slavery every day.

Videos of the crimes against the children were easily accessible on the internet. What the perpetrators did to them was indescribable. The more depraved, sinister, and painful, the more he sold. King had neither conscience nor soul. The disturbing way he directed the movies proved he did not view these children as anything more than traded cattle.

King had an army of collectors who thought nothing of grabbing a child off the street in broad daylight. These collectors often used a puppy to lure a child into a van or truck. They cared more for the little puppy than they did for the child they were kidnapping. Gavin thought King and those who worked with him had escaped hell. The pain this man caused, the absolute destruction, made the Devil dance.

Gavin looked at the picture of the kids his people rescued five years ago. The boat was found off the coast of Costa Rica and hid a dozen children. A fourteen-year-old blonde girl who took him by the hand and would not let go still put a lump in his throat. Twelve kids in all, seven of whom died from their injuries or dehydration. That little girl was damaged but appeared to be resilient. Gavin could still see those brown eyes looking up at him as she held his hand. He often wondered what became of the children he rescued, whether they found any sense of a productive life.

Gavin was a Ghost, one of a handful of the Seraphim Ghosts. His role as the original Ghost was the first one recruited by Helen Glass. The sapphire stone he wore gave his order definition from the others. The Emerald, Ruby, and Pearl came behind him, and those stones now sat with their lights turned out in Arcadia. A couple of others remained.

Gavin lived in the shadows of the relative world, with no background or identity. His life depended on Rusty and Luca keeping him hidden. Then there were the Dark 9, an army, scouts, and guards used to help the orders. They had one objective, and that was to keep the Ghosts alive.

Gavin shook the image from his head, closing his cool gray eyes.

"I just called Dark 9 in Kansas City; they will have him by the time we arrive," said Rusty, the large, dark gentleman and the Ghost's right hand and most trusted advisor.

"Kansas City will be our first stop. The jury is still out in Brentworth," Gavin told him.

Rusty glanced over at Gavin. "It's that time of year again," he said, motioning to the photograph in Gavin's hand.

Gavin looked down and tucked it back inside the envelope. "I'm fine."

Rusty knew this girl's photograph reminded Gavin of his twin sister. Celeste was abducted when they were twelve, and she and their mother had been shopping when their mother turned away for only a minute, and Celeste disappeared.

"Want to talk about it?" Rusty asked.

"Nothing to talk about; there never is," Gavin said, taking out his sunglasses to cover his eyes. Rusty could read him all too well.

Rusty looked over at his closest friend of seventeen years. They had been through hell and back together. He knew that Gavin saw his sister in each face of every child. In each pair of eyes, he dove into deep despair, a place of heart-wrenching misery. Rusty also knew that was why Gavin had so little faith in the legal system. The Ghost's brand of justice was cruel because he wanted each person involved in hurting children to suffer as he still suffered. Rusty understood the mask of the Ghost and why he hid behind it so fervently.

"You are making a difference, even if sometimes it does not seem so," Rusty said.

"Most days, I know this. The world no longer needs heroes—it needs monsters to destroy monsters. To pull the latex from their faces and expose them to the world for what they really are. Instead, now they make Gods out of criminals," Gavin said.

"There are families who will never have to go through that pain because of what we do," Rusty replied.

Luca drove out of town and listened to the annual conversation behind him. Gavin's pain was still raw after forty-two years. He peered at them from the rearview mirror.

"She would have loved today, so bright and beautiful. She loved spring and watching the world come back to life. Celeste was such a gentle soul." Gavin's heart hurt as the memories washed over him yet again. He had an image of her bright blonde curls littered with daisies and dandelions. "I often wonder if God laughs at me. As you know, my parents named me Gavriel, Hero to God. I am no hero."

It only took a minute to tear apart love, joy, and a family. The FBI was called in to help find the young girl, but they never found a trace, and the case grew cold and unsolved. His mother drank herself into the grave, and his father sheltered his son from the world. Gavin lived six lonely, dark years with empty, lifeless vessels in his house. His life fell apart because of a minute when his mother's back was turned. In sixty heart-wrenching seconds, his life was destroyed.

Chapter Three

Luca drove onto the private airstrip, thinking Gavin had too much packed into this week. Then again, it was that time of year. This meeting with Congressman Ashman, then the senator from Missouri, and, if the jury returned with any verdict other than guilty, they would head to Brentworth, Missouri. It was usually like this whenever Gavin took a holiday, and he returned with one to two weeks of personal targets and renewed energy.

The Cessna Citation flew into the jetport outside Kansas City at 5:00 p.m. Marshal, the pilot, taxied up to the side of a terminal and cut the engines. After they deplaned, Luca went for the keys and slid into the driver's seat of a blue Lincoln Navigator. Luca drove it over to meet his teammates, and Rusty placed the bags in the back. The Dark 9 members assigned to them sent Luca information on the meeting place, so he headed straight into the city. Gavin mused in the back over the scorecard he had for this trip. They would spend much time in the air, but he would accomplish a lot.

"I made dinner reservations at the Ambassador Hotel. It is discreet and quiet, and we need to have a meal," Rusty said.

"That is fine, but we need to visit the senator first. I do not understand why he voted that way!" Gavin exclaimed while acknowledging that Rusty needed to eat, especially in his condition. "It took me five years to convince Congressman Jeffries to pursue a bill that would help create an international network of law enforcement to track and catch child smugglers and to help with aid to those children."

"Do we ever understand the motivations of people?" Rusty asked.

"No, I guess not. Maybe I did not make myself clear," Gavin replied.

"You were explicit. The senator did not heed your warning," Rusty said gravely.

Thirty minutes later, Luca pulled into a parking structure in the middle of the city.

"They are a twenty-minute walk from here," Luca stated as he exited the SUV. He looked carefully around before opening Gavin's door.

The trio descended the lower-floor stairs and emerged onto the street. Gavin stopped outside the building and adjusted the collar on his wool-cashmere topcoat. The evening air had quite a chill as he buttoned it, then placed a fedora low on his head.

"Come on; we will be there in a few minutes," Luca instructed.

Luca guided them west. As they took the next left, numerous police cars turned the corner, lights and sirens blaring. Rusty held Gavin back, and they instinctively headed to the door of the nearest bistro. Their hearts beat fast. The police cars headed down the block toward their meeting.

"How is everything?" Luca asked into the com, listening to the response. "No, sit tight."

"What is going on, Luca?" Rusty asked as panic hit his chest. Rusty looked ahead at the dozen or so police cars blocking the street.

"Nothing regarding us; we are in the clear. We will need to find another route, though. The team leader said the police surrounded a store across from their position," Luca informed them.

"We will just go through the crowd; they will not pay any attention to us," Gavin replied.

They walked straight up to where a group gawked behind the police cruisers blocking the street. Several officers were already standing by their cars with their weapons drawn.

"I do not like this, sir," Rusty said, as they never publicly used Gavin's name.

Luca stayed close to the left of the flashing cruisers. The crowd swelled, and they knew the media would be on site before long. Rusty and Gavin followed Luca's path as he nudged through the people. Several folks stood around with camera phones, waiting to see the action. Then, two shots rang out from inside the store. The front door shattered. Luca immediately flanked Gavin, shielding his right. Luca quickened his steps as he guided Gavin and Rusty to the end of the block. The crowd screamed, and everyone hit the ground in a terrified panic.

The Sapphire Ghost

Once past the commotion, Luca led them up a short flight of steps to an office building with a For Sale sign in the window.

A member of Dark 9 greeted them at the door, pulled it shut, and locked it behind them as they entered the office lobby. They followed her to the office to the left of the entrance. *The acoustics would work well in here, most definitely*, Gavin thought.

Standing in the reception area of the primary office, Gavin watched the man sitting in the chair. Dark 9 placed Senator Baynard in a comfortable-looking chair, his arms restrained by soft brown elastic gauze wrapped from wrist to elbows. Electrodes were visible on Baynard's chest and temples, monitoring his heart rate and brain functions. The directions were not to leave a mark on the man. Gavin took the fedora from his head and entered the room. Gavin examined the four speakers on the wall behind Baynard, sympathetically looking at the man who would not be a problem after tonight.

"I do not suppose we need introductions," Gavin said when he took the seat in front of the senator.

"Ghost, I knew you were responsible and told you I would not be intimidated." Senator Baynard recognized the voice.

"And you were right. You voted against H.R. B47345. And that was a mistake," Gavin replied.

"I told you I was not afraid of the Ghost!" Senator Baynard retorted.

"No, apparently not," Gavin said, looking directly into his heavy-lidded, dim green eyes. His skin was tanned and aged, with smoker's wrinkles around his thin lips. Baynard's mouth turned down in an eternal frown, reminding Gavin of a wooden dummy with thick furrowed brows.

Gavin pulled a piece of paper from the inner pocket of his suit jacket. He sat and looked it over. He had no desire to harm the man, but he needed him removed from his position as the finance committee chair if he wanted to make a difference.

"Release me! I am expected home," the senator demanded, "I have Senator McFadden and his family coming to the house for dinner. Whatever you are planning, let's get on with it," the senator growled.

"Twenty-one years of service to this country. You served two tours in Vietnam, earning you the Cross of Gallantry with Silver Star, Medal of Honor, the Silver Cross, and two Purple Hearts," Gavin read from the paper. "You are a war hero. A man with your record would not be intimidated by the likes of me. However, I still need you to step down. You are a man with a whip, and if a new idea does not appeal to you, it gets rejected. Why wouldn't you allow extra resources to help the victims of sex trafficking? Children? That would seem to help your reputation, not hinder it. Could you help me understand?" Gavin was relaxed; he rubbed at the short stubble he had let grow out for this occasion.

"Throwing money at that bill would not help those children; it would only cause more abuse of public resources. It is just something else to suck at the tit of the American taxpayers. We have enough going to help those organizations; grassroots organizations are doing perfectly fine."

"Grassroots organizations can only do so much. In fact, when the government collaborates with helping criminals bring these children in, it should indeed help take care of the survivors. Am I wrong?" Gavin said.

"I do not know where you get such information! The government is not in bed with criminals who traffic children!" The senator raised his voice.

"Oh, but yes, they are," Gavin said. "And if I cannot bend you, I must remove you."

"I have been in office for twenty years, and I am not going anywhere!" the senator spat.

"Not willingly." Gavin reached into the pocket of his slacks and took out a silver and white pack of cigarettes. He carefully removed the cellophane and drew one out. "Your brand, I believe?" he said, placing one between the senator's lips. Gavin lit a match, and the senator inhaled, then blew out smoke between his teeth. Gavin looked at the man and admired his pride. "Tomorrow will look . . . different."

Gavin left the senator and went to the man on the control panel right outside the office. He watched the screens that showed the senator's heart rate, and he had an even 120 over 65 blood pressure. The man was a rock, but he was also sixty-seven years old.

"Make sure his heart rate does not exceed 140 for more than fifteen minutes. I will be back in two hours to check his progress," Gavin told the middle-aged man at the control box. "Keep the headset on—and do not allow anyone without one near this room."

The man punched a button to begin the drumbeats. Gavin looked at his watch and saw it was almost six o'clock.

"Yes, sir," the man said, adjusting the earphones.

The drumbeats started, and there was absolutely no rhythm. It was random. Sometimes two beats, long pause, one beat, a brief pause. There was something about the human mind that needed to find a rhythm. The drumbeats were of Gavin's design and carried no detectable tempo. Gavin did not want to hurt the man, just make him a little foolish and force him into retirement. He already had a replacement in mind.

"We'll be going to dinner; can we bring you back anything?" Rusty asked the team leader, a tall, light-skinned man with small wire-rimmed glasses. Attached to his jacket pocket was a sapphire stone.

Rusty knew the man was the medical doctor on duty who had also set up the equipment. None of the men or women wore name badges, and Rusty rarely asked their names.

"Dr. Brody." After noting the long bar with four sapphires on the large man's lapel, the team leader introduced himself, "No, sir, thank you. Jason will get us a pizza when the police clear out."

Gavin stepped back into the hallway, leaving the senator with his thoughts for as long as he could hold on to them. Luca thoroughly checked out the office building. Finding a side exit that would be a better option, Luca directed Rusty and Gavin toward an old break area. Gavin put his hat back on, tugged his collar high, and braced to go back out in the cold.

Chapter Four

Luca led them down the street. It never seemed to matter that Luca had never been to the city they were in; he had a keen sense of direction. Neither Gavin nor Rusty questioned that he would bring them as close to the Kansas City Ambassador Hotel as possible. Gavin glanced at his watch, determining he needed to return to the office around 8:00 p.m. to check on progress and the senator's mental state. That would give him time to find out about Brentworth.

The Ambassador was nearly empty at 6:15 p.m. on a Monday. The thick, dark paneling was reminiscent of old speakeasies, and crystal chandeliers hung from the ceilings. It smelled of warm spices, delicate fish, and the thick scents of men's aftershaves and cigars. Rusty asked for a table away from foot traffic, and the male host guided them to a table near the back.

Luca took the smartphone from his suit pocket and researched the question he anticipated Gavin would ask. He checked in to the local news station covering the court proceedings. Then, he watched the woman speaking in front of the courthouse from his phone screen. She stated that the jury had been deliberating for three days, and that day alone, it had been deliberating for six hours. Luca knew they would be heading to Brentworth first thing in the morning.

"Well, Luca, what is the verdict?" Gavin asked.

Luca took the earphones out. "They are still waiting. According to the local media, the jury is still in the jury room."

"Give them another hour, and they will ask to see the judge," Rusty said.

"Yes, it looks that way," Gavin agreed.

Too often, the theatrics of a trial either pulled you to one side or the other. It did not matter whether the defendant was guilty or innocent; what mattered was who the jury liked more—and this man had hired a brilliant performer.

The server brought their meals. Gavin observed his dearest friend and sworn protector pick over the roasted hen. Rusty ate only a few bites but politely pushed the food around his plate. All these years, Rusty served beside him, and now he felt their journey was coming to an end.

Gavin rarely ate much out but enjoyed most of the lamb chop. He preferred to drink his dinner tonight and bought a cigar to accompany the alcohol from the hostess. Luca, however, dove into the oversized bacon cheeseburger and French fries, finishing every bite but a few of the fries.

"I will never understand where you put all that food," Gavin chuckled at Luca after the server took their plates.

Luca smiled contentedly.

Rusty ordered a beer after his plate was cleared. He knew Gavin saw that he did not eat and would scold him for it. With the demanding nature of their work, Helen, who oversaw their order, required that they keep healthy and eat well.

"It was a little dry," Rusty said.

"I saw. How will you keep your strength up if you pick at your food?" Gavin asked.

"I am fine, really," Rusty replied.

Gavin gave Rusty a slight nod and let the conversation drift to something else. He did not want to make Rusty feel worse. Gavin worried about him and knew the treatments were hard on him the first time. That was around the time Luca was brought into the Sapphire Order. Gavin also understood that Rusty would not be taking treatments this time. They sat talking and drinking for over an hour. Luca drank coffee and often refrained from alcohol when there was the slightest possibility he would be driving. There was the possibility that Gavin might want to leave for Brentworth tonight. When the check came, Luca took it and placed a couple hundred in the black folder. They stood, took their jackets from the host, and started to leave the hotel.

"Would you like me to get us rooms tonight?" Luca asked.

Gavin thought a moment. "Yes, would you, please?"

Luca left them standing in the restaurant and headed to the lobby. He walked up to a young-looking bald man behind the registration desk and told him they would be paying cash and leaving before 6:00 a.m. The clerk typed into his computer and smiled.

"I believe we can accommodate you, sir," he said pleasantly.

"Thank you," Luca said as he took the key cards and slid the money across the counter.

Luca returned to the others and let them know the floor and room numbers.

Chapter Five

The night had become a cold forty degrees as it was closer to 8:00 pm. Gavin wished he had brought a thicker coat because he did not like the cold. He pulled the collar up high. They headed back toward the office building that housed six Dark 9 task force members and Senator Baynard. It was now dark, and the noise and chaos earlier had cleared. Nothing but the streetlamps guided their path. The stoplight gleamed a lonely green ahead with no cars to pass through it. One lone van sat on the side of the street with a News 9 decal in bold blue letters. Gavin tugged the brim of his hat down over his forehead as they neared the van. They headed up the steps of the office building. Gavin strolled to the office on the left, where the man with the monitoring equipment sat; Luca and Rusty stood in the lobby.

Gavin approached the man in the reception room still wearing the large earphones. Gavin leaned in and peered over his shoulder, looking at the monitors, although he could hear the senator wailing from this distance. He watched the EEG and noticed a substantial amount of brain wave activity. Gavin also looked at the arrhythmia tracings. Everything on the scans looked irregular but not life-threatening. Gavin pressed pause on the drumming CD, strolled to the adjacent room, and walked in. Studying Senator Baynard, with his head bobbing and fluids running down his face. The man had sweated through his clothes, and there was the stench of something foul.

"Senator, do you know who I am?" Gavin asked as he took his handkerchief from his pocket, wiped the senator's face, and dropped it to the floor.

Senator Baynard looked at him with hints of anger in his watering eyes. "Stop this! I can't take it!" he wailed. The Ghost scraped the chair legs across the hardwood floor, and the Senator recoiled at the sound. He sat across from the senator. *Dignity was so easily lost.*

"Not all music is beautiful, but all music is beautifully tragic in some way," Gavin said. "Try to remember me."

"I will never forget you! I'll kill you if I ever get out of here," he angrily replied.

"All right. If you get out of here, I shall look forward to that."

Gavin stood, turned, walked out of the room, and closed the door behind him. He stopped by the control panel and hit play, warmly placing his hand on the Dark 9 member's shoulder. He left the reception area and walked back into the hall. Gavin motioned to the doctor with the single sapphire pinned on his pocket. Few of the Dark 9 members held the stones, and the primary purpose was to let the orders know who could be available to offer the Ghost blood in an emergency. Gavin's blood was B negative, a relatively rare blood type.

"One more hour and turn it off. Let the senator sit for an hour and then turn it back on for three hours. Repeat that until 6:00 a.m.," Gavin commanded.

"Yes, sir," the team leader, Brody, replied, adjusting the small, tinted spectacles.

"In the morning, just before his racquetball club opens, I want you to drop him there in his car," Gavin ordered. "Someone will find him and call his family. He will be incoherent and most likely raving about the Ghost by then. Do not be daunted; this is normal. Stay out of sight but watch him until he is safe. Be careful and make sure you leave no marks on him."

"Understood, sir," the team leader said. Dr. Brody had worked for Dark 9 for many years but had never come in direct contact with the Ghost himself. He understood the sternness in the eyes of the man who stood before him. Dr. Brody had observed what those drumbeats were doing to the senator. He had been a little concerned but hearing that this was something the Ghost had done before reassured him—to a degree. The senator would be off his rocker by morning.

Gavin bid the members of Dark 9 a good night and thanked them for working so effectively. While the Sapphire Order did not have its own Dark 9 team due to a lack of trust with Arcadia, the Dark 9 army was a valuable resource in events like this. Helen, who was overwatch from Arcadia headquarters, held the reins on each order.

Luca led his colleagues back to the hotel for a few hours of sleep.

The Sapphire Ghost

Luca waited for Rusty and Gavin to close the doors to their rooms before he unlocked his own and entered. He quickly took a shower and moved to the bed in just his towel. He booted his laptop to confirm he had not missed anything. None of what they were working on were Dossiers from Helen; these were personal missions that Gavin had researched. Gavin had plenty of Dossiers, and that planning was more detailed. These were more on the fly. Luca liked these best as they were more fluid and less intense. Luca looked up Brentworth and studied photographs of the small town, the main feature of which was the Brentworth Academy, a girls-only school.

Destroying those who harmed children was Gavin's life's work—serving as an ambassador to lost children, rescuing fewer than he liked. The ones he was able to return to their loved ones, he hoped would go on to do something remarkable. Although he was aware that the internal scars would affect them for life.

Gavin sat in his hotel room bed, but sleep would not come to him. The nightmares haunted him each time he closed his eyes. He promised his sister he would rid the world of such evils when he created her memorial garden. Arcadia stripped everything away, and that was when he became a Ghost. When it was not his sister's face, he saw those kids on that dock in Georgia, their black eyes and thin arms crying for him to save them. They had enslaved his heart. Would he ever make amends to them?

Chapter Six

April 30

The following day, before heading to the airport, Gavin wanted to make a detour to the racquet club where Dark 9 was to deposit Senator Baynard. Luca safely pulled the SUV out of sight and watched the parking lot in the predawn. Several light posts lit the area, and cars filled the parking lot.

Gavin watched through the tinted window and waited. At ten minutes to seven, two cars, Baynard's red Cadillac and a large black SUV, pulled up to the side of the building. The team leader emerged from the driver's side of the Cadillac and pulled the seat forward as he was several inches taller than the senator. He then emptied a bottle of rum and tossed it inside, after which he threw the keys a few feet away. He quickly opened the passenger's door of the SUV and got in. The SUV drove to a space at the back of the lot farthest from the building, where it idled. They all watched and waited to see what would happen.

The Open sign came on in the front window. Gavin saw several car doors open, and people were eager to start their day. The back door on the Cadillac opened, and the senator climbed out. Baynard looked around, confused. He tried to talk to a woman walking past him, but she avoided him and quickly headed for the door. Two men came out a few minutes later and studied the parking lot, searching for someone. One man looked at the senator, smiled, and walked toward him. Then, the man's face showed alarm as he approached. Reluctantly, he stepped closer to the senator and looked like he was trying to speak with him, but the senator started yelling. Gavin saw the man reach into his pocket for his phone.

"He is calling the police. Time for us to go," Rusty said.

Chapter Seven

Brentworth, Missouri. Just as they had predicted, the jury was hung. The judge declared a mistrial and announced the prosecution would not pursue a new trial. The justice system failed again, and now it was the Ghost's turn to set things right.

The matter had come to Gavin's attention while he took one of his brief vacations, staying on a delightful farm in Nebraska. A daughter of a family he befriended there had attended Brentworth Academy, but they pulled her out due to suicidal behavior. The family found out later, through counseling, that the girl was assaulted at the school. It took six months for the eleven-year-old to admit to who hurt her.

The police were reluctant to believe the girl. Then, several other Brentworth families spoke up after finding out this family was pressing charges. Three other girls pressed charges, forcing the DA to file a case. The school attempted to settle out of court, and two families accepted the settlements. They did not want to drag their daughters through a trial. Gavin could appreciate this. No child should have to face what the courts did to children who testified against their abusers. Lacy Martin's Nebraska family did not settle; they wanted their day in court. That had not worked out in their favor as the defendant's attorney raked both girls across the coals. The defense called them liars. The female attorney claimed they were willful, disobedient, and simply angry as the defendant's attorney brought evidence that the girls were reprimanded.

Ronald Wilkins, the headmaster of Brentworth Academy, sat his overly polished self behind the defense table, looking arrogant. Gavin made it a point to watch in person on the first day of the trial. However, after receiving some unwarranted looks from the local law enforcement, Gavin decided it would not be a good idea to continue. Instead, he cut his visit short and went back to his team.

Gavin intended to resolve this problem. He sat in deep thought and looked out the small window of the jet. Dark clouds floated below him, and he knew the hearts of those girls must be devastated learning the morning's news. *None of the four girls would have to worry about looking over their shoulders regarding this man.* That was a promise. He watched as the plane descended through the clouds, circling an airport in Greenfield outside Brentworth.

"Luca, would you come back here, please?" Gavin called.

Luca stood up from half-sleeping on the sofa and went to sit across from Gavin.

"Do you have the surveillance on the house?" Gavin asked.

"Of course," Luca said, opening his laptop on the table between them. "I have a two-person team on the ground. The wife and children have not been at home for three months. Wilkins is to return home late this morning. Do you have a plan?"

"No plan yet," Gavin said with an assuring smile. "Thank you, Luca."

"If there is anything else, just let me know," Luca replied.

The fasten seatbelt light came on in the cabin.

"Get the silver case from the closet when we land, please," Gavin told Luca as he looked to the front, where Rusty was reading. He felt awful that Rusty would not extend his previous visit to Jamaica to rest. Granted, Rusty would say that sitting around is boring. The boss man had a point; it was hard to be bored when they did what they did.

They departed the plane, and Luca went for the car. Luca pulled up to collect Gavin, and Rusty held Gavin's door open before moving to the other side to get in beside him.

"Where are we going after we are through with the business here, sir?" Luca asked.

"I think our compound in Florida at Dremmond Beach is warmer than D.C.," Gavin stated. "That is unless you two have something else you want to do."

"No, just wondering what I needed to tell Marshal," Luca said, mentioning the pilot.

The Sapphire Ghost

Rusty sat in the back seat, wondering if he could go through with telling Gavin that he would retire. Julianne convinced him that if he was not going to take any more treatments, he needed to make the most of the time he had left. Knowing Julianne wanted him to be with her so she could care for him. That sounded nice—until he thought about giving all of this up. Rusty loved doing what he, Gavin, and Luca did. Rusty acknowledged that this was not a lifestyle most people would seek. But they looked out after one another and held an unshakable belief in the cause. There was no doubt in Rusty's mind that Luca would be fine, and he would continue to give Gavin everything he had. Rusty smiled and examined the young man in the driver's seat as he relayed the directions to the pilot. Luca was always doing something and taking on more; that man only stopped when he slept. Rusty worried a little about Luca's giving up driving to take his place beside the Ghost as his confidant. Luca would fall asleep if he had to constantly ride in the back seat, but Rusty was sure he would figure something out.

Luca took his time driving the backroads of Brentworth, wishing he had taken a croissant at the hotel before they left. He lifted the paper cup of coffee from the cupholder and sipped the cold coffee.

Luca received notification early this morning that Ronald Wilkins was leaving Springfield, where the trial was held. He had time to find a diner, get breakfast, and find a park bench where they could eat. It was sunny this Tuesday morning, and the temperature would be in the high fifties this afternoon. Luca pulled into a Denny's and went inside to order.

Luca was back in the car with the bag on the seat beside him twenty minutes later. Rusty and Gavin were locked tight in a discussion, which seemed heated.

"You do not have to retire!" Luca heard Gavin say. A lump formed in Luca's throat, and he peered in the rearview mirror. Luca did not want Rusty to retire but knew the time was coming, with his condition worsening. He also knew this was a very emotional decision on Rusty's part because the pull was strong between worlds he loved.

Luca took a left onto a street leading to a park and parked. He waited for the discussion in the back to pause.

"Would you prefer to eat in the car?" Luca asked, finding a lull in the conversation.

"No, I am not hungry." Rusty sounded battered.

"Would you care to add anything to this?" Gavin asked Luca.

"Sir, it is not my place," Luca responded respectfully.

Gavin took his paper-wrapped biscuit from Luca over the seat and stared out the window, watching a young man playing ball with a dog. Knowing he could not make this decision for Rusty, he would try to dissuade him. It was not only that he depended on Rusty; he was Gavin's closest friend. The thought of Rusty not being around sent a terrible ache through Gavin. Gavin knew this made him selfish because Julianne deserved to have Rusty with her during this heartbreaking time. Gavin's world was small, and those he trusted and loved were few, and that was by design. He looked at the half-unwrapped biscuit on his lap and rewrapped it. They sat in the car for another twenty minutes as Luca ate and looked at his tablet.

"Gavin, please understand that I will become a burden in the next couple of months, and I am unwilling to put that on you," Rusty said.

"You will never be a burden, my friend . . . if I have to stop doing anything until you take your last breath." Gavin felt selfish declaring this, understanding that Julianne had a say in the decision.

"That is not fair to you or this Order, and I will not do it," Rusty stated as a wave of determination hit him.

Gavin pondered for a long time. What if the situation were reversed? What would he want? He loved what he did and what it all stood for but would not want Rusty or Luca watching his decline. No, he would not want them to see what could become of him, not just in body but eventually to his mind. Rusty was in for a horrible end, and being with Julianne on the island would be the best place for him. Rusty could become a liability to the Order.

Gavin opened the SUV door and climbed out, "Luca, will you join me?"

Luca looked in the rearview mirror to meet Rusty's eyes staring back at him. Rusty gave Luca a short nod. Luca got out and followed Gavin onto the grassy area where he stood.

"Did you ever order that plane I asked about a few months ago?" Gavin asked.

"Yes, sir, it's in Galveston," Luca replied, thinking about the small Learjet. They needed to replace the small one they used for the local airports in remote locations.

"Good. Can you get it flown to Destin?" Gavin asked.

"Absolutely," Luca replied.

"We will give it to Rusty so he can come and go whenever he chooses," Gavin said.

"Wonderful idea, sir," Luca said.

"Luca, are you ready to step into his shoes? I think you are."

"Those are some big shoes," Luca said and gave him a nervous smile. He was uncomfortable speaking about this.

"I have complete confidence in your abilities, and I am certain Rusty feels the same. Talk it over with him when you can and reconcile any apprehension." Gavin headed back to the car.

Gavin watched as two little children played near the ditch by the road. The mother was distracted by something on her phone. Some people were simple in their naivete; others were simply stupid.

Luca stood on the grassy knoll, watching Gavin observe the boys playing out of their mother's sight, and he readied himself.

"Don't do it, Gavin," Rusty warned under his breath, noticing the set of Gavin's jaw.

Gavin closed the car door and strolled down the sidewalk. He approached the boys. Rusty looked around the park. Gavin knelt before the boys, spoke to them for a few minutes, and then took their hands. Luca stopped walking momentarily as he noted Rusty was stepping out of the car, and he relaxed. The idea that the mother could call the police was not pleasant.

Chapter Eight

The carousel horses rocked up and down to the melody of a familiar childhood tune. Jack King sat on a park bench with a bag of popcorn. King ran a hand through his curly gray hair, removed the black-rimmed glasses, and tucked them inside his shirt pocket. His deep-set black eyes watched a young girl walk by in a paisley dress.

His niece was turning eight, and his brother's family had invited him to an afternoon birthday party at the park. King watched his niece and a sweet-looking blonde girl glide up and down on two pink horses as they giggled.

The ride slowed, and King stood and went up on the platform to help his niece and the blonde from the horses. He cradled the blonde in his arms, gently rubbing her bare leg. His niece followed him from the ride.

"Jack, thank you so much," an attractive woman said as she took her daughter from his arms.

"She is so lovely," he replied.

"She is so shy; I have tried to enter her in some pageants, but she freezes so bad she will not even walk out on the stage," the mother replied.

"I see it all the time. It takes some children longer than others to adjust to the spotlight," King said as he tickled the girl while his niece yelled, "Me next!"

King took his niece by her chubby fingers, thinking his brother needed to put the child on a diet. But this was his brother's third family, and Jack knew Byron tuned out of any child-related decisions.

"Uncle Jack, when are you going to make me a movie star?" The little girl asked her uncle the burning question as he walked her back to the group.

"We'll see, honey," King answered, thinking, *never!* He took out his phone to call the head of Fox Phantom.

Byron, his brother, called earlier to tell him they had a new lead on the Ghost.

Chapter Nine

Gavin walked back up the hill and stood quietly at the young mother's side. She wore an oversized T-shirt and sweatpants with LOVE written down the side. Her hair was messy, and she probably had not done it in a year. Gavin studied the woman and recognized the look; she was exhausted. He cleared his throat.

"What are you doing with my boys?" she cried out and rushed to her sons.

"Returning them to your sight," Gavin stated.

"Don't touch them." She took her children's hands.

"It would be that easy. They have been out of your view since I arrived. Don't think it could not happen to you because it never has. Eight hundred thousand children go missing each year, and most are never found. Be more careful; I would rather not see those darling faces on the back of a milk carton."

Gavin gave her a once-over, reached into his pocket, and took out his money clip. He handed her what he had. "Get a sitter and go take some time for yourself," he said, brushing a strand of hair from her face and walking away.

Luca extracted the phone and dialed Galveston. He needed a pilot to bring the plane to Destin, and the mechanic told him he would handle it. Luca thanked the gentleman and closed the phone. Luca looked over at the car, ensuring that Gavin had returned and took to the paved trail. His eyes became moist, and he was not ready to return to the vehicle or Rusty. Luca felt like someone had kneed him in the gut, and the steak and egg biscuit he had eaten was rebelling.

Gavin watched Luca as he headed down the paved walking path in the park's center. Luca threw up the breakfast he had just eaten in the grass and took a white handkerchief from his pocket.

Rusty also noted that Luca did not return to the car with Gavin, and he could imagine what Gavin said to him—giving Luca his job, but not giving him the option of taking his place. Rusty knew that they hurt for him, and he was exhausted from seeing their concern. Luca was a good man, always following orders but not in a docile way. He always brought his concerns up that they might have yet to consider. Luca was profoundly aware of his surroundings. That was the Green Beret in him.

Rusty allowed Luca to take point whenever they would be in public. Rarely in the seven years since they met had Rusty ever truly seen Luca upset; he always had a calm temperament and an easy-going but quiet personality. Rusty was keenly aware of what Luca kept bottled up. Rusty learned about him from a commanding officer who served in Iraq with Luca. He thought about Luca's willpower to return his leg to normal. He gave complete devotion to him and Gavin. Yes, he could trust Luca with Gavin or anything else. Luca would always be a soldier, less prosaic, and a more refined soldier to their Order. Rusty felt he would take the Oath without hesitation. The Sapphire Order needed to go on, and they needed to continue their work.

Gavin returned to the car, satisfied the mother would not lose sight of her children again. He and Rusty watched as Luca made a few more laps on the walkway and returned to the car. Luca got back behind the wheel and said nothing. Picking up the tablet, Luca saw he had missed a message from a member on the ground at the house. '*Wilkins just pulled into the garage,*' the message read.

"Wilkins has returned home," Luca informed as he finished the coffee he had bought at Denny's and then opened a pack of mints. "What do you want to do, Gavin?"

"Let us head on in. We will make this short," Gavin replied, appreciating the quiet way Luca handled his emotions.

Luca turned right out of the park and back onto the town's main street, headed toward the suburban area to Ronald Wilkins's house.

Rusty stared out the window, wanting not to feel so bad about having this conversation.

Luca took the street leading to Ronald Wilkin's home. All the houses had a similar look: two-story, in varied shades of brown. They had neat, narrow front porches, immaculate white concrete walkways, and overbearing garages

The Sapphire Ghost

with doors that matched the shutters on boxy, treeless streets. Luca pulled into a driveway with a For Sale sign out front.

Rusty took the silver case from the floorboards and opened it on the seat between Gavin and himself. He took out a 9mm and attached a silencer; Gavin did the same. Neither man offered one to Luca, knowing he preferred other disciplinary methods when he had the option.

They let themselves out of the SUV and followed Luca down the tidy walkway. They walked around the bicycles leaning against the side of the house. Rusty kept watching for traffic and any people who might be out walking. But it was quiet, and it seemed that most of the neighborhood was at work.

Luca opened the lockbox with a number he had obtained by hacking into the Realtor's office's computer server. He waited for the other two to join him. Luca opened the door slowly, and they listened and heard nothing. Luca entered first, taking in the pile of children's shoes and discarded mail by the door. He went through the door leading into the kitchen, cocking his head. The shower was running upstairs, and he motioned with his hand for Gavin and Rusty to follow him.

Gavin stepped into the small, uninspiring kitchen with its bright yellow walls, pear wallpaper trim at the ceiling, and brown cabinetry. He laid his fedora on the table and investigated the open living area. Luca went ahead to assess the layout of the rest of the house, and he walked halfway up the stairs. Rusty started the teapot on the stove, took down four yellow teacups, and found a Harney & Sons Hot Cinnamon Spice tea box.

Gavin noted the toys in the corner of the space designated for the living area. He felt a little sad for the family. The For Sale sign in the front suggested that the wife and children would not return. Gavin looked at a family portrait: a handsome Black man with a giant smile, a blonde woman, three brown-skinned children, two boys and a girl. It was a beautiful family. Gavin shook his head because he could not imagine the pain and embarrassment of those children's mother.

Luca came back down the stairs and motioned Gavin back into the kitchen. "The shower just turned off."

Ronald Wilkins was dressed and headed downstairs for tea within a few minutes of his shower. The unusual quiet of the house made him aware of every creak or shift it made. He heard what sounded like water running coming from the kitchen. He stopped on the stairs, listened, and realized it was the tea kettle, but he knew he had not turned on the stove. Wilkins took the last couple of steps down into the living room when Luca stepped in behind him with a knife to his back.

"Walk quietly into the kitchen," Luca ordered.

Ronald Wilkins complied without a word. His attorney warned him that some people would still consider him guilty even if acquitted. Wilkins came in with his hands up by his head. A stone-faced man in a brown pinstriped suit met him in the kitchen. A big black fellow was pouring water into the yellow teacups. If this was a TV show, he might have laughed. Rusty placed the yellow teacups in front of Gavin and left the kitchen. Rusty turned the living room television on and turned the volume up on an old western. He returned to the kitchen and stood by the sink; his big arms folded across his chest.

"Have a seat, Ronald," Gavin said, motioning to an empty chair across the table.

Wilkins fell into the chair with a push from Luca.

Luca joined Rusty at the sink. Luca took a cup of tea but made a face when he smelled the cinnamon and set the cup down.

"Do you know why we are here?" Gavin asked.

"I presume you think I am guilty," Wilkins said.

"Do you deny the allegations from those girls?" Gavin asked quietly.

"I did not do anything to those girls!"

"How about we start with one truth, and then we can get to the others," Gavin replied. "How many girls have you abused over your tenure at the school?"

"I told you; I haven't abused any girls."

"Well, then I'll guess and give you a bullet for each one I think you hurt."

"No, no! That'll be unnecessary," Wilkins croaked, watching as the man brought up a gun with a silencer and laid it on the table.

The Sapphire Ghost

"You know, I've never understood the allure of houses such as these. They're so… average. If I were to be able to purchase a home in a neighborhood, I do believe it would be one of the old colonials over on Richman. Those have character. These little communities look like someone went shopping in the clothing area in North Korea. Too much sameness," Gavin stated as he looked around the kitchen.

"My wife picked it out," Wilkins said tentatively as he observed the strangers in his house.

"And where is the wife?" Gavin asked.

"She went to stay with her mother in Texas." As he spoke, Wilkins' eyes tracked Luca, the shorter man, who was moving to the other side of the room.

"I believe you mean to say that she fled from the embarrassment," Gavin said.

"Well, yes," Wilkins responded ruefully.

"Again, how many?" Gavin said, picking up the gun and pointing it over Wilkins's right shoulder; he pulled the trigger. Wilkins jumped, hitting the table with his leg as a scream left his throat. A teacup turned over, rolled onto the floor, and shattered. The pool of tea spread across the table. "That is your only warning. The next one will go into a joint."

"I don't remember!" Wilkins cried, bowing his head and refusing to look at the man across from him. He shivered at the idea of being shot. The hot tea began to drip onto his neatly pressed khakis.

"We know of at least four. So, take a guess: five, ten, more?" Gavin asked, still with his hand on the gun, as he laid it down.

"Ten, maybe twelve, but some of them were willing," Wilkins said as if that made a difference.

"You are in a position of trust and a person these children should be able to come to for help—you are a pillar of your community. Instead, you have abused your position and embarrassed your family, and to what end? You have a daughter, for Christ's sake!" Gavin lifted the gun and fired a shot into Ronald Wilkins's left shoulder.

Wilkins yelled at the heat and stabbing pain. Luca stepped over, and Rusty quickly reached out and took Gavin's teacup. Luca pulled the table from between them, leaving nothing but space.

"Are you crazy?" he yelled as the stain of dark red blood began to soak the crisp white shirt he wore.

Rusty crossed his arms, meeting Luca's gaze. *How did he always know what Gavin would need?*

"Some might say so, but I am constant, and consistency and truth are not crazy." Gavin's reply was cold.

Wilkins glared at Gavin. He then looked around frantically as if trying to find a way to escape. Wilkins looked at the man leaning against the sink, arms crossed against his broad chest. Then he looked in the man's direction, who'd had a knife to his back just a few minutes earlier. He did not think he could take either. All he could do, he decided, would be to try to reason with the man in front of him with the gun, the one who had the appearance of a crime boss.

"I have little tolerance for a shepherd who abuses his flock. Just ask the good church." Gavin pointed the gun at the man's right knee and took the shot. A bloodcurdling scream rang out. "That is two; ten more to go."

Wilkins slumped over his leg in the most pain he had ever felt. But that was nothing compared to the fear. *I'm going to die sitting here in my kitchen, and no one is around to help me*, he realized. In fact, there was not a person he could think of who would come to his aid. Wilkins's shoulder and knee pulsed with pain, and his vision was blurry with tears. Images of his children came to mind. The last time he saw them and the look of so many unsaid thoughts on his wife's face. Her features spelled out more than disappointment. It was fear of the man she thought he was and for her own children. The idea she married a deviant.

"It is only the wicked or cowardly who prey on children, and those are the ones I seek. Consider me justice for your sins," Gavin aimed again, putting bullets through the tops of Ronald Wilkins' loafers.

Wilkins fell from the chair, screeching in pain, his breathing short and choppy. It felt like a dozen buffalo stomping on his chest. *If, just if I make it through this alive, I'll never walk again.* The blood creating a shiny red glaze on the floor, reflecting the light from the window. His face displayed a horrid mask of anguish.

"How about you decide where the next one will go?" Gavin suggested.

"No more, please! I will do whatever you want, but I beg you, no more . . ." Ronald Wilkins choked out a childlike sob.

"Do you not feel that the punishment meets the crimes?" Gavin asked.

"Well, maybe, but I cannot take anymore," he said with jagged breaths between soggy sobs.

Rusty heard a dog barking from the neighboring house, walked to the door, and left the house. Gavin sat back, awaiting Rusty's return. He watched the formerly refined thirty-six-year-old man violently shake on the floor. There was no way he would survive the next seven shots; he was already going into shock.

"Looks like a gardener has pulled up next door. We should make this quicker, sir," Rusty advised upon his return.

Gavin knelt over the man, careful not to touch him or the blood on the floor. Gavin took the dishtowel Luca handed him, draped it over Wilkins' head, and dealt the final blow.

Rusty placed the teacups and the broken pieces, the kettle, and the tea box in the dishwasher, turned it on, and quickly wiped the stove. They left the same way they had come. Luca promptly wiped the table clean, turned the lock on the door, wiped it down, and pulled it behind him. The men in the red truck with Hawthorne Landscapers written on the side were in the driveway next door but paid no attention.

Luca backed out of the drive and headed back to the airport. Wilkins would lay on that floor for days before someone realized he was dead.

Chapter Ten

May 5

Gavin watched the morning light dance on the ocean before heading to the car. They had a wonderful evening in Dremmond, with Luca grilling lamb chops and preparing various side dishes. However, it was time to say goodbye for now. Gavin closed his eyes as he sat in the car and waited for Rusty and Luca to finish their discussion. He mentally prepared to bid his dear friend farewell.

Rusty stopped before opening the door and opened the blue box—the long platinum pin with four blue sapphires with sword-like points on both ends. The faintest of smiles crept onto his face. *I'm going to miss this.* Snapping the box closed, he got inside the car.

Opening his eyes, Gavin turned and observed Rusty, who slid in the back seat with him for what was to be the last time. Rusty looked tired but would never admit it. "Are you ready, my friend?" Gavin asked without looking at him.

"Believe so," Rusty replied.

"You know . . ."

"Yes, Gavin, I know. I will let you know if I need anything." Rusty finally looked at him. "It has been one hell of a ride and one I am proud to have been a part of."

"Yes, and if I have never thanked you . . . thank you for being with me for so many years and keeping me straight." Gavin smiled over at him.

"It's his turn," Rusty said, nodding toward Luca, who had yet to get in the car. "Trust him and his instincts."

"I will. You did well in choosing Luca and training him," Gavin acknowledged.

Rusty placed the velvet box into Gavin's palm. "Give it to him when I'm on the plane, please," Rusty's voice was slight as he motioned to the front driver's seat just as Luca got behind the wheel.

Gavin nodded. "Give Julianne my love and tell her to take good care of you," he said, his voice giving way to his emotions, although he tried to hide them with a cough.

"I will," Rusty forced the lump in his throat back down.

Thirty minutes later, the black Mercedes pulled into the airport. A new blue and white Learjet sat on the tarmac awaiting Rusty's arrival, and it was Gavin's going-away present to Rusty.

"Do not be a stranger. Come back and visit anytime you wish," Gavin said.

Rusty gave Gavin a small smile, afraid to speak. Luca popped the trunk, and Rusty opened the door.

"Bye, kid; keep an eye on him," Rusty said and smiled at Luca.

"Yes, sir," Luca said and looked away quickly.

"Don't get out. Neither of you!" Rusty ordered.

After closing the door and removing the bag from the trunk, Rusty closed it again and headed to the plane without looking back.

Chapter Eleven

Two months have passed since Rusty left. Gavin has been preparing several Dossiers. He wants to work and not think of his friend's absence.

It was the Fourth of July, a day that Luca could not celebrate as the fireworks affected him in ways that made him combative. He traveled to Manhattan to work in the city above all the chaos that would soon present itself later that evening. Gavin had returned from visiting with Rusty that morning, and Julianne had been gone all weekend, so Gavin and Rusty decided to go sailing.

Rusty was the man who had trained Luca to work with Gavin Garrison. He had also taught him how to direct the ground teams. That had not been hard since he was a former Green Beret. Gavin's life was meticulously disguised, and nothing was left to chance. Luca realized that Rusty had been training him to take his place since the first time he was diagnosed with cancer. Luca sat back down in the leather-bound desk chair and placed his hands behind his head, interlacing his fingers. He stared far off into a different place, just seven years prior.

Luca was depressed, limping outside the VA hospital, refusing to use the doctor's prescribed cane. While in Iraq, he took shrapnel to his left leg, and the injury gave him his second Purple Heart and a medical discharge.

Rusty approached him, eclipsing the light with his height and broad form. Rusty sat with him on a bench for an hour, asking questions about what he would do from this point forward. It was an odd conversation because it was rare for Luca to speak openly with anyone. He did with Rusty. The big guy gave the impression that he did not afford fools.

Luca smiled to himself and at his old self because he had no clue. Luca thought that at the age of twenty-six, his life was over because he loved being a Green Beret and the Army. Mostly, though, Rusty listened to him, and Rusty understood how lost Luca felt. Afterward, Rusty introduced Luca to Gavin Garrison.

The Sapphire Ghost

Through them, Luca found a new purpose. They did not care that his leg would never be the same; they wanted Luca, the man, and the soldier. Plus, the war his new team was fighting was one he could embrace. So, Luca dedicated his life to serving the Sapphire Order.

Luca awaited the impending storm. It was 3:00 a.m. Tuesday morning, and he was working in the study of his East Side apartment. Reaching for his coffee, the steam still whiffing into the air, Luca took a sip to test the temperature. Luca could hear the thunder in the distance. It would not be long before the large windows overlooking the city would drum with the sound of rain.

Luca had been awakened by Gavin's cries in the dark earlier that evening. Rusty always handled the situation with Gavin's night terrors. He opened Gavin's door, finding him tossing in his bed. Luca turned on the light as Rusty did many times. The light brought Gavin out of his dream, and he sat up.

Gavin saw Luca at the door. "Thank you. I am fine. Go back to bed," he said, wiping his eyes. His heart raced.

Luca had left the door open and went back to the study. Gavin never spoke of the nightmares, but Luca knew they came often. What could give someone like Gavin Garrison such terrors?

Thunder erupted as if angry demons played the drums and had buckets of rain slamming against the glass. Luca gathered the map, went to the window, and leaned against the cool glass. Looking over London's Bloomsbury neighborhood map, Luca paid attention to the red, blue, and yellow dots. The red dots indicated security cameras facing the street; the yellow dots were restaurants that Dark 9 ruled out due to security cameras inside. The blue dots represented the only three possible meeting spots with no cameras or frequent police patrols. The most probable meeting location would be a tearoom on Great Russell Street, across from The British Museum. It was small and quaint, with a bookshop attached and on a busy street. They could remain unnoticed. Luca would keep the other two sites as backups in case the owner or the manager was uncooperative. Gavin preferred to buy cooperation rather than strongarm someone into giving up a lucrative day of business. Since Luca had been with Gavin, he had not found anyone unwilling to take double what they would have made in sales for a couple of hours of use.

The upcoming meeting with the prime minister must have Luca's undivided attention. It was just six weeks away. Leaning against the cool glass and listening to the rain, Luca was unsure why he was staring at the map. It was mainly a habit, as most things were. But he was alone, and no one would notice him. The exits, the side streets, and the parking spots were permanently imprinted in his head. Closing his eyes, he mentally shifted the map and zoomed in on the streets. He needed to fly over and take pictures, which Luca would do when they finished their business in Nevada in three days, too much in such a short time. Luca thought of Las Vegas, where the next named Dossier was located.

Luca was the point man on the London assignment and the case there. Unfortunately, he would be in that position from now on, having been promoted from second to first in command—after Gavin, of course. The Sapphire Order had been passed to him, which some would have considered an honor, but Luca would gladly have declined if the situation differed. However, he did not intend to let Rusty down. Luca secretly aspired to move into another position, the highest position within an order, if the opportunity ever arose. He would keep that idea to himself, though, because Luca knew he still had a lot to learn. He also had the presence of mind to keep his mouth shut. Noting the time, Luca went to turn on the teapot for Gavin.

Gavin had left his bedroom and fallen asleep in a chair in the living room. That sketch pad was lying open at his feet, and the charcoal pencil was still in his hand. Rusty had told him never to ask about the sketches or open the pad. Luca was not a person to snoop, but curiosity and Gavin's nightmares made him want to know what they were about. He slipped over and picked up the drawing pad.

Sitting on the sofa's edge, he carefully looked at the current drawing. If torment could be drawn with charcoal, pain was etched on this page. It depicted children's images with outstretched hands. The eyes, though. Those eyes were piercing Luca's heart. He turned the page back and looked at another, this time a boy, maybe five, his face bruised, his body thin, and starved. Again, the eyes were heart-churning wells of helplessness. Luca's heart ached as he turned the pages and saw each image of suffering and how Gavin captured their hopelessness. The devastation could not have been captured better by camera.

He flipped through the book and settled on a grave marker. **Angel 446, 2013,** was on the headstone, and an engraving of an angel was etched onto the monument. The drawing showed a shadowed Archangel Michael kneeling over the grave, a sword by his side, his wings laid gently against his back.

Gavin awoke and saw Luca looking at his drawings. He sat still, observing Luca look at each sketch. A tear fell down Luca's cheek. Gavin's instinct was to take the tablet, knowing Luca did not need these images in his head. Instead, he looked on as Luca turned the page. No one, including Rusty, had ever seen his drawings.

Luca turned to a page of five children, naked, but their bodies were drawn blankly to protect their nakedness. They sat in a dark cell, dirty, their ribcages exposed beneath paper-thin skin. Luca ran his hand over his mouth and shook his head. The absence of life in those eyes, the apparent lost opportunity to believe that anything good still existed. Luca was moved by the art and surprised at the skill of the artist.

"Luca," Gavin said when he saw more tears fall, "give me the book."

Luca looked at Gavin, realizing he had been watching him. "I'm sorry," he said and gently closed the tablet.

"I know. This is personal. Something I keep to myself. I am allowed that," Gavin said.

"Yes, but tell me about them," Luca requested quietly as he felt grief in his chest.

Shadows danced over Gavin's face. "They haunt me. I've failed each one. Each child appears in my dreams, asking why I couldn't save them. I see them every time I close my eyes."

Luca opened the book and turned back to the page of the grave. "And this?"

Gavin studied the image for a moment. "I provide a burial for the ones we find, but no one claims." The sadness in his voice was just as heartbreaking as the images.

Luca gazed down and traced a finger across the image of the marker. This marker did not contain a dash, the simple indication that they lived between the years of birth and death.

He closed the book and handed it back to Gavin. "I am sorry I invaded your privacy, but I am glad I did. I see them, too, the ones we've lost. I see them when I am alone when things get too quiet—I think I can hear them crying. Sometimes I think I'm crazy."

"Luca, you're not crazy, just damned. I am sorry for you as well," Gavin said.

Chapter Twelve

July 8

Several Dossiers had been sent to the targets in the previous weeks, and now it was time to meet the Ghost.

This target was Governor Mark Cydet of Nevada. His hand was in the cookie jar of one of the largest human trafficking rings in the western United States. Many of those hostages were used in the casinos and clubs, and the patrons of those organizations would have their time. It was the good governor who had allowed this in his state, who had protected these vilest of creatures to continue their assault on people—Cydet disgusted Gavin. People in power could do awful things, but this was the foulest thing a person could do. This, however, was the reason the Ghost existed, how he had built such great wealth and influence. This had been his purpose: to set a ceiling on depravity. Drugs, that was a choice. Guns, there was always war. This was different.

However, with people like Governor Cydet shielded by the highest levels of government, the Ghost had taken it upon himself to be judge, jury, and executioner.

Cydet had denied these children their right to life, the right to pursue happiness. The Governor of the great state of Nevada had deprived these women and children of the future they truly deserved. The sanctity of life mattered. The Governor had sworn to protect and serve the residents of Nevada, but he had sold some of them out to the highest bidder.

"Governor, do you know who I am?" Gavin asked as he sat across from him, hanging by his wrists, hands together as if in prayer, from the highest platform of an abandoned concrete manufacturing plant.

"No, I don't know who you are or why you've brought me here. Get me down now. It hurts!" Cydet screamed. "Get me down!"

Gavin listened to the tearing sounds of joints, ligaments, and limbs popping and pulling apart. The governor was at least three inches taller than he was several hours ago.

"Didn't you get my package? Surely you would remember," replied Gavin.

"Yes, I remember the package, the red *G*, but it's not true, I swear!" Cydet protested.

The Ghost leaned back in the chair, interlacing his fingers on his navy suit vest. Staring off into the gray morning darkness, the Ghost's face was emotionless. He hated the desert—so much vast nothingness clearing out to even more nowhere.

"You'll hang there and tell me you were not in the fourteen photographs I sent in that package? Really? That is so unremarkable. Just once, I would like to hear a real confession, and it would make my life complete. 'Forgive me, Father, for I have sinned;' I'd hear that and tell you to say five Hail Marys and jump off a roof," Gavin said. "Trust me, the last seven hours of your stretching is no comparison to the pain you have caused."

Gavin first pulled out a photograph of the man hanging before him playing golf with Manuel Hernandez, the second-in-command of the largest criminal organization in Los Angeles. Then, the one where he was having dinner with the Armenian nationals whose most significant business was child trafficking.

"You've grown quite wealthy on a governor's salary in the last three years. I know you accomplished that by getting involved in this sinister business and making deals with these devils. That's bad for your health," Gavin lifted the photographs for the governor to see.

"I didn't do anything!" Cydet cried.

"You allowed children to become prey," Gavin stated.

"Sir, the sun will be up soon," Luca reminded him from behind, where he was keeping watch.

"Governor, I will let you in on a little secret. The fall's not so bad. It is the foreplay that gravity plays with you, that anticipation of a climax that scares you. It's a lot like sex, without the happy ending. That said, I believe I will let you hang there a bit longer. The Reaper deserves her fun."

Gavin opened a short-handled knife, then cut into the rope—but only a little over halfway—and stood back, watching the threads of fiber begin to break. Gavin strolled away, and Cydet realized there was only one way down. He screamed again, this time for mercy.

Gavin would be in the car for the conclusion. The governor's pain would end shortly. He dialed his friend at the FBI to let him know where to pick up the truck with four souls—the two women and two children they had rescued that night.

Gavin looked at his phone when he hit the end button. Something in Agent Fagan's voice wasn't quite right.

Chapter Thirteen

July 9

Luca rented a house on the outskirts of Las Vegas, but Gavin insisted on returning to Dremmond, Florida, once the operation with Cydet was complete. Luca headed back to the house to pick up their belongings before driving to the airport. It was just before 6:00 a.m. They were tired, having been up all night. With all the traffic, it would take at least an hour and a half to get back to the rental house and then to the airport. Gavin called to check on Rusty and left a message with Julianne.

Luca pulled into the driveway to retrieve their bags. Having anticipated traffic, they found the roads unusually dead for this time of the morning. *Why weren't people heading to work?*

They heard sirens, and Luca gazed over at the highway south of the house, not thinking much about it. The sirens grew louder and seemed to be coming in all directions.

"I'll be right back," Luca said, jumping out of the car and looking over at the line of blue lights, creating an eerie haze in the desert horizon.

By the time Luca reached the porch, the sirens were louder, and the blue and white light lit up every sightline.

"Luca, find a place to hide!" Gavin called when the first car pulled onto the street.

"But . . . *Sir*!"

"Go! Now!" Gavin yelled above the sirens as he tossed him his briefcase. "Go! Luca, that's an order!"

The cars surrounded the house. Gavin crawled over and wiped down the steering wheel and handles before the first car stopped. Gavin's team members had learned to touch as little as possible, but these items could not be avoided. Gavin could feel the air grow hot as the police vehicles surrounded the car. He knelt on the driveway with his hands on his head. From his short conversation with Fagan, his FBI pal, he felt that something was wrong.

Luca ran inside, grabbed a kitchen cloth, and wiped down anything he might have touched. He placed everything possible into the dishwasher and turned it on. He ran back to the bedrooms, took anything linking him to Gavin, and tossed it into the washing machine, including his computer. Luca extracted Gavin's silver dollar money clip from the briefcase before dumping the contents into the washer, turned it on hot, and poured in bleach. Luca cringed, remembering his tablet was in the car.

He ran from the back of the house, allowing the protocol, when compromised, to lead him. Luca ran behind six other homes and emerged on the street where the blue-light party was being held. The cacophony of sirens, radios, and officers yelling was deafening in the early morning. He took out his phone and attempted to walk casually—his nerves bit at his insides. Luca texted the Fortress, *Sapphire Code Red*. He lifted his phone as the growing crowd of bystanders was doing and got several pictures of the scene.

Luca felt pain hit his chest at seeing Gavin on the ground while Thomas Fagan put him in handcuffs. His phone rang, and he almost dropped it in surprise.

"Luca," Wright said.

"Yes."

"What's going on?" Wright asked, looking up where the Sapphire Ghost was due to be today.

Wright was the lead Dark 9 on the East Coast and a trusted advisor to Helen. Not to mention, Wright was an assault weapon of a man.

"Gavin's being arrested. Ping my current location. I've sent pictures of the scene," Luca replied.

"Stay out of sight. We will have a retrieval team there shortly," Wright disconnected to call Helen.

Special Agent Tonya Simons, with the FBI's Ghost Task Force, issued the tail numbers of the suspected Ghost plane to the FAA. She had not expected to hear back so soon. Then they searched for the car that had driven away from that plane. The hunt was long and exhausting, involving hours of video surveillance. The Cessna flew into the private jetport the previous morning, and every single agent she could muster started reviewing the footage. They found the car on a traffic cam and issued a BOLO, a combination of sheer luck, good timing, and hard work. With another stroke of luck this morning, an off-duty detective was nearby in an unmarked car and called in the vehicle. Then, the officer followed it.

Special Agent Simons stepped out of the government-issued SUV. Tonya Simons was nearly six feet tall and walked like an athlete. She found her former Ghost Task Force partner, Deputy Director of Special Operations Thomas Fagan, already cuffing the suspect. No one knew what to expect from the person known only as the Ghost.

The files had been stacking up for two decades at FBI headquarters in Washington, yet all they knew about the Ghost was that he targeted the highest profile figures involved in the most despicable form of child abuse. Most of the agents on her task force rooted for the Ghost in their off-duty hours. This person killed many the FBI could not touch, leaving the evidence of his victims' crimes at each scene. The Ghost took his role as executioner seriously. This man evaded capture many times—with them right on his heels.

However, ever since the U.S. Secretary of State and his wife had become Ghost victims, the powers that be wanted him tracked down. It did not matter that the gray file contained enormous mind-bending evidence. It was time for the Ghost to give up his gavel.

Special Agent Tonya Simons marched up to Fagan as he lifted the older gentleman off the ground. "Do you think it's really him? He doesn't look menacing."

"Guess we won't know until we get him back to the box," Fagan said and escorted Gavin to the backseat of his SUV. Gavin never looked at Fagan. Instead, Gavin took notice of the tall woman, recognizing her from a previous pursuit.

Simons examined the older man in a stylish suit and gentle manner. "Is the house clear?"

"Yes, we searched it," replied a Nevada State Patrol officer. "If there was anything in there, it's been washed."

Simons gawked at him, revealing deep creases around her dark eyes. "That's an odd statement. What do you mean?"

The Sapphire Ghost

"I mean, everything is in the wash. A computer, clothes, and a lot of paper are in the washing machine and the dishwasher. Everything is bleached out. It's a total loss. There was someone inside," the officer said and walked off.

Simons ran her hand through her short brown hair. "Okay, let's get him back to the station and see what we can get," she said to Fagan.

Fagan and another agent sat up front and led the two other SUVs back to the field office, where they would conduct the interrogation. He wanted to speak with the Ghost, but, due to the presence of the other agent, he kept quiet. Fagan glanced in the rearview only once, and it sent a shiver into his bones. Fagan had not worked in the Ghost task force for three years. Not since the Ghost recruited him, and he advanced to his current position as a reward for the number of children he had found.

Two hours later, Gavin sat quietly inside an interrogation room. The clock ticked on, and the slow clicking sound seemed to mock Gavin. He looked over at the clock for the third time in thirty minutes. The FBI left him to think since he had not answered any questions. The memory of Thomas Fagan pulling the zip ties tight around his wrists kept going through his mind. Fagan did not say anything, and Gavin failed to be disappointed because he understood it was risky to trust someone in law enforcement.

Still, the clock ticked on; long, monotonous strokes of time. Luca would have called Helen if he evaded capture, but perhaps he was in a similar room. Helen would have a retrieval team in transit. Gavin just needed to give her time for a transport rescue if necessary. Helen never failed her assets.

Special Agent Tonya Simons stood behind the two-way mirror for almost two hours. The man who sat there had no prints to run. Facial recognition also came up empty, but she was sure she held the elusive Ghost—although it would be hard to say for sure since he looked nothing like any of the descriptions. This man was much older, and the deep carvings on his face indicated he might be seventy. Now, the question would be how to get him to talk. Her former partner on the task force, Deputy Director Thomas Fagan, was on-site to conduct the questioning. Fagan had a reputation for getting people to spill their souls. Fagan was humble and easygoing, and people related to him better than most cops. Plus, the FBI Director wanted to find out where Fagan's allegiance lay.

"Has he said anything yet?" Fagan asked when he came in to join her.

"Not a word," Simons replied.

Fagan studied the man handcuffed to the stainless table. He thought he could feel him staring straight at him. The Ghost was the one who fed him the locations to find missing children. His heart hung heavy. Quantico ordered him to work on this operation, and the Ghost would never forgive him. *What will my death be like?* Fagan shivered.

"I would like the opportunity to speak with him," Fagan said.

"I was hoping you would." Simons looked at the man wearing a lightweight Ralph Lauren jacket over his dress shirt and tie. Fagan rarely looked the part of an FBI agent.

Fagan took the file from her and walked through the door to the interrogation room. "Deputy Director Thomas Fagan," the FBI agent said, as if they'd never met.

Gavin never looked up as Fagan sat with his back to the mirror.

Fagan set bottled water down in front of the Ghost. "Would you care to tell me your name?" Fagan sat and took a pack of gum from his pocket.

Gavin watched as he rolled up a piece of gum and pushed it into his mouth. The foil wrapper lay on the table, and Gavin read the block lettering written inside.

Fagan followed that with a series of questions, then pulled his lips back tightly after getting no response. Standing, Fagan jerked Gavin up by his shirt. "Who are you?" he demanded while discreetly dropping a key into Gavin's shirt pocket.

Gavin whispered in his ear. Fagan's eyes met Gavin's, and an acknowledgment passed between them.

Fagan threw him back in the chair. "Maybe my partner can get you to talk. She is not as nice as I am."

Fagan snatched the wrapper and left the room, and, for Simons, who was watching, he appeared angry.

The Sapphire Ghost

Gavin sat back in the chair and thought about the message on the foil wrapper, *check your pocket*. He relaxed a bit, feeling that Thomas was trying to help.

Gavin needed to keep his mouth shut because he could not pass voice recognition tests. Many recorded lines at the Capitol and the Pentagon had his voice on them, and he would never risk his contacts or their careers. He needed each relationship he had built.

After another hour, Special Agent Simons entered and sat across from the Ghost with a notepad and a file. When Gavin sat back, the chains rattled on the table, and he watched the woman.

"Apparently, we are asking the wrong questions. What are the correct ones?" Simons asked. She noticed the untouched bottle of water.

Simons began to take photographs out of the folder. There was a picture of the two men from Anaheim whose throats were cut—a plastic surgeon from Phoenix who had been sun-dried in a date orchard but died from bee stings. The real estate tycoon from San Jose was covered in a blistering rash.

"Are these yours?" Simons asked.

Gavin gazed down at the photographs, shifting his eyes across the gruesome pictures. Gingerly, he took the one from the date field; this one was his. The other two were not his work. He shook his head and motioned to the notepad. '*What are these?*' he wrote.

"People you have killed," Simons said after reading the note.

'What are you talking about?' he wrote.

"Are you not the Ghost?" Simons asked in sign language, curious if this man could speak.

Gavin smiled and signed back, "I can hear perfectly fine." Then he feigned confusion. "Ghost?"

"Who are you?" Simons asked again.

Gavin smiled and shook his head.

Simons sat across from the unidentified man and waited for him to say or do something—anything. The man across from her looked thoughtfully at the photographs. The room was growing warm, and Simons waited for him to drink the water.

"I know you have a name, a history, and I am curious to know something about you," Simons said.

Gavin observed Special Agent Simons. She patiently waited for answers to the questions that had plagued her for so long. Simons had been the lead on the Ghost files for over six years. There were several near misses for a couple of the existing Ghosts, and Gavin had walked right past her on one occasion. Gavin knew Tonya Simons had no life outside the FBI. No spouse, no children, but Tonya Simons appeared content from the research he gathered. You must always know your enemies as well as your friends. Then he took a long look at her. Maybe she hated secrets as much as he did. This was a great big treasure hunt, and he was her X. Just as King was his.

"You can sit here until the paint peels, but eventually, you are going to tell me your name," Simons demanded, looking into the man's brown eyes.

Gavin signed, "James, Chad, Dean, choose one. What am I being charged with?"

"Murder," Simons said.

"Evidence?" Gavin replied, signing.

Simons studied the man, who was not sweating or showing any discomfort. She thought his fingers moved in a way as familiar as her own father's, who was deaf. She also knew they had nothing concrete unless they could convince the Ghost to speak—six hours in here and nothing but a few signed words.

Chapter Fourteen

I need to use the restroom, Gavin wrote on the pad an hour later.

Simons read the writing and nodded. She waved at the mirror and motioned for someone to come in.

"Please take him to the men's room." Then she added, probably unnecessarily, "Keep a close eye on him." The man seemed old but had revealed some knowledge of the legal system. They would have to charge him soon to hold him.

The much younger agent unlocked Gavin from the table and guided him out by the arm. Gavin looked down the halls and for the exit signs, but he could not see any windows or doors leading out from the long, narrow hallway. Once they got to the men's room, the agent stood behind him as he did his business. It would not take much to overpower the young man, who stood posturing authority but shifted nervously on his polished black shoes. Gavin glanced through the mirror up at the ceiling. He took in the bathroom with its four blue stalls.

Gavin washed his hand and, with mastered precision, stepped back quickly and pulled the handcuffs around the agent's neck. "Shh . . . just sleep for now. Later, you will have a story to tell," Gavin whispered.

The agent quit struggling, and Gavin laid him down on the cold tile floor. He checked for a pulse; it was steady. Gavin dug inside his front shirt pocket, retrieved a small silver key, and unlocked the cuffs, which fell to the floor.

Five minutes later, Simons nervously checked the clock, stood, left the interrogation room, and went to the men's room.

"Motherf——!" she yelled when she saw the agent on the floor.

Fagan came running at the sound. "What happened?"

"Shut down the facility. He is still here somewhere!" Simons stated as she threw back the stall doors.

"His gun's missing, but he's breathing," Fagan noted, kneeling to the agent.

"Well, that is something. I figured that poor guy was added to the Ghost's list of victims," Simons said.

Thomas shouted into his radio, "Shut down the building! No one in or out. The suspect is armed." He needed to message whoever was now on the other end of the phone number that Gavin whispered to him. He ran into the hallway like he would hunt for the man. He took the stairs to the second level and typed in a message.

Call - Ghost in danger.

Chapter Fifteen

Luca paced the empty house, his energy demanding a way out. Gavin Garrison was caught and arrested. One thought kept running through his head: *How had they known?*

He picked up the phone and dialed. "Helen, it's Luca."

"Luca, I just spoke with Wright. They have teams on the way," she replied.

"I don't know what happened. We were careful," Luca seemed to plead.

Luca stood to the side of the window, watching a police cruiser crawl by in front of the house he sheltered in.

"We will get him back. Was he wearing a disguise?" Helen asked.

"Yes, of course."

"That's good. He will get out, or we will intervene. He has done this a time or two," Helen reassured.

That made Luca's head explode. He had not known this. "Really?"

"Yes, the last time, it was for drunk and disorderly," Helen stated with casual indifference. "Wright said it is FBI; it may be a little trickier. Gavin will follow protocol. If that doesn't work, we have a backup plan," Helen said. She had already located the FBI Director, Matthew Barns. If necessary, they would force a trade.

"What can I do?" Luca asked.

"Where are you? I will have you picked up shortly," she replied. "Just sit still."

Luca gave her the address, and they hung up. He had never been this scared.

Helen sat at her computer with the Sapphire Ghost's location on her screen. Every Ghost held a pin with a GPS so she could lock into their location. She needed to keep an eye on it in case the Sapphire Ghost managed to get out of the building on his own. It would be critical to pick Gavin up immediately. The FBI was a first, but she did not want to scare Luca any more than he already was. Gavin would have to bring him in to be sworn in so he would know the codes. The FBI had never bothered the Sapphire Ghost before, and the Orders had many contacts within the agency's walls.

Gavin was not a novice to complicated situations. He stood on the back of a toilet and heaved himself up into the ceiling. Once he returned the tile to its place, he crawled backward, flattened himself on a supporting wall, and eased into a comfortable position. Within minutes, the bathroom door below flew open. Agent Simons nearly cursed but stopped herself, and then he heard Fagan. Fagan checked the agent on the floor.

Luca sat in the empty house, wondering where the FBI had taken Gavin. The thought that Gavin had been arrested before caught him off guard—and for being drunk, of all things. That made no sense. There must have been a reason he had wanted to be arrested. The most calculative man he knew would not do something so irrational.

Luca's phone rang and he did not recognize the number. The small red dot at the top showed a forward from the informant line.

"Yes," Luca answered cautiously.

"The Ghost gave me this number," the voice said. Fagan waited five minutes for his text to be returned and then called because he wanted to tell someone he was not the enemy.

Luca's mind cleared, "Who is this?" he asked.

"Thomas Fagan. He's gone missing, and we think he is still in the building. I was going to find a way for his people to retrieve him during transport; now I am unsure what to do."

"Thomas, when did he go missing?" Luca's mind wandered to horrible black sites.

"Maybe twenty minutes ago. The Ghost knocked out an agent on a trip to the restroom," Fagan explained.

"Give me the address," Luca said, his mind swimming with questions.

Fagan relayed the address and looked around when two other FBI agents entered the stairs. "Gotta go, call again when I can."

Luca sat for a moment, relieved that Fagan was not betraying Gavin. Because Fagan had no idea what a ridiculously bad idea that was. Apparently,

The Sapphire Ghost

Fagan was ordered to work with the FBI's Ghost task force, and thankfully, he was still on their side. As Luca contemplated this development, he heard a car pull up outside.

Gavin nested in place for several hours while the station went wild with activity. Clicks of radios and clipped voices resonated through the rooms he was above and between. He heard doors slam on the other side of the wall. The exits had to be over in that area, and he continued to listen, taking in all the information. He heard keys tossed onto a desk, file cabinets jerked out and slammed shut, and someone clicked a pen within a few feet under him. Gavin made mental notes of where everything was located according to what he was hearing. He counted eight within his hearing range. Footsteps in and out, heavy tromping of rubber soles, the padding of expensive loafers, and the lighter sounds of female steps.

Gavin was growing tired; he had not slept in over twenty-four hours. His thoughts wandered to Luca and what he must be going through.

Gavin thought about taking him to Arcadia to swear in. As his first-in-command, he only worked for him. When Luca swore to the codes, he would become Helen's Warrior to the Sapphire Ghost. Helen would then be able to call him in under the Warrior Codes. Until Luca swore to those codes, he was unaware of the consequences of not obeying Helen's directives. Gavin controlled his order for the first time and wanted to keep it that way for a bit longer. Once Luca was sworn to Arcadia, he belonged to it just as much as Gavin did.

Luca sat in the back of the Suburban, logged into his tablet that he left in the car, and wiped it clean. They headed to the FBI field office in Las Vegas to observe activity outside the facility.

They arrived late in the afternoon, and the commotion had died down. Gavin was stiff from lying so still and caught himself drifting off. He scratched at the glue around his eyes and mouth and tore the material from his face. He was hot and sweating, so it came off easily.

Gavin continued to lie still, awaiting a sign that Arcadia was involved. The rustle from below grew quieter, and the angry phone calls and hasty words became muted.

Helen took the address from Gavin's pin and found her way into the security system. The FBI field office was a small-two story building west of the city. She sat with her fourth cup of tea for the afternoon, looking through the camera feeds. Luca called her and relayed what an FBI agent told him: Gavin disappeared during a bathroom break. She looked at each face, trying to see him. The Sapphire Ghost was nowhere on camera, but she knew he would be waiting on a sign that it was clear for him to move.

Helen backtracked her way into the power grid for the city. Targeting just one building in the maze would be impossible, but she could take out a block.

Luca sat with members of Dark 9 in the SUV at the end of the parking lot. They watched for any sign that Gavin would come out in cuffs or on his own. He forgot his tiredness and was working on fear and adrenaline. It was one thing to evade bullets but another to think of public courts and the media for all the Ghost's crimes. He couldn't imagine the circus that would surround something like that.

"Wright, are we going in to get him out or what?" Luca asked into the comms.

"No, stay calm. Garrison prefers more calculated exits with limited bloodshed," Wright spoke back.

Again, Luca was caught off-guard at the reply. *How many times had Gavin been caught?*

Gavin waited. The smell of coffee burning on a forgotten burner drifted into the ceiling vents. The footsteps below had decreased, and the pings and bleeps of scanners drowned out the voices. Simons was sitting directly below, and Gavin could hear her on the phone.

Fagan came in a determined but exasperated tone. "We have searched this building from top to bottom, and I don't know how he made it out."

"He's a ghost," Simons said. "I'm unsure he was ever really here. Maybe I dreamed it."

"The Director wants to know if we found anything concrete, and I told him the man said nothing, absolutely nothing," Fagan said.

"Twenty years of gray files, and we still have no idea who he is. What gets me is that the MOs are never the same. Hangings, burnings, poisonings.

The Sapphire Ghost

It's teachers, professors, doctors, politicians, corporate executives. He doesn't miss any group. Over a thousand files, and we cannot find a clue to his identity. We have no idea who we had in custody, and there's nothing to say he had any such business here." Simons tossed the file on the desk. "Why, that's my main question. Why?"

Simons looked at the blurry photograph from last year of a middle-aged man in New York City. It was one of the few sightings of the Ghost captured on camera. She lifted the photograph and another behind it, this one of a brunette woman picked up on a nanny cam. The victim was an attractive blonde, a modeling agency owner. The victim was dosed with cobra venom.

"Yes, I'm afraid we do." Fagan relayed that the governor's office called to report that Governor Cydet never came home last night.

Simons stood and grabbed her keys. "I guess we need to track the governor's movements and see if we can find him. Hopefully, we found the Ghost before he finished whatever deed he had in store."

"I'll be out in a few minutes. I need to call Director Barns," Fagan said.

Suddenly, the lights went out in the building. Every computer monitor went dark, and the air conditioner went silent. The lower level was black. Alarms squawked, penetrating the room from the hallway.

"Well, you might want to wait," Fagan said. He looked around in the dark, and he could not make out Simons sitting at her desk near the wall.

Simons sat still, allowing her eyes to adjust to the dark. Running her hand over the desk, intending to locate her coffee cup so she wouldn't spill it, she inadvertently tipped it over anyway. Coffee ran over the table and down the side of the desk as she cursed again. Simons reached inside a lower desk drawer, taking out a stack of fast-food napkins, attempting to soak up the mess. Simons bumped against the desk in the dark.

Gavin heard everything go quiet. The noise from the air ducts came to a sudden stop. This was his sign. Lifting the tile, Gavin peered into the room below. Of course, Gavin had been in the dark for hours, so his eyes had adapted and could make out the two agents. Quietly, Gavin extracted the tile, slid out, and dropped into the corner of the room. Gavin heard Simons muttering under her breath, covering Gavin's movements. A few feet over, he had previously listened to a set of keys discarded onto a desk; he cupped them in his hand and stood still. Gavin watched Fagan's shadow over by the door. Gavin slid the navy FBI jacket from the chair's back, pulled it on, and knelt behind the desk. He spat out his Sapphire pin and tucked it into his pocket.

Simons jerked her desk drawer open, retrieved her weapon, and felt for the flashlight she thought was on the desk. "We cannot just sit here. Let's see what is going on. Your phone call is going to have to wait."

"Let's go," Fagan said, looking out into the dark hallway.

The door opened and closed, and Gavin slipped a keycard from a desk and clipped it to the jacket. Turning on the flashlight he found in the windbreaker, Gavin scanned over Simons' desk. The Ghost file lay open, and he scooped it up and tucked it into the back of his pants. Putting on an FBI cap from another desk, Gavin padded to the door. His face looked vastly different without the wrinkles around his eyes and mouth. The leather soles on his shoes made no sound as he walked out the door and down the hallway. He strode with purpose when another agent headed his way with her flashlight.

"Have you seen anything?" the agent asked.

"No, not a soul," Gavin replied. "Keep looking."

Gavin walked past the woman and opened the door marked stairs. Then he saw Thomas Fagan.

"Thomas." Gavin's voice was firm as a rock.

Upon hearing the familiar gruff voice, Fagan turned around, lifting his eyes from his phone where he had been reading a message. "Sir . . ." He felt his mouth go dry.

Gavin motioned to the key code pad on the door. "Care to punch in the code?"

"Sir, Special Agent Simons is outside," Fagan replied. "I am sorry, I did not have a choice."

"The code, Thomas," Gavin instructed.

Fagan turned around and punched in the code. The lock clicked open.

"I'm truly sorry about this, Thomas, but it is for your own good," Gavin said and struck him across the side of the head with the gun.

The Sapphire Ghost

Gavin took the phone from his hand and walked out into the sun. Simons was standing off to the side of the door, speaking on her phone. Gavin ambled past her and nodded. He felt for the key fob in his pocket. Although Gavin was sure Dark 9 was out here, he had no idea where to look with all the black vehicles. He clicked the fob and walked the parking lot as if he belonged there, the navy windbreaker with the big FBI across the back shielding him from a second glance.

Gavin was walking toward a blue Honda when an SUV pulled alongside him.

"Get in," Wright said.

Gavin opened the back door and got inside. Wright drove out slowly and headed out of the parking lot. He spoke into the comms. "I have the Sapphire Ghost."

Luca heard the words and, at that moment, nearly fell apart. All the fatigue and fear had become almost more than his body could bear. Luca began to shake all over. The driver started to drive away, and Luca stopped him and jumped out. He fell to the ground and dry heaved.

"Sir, are you okay?" the second Dark 9 member asked Luca, getting out and assessing the front lot, studying to see if they had been noticed.

Luca slowly wiped his mouth with the back of his sleeve. Luca nodded to the member and climbed back inside the SUV.

"Did Luca get away?" Gavin asked Wright.

"Yes, sir, and he was also in the parking lot," Wright said.

Gavin nodded his head gratefully. "So, he heard you say you had me?"

"Yes, sir, Luca is with two other Dark 9 members," Wright said. "He got sick at the news."

"I see. Luca must have been scared," Gavin said.

"Terrified," Wright corrected. "We will meet up with them outside of town. Your jet is compromised, so you must lay low until we get you out of here," Wright replied.

"I understand. I need to call Helen," Gavin said, taking the phone when Wright handed it over the seat. "Here, take care of these," Gavin said, depositing the phone and gun he had collected on the center console.

"Gavin, thank goodness," Helen said, sounding relieved.

"Yes, thank you for the assist," Gavin said.

"You are out and safe. Tell me what I need to retrieve," Helen said.

"No DNA, and I had on a face," Gavin said. "They still have nothing. I am exhausted and hungry, and I've not slept since the night before last," he complained.

Helen observed Gavin's pin on the screen moving away from the FBI field office. "I have secured a location, and Wright will ensure you eat. Go rest. It might be forty-eight hours before I can get you safely out of Nevada. Oh, and you might have to explain to Luca how you were arrested for drunk and disorderly."

Gavin chuckled. "Oh, okay. Is he all right? He looked panicked when I ordered him to run, and I heard he was just ill."

"Luca is shaken, but he will be fine. You need to bring him in, and he needs instructions for these situations."

"I know, and I will—you don't have to keep reminding me. I understand it's time. Thank you again," Gavin said. Still holding the phone, he retrieved the file he had taken from Simons' desk. You might want to send the Opal Ghost to see Dr. Kiss; she needs to have her face altered."

"Why?" she asked.

"I have a clear picture of her in front of me and another of our former Ruby Ghost, Emanuel. I'll send you the file," Gavin said.

"I will make her an appointment. Get some rest," Helen said and hung up.

Gavin returned the phone and peered out the window, "Could you stop and collect Luca for me?" Gavin asked.

"No problem. I'll call that driver, and we will meet up, then get you both something to eat." Wright handed back a bottle of water.

Three SUVs pulled up outside a half-star establishment, and a Dark 9 member went inside to order. Luca went up to Wright's SUV and deposited himself in the back.

"It is so good to see you, sir," Luca said, examining Gavin.

"I thought it might be best if we rode together and you could see I was fine," he said, his expression soft and apologetic.

"How? Fagan called me to say you'd disappeared. How?" Luca stumbled through his words, and hints of his Hispanic accent came through.

"I'm unsure of the story, but Thomas was a reluctant participant of the arrest. I found my way into the ceiling until I had a sign that Arcadia had Dark 9 onsite."

"You are so calm. How many times have you been through this?" Luca asked.

"Only three times in this country," Gavin stated. "I was overdue."

"Overdue? This nearly gave me an aneurysm!" Luca quipped.

"Calm yourself, son. Everyone is fine, and everyone works as they should. Thank you for listening when I told you to run. If you hadn't, it could have ended differently because no one would have called Arcadia. Helen reminded me you have not been training for this," Gavin said.

"There's training for this? Well, hell, sign me up." Luca's voice shook.

Gavin could tell Luca was irritated, which meant he was tired and hungry. He would be fine after eating and resting. He watched as Luca picked at the glue on his fingertips, which he applied while hiding in the empty house.

Chapter Sixteen

Simons sat in the ambulance while Fagan was being cared for by a paramedic—although reluctantly. Simon's suspicions were dissolving seeing the gash on Fagan's head.

"I'm fine," Fagan said to the paramedic.

"You're going to need stitches," Simons said. "Now sit back and relax." Turning to the paramedic, she added, "Just do it," Then she climbed inside the ambulance. "I'll ride with you."

Fagan glanced at his former partner. It had been three years since they had worked together on the Ghost Task Force.

"Not a coincidence that the lights just came back on," Simons said.

"No," Fagan said, grimacing as he felt the side of his head.

"How does he do that?" Simons said, thinking of the three who had walked out the door while she was on the phone. None had been an older man. The first was the agent leading out the younger agent, who was knocked unconscious in the men's room. The third was an agent of her height, maybe fifty. She thought more about the third agent's height and build. But she sat quietly on the ride to the hospital.

"Just once, I would like to know who he is. But I have a new theory because I don't think it's the same person anymore," Simons finally said.

"What do you mean?" Fagan asked.

"I have two surveillance photographs at two different victims' residences. One is a woman. Last year, we had four victims show up within three weeks, and a woman appeared on a nanny cam," Simons replied.

"I always suspected he did not work alone," Fagan said.

"I know you aren't stupid. You must realize that anytime you get one of those phone calls, it's just before we get another gray envelope?" Simons asked.

The Sapphire Ghost

"Yes, each and every time. The bureau has tried to trace the calls, but they have been untraceable." A note of contempt hit Fagan's voice. "What do you think I should do? Not take the calls!?"

"No, that's not what I'm saying. Why did the Ghost choose *you*?" Simons asked.

"That'd be a question for him—or her or them, for that matter. How do you find someone who's that invisible?" Fagan replied. "I'm having way more success on this side, and I can't say I want him caught."

The Ghost never mocked law enforcement by leaving behind any clues, either to who he was or who his next victim would be. No one he killed was revealed with circumstantial evidence. The Ghost was not a catch-me-if-you-can serial killer; it was as if he was working with some deep secret police force with massive resources. Now, Simons was unsure if it was, he, she, or both.

"Found out anything about the plane?" Fagan asked.

"Registered to some company out of Denmark. We found some weapons but nothing else," Simons answered.

"Weapons, you mean guns?" Fagan asked. "Has he ever used a gun?"

"No, but we found four clean handguns. They are looking for prints on the bullets, but I don't hold out hope. I've learned that the Ghost is careful, and the people he works for must be as professional as he is," Simons said when her phone went off.

Agent Simons was not the most tactful of agents, and she bit back the words like a scream after she hit her toe on a corner table in the ambulance. Simons allowed those words to swim around momentarily before opening her mouth.

Fagan observed her while she spoke to the person on the other end of the line. Her face grew tense, and Fagan realized they had found the governor, which was not good.

"They found Cydet. A couple of kids riding motorcycles out at the concrete plant," Simons relayed. "We had him. We had the Ghost." Simons decided to take out her frustrations at the range later.

Chapter Seventeen

July 8

Rusty sat wholly immersed in Nicholas Sparks's novel *The Guardian*, one of his guilty pleasures. He was lying in a hammock tied between crooked palm trees, gently rocking in front of that ever-blue, clear water. With all the violence and suffering he saw, sinking into a sappy book took his mind away to a simpler, kinder place with a happy ending.

Rusty was dying. He knew he would not see his fifty-third birthday in December. He decided to live out his remaining days in Jamaica, where he was born. However, Rusty grew up in Florida. Gavin kept in close contact and gave him everything he could want or need. Rusty smiled. He watched the sailboat struggling to catch wind about a hundred yards out.

Gavin was a character. Although the Order paid him well, he had never been able to spend very much. Arcadia took care of everything when they were on assignment, which seemed to be most of the time. If Rusty were to be truthful, he thought, he missed the constant danger of the work. More, he missed the camaraderie. On the other hand, Julianne deserved more than he had given her over the years. Then, it was getting more and more challenging to keep Gavin in the dark about his biggest secret. His dearest friend had no idea Rusty had a child that carried Gavin's original name.

"Babe, I've made you some tea." Julianne's voice came over the rush of the waves. Rusty watched her extra curvy body walk across the sand from the little turquoise and yellow house less than a hundred yards from the water.

They were located ten miles from Negril. Rusty had bought it because he loved this side of the island, where he and Julianne enjoyed snorkeling the coral reefs. Twelve years younger than he, Julianne had been the calm center of his storm for the past eleven years. Her tender nature had calmed many rages. She never asked for anything and had always been there for him. When the evil was too much at times, she always reminded him of the man she loved: the one who had built the basketball courts in the middle of town so youth would have somewhere safe and well-lit to play, the man who helped with disaster relief when a hurricane hit the island. Julianne knew these things—everything Rusty did for the island residents, he did anonymously.

Moreover, Rusty loved her and had given her the biggest blessing. Although he was not around much, he was there when he was with them. Hence, Julianne would be the only one to know the legacy Rusty would leave behind. Her heart swelled as she looked at him.

Rusty had bought Julianne, who was born and raised in Jamaica, this little house nine years earlier, and together, when he had downtime, they had turned it into a perfect sanctuary. It was her, after all, who had brought some balance to his life and tamed the demons when they threatened to take over. It became Julianne's permanent home five years ago after she left teaching. Rusty trusted her more than anyone outside his order, and she knew what he did.

"Julianne, you're beautiful this morning," Rusty said as he took in her ebony legs, which peeked seductively from a green-and-blue wrap tied at her waist's right side. Her white bikini top contrasted beautifully with her skin, and she topped it with an emerald green scarf around her head, hiding her short brown hair. When Julianne smiled at him, her whole face lit up.

Rusty swung his legs around, sat up in the hammock, and took the tea from her; the aroma of strong mint clung to the blue teacup. He moved so she could sit beside him.

"How you feeling this morning, Boonoonoonoos?" she asked as she gently brushed her hand against his forehead.

"Actually, I'm feeling very well. I haven't felt dizzy at all this morning." Rusty smiled over at her and kissed her forehead.

"That's good; that's what I like to hear. Island air is good for you," Julianne said as she leaned her head against his lips before he pulled away. "Gavin left another message asking about you."

"I'll call him later. I thought we could go snorkeling if I still feel stable this afternoon." He looked off into the water, where the sailboat picked up the wind, then at Gavriel, who came running to them. "That is, if it's okay with you."

"Yes, I think we can. But first, you must eat more than two bites." Julianne looked him in the eye, which meant she was not playing. Julianne reached out and drew the boy onto her lap.

"Yes, my love," Rusty said as he took the last swallow of the tea. He set the cup down on the makeshift table.

Julianne watched Rusty closely, knowing when he was hiding something from her. He hid a lot. She accepted that she would not know everything; however, she expected nothing less than the truth regarding his health. The cancer was spreading, and Julianne would use any resource available to give her just a little more time with him.

Chapter Eighteen

July 13

Luca was still apprehensive and quite upset that Gavin shrugged off the arrest in Las Vegas. Gavin was his typical analytical self and reviewing the next Dossier.

Luca insisted they go to Manhattan, where he felt safer and was more aware of his surroundings. Helen received Luca's request to keep an eye on Agent Simons and waited for her to complete that task.

Gavin, however, was not thinking anything more about the incident in Las Vegas. He did not appreciate Helen's getting on his case again about getting Luca to Arcadia, their headquarters. Then, there was Luca's drama over the arrest. No matter how much Gavin reassured him, something other than his usual calm had overtaken the young man.

Luca left the penthouse and went for a walk. He needed to call Rusty.

Rusty took the satellite phone when Julianne said it was Luca, and he sounded upset.

"Luca, what's wrong?" Rusty asked.

"How many times has Gavin been arrested?" Luca replied without pleasantries.

"Three, maybe four times. Why, has he been arrested?"

"Yes, four days ago. Gavin is out, and everything is back to normal. I could use a sit-down."

"I can hear it. Scared you, huh?" Rusty asked with an attempt at humor.

"Scared is not the word I would use; all I could see was tabloids and headlines," Luca replied.

"You will learn that these situations are taken care of easily. There are measures to make sure he does not stay in custody. Which force was it?" Rusty asked a little more compassionately, hearing the fear remaining in Luca's voice.

"The FBI. They had him for almost nine hours," Luca stated.

"The FBI? Well, yes, that does sound tricky." Rusty thought about how the extraction team would have worked. "Did they find any evidence of who he is?"

Rusty muffled the phone to keep from laughing into the receiver. When Luca was upset, his Colombian and New Orleans accent came through in a scrambled mess that sounded like another language altogether. New Orleans came out *Norlens* and tabloids came out *tibleds*, and all other words had to be deciphered. That was until Gavin got to him with intense articulation.

"No, he told me to get out and run. I had ever'thing. But felt like I was abandoning him." The Hispanic accent which was mingled with New Orleans was falling out fast.

"You did as you were told, and that was right. Helen would not have been able to work so quickly if you were caught." Rusty said. "He once stayed in a Pasadena jail for three days. We had kidnapped the police chief's wife for a trade. Things are in place to ensure he does not stay in custody long. It seems like I need to talk with Gavin about getting you into training," Rusty said.

"Training? I am unsure if training will help keep me from becoming volcanic!" Luca shouted.

"Luca! Keep your head; everything worked out. You are fine, and so is he. Remember why you are with him. You have to be calm even when things get screwy," Rusty replied. "Come down to the island soon. We can speak, and I'll tell you what I can."

"All right, I think I could do that. Gavin is locked away again and working; I can fly out this afternoon. We just received another plane because the FBI kept ours." Luca already felt better. Speaking with Rusty always had a calming effect. "I'll pick up your favorite pastries from Two Little Red Hens. See you this evening."

Rusty set the phone down and looked out into the waters. Gavin seemed reluctant to take Luca to Arcadia, and that was something he needed to quit putting off. Gavin needed to resolve this situation immediately.

Chapter Nineteen

July 20

Luca wrapped his head around every situation imaginable. He kept a close eye on each move leading up to the operation. This time, he insisted on being well-rested and refused to be unaware of his surroundings again.

Gavin listened to Luca's concerns. So long as Luca stayed off Arcadia's radar and allowed Helen to think everything was under control, she would lay off insisting on a visit. She did not have Luca's Oath, but that did not mean she was without resources to bring him in if required. It had been years since Gavin had felt he had any real control of his life, and he would bathe in this for a bit longer.

Luca drove to an abandoned office complex on the east side of Annapolis and parked beside the metal structure. He looked at his watch and noted the time: 6:30 p.m. He stepped out to open Gavin's door.

Mitch Anderson was the husband of a chief operations officer of a mega-giant communications company. He was also known to Gavin for his secret trips to Vietnam, where he had purchased children for his sexual pleasure. Anderson would turn the children out into the street for someone else to capitalize on the young blood when Anderson was ready to dispose of those kids.

Gavin sprayed down his clothing with Off! Deep Woods spray before walking into the room. Anderson was in bed with the Bruscoe Crime Family. Duncan Bruscoe, Jr. was on Gavin's radar as his father had been. It would not be long before he had a location on the family patriarch.

Gavin stood quietly at the door of the abandoned warehouse, watching Anderson squirm from the fire ants crawling on him. The man was tied shirtless to a wooden chair and had a hood over his head. He screamed at the agony of each bite. Dark 9 sprayed Anderson down with sugar water, and painful-looking welts already covered his bare arms. Soon, the poison would cause fatal anaphylaxis.

Gavin carefully tugged the hood from Anderson's head so he could see him.

"Do you know who I am?" he asked as Anderson looked at him with an expression of pain.

"No, should I?" he asked, twitching.

Anderson's lips were the color of a purplish-blue violet.

"You got my package; I assume that's the reason for the extra security you recently hired," Gavin said.

"Oh! You're the Ghost!" Anderson said, fright now in his eyes because he knew what this meant.

"Yes, few people have the pleasure of meeting with me personally."

"Yes, but I can stop, I can change, you don't have to kill me, please!" he pleaded.

"I am Death's sickle," Gavin said, leaning in.

The Ghost stared into the man's bloodshot blue eyes.

Gavin held copies of the photographs. "The value of a person who can look at a child and hurt them is zero, worthless," he said, throwing the pictures face up on the floor. The photographs showed the lifeless bodies from the morgue. Six small children lay on cold steel slabs. No one had claimed them, so Gavin saw to their arrangements.

"I am just the instrument. Do not take it personally; I don't." Gavin stood and stared at the 8x10 photographs lying on the floor, the small faces staring up at him. His heart wept at those lost babies.

The more Mitch Anderson tried to find air, the more he struggled to breathe. He rocked back and forth on the chair.

Gavin stared him in the eyes just for a moment. Mitch Anderson's throat swelled and slowly closed.

"Do you know what that feeling is? It's fear, fear you cannot breathe, and fear you will die. Blood-thirsty fear. Now you know what those children felt like when you raped them."

Gavin took his hat from the Dark 9 member at the door and placed it low on his head when he heard the slow gasping for breath.

"Leave the scene. Call the police in, say, fifteen minutes," The Ghost said, looking at his watch and heading down the stairs.

Once Gavin was in the car, Luca got in the driver's seat and pulled away.

Chapter Twenty

August 15

The last few weeks flew by while Luca worked with Gavin on the London assignment. He just returned from a field trip with Dark 9 to make assignments and take photos. This operation had taken more time and infiltrating the prime minister's security had not been easy. But this Dossier was nearly six months in the making and needed more time. However, due to new evidence, the timeline had to be moved.

Back in Manhattan, Luca dismissed Dark 9, assigned to watch Gavin while he was away.

Luca knocked on the office door. "Gavin, I am back," he said, and then he left to repack and prepare to leave for London.

When Gavin emerged, Luca was on the phone. Gavin noted that his friend looked tired. They would need to take a break after this assignment. Maybe they could go sailing.

Luca was on the phone with a Dark 9 team leader about surveillance. He felt overwhelmed by his responsibilities. His mind had become a whirlwind of ensuring each situation was as safe as possible.

Luca had requested Helen keep tabs on Special Agent Simons. Helen had sent someone to her apartment one evening while Simons was off duty. The Dark 9 member placed a transmitter on the back of Simons' shield. Now, Luca could pull her location at any time. Simons was currently in Miami.

"Luca, are you ready to leave?" Gavin called as he put on his black suit jacket over his white shirt. He wore a royal blue and black Italian panel tie. Appearances were important to Gavin. Maybe it was his love of the old 007 movies.

"In a moment. I am repacking," he said as he closed the phone. Luca did not understand all of Rusty's responsibilities until now. He now grasped why they divided them, and they did not seem so overwhelming.

Luca shook his navy box-checked jacket off the hanger and slipped it on. He tied a Windsor knot on the green silk tie and tightened it. He examined himself in the mirror to ensure the knot was straight, grabbed his laptop and tablet, and shoved them in his bag.

Gavin had two interests in London. The first was to make sure the prime minister remained with the living. The second was to conclude the life of one Steve Bains, CEO of Hollinger Enterprises. There was more than enough evidence that Bains amassed his wealth not from his salary but from the sale and online distribution of child pornography. Gavin was searching for information to tie Bains to King himself. Although Gavin did not have proof that Steve Bains was in with Herbert Enterprises, he hoped to rectify this with evidence from the man. Gavin felt more optimistic than he had in a long time.

Chapter Twenty-One

August 17

Gavin sat quietly in the back seat as the driver took him to the meeting spot. He studied the streets of London, and the heavy traffic and the cyclists created a current of continuous movement in the streets. The driver was a salty-looking woman of thirty with dark hair, a fair complexion, and a dragon tattoo peeking from the cuff of her gray suit sleeve. She sat quietly in the front of the black SUV and stared straight ahead.

Gavin did not use any disguises on this trip. He did not feel the need because he was sure the Ghost could convince the prime minister to see things his way since he was here to save her life. Gavin rarely took work in the United Kingdom, but this concerned King and Gavin would move mountains when it came to King.

Gavin thought about the PM, Mary Lawrence, with nothing else to do besides look at traffic. The prime minister had received a threat from Hollinger Enterprises, which wanted a particular land purchase approved at any cost. No, these situations were not something the prime minister got involved with, but she had the influence over those who did. Gavin liked the prime minister, and by all accounts, she was suitable for the British people. However, she did not play by the usual rules and did not heavy-hand others to do her bidding. The prime minister did not take bribes or use her influence outside her role. Or, as in this case, to influence land sales.

Hollinger Enterprises pushed, threatened, and even tried to intimidate her. Ninety families currently occupy the property in a purpose-built flat complex. Nothing worked, and Gavin knew Steve Bains intended to ensure the prime minister went away permanently. She was due to address the Thames Valley District School Board on August 20[th,] and Gavin had it on good authority that an attack on her would happen on that occasion.

Luca had reviewed the arrangements secured by the Protection Command of Dark 9. Luca's friend Rango was his former medic from their military days with his DRAC unit. Luca planned to prevent any unforeseen trouble. Luca had been hyper-alert ever since Gavin's arrest in Las Vegas.

It was midday on 17 August. The air was thick and syrupy and just miserable. The sky was a lazy battle gray. Arrangements had been made with Mary Lawrence's protection detail, which had been infiltrated by a member of Dark 9 over four months ago. This had not been easy by any stretch of the imagination, but they had gotten lucky to have a Dark 9 who had served the prior prime minister, which had helped tremendously. It was unfortunate that the prime minister did not have previous knowledge of her forthcoming meeting with the Ghost.

The prime minister's car arrived first, and a security officer opened her door. The prime minister exited the car, looking confused, when the bodyguard motioned for her to go inside. Another bodyguard got out of the other side and followed her inside, ensuring everything was as it should be.

"What is this?" she exclaimed.

"Your appointment," the security agent answered.

"Not quite," she protested. "What appointment do I have here?"

"Ma'am, it's secure, and you will want to listen," he assured.

"I'll have your job for this!"

"Yes, ma'am, I still believe it's worth the risk," he insisted.

Gavin's black SUV pulled up after the prime minister's. The driver went around to the side door of the building where Luca was waiting.

Luca led Gavin to the table, where Prime Minister Lawrence waited nervously. Gavin observed the short, sturdy woman, a tad over sixty, with an easy round face framed by too-short bangs. The massive clump of silver beads accentuated the slate blue blouse she wore.

"Prime Minister, I am sorry to be meeting in such a manner; however, it could not be avoided," Gavin said, smiling.

"Who are you? Do you know what you are doing?" she asked curtly, brushing her hair behind her ears.

Gavin looked around the empty tearoom, smelling the familiar scent of Earl Gray along with some distinctive minty and fruit fragrances. Like many establishments in the UK, it had the feeling of a place that had not changed in a hundred years, where ladies dressed in their finest dresses and hats and men wore suits and tall hats and carried canes with elaborate handles. It had the wide dark trim of highly waxed walnut of a bygone era. The tables were strong, handmade of wood, old enough to have well-worn edges due to years of use. The walls above the walnut wainscotting were neatly wallpapered in a charming mint-green and white floral pattern. He concluded that it was a charming place, pulling the chair out and unbuttoning his jacket before sitting down.

"I always know what I am doing." Gavin smiled and spoke softly. "Who I am is not what is important today. Who you are is of grave importance, Prime Minister Lawrence. I have a preference for you living, and I have documents you need to see." Gavin slid a gray envelope to her.

Transcripts of conversations between Steve Bains, Hollinger's CEO, and an unknown person were in the envelope. Bains talked about dates and details of the prime minister's daily activities. On page three, they were discussing the District School Board meeting. She saw the words "single shot to the head." She dropped the papers on the table.

"How did you get these before my people did?" Lawrence asked, her round face pinched, her jaw slack.

"I find the *how* rarely matters," Gavin replied.

Her hand went to the large beads at her neck. "A plan is already in place; I'll just increase my security. May I have these?" she asked.

"That's only one plan. These evildoers have contingencies," Gavin replied, tugging at the collar of his shirt as he watched the pedestrians out the window. He did not like being so public, especially sitting with a head of state. Gavin observed her protection detail standing guard by the door. If she did not believe him, this could be the end of the line for his Ghost. It was time to reveal who he was and see.

She picked up the papers again and flipped through them, not seeing any more threats, and looked at him.

"Madam Prime Minister, I have a reputation for recovering and often disseminating information. I deal in knowledge, and at times it is devastating material. It is mostly that intelligence that has kept me safe over the years. A lover, drug problems, and often a person's pockets cannot account for their lifestyle. These and many more are secrets that ruin lives. Perhaps, if I told you who I am, you might be more inclined to consider that I am sharing a true transcript of a conversation." He reached his hand across the table to shake hers and introduce himself.

"I am the one referred to as the Ghost. Maybe you have heard of me?" he said. "Very pleased to meet you."

The prime minister's face went white while her hand was still in his. A sticky, sick feeling filled the prime minister's stomach, and the air thickened around her. She had heard stories told by older men of people having their lives hijacked by such a person, a person capable of finding the most toxic information. That information could bring even the most seemingly upstanding men or women to saunter through the dredges and their worldly possessions ripped away without a trace. The Ghost made leaders flee and toppled industries. For years, he had been on Interpol's Most Wanted, a simple silhouette with **The Ghost** written underneath. There was never a picture nor a face, and those who encountered him rarely gave a description. When they did, the account was vague. He was indeed a ghost. The Ghost did not exist anywhere. This person had no DNA, no fingerprints, nothing. There was never a name, just a ghost story people told to scare each other. The Ghost stories are cryptic tales, except they were imposed upon those with less than ethical practices.

"The Ghost," she said aloud, staring at him like he had grown a third eye.

"No man or woman is either a mouse or a lion. In each lives both; it only depends on the proper motivation," Gavin replied.

"Which am I?" she asked.

Gavin looked at her thoughtfully. "That depends on whether you will give in to Hollinger's threats."

"Is that why you are here? To convince me to influence the sale to dislocate all those people? I will not be responsible for that." She spoke more bitterly than she intended, her jaw tightening. She bit into her lower lip, trying to remain composed.

The Sapphire Ghost

"Then a lion it is. I knew you were a good woman, and I'm pleasantly surprised to find a few politicians with ethics. That is precisely why I will help you," The Ghost stated.

"How do you intend to do that?" she asked skeptically.

Before Gavin could answer, a front window of the tearoom shattered, and smoke filled the air.

Chapter Twenty-Two

Luca heard the object hit the window, and the glass shattered; two more flew through the now open front of the tearoom. Luca stumbled to the table and hastily pushed Gavin and the prime minister to the floor, pulling the heavy wood table over them. Luca had just toppled the second table and drawn his weapon when everything went bright white as the first bomb went off. Debris hit the surrounding crockery in a storm of shattering porcelain. Then, just as suddenly as the smoke filled the air, it went dark. The ringing in his ears reminded Luca of Iraq and those images had him disassociated for what seemed like a long dream. Then, his body was thrown backward into the waiter's station. Within a few seconds of the first bomb, the second ruptured with a violent cracking noise.

The bombs sent shards of glass and wood splinters into a cyclone within the tearoom. Luca was dazed and hit his head when the force of the first blast flung him back. Just as he made it to his feet, the second blast erupted, throwing him down again. Thoughts of distant lands, hot sand, and heavy gunfire permeated his mind. Finally, Luca forced his thoughts into reality as he staggered toward the table where he had covered Gavin and the prime minister.

Luca lifted the table off Gavin, noticing he shielded the PM with his body. Luca began to tug him to his feet when Gavin said, "Get her out first!" Mary Lawrence was unconscious and bleeding from a head wound. With Lawrence in a bridal carry, Luca headed to the side door where an SUV should be waiting. The SUV was gone, so he went to his car.

"Secure the area! Find Gavin's driver, and scatter." Luca spoke into the earwig.

Luca got the prime minister into the back seat. Knowing he had no time to spare before the weight of London dropped down on top of them, Luca went back after Gavin, noticing the stark red across his employer's white shirt. Luca helped him to his feet, leading him to the door and into the car.

The Sapphire Ghost

Luca noted the scurry of official bodyguards picking themselves off the concrete walk, and they headed inside. *This is bad, really bad!* He wanted to call on the help of Dark 9 but was still determining who he could trust. This place should have been secure. Where was Gavin's driver?

Luca nearly collided with a police car as he tried to pull out. The massive headache had lights flashing in front of his eyes, and he wasn't sure which were from PTSD and which were from the metropolitan police force. Luca finally pulled into the street and took off just as the fire trucks slowed in front of the tearoom. This was bad. Not only was the prime minister injured, but Luca was kidnapping her. He did not feel he had a choice because someone leaked this location. Gavin looked awful, and his color resembled burnt newspapers in a wastebasket. The blood crept out around Gavin onto the leather.

Luca finally pulled over when it was safe. He grabbed a blanket from beneath the passenger's seat and approached Gavin. Tearing open the injured man's shirt, Luca saw a small piece of a wooden chair leg penetrating Gavin's left side, just under the ribs. Luckily, Luca heard Gavin was not straining to breathe, so he knew the lung was fine. Luca pressed the blanket around the wooden shrapnel and asked Gavin to hold it there. Looking into the face of his employer and friend, Luca began to panic as he saw the color of his face. Then reached across Gavin, feeling for the prime minister's pulse, which was strong. Luca returned to the car and took off for the Surrey Hills as fast as possible without drawing attention. He and Gavin were the same blood type. Luca could handle it if Gavin needed a field transfusion before getting to Rango's house. He messaged Rango to let him know he needed that favor after all.

Luca paid no attention to the landscape as he turned onto a long dirt road leading back into a wooded area. His head was splitting, and red dots danced in front of his eyes. Rango stood in front of his farmhouse. His large, tattooed arms crossed over a rather hefty belly, and Luca could see the confusion in his dark, prominent features when he pulled up to the front door.

"Get her! I'll get him!" Luca commanded.

Rango did as Luca ordered and quickly lifted the limp body of the prime minister out of the car. Luca helped Gavin from the vehicle. He could walk but leaned heavily on Luca, but Gavin was weak from blood loss.

Once inside, Rango assessed both patients. Fortunately for the prime minister, she was hit in the head and knocked out cold, and she had a minor laceration but nothing life-threatening.

Gavin was another matter. Gavin went limp, and Luca and Rango caught him and placed him on the transport bed. Rango moved him quickly to the barn. Rango had transformed the barn into a makeshift radiology lab, small scanner, and an ultrasound machine, although a field medic—such as he had once been—could work wonders with less advanced tools. Assorted chairs sat against the wall on the clean concrete floor. Once they moved Gavin to a bed, Rango managed to get some pictures while Luca called Helen.

"Let me know when you can get him back on the jet, and I will give you a location for a hospital where he will be safe," said the voice on the phone.

Luca knew what that meant. A year earlier, outside of Pittsburgh, they had taken fire, and he and Gavin were hit. Although Gavin was grazed on the side, Luca had taken a small caliber to his right shoulder. Helen sent them to a monastery outside Youngstown, a small borough.

"Yes, ma'am, I'm very sorry," Luca said. "Seems I am not as good at keeping him as safe as Rusty was."

"Luca, listen, you did nothing wrong. Sometimes things happen." Helen spoke quietly on the phone. "We cannot predict everything."

"Luca, get in here!" Rango's voice called from behind him.

"Got to go." Luca stuck the phone in his suit jacket and ran back into the barn.

"What is it?" Luca looked more panicked than before.

"You told me you're his blood type, right?" Rango asked.

"Yes," Luca confirmed, already removing his jacket and pulling up the sleeve on his shirt.

Helen laid the phone by her keyboard, and her fingers quickly moved across the keys. She was the one who quietly ran the orders from the headquarters in Maine, and finding help in another country was more complicated and costly. However, Helen would spend whatever was necessary to ensure Gavin was cared for. As for Luca, she understood he needed help, but first, she needed his commitment. Maybe this situation was precisely what Gavin needed to quit putting off the inevitable.

"He needs blood, enough to give him strength back. I have him stable. Removed the wood, cleaned the wound, and stitched him up," Rango called to Luca.

Rango swabbed Luca's arm, and Luca took the FBTK from Rango and inserted the needle into his arm. Rango then inserted the needle into Gavin's central vein in his neck.

"I'm going back to the house to take care of the prime minister," Rango said and left them.

Luca watched as the dark red material led itself through the line when Rango opened the port. Luca studied Gavin's face and the hollow gray features, unlike his own. He waited for the blood to reach Gavin's neck. Gavin was not an ordinary man. He was one of the Seraphim—a guardian. The angels knew that the world was not sunshine and roses. That is why God gave them weapons. Luca felt that Gavin had that role on earth.

Luca's thoughts wandered off as he sat in the chair beside Gavin. The Holiest Order of Angels is how the Ghosts began. At least, that is what Luca was told. The only one who knew for sure was Helen Glass. The Glass files were the Dossiers Gavin Garrison retrieved every week by courier, and the files were delivered directly to Gavin's hand no matter their location. It was fantastic to think about, to say the least, but it was Luca's world now. Thinking back to his earliest days with the Order, he marveled at how easily Gavin described what he did and how he justified it. It was an awakening to the darkness that seemed like a natural next step for Luca.

The revelation that people out there had causes such as this gave him hope. Luca put that devotion not just into the Ghost but into the cause. Rusty once said it would only take once for a mission to fail, and it would all be over. "Then what? Could you go back to how you were before?" Luca thoughtfully shook his head. *No, I could not.* Luca would never be able to go back. He would strive to reach so far forward, stretch to whatever length possible, to become half the man Gavin was.

Luca's thoughts jerked back to the present when he heard his phone ring. Looking over to Gavin, lying too still, Luca stuck his free hand in his jacket pocket and retrieved his phone.

"Luca."

"Luca, it's me," came Helen's ever-calm voice.

"Ma'am," Luca said.

"There's a helicopter on its way to your location. Is Gavin stable?" Helen asked, concern, sneaking into her voice.

"Yes, I believe he's stable." Luca sounded more confident than he felt.

"Medical staff will be on board. Let them take over when they arrive." Helen's words were quiet and calm. "ETA, ten minutes. It will be all right, Luca."

"We'll be ready," Luca said, placing the phone in his pants pocket.

It was now time to make this right. Luca Medina allowed a rage he had not drawn on in nearly a decade to return.

He watched Gavin for several minutes and noticed he had recovered some color. Rango walked past him to remove the FBTK.

"We've got a chopper on the way," Luca told him.

Rango's attention was on Gavin's vitals. "Much better," Luca heard him say to himself.

Then, he began adding more tape to the IV on Gavin's hand. Luca withdrew the needle from his arm and, taking the cotton Rango offered him, taped it over the mark. Luca took the other end of the FBTK and stuffed the cord and needles into the red plastic bag hanging on the wall.

"Now, let me take a look at you," Rango said, looking at the gash on the top right side of his head.

Luca touched the bump and felt the crust of dried blood congealed in his hair. "I'm fine."

"Sit," Rango ordered.

Luca sat while Rango cleaned the laceration and added a couple of butterfly strips. Afterward, Luca quickly left the room. When he returned, he held

The Sapphire Ghost

a gallon of bleach and some towels. Methodically, Luca began to wash everything down. Luca quickly wiped any remnants of blood off the floor and counters. He would also wipe down the table that Gavin was lying on after he was moved. Luca collected everything with Gavin's blood and stuffed it into a large black trash bag.

Rango left the barn to check on Mary Lawrence again and download the ultrasound pictures of the object nearly penetrating Gavin's left kidney onto a flash drive for Luca.

Rango stood at the barn door, studying Luca, cleaning the surfaces carefully upon his return. Rango wondered to himself who the man was. He trusted Luca Medina, and Captain Medina was his army unit's commanding officer. Whatever he was involved in, whoever this mystery man was, Rango was sure he mattered. Both men looked up simultaneously as the chopper sounded overhead.

"I hope you don't mind; it's landing in the field beside the barn?"

"I don't mind at all," Rango said as he spotted the white and green helicopter when it began to descend. "This is the most exciting thing I've done in a long time."

"Thank you, friend." Luca gave the man a one-armed hug. "Your payment will be here by morning."

"Payment? I don't want payment!" Rango looked hurt. "I owe you everything."

"You owe me nothing, brother, ever," Luca said, placing a hand on Rango's shoulder. "Please don't speak about what happened here."

"No worries, brother," Rango said.

The side door to the barn opened, and Luca watched as two men in identical black uniforms entered. The first was a tall black man with round, tinted glasses and tight, neat, small dreads. He approached Luca, studying his lapel pin. Luca noted the man's small square sapphire pin on the pocket of his uniform shirt. Luca also remembered the face; he had seen this man before with Senator Baynard.

"Dr. Brody, sir," the man said, holding out his hand. He eyed the four-stone sapphire pin Luca wore on the collar of his jacket and knew it meant

Luca was the Ghost's right hand, to be held in the same high regard as the Ghost himself. One life depended on the other. It was a long, narrow platinum bar with four perfect square blue sapphire stones.

"Luca Medina." He introduced himself. "Brody, this is Rango," Luca said, recognizing the distinct military persona and using the doctor's last name. Luca took a step back so Rango could inform the doctor of the Ghost's condition.

Rango came forward, took control of the situation as if it were normal, and proceeded to tell Brody what he had done and his thoughts about the man's condition.

"Thank you for everything you have done," Brody said, shaking Rango's hand. Brody then stepped back and handed a light blue envelope to Luca.

Luca recognized the offering and stepped forward to give it to Rango. "This is for you. Do with it what you want. Also, there is a card with a phone number. Call that number if you ever need anything, day or night. Or call me." Luca turned to Brody and the other man, already looking over Gavin.

Luca overheard Brody on the mic, and almost immediately, more men headed into the barn, carrying a stretcher and a case with cleaning supplies. Luca knew it would be no use telling them he had already cleaned the area. They had instructions from Helen to leave no trace that Gavin was ever in the house or barn.

Luca stood by as they loaded the Sapphire Ghost into the helicopter. Helen had spared no expense in getting transportation here for Gavin. Luca knew that from this point until Gavin was well, all those attending would regard him with the highest respect and attention as the Sapphire Ghost.

Once Gavin was safely inside the medevac copter, Luca took Brody by the arm. "Take care of him. I have got to get the prime minister back, and I have a few things to handle on this end. Give me your cell number. I'll call you when I need to find him. If he is well enough, he will demand you take him here," Luca said, writing down an address in Florida.

"Sir, what about your pho—?" Brody had started to say before Luca dropped his phone to the ground and stomped on it.

The Sapphire Ghost

With an ominous stare, Luca said, "I'm going dark, and, as I said, Dr. Brody, take care of him and stay with him until I return." In his tone, it wasn't an implied threat but a promise.

Brody handed the man his number and could feel the tiny pinpricks up the back of his neck. Luca looked down at the doctor's number, returned the paper, and walked to the main house to get the prime minister.

Chapter Twenty-Three

Luca was falling, and there was no coming back until he was done. He was extremely calm—that type of calm where everything seemed to move in slow motion. The part of him from the war, always analyzing, picking away the wreckage, losing himself in the full-on take-over. This part allowed him to see the dispersed clutter in absolute quiet. Luca was not a man who angered or had any outward tells. When he slipped past comfortable, he was deadly. He warred with his two wolves daily, and it was clear which one fed today. And with Rusty gone, Luca was off leash.

When Luca returned to the house, Rango was cleaning out the backseat of the SUV with ammonia and scrubbing it with a scrub brush.

"I'm unsure what you will do with the car, but there is no need to take that lady anywhere with this back here," Rango said when Luca walked up. The hairs on Rango's neck instantly stood up. Unfortunately, he understood the attitude he was seeing. Medina was not himself when he went here.

"Thank you. Do you still have any of my clothes from my last visit?" Luca asked.

"Yes, up in that room," Rango replied, gesturing to a window on the second floor.

"Would you mind if I cleaned up before I left? I need to return the prime minister to her driver," Luca asked, watching him add more ammonia to the car seat.

"Do what you need to, Medina. If I can help, let me know." Rango knew what lay beneath that cool outer appearance. And Rango felt his gut churning slightly, knowing that monster was about to come out.

Luca stood in the doorway to the den where the prime minister was waiting. She was sitting up, drinking something hot, looking around in the modestly decorated den of the farmhouse.

Coughing as he entered the room so as not to startle her, Luca spoke. "Prime Minister? Are you okay?"

The Sapphire Ghost

She looked up at him sadly. "I think you should call me Mary. How is he, the Ghost?" Something inside made her feel great empathy for the man who had covered her and probably saved her life; he was no longer a myth.

"He will be fine; he is in excellent hands," Luca told her.

"Good. Hollinger wants me dead," she spoke as if she had just now concluded. "Thank you for protecting me."

"Yes," Luca said. "You weren't meant to die today."

"What should I do?" she asked, her face wracked in confusion.

"I recommend calling your family and meeting them outside the city center. Then, go to a secure location. Think of a home that allows you to see in many directions. Get your family and as much security as possible but be sure you can trust the personnel. It wasn't an accident that Hollinger knew where you would be," Luca said, running his fingers through his hair.

"I am unsure I can trust any of them." She sighed and shook her head.

"Talk to Rango. Perhaps he would be interested in going with you. He is a good man and a better scout you will not find. I'll give you a few moments to gather your thoughts. I've got to have you back at the meeting spot in an hour," Luca said, walking out.

Luca spoke with Dark 9, who was currently acting as security detail for Mrs. Lawrence. The team member was also a former SIS and understood the protocols. Luca decided his window to return the prime minister was growing shorter. The PPO was scouring London, and her kidnapping had already hit the news.

Shortly after 4:00 p.m., Rango pulled onto a little-used street outside London. The prime minister asked Rango to work with her for a few days. Luca helped Mary Lawrence out of the car and gave instructions to the driver, the Dark 9 member that Luca spoke about. Luca instructed him to stay with Prime Minister Lawrence until further notice, or his superiors dismissed him within the PPO.

Chapter Twenty-Four

St. Catharine's Convent of Mercy waited for the arrival of the Ghost.

Brody walked in and spoke to the sisters. "I need to speak with Sister Rebeka, please."

"I am Sister Rebeka," said a voice to his left. A noticeably young woman, not wearing a habit, stood there. She was perhaps in her late twenties with shaggy, short red hair, freckles, and a reassuring smile.

"You are the one who knows of the Ghost?" Brody asked.

"Yes. What Order are we caring for today?" Sister Rebeka asked.

"The Sapphire, Sister," Brody responded respectfully.

"I have not had him here before, and he is far from home," Sister Rebeka commented.

"No, ma'am," Brody replied.

He looked around the building's rock walls. It was hot outside, but inside the stone structure, it was cool.

"We are set up for him. I am unsure if we have everything you need, but we are adequate. The sisters are waiting on him."

"We just need to get him in and prepped for surgery."

"Bring him in through the lower side. I'll have the sisters assist you," she said.

The facility was not large, but its stones had stood for hundreds of years. Updates were evident. St. Catherine's is in the Norfolk Broads, the farthest east one could go and still be in England, and it was miles from any other building. On the flight, Brody had noticed the hundreds of acres of wheat grown in East Anglia.

Brody completed a scan of Garrison's condition and then prepped for surgery. The sisters' setup was good. The room was pristine, and every stainless surface was scrubbed and shined.

Forty-five minutes later, Brody removed the rest of the debris and cleaned the wound. He allowed the sister to assist him in stitching the Ghost back up

The Sapphire Ghost

as he watched. The nun's skill was incredibly good. He would heal without much trouble unless Gavin did something to pull the stitches out. The first in command, Luca, ordered Brody to stay with Gavin; Brody knew he would soon see what kind of patient the Ghost would be. He served as medical support for two other Orders but had never learned anything about the Ghosts he treated.

Chapter Twenty-Five

New York, New York

King walked into the studio in a bad mood. His brother had called to tell him that again the Ghost escaped their army of mercenaries. This man had been a thorn in his side for nineteen years.

"No, no! Don't you people ever listen?!" He ranted in the studio about these not being the right kind of kids.

Seven small children from ages four to seven or eight stood naked in front of Jack King. The set they stood on was a large room with a small bed, table, and two chairs. The room was completely white, with dimmer lights around the bed and bright daylight-infused lights around the table. Cuffs were fixed to the table, along with chains and ropes.

The King walked the line of children. "Get rid of this one. Features are too angular and don't have that sweet look."

A slim man in rectangular glasses took the boy by the arm and led him out of the room.

"This one looks sweet." He placed his hand under the small girl's chin. She was no more than four. "Clean her up, curl her hair, and put her in something white."

The next one was a boy of about seven. The small boy had dark curly brown hair, and already, at his young age, his eyes were permanently scared. He shivered as the director approached him.

"Yes, you are a pretty one, aren't you? Nice dimples," King turned to his assistant. "This one, get him ready for Adam's room. Let Adam have some fun with him first. I want to see the terror on his soft face. Dismiss the rest for now; two is all I have time for today. Let's not dawdle! We've got movies to make and a couple of fresh faces for the fans. Let's not disappoint."

An hour later, the little girl came out with two men who held her hands. They danced with her and made her laugh, and she twirled around in a fluffy white dress with a cute white bow in her hair.

The Sapphire Ghost

"Quiet!" said King.

The sheer torture that child was exposed to was terrible.

"I think we will lose this one, King," said a man from the stage.

"Get rid of the body and bring in the boy," King said.

King did not care that these children belonged to someone or that someone was missing them. It did not even cross his mind that there was a mom or dad someplace hoping and praying that their child would return home safely to them. It didn't matter; they would never be seen again.

This filth made King the most unknown but richest man in America.

Chapter Twenty-Six

August 19

Luca spent nearly two days looking through public records to acquire the blueprints for Hollinger Enterprises' offices. He also printed the one for Steve Bains' home as a backup. Luca thought this would soon be finished, one way or another.

The plan Dark 9 made to snatch Bains from his morning coffeehouse on the corner of Ridge Street had been abandoned. All the research that had gone into it was a bust—and he could not find the documents in Gavin's bag when he went through it in search of Steve Bains' itinerary. Luca would have to make his own plan. Luca thought he'd like nothing better than to snatch Bains from the comfort of his bed in the middle of the night. He would love to see the alarm on his face as he was gagged and dragged from a deep sleep quietly without waking the wife.

Right now, however, time was short, and he would be working alone. He'd have to go with the most readily available opportunity. Unfortunately, since Bains spent so much time at his office, that location would have to do. Now Luca needed to figure out the details with, of course, minimal risk to himself. He would need to cut the power, but they might have automatic generator backup. This was the problem with working alone, but there were also many advantages. Luca would have to figure this out for himself. Then, the light bulb went off in his head.

He tapped into the building management company's server, looking for the controller's records. It took several hours to review the paid bills, but he finally found what he was looking for: janitorial service records. NCI Inc. was the custodial service for the Hollinger floors. Then Luca went through NCI's employee directory. Andy Rollins was a night shift janitor assigned to the building, with badge number 1843.

"Okay, Andy, let us see what you like to do. How much money do you owe?" Luca said aloud, searching bank records. Andy Rollins used the most common bank in London.

Ouch! Poor Andy, who was almost five hundred thousand in debt. Astounding on a janitor's income.

The following night, Luca visited Andy Rollins' home. A million in American dollars because he did not have the time to switch to sterling. The money should keep him from work tonight, and the only other thing he'd have to do is give Luca his badge.

Luca and Andy had a long, friendly chat. He seemed extremely nice, working two full-time jobs and barely making ends meet. Donnie, his partner of thirty years, had needed several operations, leaving them with a lot of debt and Donnie unable to work. Andy willingly gave up his badge and keys to every office on the two floors and sketched a detailed drawing. Luca listened intently but only wanted to know where one office was.

"Anything special for the CEO's office?" Luca finally asked.

"No, the usual, clean his coffee pot, start a new pot because he is an American and hates tea. Mr. Bains will be there for hours; he works all the time. He is a nice guy. Clean his bathroom and take out his rubbish. He doesn't like you to vacuum while he's working, so don't do it," Andy explained.

Chapter Twenty-Seven

August 21

Gavin Garrison sat on the balcony of his only real home on the beach in Dremmond—a quaint, idyllic blue and white house in the tiny compound outside of Destin, Florida. Gavin sat on the balcony, sipping on a glass of brandy. Dr. Brody insisted on staying with him while he recovered.

Gavin hated being coddled, especially by someone he had no relationship with. Yes, Helen trusted Brody, and he knew beyond a doubt that he could trust Helen's instincts. Still, he was not fragile and did not like being treated that way. And where was Luca? Helen had nothing; Luca was gone.

Gavin figured Luca was out to complete the operation. That Dossier was probably the person who wounded Gavin so seriously. Luca was going after Steve Bains alone, although Luca knew that was against the rules. What was he trying to prove? Gavin thought about what Luca Medina was capable of and how many pages of his Army files were redacted. He still had many questions about Luca's past, but the man always followed orders and was entirely devoted.

Brody came in holding a phone. "Is it Luca?" Gavin asked.

"No, it's Congressman Ashman." Brody looked a little baffled and hesitated, but Gavin took the phone.

"Phillip, so good to hear from you," Gavin said politely. "I am so sorry I missed your fundraiser; I was looking forward to it but was unexpectedly delayed in the UK."

"First of all, thank you for the cakes. They were well received." The congressman cleared his throat. "Well, sir, it was not what you would have expected." Ashman's voice sounded defeated. "Herbert Enterprises sent an actress, Elaine Pratt. She came to get the invitation through a friend, Ms. Pratt, who is researching how campaign money was raised."

"All right, so she knows somebody. We can follow up on that," Gavin replied.

"There's more, sir," Ashman stated. "Elaine Pratt has ties to Duncan Bruscoe, Jr. It's rumored she is Bruscoe's girl of the hour."

"Interesting. The Bruscoe crime syndicate out of Maryland. I'm aware of them. Duncan Sr. and I had an ongoing game of chess, but he eventually lost."

Congressman Ashman ignored the remark since he was unsure if he wanted to know whether or not they had played chess. "The information you requested on Isaak Heinrich, the German Ambassador. The U.S. has nothing; he is clean as far as we know, as is his wife's. Does this help you?"

"Thank you, Phillip; I needed some good news today," Gavin spoke softly. He enjoyed hearing Ashman's familiar southern accent.

"I wish I could've been more helpful in getting that filth off the streets." Ashman's voice spelled out everything that justified Gavin's having trusted him.

"Phillip, we'll have drinks when I am up and about. We can discuss any further help from your side if you wish. Feel free to call me Gavin."

Ashman paused momentarily at being given a name. "Up and about? Are you okay?" The congressman spoke in an endearing southern drawl. He thought about the news in London a few days earlier and Prime Minister Lawrence's strange disappearance for several hours.

"Had a small setback, but I will be myself shortly. Don't you worry yourself because it is the nature of the beast." Gavin smiled at Phillip's concern.

"You were in London, weren't you?" the congressman surmised quickly.

"Phillip, keeping up with the news, I see, good man. Take care of that family of yours and if you need anything, call." Gavin hit "end" before anything else could be said. He handed the phone back to Brody.

"I'd like to get out of this chair and go for a walk," Gavin said.

"Yes, sir. Let me help you up, and I'll go with you," Brody said.

"Brody, you are suffocating me. Back off a bit. I can do this!" Gavin said with a grimace and sounding irritated.

Gavin started to sit upright when the pain in his side stopped him short. It was not as bad as being shot, but it gave him some deep-down stabbing pain that made him sweat. Nevertheless, he pushed himself up and stood without assistance.

"I'm walking with you or behind you, but you're not going alone," Brody said, matter-of-factly and precisely like the doctor he was. "Would Medina let you just wander off in your condition?" Brody said, barely holding back his annoyance.

"I suppose not, but do not raise your voice to me, Brody, because I've shot men for less. Get my shoes, please," Gavin said, feeling wobbly but determined to get on his feet and not lay around that house for another day.

Several houses were within the Dremmond Beach compound. Most of those who stayed here were those under Gavin's protection. Gavin looked over at the house next door, which was usually empty. He had seen a woman the previous night, and now, noticing the white and black Mustang in the drive, he knew he had not imagined her. The caretaker had said nothing about someone staying in his other house. Then again, he was not sure anyone had notified her that Gavin was coming in. He could not stand convents, which were too quiet and pious for his liking.

Gavin's role as a Ghost allowed him certain entitlements, which were not numerous. Nonetheless, he always received excellent medical care from sisters who were more than adequate in their roles. And they were never hurried or restricted by bureaucracy.

Gavin's thoughts turned to Luca, now his first-in-command, who still had not breached the entry hall. Gavin was growing concerned, and it had been four days without a word from him.

Brody walked quietly alongside Mr. Garrison as he stared off to someplace else. Brody wondered if he should tell him what Mr. Medina had told him.

"Sir, may I speak freely?" Brody approached the subject with care.

"As freely as you wish," Gavin responded.

"Mr. Medina told me he would be dark for a few days after asking for my cell number," Brody said.

"I see. What was Luca's state of mind when he told you this?" Gavin asked.

"He seemed resolute. Yet I felt threatened when he told me not to leave your side until he returned. So, he must be returning, and I thought you should know," Brody said.

"You felt threatened—by Luca?" Gavin asked, surprised. He thought about the mild-mannered man with zero attitude. If Brody had felt threatened, it meant Luca was beyond being himself; maybe what was blacked out in his military records. The revelation had Gavin's curiosity piqued. He studied Brody and did not see a man who often felt threatened. Although Brody's tone was polite and gentle, it held authority.

"Yes. Not by Medina's words but by his tone, which was unnerving. It almost held a hint of death," Brody said reluctantly, thinking back also to the expression on Luca's face as he instructed Brody.

Gavin listened carefully to Brody's assessment of Luca's state of mind. He was apprehensive about Luca disappearing but thought Luca was his usual, highly analytical self. Then again, Luca had never been in this situation before, entrusting Gavin to another's care, so it was reasonable that Luca would react strongly. Gavin wondered what it meant. He thought about calling Rusty for advice, but that would only result in heaping worry on the ill man.

"Do you mind me asking . . . what are you thinking? I just assumed this was normal for him," Brody continued.

"No, Brody, he's normally anything but unnerving. Luca is always calm and calculative, and he has never shown a measure of anger in the seven years I have known him. He has always been the center of the hurricane between Rusty and me."

Brody broached the subject he wanted to bring up. "Do you question my judgment in any way?"

Gavin responded quickly. "Absolutely not. I do not question you, Brody, as I see that you are not a weak person. I do, however, question just where Luca's head is."

"I felt you needed to know he did say he would return, and he has not abandoned you, sir," Brody said.

"Thank you. I believe I will go back to the house now," Gavin replied with an air of finality.

Chapter Twenty-Eight

The night of August 23rd, Luca went to work on the night shift, completely jacked on coffee. He played all day at getting into the character of a mild-mannered janitor. Luca used the secured entrance at the back, as Andy had instructed. Luca contacted the security office to inform them that a new person was on-premises because Andy needed to care for Donnie. NCI sent him in Andy's place.

A three-day beard covered his face, and he wore a ball cap. He had put on an extra layer of clothing under the shabby green uniform to fill him out and help in his escape. By outlining his eyes with a bit of eyeliner smudged to form deep circles, he had created the impression of a man who worked nights—perhaps a second job.

After leaving the security desk, he made a beeline for the electrical closet. He pulled a small device from his pocket with a cell phone attached. The distraction would at least cut the power for approximately five to seven minutes before the generators were engaged if they existed. Luca could not confirm the generators' existence or the generator switches' location. This device could effectively keep the power off indefinitely; at least, he was hopeful. Luca also left a mild diversion for the guards behind the water feature as he passed.

Luca quickly found the janitor's closet. He grabbed the cart and added a gallon of bleach to the mop bucket. Shoving a new roll of duct tape in his pocket and filling his cart, Luca started his rounds, beginning at the last office on the ninth floor. Luca would systematically make his way to the corner office, where he knew Bains was still working.

Luca ran the vacuum in every office and corridor and tipped the rubbish into his large bin. He knew he had only a few minutes to move once he got to the CEO's office before security was triggered. This unknown was the part he loved best. Luca memorized the schematics of the office building, knowing exactly where each camera was placed. He knew all the vents and every exit. The power would go out at precisely 11:30 p.m.

The Sapphire Ghost

At 11:25 p.m., Luca rapped on Bains's office door and turned the knob. A slender, well-groomed man with a loosened blue and white tie sat behind the desk. He had styled black hair, the kind you would see on the evening news, his features chiseled and taunt. Luca knew vanity played a key role with people of his status. Bains was sitting at a glass desk, neat and uncluttered. The city's light reflected behind him in the oversized windows, and he was intensely working on something on his desktop.

"Who are you? And where's Andy?" Bains asked immediately.

Luca was impressed that the man had the decency to know Andy's name. "Sir, I'm sorry. Andy has some personal business to take care of," Luca spoke quietly.

"Donnie sick again?" Steve Bains asked, leaning away from the desk.

"Hmm, yes, sir, real bad," Luca replied in an exaggerated lisp as he took the paper towels from the lower shelf on the cart.

"Your name?" Bains asked, almost interested, looking directly at the smaller man with slumped shoulders.

"It's hmm, Chad Tate. The lads call me Tater." Luca gave a slight smirk.

"Well, Tater, I don't know if Andy told you, but please be quiet and do not use the vacuum."

"Yes, sir. Andy was thorough in his instruction. No problem, I'll be real quiet," Luca said as he fitted his hands with clean blue gloves.

Then the lights went out. The battery-operated security lights came on immediately, but Steve Bains still cursed.

"Dammit, I may lose two hours' worth of figures if the autosave fails!" Steve Bains shoved back from the desk with a few more expletives rolling off his tongue.

Chapter Twenty-Nine

The security lights were so bright that their reflection danced off the floor-to-ceiling windows, momentarily blinding Luca. Luca moved fast and was behind the CEO in a moment, taking advantage of Bains's distracted state. He worked with quick, precise movements that instantly took Bains off his feet. Bains hit the floor with a hard thud which knocked the wind out of him. As quickly as he took Bains down, Luca sat on his back, taking the duct tape from his pocket and wrapping the man's hands and feet together.

Unexpectedly, Bains rolled over, pulling his tied legs back, and kicked out at Luca, knocking him off balance. Luca rebounded just as Bains managed to get awkwardly on his feet.

"So, you think you're the little shit who'll take me out? I have friends that can squash even a bug like you in the dark. The people I know will be relentless in making you pay," Bain spat out as he struggled with the tape on his wrists. "Better people than you have tried to kill me."

"Doubtful, but maybe you are right. Tonight is your last one breathing. You screwed up uploading that trash from your business servers, which was stupid. I will be the one to punch your life card. The Ghost sends his regards," Luca said.

"The Ghost is a fool's tale; I received that garbage in the mail. You are just some sad little man trying to scare people, and have too much time to take pictures. The *Ghost* does not scare me, and you? You're like a buck-twenty. I am a boxer, shrimp; what have you got?" Bains spit out the words, not a hint of fear in his tone. "I am untouchable."

It felt to Luca that he moved in slow motion as he crossed to Bains, still attempting to free himself from the restraints of the tape. Luca slid the thin blade smoothly across his throat. Their eyes locked for what seemed like an eternity before the blood began to spill. Luca stood still and watched the recognition hit Bains's eyes at the knowledge he had been touched, and there was nothing he could do. Luca looked into those pale blue eyes as life escaped through the blood running down his forty-five-hundred-pound suit trousers. His body collapsed to the floor in a heap. In one priceless instant, Luca could feel what it was like for the Ghost. One more childhood monster sent to the deepest recesses of hell.

Luca quickly and efficiently wiped down each surface and cut the duct tape from Bains's wrists and ankles. He ran the vacuum over the floor where they had fallen. He tipped the rubbish and his gloves into the bin. Shrugging out of the uniform before tying the bag, he would shower in the CEO's office private bathroom and set the bag on fire in the wet shower. Luca took out another pair of gloves, put them on, and went to the computer.

Luca peered out the window twenty minutes later, seeing blue lights flickering. The MET was called as he expected; time to retreat.

Chapter Thirty

It was August 24th, and the temperatures had tempered just slightly. It was about 10:00 a.m. Gavin watched the woman down on the beach, reading a book. Henley Scott seemed to be in her own world, unaffected by anything around her—a single woman alone in the middle of nowhere. Gavin had to admit that he was curious about who she was and loved a good mystery.

Gavin wanted to speak to her but could not, because currently he was far from a hundred percent, as it had been just seven days since his surgery. Dr. Brody continued to stand over him, ensuring he did nothing to strain himself. Gavin thought he would have done better being shot. His body was littered with scars of near misses, from head wounds, bullet holes, and being hit by more than one car. He did not have patience for downtime.

Gavin analyzed every detail of every action anticipated in the next couple of weeks. Those storyboards in his head were always covered in problems, and at the moment, he had no solutions. Distraction was not his strong suit. Although, that pretty lady down below had him down to one and a half storyboards. Gavin was feeling a need for feminine companionship.

It had been a week since anyone laid eyes on Luca Medina, and now even Helen was growing concerned. The tracking chip in his pin was still offline, and there was no activity to say whether he lived.

Suddenly, a large smile spread across Gavin's face. He heard a familiar bump of a shoe hit the bottom of the door, then the door handle turned. Gavin turned to watch the door open and saw Luca strolling through it, not realizing he was holding his breath.

"Luca!" Gavin exclaimed and began to get out of his chair.

"Don't get up, sir; I'll come to you," Luca said, walking to where Gavin sat.

"Are you all right?" Gavin questioned. He looked at the several days-old beard on Luca's face and the jagged cut on his head.

Luca smiled a genuine smile; complete admiration. He hoped Gavin did not think he was abandoned, and now he was sure Gavin trusted him, even if he did not yet know what he had done.

"I'm good. And you! You look so much better than when I left you with Dr. Brody. How are you feeling?" Luca asked.

"Ahhh, Brody. He hovers." Gavin sighed but smiled, expecting to see the man nearby. "Feeling like a train wreck, but I'm getting stronger."

"Brody's outside smoking, and I asked him to give us some space," Luca said.

"Sounding like a First-in-Command," Gavin said. "I didn't know that health nut smoked after the crap he has been trying to get me to eat."

"No, sir. You are in command, but I always have your back." Luca dug into his jacket pocket and fished out a flash drive. "Everything I recovered from Steve Bains's computer and his security feeds; all of it."

"Honestly, Luca, I have not been sure who's in command these last seven days," Gavin said. He did his best not to sound like he was rebuking him or questioning the decisions Luca felt necessary.

"The Ghost was, sir," Luca replied to the statement. "A poor understudy, I will admit."

The phone rang before Gavin could overthink that last statement.

"Guess who is late to the party?" Gavin asked, wincing as he turned to take up the phone.

"Helen. She has news, so you might want to answer it." Luca smiled. He was impressed that Gavin neither questioned him nor interrogated him, and Gavin just showed he was glad of his return. Now, that was the familiar feeling of family that Luca had grown accustomed to. Except now they were, sadly, one short.

"Yes, Helen?" Gavin said as he hit answer on the satellite phone and put it on speaker for Luca to hear.

"I think I know what Luca was up to," Helen said, sounding smooth on the phone. "Have you looked at the news?"

"Dear, you know I do not have a television here, and I have not read the paper today. I was distracted," Gavin said as he peered onto the beach. "You must deliver the news yourself."

"Steve Bains, CEO of Hollinger Enterprises, was found dead in his office around 4:00 a.m. The electricity went out, leading to many monitors and generator backups going offline. Also, whoever was there erased the security footage for the day before, and the MET has no idea who did it."

"Just how did he meet his demise?" Gavin asked.

"His throat was cut, ear to ear. The police revealed that his hands and feet were bound. But they cannot find evidence of the other person in that office. According to reports, the office cleaning was professional. Your friends at the FBI are headed there since Steve Bains is an American."

Luca could not resist any longer. "Good morning, Helen; I hope you are well."

"Luca, you are there!" Helen exclaimed, surprising both Luca and Gavin.

"I thought you were the all-seeing Oz," Luca said, grinning.

"You are good, Luca, incredibly good. I hope you are ready to go back to work. Once Gavin is well enough to travel, I need to see you both."

"What for?" Gavin asked, taking the last sip of the tea in his cup and making a face because he had let it go cold. He knew what for; it was time for Luca to take his Oath, and Gavin had resisted going to Arcadia before the accident. Honestly, the reluctance was all Gavin and less about the Oath. Gavin wanted to be selfish for a little longer because it made him feel more in control.

Helen expected Gavin to be stubborn; it was his nature. "The first reason you are more than aware of, I am sure. The second is that you have a decision to make. I have selected and vetted five files for your review for a Second. You had to fill that position yesterday," she said sternly. "Luca, you did know you were breaking the rules, and you must never do that again. It is unsafe for you to go out alone without someone to back you up. Please understand that I only say this because we were genuinely concerned about you."

"I understand, Helen, and I respect the rules; on the other hand, this was something I had to do. There would not have been a soul on earth who could have stopped me," Luca said.

Gavin looked at Luca and digested the words that told him exactly what he had feared. Luca went to complete the mission, and he could not stop himself. There was more to this man than Gavin knew. It gave him a chilling thought about his mindset when Gavin became the Ghost. Luca said the Ghost was in control. Gavin examined him thoughtfully for a long moment before returning his attention to the phone.

"I guess you'll be seeing Luca. Rusty chose him; I'll leave it a tradition, and Luca will choose our Second. If he chooses not to pick from your files, that'll be fine."

"Gavin, Luca is not Rusty," Helen said. "And I still need to see you both. It's time."

Helen thought of the dangerous situations Gavin could get into, and she could not call him in under the circumstances. Currently, Lucani (Luca) Medina was only Gavin's first in command. He was not sworn to Arcadia, and when he committed, he would become her Warrior to the Sapphire Ghost.

Gavin replied quickly. "No, he's not, and I don't want him to be. Luca's exactly who he needs to be. We will discuss it if I disagree with his choice, but otherwise, the subject is closed." Gavin ignored her request for him to bring Luca to Arcadia but did not disconnect the call.

Luca finally collapsed into the chair across from Gavin. He thought deeply, wondering if it were too soon. Luca felt a pull—the kind you get when you are near someone of truth and value. He recalled seven days ago when he turned over a significantly injured Gavin Garrison to a stranger.

However, Brody did not feel like a stranger. Nate Brody felt trustworthy, especially seeing he was still with Gavin. Although Luca had warned him menacingly, Brody showed regard for Rango, which had earned his respect.

Moreover, Brody carried that discontent in his eyes, a look that spoke of a desire for something his life was not offering. After studying Nate Brody, Luca concluded he would be a beneficial member of their Order.

"Helen?" Luca finally spoke into the speaker.

"Yes, Luca," she replied. Gavin was pleased she had been so patient.

"What if I've already chosen?" Luca did not look at Gavin but directly at the phone. "What's the next step?" There was a long pause on the other end of the phone. "You have chosen someone?"

"I suppose I have, and I believe you'll approve. Gavin may not, however," Luca said, smiling at Gavin.

Gavin immediately looked back at the door. "Let me get him," Gavin said as he carefully picked up the teacup.

Luca started to rise to help him but decided against it. Moments later, Brody entered the room.

"Luca, will you tell me who you have chosen, or do I need to guess? Rango from the farm? An old Army buddy?" Helen asked, finally showing impatience. "You know they must be vetted, and their background must be clean."

"Shh," Luca said, "Just wait a moment longer, please. I'll be back," Luca could hear an irritated sigh on the other end of the phone. *Did I really just shush the great and powerful Helen Glass?* Luca rolled his eyes at himself and envisioned his head being lopped off and rolling across the floor.

Heading to his room, Luca opened his closet and found the little blue velvet box. He opened it with reverence and took a long look at the little gold bar that he had worn so proudly. Luca had not started from the point of trust within the organization. He did not even know organizations like this existed when he was initially contacted. Rusty had researched, reached out to, and finally chose him. At least Luca had noticed that Brody had insight; he knew how to keep his mouth shut and his eyes open. But the most important thing was he knew how to care for Gavin if something happened. Brody was a good medical doctor, according to what he had found in Dark 9's database. After admiring the gold bar with the two square blue stones, Luca snapped the box closed and left the room.

"Helen, are you still there?" Luca asked.

"Yes, Luca," Helen said.

Luca smiled and looked over at Brody, who tried to keep his face placid but failed. Brody pulled off his glasses and cleaned them with a soft cloth

The Sapphire Ghost

from his pocket, and curiosity about what was going on written across his face.

"Helen, I have chosen Dr. Nate Brody to be my Second. Do you approve?"

The phone was dead silent.

"Helen?" Gavin asked.

"Very well, let me know when he accepts," Helen said after another lengthy pause.

Gavin studied the doctor, and lines formed on his dark face gave way to copious apprehension.

"Stay on the line, please." Luca turned to Brody and carefully opened the box. "Brody, will you marry me?" Luca asked. Gavin busted out laughing, and Luca thought he could hear a snicker from the phone speaker. Luca stood there with the most serious expression. Brody's face showed sudden confusion and then amusement. "In all seriousness, it'll be a lot like marriage, maybe an arranged marriage. As the First-in-Command of the Sapphire Ghost Order, Brody, I'm asking if you'll take the position of Second?"

Brody glanced between Mr. Garrison and Mr. Medina. He was looking again at the bar in the box. He removed the tinted wire-rimmed glasses, revealing his light green eyes. "Really? Me?" He stared at Luca Medina. *Is this the same man I met seven days ago?* Medina acted completely opposite of the man in London, and he found it baffling.

"Why not you? You have shown me you are already committed to the cause and earned our trust. This assignment is just about as full-time as it gets. You have earned my trust because you've not left Gavin since I placed him in your care. The choice is yours; you would no longer be only over the medical; you would be both medical at our side and a one-person army if needed."

Brody glanced between the two again, completely caught off-guard. Nate Brody knew what such an offer meant and knew there could be consequences if he declined. He also understood that he would be giving up much of his life by taking such a position, and his life would become one of complete service to the Order. But then there was the honor of being by the Ghost's side in the thick of it all. Brody had no family, which was why he was able to sign on initially.

Although Brody held a poor record of obeying the bureaucratic rules with the Marine Hospitals and at the civilian one, he tried when he was discharged. Dr. Brody was an excellent trauma doctor. He never cared if a procedure was medically necessary by a desk jockey at an insurance company assigning a dollar value to someone's life. Often, he was referred to as the black *House*, a nod to the hit TV show. Just as often, Brody was reprimanded for his practices and the cost he incurred on behalf of the hospitals. Dr. Nate Brody hated giving poor medical care due to a budget.

Chapter Thirty-One

Brody sat in the den where he camped out for the last four days. The sofa was too short for someone 6'2", but he had slept in worse places.

It might have been a mistake, but he asked them for time to think about the offer. *Why?* was Brody's primary question. *Why did Luca Medina offer this to him? Was this some sort of test?* Medina was younger than him. He wondered how he had become the first-in-command at maybe thirty. Medina may have been six or seven inches shorter, but Brody recognized the man's look. It was of a man who owned and fisted any fear he had. Medina was the kind of man you would want on your side and never on the opposing team. Again, why him? Medina had spoken to him for all of ten minutes. It was a test of some sort, he was sure. In the world, he knew, men did not place better-educated men below them because it was an excellent way to get shoved to the side.

Not to be cocky—well, maybe a little—but Brody was a force to be reckoned with. He was a former Marine, had graduated in the top three percent of his class from Columbia Med, and spoke five languages fluently. Brody could have done anything; joining the military had been more about fleeing than paying off college if he were to be honest. He had no family left and no real friends. His father died only weeks after he graduated from medical school. Dr. Nate Brody went looking for a place to belong. Brody thought he might find that connection in the Marines with all the talk of brotherhood. But he did not find what he was looking for there, either. Brody saw war, death, and sacrifice. He also saw beauty, having been stationed in Hawaii and Japan and visited other beautiful locations. Brody also frequented places like Costa Rica and St. Thomas to enjoy sailing, drinking, and entertaining company, not necessarily in that order. Brody made vanity friends easily, as he was shallow but had no close friends. Developing close relationships was something he had avoided all his life.

Brody's mom had died of cancer when he was thirteen, and why he'd become a doctor. His dad had lived only long enough to see Brody graduate from medical school before COPD took his life. *Yet I smoke,* shaking his head as he looks at the pack of cigarettes lying on the coffee table.

Brody watched Garrison and Medina through the closed French doors from where he sat. Medina had a way with Garrison, and he did not attempt to assist when Garrison wanted to stand. Brody could see the pain in Gavin's features. Garrison was one obstinate patient, but he dealt with worse, and one would not expect compliance from someone of Garrison's discipline. Brody watched as Medina stood and went with Garrison into the kitchen. He put on the tea kettle, and Luca began to write on the notepad on the bar.

Brody was not privy to many facets and wanted to know more. With Dark 9, it was not his job to question why; he just had to show up when called—which was not often. Brody was assigned to be medical, retrieve people, watch places, take pictures, and clear buildings. However, he had plenty of weak spots. Take the computer. Brody used one, knew how to create documents or browse the web, but he had no clue how that thing worked.

Nearly every Dark 9 team member he'd encountered had a particular skill, and they had been from a branch of the military or secret government agency. Many were from other countries, like former agents with SIS, BDN, MI6—or GU as it was now known—and many other initials he was unfamiliar with. And there was that fifteen-year-old computer genius he had retrieved to help on an assignment. Dark 9 recruited some of the best people from various organizations worldwide.

But the Ghost Orders went beyond that. It reaped the benefits of many people who had become disenfranchised. Brody could not understand how this organization went undetected, even though members seemed to be everywhere. Many of the Dark 9 Brody encountered held full-time jobs working in IT with major companies; also doctors, nurses, coaches, police detectives, real estate agents, and parking attendants. These didn't include those who never passed the stringent requirements of the Dark 9 training—those who were sympathetic to the cause and would step in if needed.

The Sapphire Ghost

People wanted to be part of something bigger than themselves. They all showed up when Helen called, yet no one had ever met the elusive Helen Glass, who seemed to exist only on the other end of that phone.

Gavin was a Ghost, one of a handful of Ghosts, and Brody had the opportunity to work with other Orders. Under hushed tones and in house only, they were called the Seraphim Ghosts—the guardians. Watching Gavin Garrison and his habits this last week, he wondered if Gavin had once been a spy or something remarkably close.

Brody loved the network he built within Dark 9. He enjoyed both the camaraderie and the mechanics of the outfit. Brody especially enjoyed the work and the freedom to handle the assignments. For example, building C needs to be taken down; there are no instructions, just left up to those on that assignment. That in itself was exhilarating.

Brody wore the single stone of the Sapphire Order. Those of the Dark 9 army were often granted colored pins, which signaled they were assigned to that Order. Or, in his case, he had a blood type that matched the Ghost of that order. Therefore, he would accompany the Order in dangerous situations. That was why he had been on standby in London.

Brody was point on his unit for three years and worked with another team before that. He'd met the Sapphire Ghost just one other time in all those years, and then the FIC was another man much more prominent than himself.

The Ghost did not operate under vengeance but toward true justice that presently had faulty scales. Criminal courts were just that: criminal and seemed to be paid off by the deepest pockets.

It was time to have a heart-to-heart with the Ghost.

Chapter Thirty-Two

Luca and Gavin went for a walk on the beach. Luca noticed Gavin observing the woman lying in front of the only other house remotely close to theirs, and Gavin turned and walked in the opposite direction. The caretaker returned Gavin's call, explaining that the woman had sought refuge and that her name was Henley Scott.

"I need you to make arrangements to go to Maine on Saturday," Gavin remarked quietly.

"Sir, that's two days away," Luca replied. "Do you believe you are well enough to travel?"

"It's a request from Helen, and I need to discuss something with her in person. Do we have a team preparing for the Dossier next Friday?" Gavin asked.

Luca recognized the tone and backed down. He watched Gavin's careful steps. Gavin was more than capable of knowing his limits.

"Okay, I'll make the arrangements," Luca said. "A scout team is in D.C., and preparations have begun. Are you sure you're ready, sir?"

"Yes, I can travel. As far as D.C. is concerned, I can do what I have planned." Gavin understood Luca's concern and appreciated that he did not baby him. He could still feel the stretch on the stitches.

"Once we return to the house, I thought I would go to the store and pick up salmon and grill this evening. How does that sound?" Luca asked, and he knew how much Gavin enjoyed grilled salmon.

"Yes, that sounds wonderful." Gavin thought about a nice, thick salmon steak, so different from the soups and dry sandwiches he had endured the last few days. "And get a bottle of Pinot Gris while you are there—that vineyard in California; I cannot think of the name."

"Shadow Mountain?" Luca responded.

Brody heard Garrison and Medina return and watched Medina leave again. He took a deep breath to steady his nerves, which he was surprised to

The Sapphire Ghost

find had him shaking. Brody was intimidated by Garrison and what he could do to him, not to mention what he saw him do to a senator a few months back. Killing the senator would have been mercy. Brody walked out of the den and across the room to the balcony, where Gavin seemed to stay.

"Sir, may I speak with you?" Brody asked.

"Certainly. Have a seat," Gavin said, gesturing to the chair beside him. I'm sure you have many questions," he said, laying his cigar on a tray.

"Yes, sir," Brody began cautiously, wondering what would happen to him if he turned the offer down.

"Well, shoot," Gavin said with a tired smile. He finally felt relaxed now that Luca had rejoined them.

"Let's not but say we did," Brody said, trying to steady his nerves.

Gavin laughed aloud. Okay then, he has a sense of humor.

"I will not shoot you, Dr. Brody; that's not my style. At least not just yet, as I still have use for you." Gavin winked but didn't go further. He could tell something was weighing on the doctor.

"Can I be frank?" asked Brody. His apprehension was almost breathable.

Gavin spoke with a straight face and still attempting to lighten the mood. "Most certainly, or Bob or Tom, but you look like an Alexander."

Brody sucked in a breath and exhaled. "What happened to the man before Luca?" Finally, Brody asked the question he most wanted to know.

"Ahh, I see where this is going," Gavin said. He relit the cigar and watched the tense man in an ill-fitting dress shirt and tie who had yet to feel comfortable enough to dress more casually. "Rusty is a dear friend, and he is still living, but he is quite ill and took retirement."

Brody blew out a breath. "Okay, then, why me? I am sure there would be someone who would benefit this team more than I would."

"Brody, putting this team first is a good place to start, which shows you care. I don't know what Luca's motivations were for selecting you. I'm certain, however, that he gave it a great deal of thought. Luca rarely does anything without careful consideration, and knowing that, I'm confident he knows exactly what you have to offer. Luca is a man I can trust to make the best decision for this Order, but I always reserve the right to say no."

"What about you?" Brody asked. "Do you think I'm what this team needs? That what I offer is enough?"

"I am guessing you prefer to be called *Brody* to *Nate*, as you have not corrected Luca's use of your last name. Brody, each of us has things we excel at and certain things that we do not do as well. I'm certain your talents are particularly useful to your place within Dark 9. As for this situation, you will have to consider what you can offer and decide if you are up to the task. No one can decide that for you. The offer stands." Gavin circled the question back on Brody. "Speak with Luca and see what he says."

"Brody is fine; Nate was my father. Would you tell me why you chose Mr. Medina?" Brody ventured.

Gavin contemplated his answer and considered what Brody wanted to hear versus what he needed to hear.

"Rusty, my former FIC, chose Luca when Helen decided we needed a Second to assist him. Rusty didn't like any of the files Helen sent, but he heard of this injured, young Green Beret sitting in a VA hospital in California, who had something Rusty found valuable. I will be the first to admit. I did not see what it was then," Gavin stated.

Gavin toked on the cigar, and smoke drifted into the air. He examined the doctor and thought again before he answered.

"We were heading into a need for massive amounts of computer technology, something neither Rusty nor I had more than a thimble's amount of knowledge. Luca has a lot of talent in that area, and I have found he is very clever in other matters we have encountered." Gavin looked over at Brody with his intense gray eyes. "Plus, he needed a reason to exist. I would guess you question that from time to time as well. You have a considerable education and cannot settle anywhere. Finding purpose isn't easy, is it?" Gavin asked and relaxed back in the chair, looking at Brody sincerely.

Quiet for a long time, Brody contemplated Gavin's answers. "No, sir, it's not. But back to the question, I'm not sure I am the right fit for this position, and I certainly do not want to disappoint you," Brody said.

The Sapphire Ghost

"I would not be disappointed. Speak with Luca before you make your final determination. I think you will find the answers you seek with him," Gavin said.

"Yes, sir, I will. Is he coming back tonight?" Brody asked.

"Yes, he has gone to the store to get some real food," Gavin replied.

"Right, I understand," Brody said and finally smiled.

Chapter Thirty-Three

Luca grilled that evening. Afterward, Brody checked Gavin's stitches before the patient turned in for the night. Then Brody followed Luca to the kitchen to help with the cleanup.

"How's he coming along?" asked Luca, hearing Brody's footsteps.

"Better every day. Mr. Garrison is tired, though, because he didn't sleep well while you were gone. I think the stitches in his back can come out in a few days, but the ones in the front are taking longer to heal," Brody answered. "Your friend Rango did well with that one."

"Thank you for tending to him in my absence." Luca was focused on scrubbing a skillet and didn't look up.

"It was my pleasure. I've only met this Ghost once, but we have heard the stories." Brody began to wipe down the counter. "He is different from what I imagined."

"And you imagined what?" Luca asked curiously, turning to face Brody.

"I'm not sure. Less humility, maybe," Brody said after a moment.

"Oh, Gavin is a good man. I admire and respect him. But he's also everything you have heard about him."

Brody scanned Luca's gun and knife set on the wine bar. "I believe he admires and respects you. He was going a little crazy not knowing where you were." Brody paused before asking, "Do you like working for him and doing the things you do?"

Luca listened to Brody's pleasant tone, which could coo a child to sleep. "Brody, I do not work for Gavin. I work with him. I've found it an honor to be here, and I never expected to be his right hand. Then again, I never considered myself second, either. Does that make sense?"

"Not really," Brody said. He appreciated order in things.

"I never thought of being Second. Rusty offered me the position, but it was never brought up again. That's until Rusty left. The lapel pins . . . not sure they mean anything other than the proper order of things. I'm responsible for keeping

The Sapphire Ghost

Gavin alive. Without him, this Order dies. My mentor and friend Rusty told me that Gavin is to remain the Ghost, not become one. That is my job, but I felt like it always was. I did not feel like I was a backup."

"Speaking of jobs, what would my job be? I'm unsure what you think I can contribute."

"Hmmm . . . that is a complicated question." Luca braced himself on the kitchen island. "Rusty was far better than I am at dealing with the occasions when Gavin gets hurt. I don't deal well with certain situations." Luca walked over to the bottle of whiskey on the bar and poured a glass. He gestured to Brody, who nodded his head, and Luca filled a second. "I still have flashbacks from being injured in Iraq, not as bad as they used to be, but they showed themselves again during those bombs in London."

Luca handed Brody the glass. All of this was hard for Luca to admit, but he felt he needed to be honest with Brody as Rusty had been with him seven years earlier. Rusty had said, *you start with trust and expect someone to keep it, not earn it.* Betrayal was a death sentence.

"Let's walk and talk. Sitting makes me sleepy," Luca said as he headed out of the kitchen through the balcony doors.

Brody followed Luca out on the beach. They walked silently for the longest time, half drinking, half thinking.

"Rusty confided in me after I accepted this job that he needed someone with skills that he did not have—in Rusty's eyes, bringing me on completed this Order. It is not a power trip; everyone has something unique to contribute.

"Gavin Garrison's Ghost is first. He is the head of the table, so to speak. We are here to ensure he can do his job. You, my friend, have something that I don't have. I feel you are equipped to handle situations like London. I've read your jacket, and you can handle much more than that. It's not only your medical degree I am interested in but also your capacity to adapt easily to any situation that appeals to me. You can relate to people, which shows up in an amazing bedside manner. I'm better with computers than with people."

Luca knelt and picked up a seashell, turning it over in his hand. "There is another reason, Brody. Everyone who has reviewed your resume has noted your extreme attention to detail. Brody, I feel I can trust that you would have my back."

"That means a lot, sir," Brody replied, feeling gratitude. He also felt awkward that Luca had studied his documentation while he was gone.

"Brody, I'll be honest with you. It is hard, sometimes casting the nets we do and those nets continually coming up full. Sometimes, it seems like we're not making a difference. However, for the most part, it can be satisfying, knowing somewhere a child may be sleeping in their own bed because of what we do." Luca spoke from the heart. Thinking of children reminded him he needed to send his nephew a birthday present before next week.

Brody took the last drink from the glass and stared at the large crescent moon over the water.

"Are the deaths . . . as cruel as I have heard?" Brody asked.

"Some are worse, I'm certain. There is a reason behind the brutality, and you will soon learn what that is."

"And he plans each one? Do you have any input?" asked Brody.

"Yes, he does all the planning, and his reputation for that is accurate. Some can be ruthless. No, I have never planned a Dossier. Set them up, yes," Luca said and then thought. "Well, that is not exactly true. I planned the one from London but lack the flair for the dramatics."

"Are they all guilty? I mean, he does not go after the innocent?" Brody asked.

"No, there is always an extraordinary amount of evidence. That is Helen's number one requirement. We never shed innocent blood." Luca cast the shell into the water. "But Brody, that is not the hardest part. There are those who know about the Ghost and are determined to find him and stop him—entities with better skills than the CIA. Certain mega-giant corporations with substantial wallets would love nothing better than to lay the Ghost in a permanent grave. The Order has collected hundreds of millions of dollars from corporations, politicians, and philanthropists. Accounts are currently being drained, like Steve Bains' ledgers. We do not allow those people to keep the money they made off human flesh," Luca paused, downing the still untouched whisky. "Some would make you never eat certain products again or use certain services once you learn what the company's leadership has done. People you would never guess would be involved in child trafficking. Then, there are the children who are stolen for experimentation or organ retrieval. That is the sole reason we are here. The research is extensive and complete before we go anywhere. That alone can be exhausting. I still fear I missed something running the operation alone in London."

"I think you did well. The prime minister was the primary target," Brody said reassuringly.

"I keep telling myself that, but I'm not afraid to admit I need help. If it is not you, it will be someone." Luca was not fond of taking on a new team member, but he could not deny his need for a second set of eyes.

"I'd like to take some more time," Brody said, not feeling confident. He did not have a great track record of staying in one place and giving total dedication. *Could I dedicate my entire life?*

"Take time. Gavin and I will be going to Maine the day after tomorrow. But I will expect an answer when we get back. We'll be gone for three days. If the answer is no, come back and tend to Gavin, and we will leave it as such," Luca concluded.

"I would recommend against any strenuous activity for at least two weeks. I do not think it is wise for Garrison to travel out just yet."

"I'll take that under advisement." Luca smiled as he continued walking, leaving Brody behind.

Chapter Thirty-Four

August 25

Congressman Ashman was in his Washington office early. He read the bills due to be voted on in the next session. Congresswoman Ashley Jeffries's bill was the second one on the docket. He would definitely need to make some calls to gain support for this one, but it was necessary. The Ghost would expect it. Ashman would trade off a vote or favor to ensure this bill passed both houses this time. Senator Baynard's vocal objections to the bill influenced its failure the first time. At 7:30, his phone rang. He considered letting it go to voicemail, but on a whim, he picked up.

"Congressman Ashman," he answered.

"Yes, congressman. I am glad I caught you. I apologize for calling so early. This is Will Jones with Herbert Enterprises, and I am calling in a request from our CEO."

Congressman Ashman sat upright at the mention of the company. He swallowed hard through the lump forming in his throat.

"How can I help you, Will?" Ashman managed to ask without a hint of the apprehension he felt.

"Well, this is a delicate matter, and I was informed you are the man who can assist us. We have two shipping containers held up in Miami, and the ATF is on some type of mission and will not release any cargo that came in this week. The CEO wonders if you could make a call to inspire them to release those containers," Will explained.

This man was phony. Will Jones? He could be speaking to the CEO since the man did not appear to want to give him a name.

"I'm unsure what I can do if there is an investigation. But tell me the container numbers, and I'll see what I can do," Ashman suggested.

"You have a pen? They are 84173 and 36741. That's 84173 and 36741. Please read them back to me."

The Sapphire Ghost

Ashman repeated the numbers back to Mr. Jones. "May I get a number to call you back?" Ashman asked, wanting as much information as he could get.

Will Jones rattled off the phone number. "Just call me when the containers clear." The caller hung up, leaving no more time for questions.

Congressman Ashman sat back in his chair and stared down at the notepad. These people thought he was in their pocket. Sure, they had donated money but so had a lot of others. He had a little news for them. Ashman fished inside his wallet and took out the small gray card.

"Yes?" Luca answered the phone line designated for informants.

"Good morning. Sorry to call so early. May I speak with Gavin? It's Phillip Ashman."

"What's the nature of your call, congressman?" Luca asked. Gavin was sitting on the deck having his morning tea.

"It concerns the Ghost's request, and they have called my office," Ashman replied.

"Say no more. I will have a secure phone sent to you immediately." Luca hung up and dialed a contact at the Capitol.

Once he received a response from his Capitol contact, Luca left the phone on the table for Gavin. "Phillip Ashman is being sent a secure phone and has information on Herbert Enterprises." Luca went to make breakfast.

Congressman Ashman wondered just how they would get a phone into the Capitol. He dismissed the thought and emerged from his office to speak with a clerk about some letters he was preparing for him. Ashman passed by his assistant, Camille, a bright twenty-seven-year-old who spoke four languages, prepped all his speeches, and handled all press-related information.

"Good morning, Camille," the congressman said as he passed her desk. He noted the small square blue sapphire on her necklace. He shook his head at the thought that was forming. Many people wore blue stones, and it could be her birthstone.

"Morning, congressman," she replied. Camille waited for Ashman to leave the office, then took a phone from her bag and installed an SD card. Per Luca's instructions, she programmed one number into the phone. She stood, walked in, laid the phone on the Congressman's desk, and quickly left the office.

Thirty minutes later, Ashman returned to find the phone on his desk. He looked around the offices, and there was no one around. Then Ashman thought about Camille; she was the last one he had seen. The congressman figured they had eyes and ears everywhere, but Camille was young; he could not figure out how she might play into their plans. He closed his door, turned up the radio, picked up the phone, saw the number, and hit dial.

"Phillip, I hear you have some news for me," Gavin said, dispensing with any greeting.

"Yes, I do, and I believe it will give you something concrete," Ashman responded.

"Go on."

"Someone named Will Jones called me from Herbert Enterprises. They have two containers detained in Miami, and Jones wants me to convince the ATF to release those containers."

Gavin stood at the information and headed into the house to find a pen. "The name is fake, but did you get the container numbers?" Gavin asked.

"I did," Ashman replied. He read them off, along with the phone number.

"Do you know why the ATF is in Miami?" Gavin asked.

"I believe it's a routine check; the ATF does them every few months. I have emailed the director to find out with certainty."

"All right, I'll take it from here. Get the containers released if you can. If not, I will. Call Jones back and tell him you are working on it," Gavin said. "Keep this phone with you," Gavin disconnected the call.

Ashman wondered how the Ghost would get the containers released if he could not. *That organization's tentacles run deep*, he thought.

Chapter Thirty-Five

Gavin punched in a number. A gruff voice answered.

"Thomas, are you busy?" Gavin asked.

"Sir, somewhat, but not getting anywhere. What can I do for you?" Thomas Fagan asked. He was excited at the possibility of another big confiscation.

"I need you in Miami. I have it on good authority two containers are of particular importance to me," Gavin replied. "The ATF is doing a routine check of the dock and holding them."

"Okay. Give me the numbers, and I will get right on it," Fagan replied. After arresting the Ghost, Fagan wanted to reassure him he could still be trusted.

"I don't want you to take possession of these containers. They need to get on the road, and I need to know where they are going," Gavin said.

"So, you need for me to track them?" Thomas asked, a little surprised.

"No, Thomas, I'll have them tracked. What I need for you to do is get me the shipping manifest and truck numbers. I'll have someone waiting for you outside of the Miami International Airport. Take the package from my person and place a tracker on each container. The container numbers will be inside the package. I would do it myself, but the ATF is there, and I've never required someone within that agency. Let me know when your flight will land," Gavin said. "Thomas, you can have the containers when they get to their destination, but nothing more. The rest of the information I'm seeking is not FBI business. Do I make myself clear?"

"Crystal, sir," he replied, knowing he did not want to be on the deadly side of the Ghost, and he had already come too close with the arrest.

Thomas felt grim at the idea of getting out of Kentucky and to Miami before this Haven Center mess was straightened out. Then again, it would lead to another large count of trafficking victims, and he would try to cover in the meantime.

Thomas decided to fly to Miami that afternoon and picked up the phone to book a flight. He would do as he was asked and have ATF free the containers. He would get the Ghost the information he sought, fly back tomorrow for the search warrant, and await further instructions.

He wondered about the Ghost's motives for letting those containers out on the road. He surmised it was because he was looking for someone and that someone and another gray file would make its way to that back room of the FBI. Pain ran through Thomas's stomach, and he reached for his oversized bottle of TUMS and chewed up four. He was looking forward to another large confiscation. And his superiors wanted him to arrest Henley Scott, but he did not have enough evidence.

Gavin stood by the breakfast bar in the kitchen and looked down at his notes. This was a big deal. He would have the containers tracked to their destination, hoping it would lead directly back to Herbert Enterprises. He needed to call Helen and let her know of the current development.

The next afternoon, Gavin received a call from Thomas Fagan confirming that the trackers were on the cargo. Fagan then emailed him copies of the shipping manifest. The shipping company was Camden Harbor Quest, and the containers were bound for a warehouse in Maryland. The location was not an hour's drive from his Dossier on Friday. Gavin was elated with the news.

Chapter Thirty-Six

August 26

Brody landed in Detroit just before 6:00 a.m. on Saturday. He slept on the plane for a couple of hours, hailed a taxi, and headed home to try to sleep for a few more.

The cab drove up in front of his white two-story bungalow with a narrow front porch. A white picket fence ran along the sidewalk. Although the fence was run down and broken in places, he thought at least the grass had been cut. As always, when he arrived home, Brody heard his dad's voice telling him he needed to fix that fence before the neighbors started to complain about declining property values. He remembered as a teen painting the fence with his dad, and his dad always told him: "Son, you better take care of what takes care of you."

The young Nate never understood how a fence took care of him as he miserably hand-brushed the paint onto every picket, which he had done for too many years to remember. Now, Brody understood it was about having pride in what you worked for and having a measure of respect for the money you earned.

Brody's thoughts turned to Gavin Garrison, and his father's words rang out again, "Take care of what takes care of you."

Nate Brody realized he had just made his decision. He saw how Garrison worried over Luca Medina and how he spoke of him with admiration. Brody wanted that. Yet, he had two more days to give Mr. Medina his answer.

Walking inside, Brody dropped his bags by the side door that entered the kitchen. He went to the fridge, knowing it would be empty, but he opened it anyway and stared inside.

Why did he keep this place? He did not live here, and Brody did not live anywhere except out of those two Gucci bags on the floor.

The last relationship he'd had pretty much broke him of wanting another one. Dr. Brody would never father a child again; he had ensured that. It had been twelve years since Brody watched his newborn son die in his hands; the baby was so small. August Nate Brody III died nearly five years to the day of Nate's father's passing. All because the dimwit who gave birth to him hadn't taken care of her health during pregnancy. Brody did not love the woman but was determined to have a place in the child's life. Brody had loved that baby even before he'd been born, and he had wanted to be a father, but Brody refused ever to feel that pain again.

Brody took the keys from the hook beside the fridge and headed out to the garage. He opened the garage door and looked inside. Nate Brody had no family left and struggled with letting go of the things that reminded him of his parents. It had been hard for him to figure out where he belonged with a Black mother and White father. Often, he felt he didn't fit in anywhere. Brody smiled at his dad's brown 1987 Dodge truck and tugged off the tan cover from his 1968 Camaro in Apple Red. Brody picked the color when he was thirteen, just a few months after his mother passed. The Camaro had been a Bondo putty gray when his dad towed it into the driveway. He and his dad worked on this car every night for two years. Brody's dad, suddenly a single parent, had left his job so he could be home with his son. Brody replaced the cover on the car and headed to his dad's truck.

Brody needed to think, and to do that, he needed to work. A couple of hours later, Brody pulled back into the driveway with a truck bed full of supplies. He had waited for the local nursery to open, which took its sweet time, but he'd purchased twenty red rose bushes to go in front of the fence. He filled the fridge and decided not to buy cigarettes—another reason to stay busy. He called when the dental office opened to have his teeth cleaned and committed not to pick the cigarettes up again.

Brody cut boards and replaced pickets on the fence. Then he pressure-washed the old paint off and went inside to make a sandwich while waiting for the wood to dry.

It had been a long day. It was 7:00 p.m. when Brody finished painting and swept up the sidewalk. He'd dug fifteen holes and planted fifteen rose bushes; the last five would not fit. He'd plant those outside the kitchen window tomorrow. Brody looked at the freshly painted fence and thought his dad would be proud and the neighbors would be satisfied. Brody pulled out the hose and tugged it to the front of the house to water all the new bushes. It had been a long and productive day, but now he was dog-tired and covered in dirt. He would have to remember to call the gardener tomorrow morning and adjust the rate so the fellow would take care of the new plants.

While showering, he thought about how the Order would change his life. He began to look forward to the new direction. Brody knew his life lacked something real, something that gave him purpose. Repairing the fence and replacing the rose bushes had made him feel his parents would be proud, but what about the living? Leaving medicine had severed some of his connection to humanity, which he deeply craved. Working to save those who could not protect themselves had kept him humble. Brody wanted, no, he *needed* a place to belong.

Chapter Thirty-Seven

August 27

Luca packed their bags into the SUV. Gavin was quiet, as was his custom when prepping for an operation. He had hardly spoken to Luca since the day before. Brody left for Detroit the previous morning and would return in three days.

Luca was feeling apprehensive about going to Maine. This was Luca's first visit to Arcadia and meeting Helen Glass.

Gavin sat back in the seat and pulled up his brown satchel. He took the small bottle out of the side pocket and shook out two oval pills.

"Luca, do you have any water up there?" Gavin asked.

Luca reached over to the seat beside him and handed back a bottle of water. Gavin gratefully took it and swallowed the pills.

"The pain must be bad," Luca said, watching Gavin in the rearview mirror.

"Just lingering, that is all. I'll be fine," Gavin replied.

"Sir, might I suggest we stop in Springfield, Massachusetts? I believe you have a confession to make." Luca knew it was a top priority.

"Ahh, yes, I can do that. Father Paul, I believe," Gavin stated.

"Yes, sir," Luca agreed. "Helen called to say she could have someone else take care of it if you do not feel up to it."

"Not a problem. Make the arrangements," Gavin said. "We have some news on Herbert Enterprises, and I think Helen will be able to find the information I seek."

Luca soon pulled up to the airstrip. Marshal was waiting beside the plane. Maybe a twenty-five-year-old young man stepped to the car and opened Gavin's door.

Luca threw him the keys and said, "Gas it up. We will be back in a few days."

"Please and thank you," Gavin added as he tipped the young man. "Manners, Luca!"

Chapter Thirty-Eight

August 27

Thomas Fagan was back at a desk in the police station in Independence, Kentucky, looking over the file contents on Henley Scott. She was a pretty woman with small, delicate features, bright, bold brown eyes, and brown hair. There was something familiar about her, but he could not put his finger on it. Over two weeks ago, someone matching her description drove off with a truck from the Port of Baltimore, and the cameras had captured a good picture of the suspect.

Henley Scott was born on August 19, 1966. No current address is listed; the old address is in Statesville, North Carolina. Bachelor's degree in Forensic Accounting and another in Bio-Metric Engineering. *Whatever that is*, Fagan wondered. Intelligent woman, it would appear. So, why would she be transporting a cargo container of children? It had to be for less-than-desirable reasons.

Thomas had a lot of experience with people who went to the wrong side of the law for profit. However, he did not get that impression from this woman. Henley Scott had roughly $4,800 in her bank accounts. But what worried him was she had a daughter who attended Laughton School of Science and Mathematics, which was not cheap. Fagan had already gone through her bank statements and had no typical purchases. She had a gym membership but neither gas nor groceries purchases, which to him meant she was hiding money somewhere. *Where was it?* With degrees like that, she could hide it.

Haven Center, however, looked promising. Home for runaway teens, and that could be a tricky situation. How often had he known of people fostering children only to use them in the sex trade? Fagan did not like where this seemed to be going.

The FBI was obtaining a search warrant for Haven Center at that moment. From what Fagan could see on the satellite view, there was one main house and a smaller cottage off to the side. A large barn and five other cottages were near a lake. Henley Scott was the current owner and director of Haven Center, with a staff of fifteen. Fifteen employees for what seemed to house only four girls over age fifteen and one seventeen-year-old boy. The center employed four full-time nurses, three therapists, a horse groomer, and other support staff that did not include the groundskeepers. To the deputy director of special operations, that seemed like too many specialized people for a handful of teenagers. The center was operating an above-average budget for a small group home; the payroll alone was $270,000 annually. Where did they get that kind of money? Fagan sat back in the chair and closed his eyes.

There was something not right about that center. The bank records did not support what they had going out. So, they would just wait for the search warrant and then see what was going on.

As for the Ghost's request, Fagan ensured that the tracking devices he had been given were securely attached to each container. It took some convincing for the ATF to allow their release, but they had gone along because of Fagan's reputation, and it was the FBI.

He turned to the copies of the shipping information but could not see anything that might have tipped off the Ghost. Fagan wondered if the two containers were full of kids, and he had not had a shipment that big in a few months. Fagan knew the containers were bound for Maryland, but he also knew they could be redirected—and apparently, so did the Ghost. Fagan opened his laptop and connected to the satellites in Flintwood, Maryland. Patience was not a strong suit for him, and he wanted Scott's arrest or those containers soon.

He had noticed that Special Agent Simons had been monitoring him, almost too close for comfort. His phone rang. "Speak of the devil," Fagan said under his breath.

At about that time, Congressman Ashman received a call from the ATF director concerning the shipping containers in Miami. The director explained that the ATF did routine checks, which was all that was going on. The director also informed him that the FBI had shown interest in those containers, which were released to its agent. Ashman asked the agent's name on the release form and learned it was Special Deputy Director Thomas Fagan. He wondered, *another Ghost ally, or was he being blackmailed?* The congressman decided to do some research.

Chapter Thirty-Nine

Gavin sat in a leather recliner on the jet, the pain pills taking the edge off his side and creating a fog in his mind. He knew the pain would eventually be nothing more than another scar, and his body was a roadmap of near misses. He wondered how the prime minister held up and made a mental note to call her this week.

Gavin's mind wandered to the day he had quit The Agency, which was too dark to have letters to abbreviate. They were not even a line item with the fiduciary committee. *Quit* was not actually the word for it. It had been after he called the FBI on those trucks because he could not comprehend what The Agency was doing. Gavriel Masterson, Gavin's former name, was attacked and hospitalized. Four men in masks had ambushed him outside his favorite bar and left him for dead. Masterson had begun to drink heavily to drown those eyes from his mind. The police said it was a mugging gone wrong, but he was sure it was not. It was a message from the top to keep his mouth shut.

Confiscation and relocation. That is what The Agency called the process of making criminals pay a heavy price to get their cargo back. The day had dawned miserably hot in late August, and even the breeze smelled like bad breath after the flu. It was supposed to be a routine visit to Garden City, Georgia, an industrial high-crime suburb just inland of and upriver from Savannah, near its airport.

Special Agent Masterson looked over the dockmaster's log. Something seemed off about those four containers. The logbook stated they contained antiques from Nepal, but the draft declared this cargo came from a company called Camden Harbor Quest in Australia.

Masterson had walked over to one of the containers. In the background, the high-pitched sounds of docking cargo ships and the excessive beeping from the trucks wailed.

"Don't open that door, Masterson!" instructed Special Agent Shiffite.

Masterson opened the door anyway. The smell was pungent: urine odors, feces, rotten food, death, and misery sucking the air from his lungs. The overwhelming urge to vomit overtook him. Looking inside, he had seen small faces and dark eyes staring back at him. Those tiny faces were hungry, and their eyes were vacant. Gavin would never forget the eyes.

"Masterson, shut that door!" Special Agent Shiffite ordered.

Reluctantly, Masterson stepped back, closed the door, and walked away. Those eyes continued to haunt him each night as he fell asleep.

Gavin attempted to shake the memory from his mind and laid the recliner back, feeling lightheaded from the pain pills. He continued to reminisce about the day he had changed.

It had been another night of drinking—Gavin's custom since he had been unemployed. Fate was not smiling at him for doing nothing. He had been unable to sleep, and the world he had known had spun out of control. There was something incredibly wrong about his government working to allow these criminal acts to continue. *Where was the justice?*

He'd been sitting on that beach contemplating the worst. Gavin felt he could not live knowing that those children had been sent on to their abusers. There must have been something more he could have done. But what? No one would listen. They declared he was disgruntled for returning him from an overseas assignment.

He looked up to see a tall, thin woman coming toward him. She was dressed in a soft, white overcoat and white slacks. Her hair was neatly cut short and fair blonde. As the woman drew closer, he realized she was approaching him. Gavriel Masterson sat still and was surprised when she sat beside him, pulling her knees toward her chest.

"Mr. Masterson, you have been hard to track down this week," she said, looking down at the folded sports jacket with a silver dollar money clip and a college class ring.

He looked over at the woman; her eyes were the clearest emerald green he had ever seen. The right side of her thin, angular face was scarred, and her features were sharp. She looked like she had emerged from a drawing in a children's book about fairies.

The Sapphire Ghost

"How do I know you?" he asked. The smell of whisky was still rich on his breath.

"You do not know me, Mr. Masterson, but I know you. I have been watching you since before you left The Agency," she spoke softly.

He looked her over, taking in her presence, which was slightly surreal. Had he already walked into those dark, churning waters?

"Why?" he asked, unable to look away, "Who are you?"

"Forgive me," she said and smiled. "My name is Helen Glass." She extended her small hand with long, delicate, childlike fingers.

He shook the woman's hand. He noticed the scar on her right cheek: burn marks, and her delicate features and pale skin had made it nearly invisible.

"Ms. Glass, it is nice to meet you out here. Strange but nice. What can I do for you?"

"It is not what you can do for me, but it is what we could do together. You want justice, as do I."

"Yes, I want to burn it all to the ground," he said bitterly.

"As do I, to even the scales," she replied. "And in order for us to do that, we will need a plan, and lucky for you, Mr. Masterson, planning is something I do quite well."

"A plan for what?" he asked.

"To serve justice, real justice." She smiled at him once again, then looked down at the water's edge.

Helen Glass reminded him of the stone angel sculpture he had once seen in a cemetery in Hendersonville, North Carolina. When he was twelve, he was on a trip to see the Biltmore House with his family. The light hitting her face as her eyes cast down was impressive. The woman's skin looked like the white marble of the statue, Thomas Wolfe's angel from the book *Look Homeward, Angel*. The likeness seemed uncanny.

That trip was also the last good memory he had as a boy. Two weeks later, his twin sister, Celeste, was taken while shopping with his mother.

Helen observed Masterson, and he was lost in thought. She had developed a fondness for the man. Helen knew his moral compass was tarnished, yet he felt it was broken and was on the verge of the unthinkable. She looked down again at the jacket and jewelry. She wanted to give him a reason to stay. He did not know the strength he contained, but she did. In his broken state, he could be molded. This legal system he so wanted to believe in; could he bend against it?

"I am working on putting together files of the most amazing individuals. I believe you are the right person to start that plan. Helen said, tucking her hands behind her knees.

"For what exactly?" he asked.

The warm air came off the water, but he noticed she appeared cold. The long white Chanel jacket pulled comfortably around her. Gavin did not know it at the time, but Helen was recovering from breast cancer when they met.

"An order of men and women of high moral value to make up the difference where our justice system fails us," Helen replied.

"Vigilante justice, you mean?" he asked.

"As defined by Webster's dictionary, perhaps," she replied.

"Can you actually make something like that work?" Gavin asked. "I mean, without someone like me going to jail?"

"I believe I can, and you are the first one I have approached. I could not risk losing the momentum behind your broken illusion," Helen said.

"Broken, torched, and the ashes have yet to hit the ground. I thought I would be ridding the world of criminals, not helping them. They just took those kids off to some unknown location to sell them back for a price. How could our government become so callous?" Rage and pain quaked in his voice.

Helen examined him as he spoke and saw the anguish deeply embedded in his eyes. "Money, greed, the slow drift away from humanity," she replied quietly.

After several long minutes, he simply asked, "How?"

"First, Gavriel Masterson must die," she said.

"He is already dead," he replied.

Chapter Forty

The Cathedral in Springfield, Massachusetts was a beautiful old Catholic church with huge organ pipes at the back of the nave.

The very first assignment that Gavriel Masterson, who had taken the name Gavin Garrison, received from Helen was a confession in Philadelphia. Helen had an agreement with the Archdiocese of New York to help with the ever-present problem of priests' abuse of altar boys. The church wanted it handled quietly without any link that could be traced back to itself. Cardinal Chapman made available all churches and any convents or monasteries to aid and provide sanctuary to anyone under Arcadia. Helen agreed to have the Ghost Orders take care of the nasty business of removing wayward priests for the protection of the church. It was a mutually beneficial alliance. The first rule was to take *care of all requests on betrayals of trust within the Church*. In each church, one employee was sworn to secrecy of the Seraphim Ghosts.

Gavin entered the beautiful cathedral. He admired the architecture and stained glass, which he loved. Luca waited in the vestibule and observed. Gavin leaned heavily on the silver-handled cane as he walked down the nave. A young priest was wiping down the seating. He stopped, looked up, and greeted him warmly.

"Good evening, I'm Father Michael. Can I help you?" he asked politely.

"No, thank you. But would Father Paul be available to take a confession?" Gavin asked.

"I will check. Father Paul is due to be transferred next week, so I believe he's in the back, packing." Father Michael left to check.

Gavin walked farther into the church and wondered about the age of the organ. Antique handmade glass pendant lamps hung from the ceiling, and the Gothic arches framing the space reminded him of his time in Europe.

So many things were hidden behind a lovely façade, he thought. Gavin had served as an altar boy growing up. Later, he found he was fortunate to have never been subjected to the abuse of some of the priests. He understood not all priests were bad, and most were genuinely dedicated to God.

The US Catholic Church was facing payouts in the millions of dollars; in 2007 alone, it had paid out $660 million to five hundred victims of sexual abuse. The cardinals were on board with the new plan to remove these priests instead of moving them to new churches.

Father Paul's expenses were more than $200,000, involving four children in this church. Money could never buy back lost innocence, and it could never buy back the idea that the world was good.

"Good afternoon." A man in his mid-forties came up to Gavin. "Father Michael said you requested me to make a confession?"

"That would be correct. Do you have a moment?" Gavin asked.

"Absolutely. Are you a member?" Father Paul asked, noticing the man looked ill.

"Not of this church, no; I am only passing through," Gavin said, looking at Father Paul. The priest wore jeans and an open-collar shirt.

Noticing the look, Father Paul said, "I apologize for my appearance. I am being transferred next week and have been cleaning out my office."

"Shall we?" Gavin motioned for the father to lead him to the confessional.

Gavin opened the small door and took the bench on the left. He removed the gun from his belt and quietly screwed on the silencer. He waited for the screen to open and for Father Paul to begin.

"Forgive me, Father, for I have sinned. It has been three months and twenty-three days since my last confession," Gavin began.

"What do you seek forgiveness for today?" Father Paul asked.

"I have killed five men for immoral acts against children and have demented a sitting senator," Gavin confessed.

"There is never a good reason to commit murder, but the Lord forgives and absolves you of your sins if you are truly repentant," Father Paul replied.

"Father, I am going to kill again very soon. Would you like to confess before I do?" Gavin asked, glaring through the screen.

Father Paul studied the man through tiny holes. "The Lord knows of my sins and forgives me."

The Sapphire Ghost

"The Lord can deal with you in heaven. The church decided it does not wish to offer you absolution," Gavin said, lifting the gun and, in a single silent shot, he took the priest from this life. Father Paul could explain himself to God.

Gavin quietly left the sanctuary and waited for Luca to pull the rental car around to pick him up. Fortunately, Father Michael was nowhere to be seen.

Chapter Forty-One

August 27

On the plane, Gavin instructed Luca to call ahead and rent a 4x4. When they arrived, a white Range Rover awaited outside the hangar doors. Gavin took the keys from the woman who had brought the SUV. He opened the driver's door and got behind the wheel, and Luca opened the passenger door and stared at him, confused.

"You have a driver's license?" Luca questioned.

"Of course, from the great state of South Carolina. Easiest one to forge. Have you ever driven in South Carolina? Folks there get their licenses from the local Walmart, on the gift card aisle," he joked. "Now get in."

Luca reluctantly sat down in the SUV, pulling his seat belt tight. *This is going to be interesting.* "Have you ever been in a Walmart?"

"No, just seen the commercials," Gavin chided back. "Wright went to get mine," Gavin said, grinning.

Luca shook his head. Gavin was not feeling much pain right now, and he was in rare form.

They drove north. The scenery was lush, and the view was a sewn tapestry of bold greens, scarlets, dark copper shades, and yellows that dripped like liquid gold, draping the mountainside like a delicate handmade quilt. The sky was stunning in its glorious cerulean blue.

Gavin turned the Land Rover onto a well-kept gravel road leading farther north nearly two hours after landing. Autumn came early in northern Maine. They climbed a seventy-degree grade steadily, and Luca found himself surprised at how well Gavin could drive. Luca now understood why he was sitting in the passenger seat. There were no directions to this remote location. He looked to the left, where hundreds of solar panels glinted like mirrors.

Gavin was quiet, still trying to figure out how to tell Luca about the coming visit. However, Luca was often silent, and Gavin found it hard to find an opening.

The Sapphire Ghost

As they steadily climbed further up, a large log home appeared. The two-story house was made of exceptionally large gray logs, and Luca estimated it was over a hundred feet across the front and two stories. The pillars on the porch that held up the enormous roof were still in tree form, with the branches scattered out at the top. The house looked more like it belonged in a painting, with the backdrop a highly energized display that would inspire awe in any artist.

Gavin smiled as the woods opened to the idyllic setting. "Welcome to Arcadia," Gavin said. "The very definition of visual peace, beauty, and unspoiled nature. More to the point, this is where the magic happens. This place is known to only a very small number of people, and now you are one of them."

Luca began to feel a little anxious about meeting the as-yet-invisible Helen Glass. He had trouble imagining the visage behind the voice. Luca knew Helen was the real head of the Orders, the one who collected most of the information they used. It was understood that when Helen called, it was to be done. Gavin could stand up to her, but neither he nor Rusty ever felt it would have been in their best interest.

A thought struck him. Nate Brody! What would she do if he turned down the position? Would he disappear? Gavin would not make that call—he was not that kind of man. But would Helen?

Gavin had begun to slow. He stopped about twenty feet from a white Cadillac. Luca's eyes fell on the beautiful redhead descending the steps.

"Who is that?" Luca asked in a hushed tone. "Is that Helen?"

Gavin chuckled. "No, that is Grace, also known as Pandora. Her box is most definitely in that truck."

Luca could not help but stare at the beautiful redhead.

"Pandora, as we sometimes refer to her, is Helen's information bulldog. What Helen cannot obtain through computer channels, Grace uses her powers of persuasion to obtain. She has a way of making people talk," Gavin said. "That is why we call her Pandora. You never know what information she can get people to release. Not to mention, she's the chemist who creates those toxins we use."

"I would still talk and talk," Luca said somewhat stupidly.

"Down, boy," Gavin said with a knowing smile. "She is dangerous and likes snakes, especially her black mamba, Joy. That thing is just plain creepy." Gavin shuddered at the thought.

Gavin inhaled when he saw Grace look in his direction. She was indeed beautiful, and she let that work for her. But those snakes! Gavin shivered again and began to roll down his window for the approaching redhead. "Keep your tongue in your mouth," Gavin said out of the side of his mouth.

Luca watched the stunningly attractive woman approach the SUV. Her hair was copper penny red and laid like silk down her back, and the royal blue CHANEL dress she wore fit every curve. Her face was perfectly painted, with a hint of green shadow around her pale greenish-blue eyes. She had long, thick lashes, and her lips were painted a perfect tulip pink. Everything about her screamed that alluring combination of sex appeal and confidence.

"Lovely seeing you here, Gavin." The words rolled off her tongue like a song. "I have missed you—it's been a while."

Gavin's thoughts were taken back one year ago to Madrid, one of his favorite cities. She was there on business, and he was there for pleasure—and pleasure it was. Yes, she was a treat for sure, but that snake went everywhere with her.

"Yes, Grace, it has been a long while since Spain. Would you mind staying a bit? I may need your particular services."

"Not at all, handsome. What particular services would you be referring to?" Grace gave Gavin a wicked smile as she playfully touched a perfectly painted fingernail to her bottom lip.

"Not the ones you are thinking of, my dear. It's work-related," Gavin said, dismissing her pout.

"Okay, speak to Helen and let her see if it's something I can help with," Grace said before strolling back to the house.

Luca watched with some surprise at the exchange between Gavin and the lovely redhead. Luca concluded the Ghost had, at least once, had a thing with Pandora from those brief words. The image was amusing.

Luca's thoughts were jolted back when his phone dinged.

The Sapphire Ghost

"That will be Helen," Gavin said as he began to pull around the Cadillac and to the back of the house.

As the Range Rover turned the corner around the house, Luca realized there were at least two more floors in the large log home, which were not visible from the driveway. River stones constructed the basement portion of the house, with several narrow windows at the top and one large, thick, natural wooden door. This house was massive but fit well into the scenery.

Gavin turned to Luca. "Helen will not be what you think. Just remember that."

"What does that mean?" Luca asked as images of Medusa jumped into his head.

Gavin smiled one of those rare smiles of pure amusement. Luca was in for a treat. This was his first time seeing just who was behind all the Dossiers.

They were also here for Luca's swearing-in ceremony, which Gavin had yet to mention.

Gavin hit the trunk latch. Luca stepped out and went to the back to retrieve the bags. If Luca were to admit it, he was a little scared to meet the person behind the voice.

Gavin took his bag from Luca and headed for the house.

"Reception has been bad. When I get a signal or Wi-Fi, I will check where those trucks are," Luca said.

"Thank you." Gavin headed up the hill to the backdoor.

Luca could see the pain on Gavin's face as he started up the slight incline to the door. Luca stared at Gavin, realizing Gavin looked old and tired. It was not the tired he usually saw before, after a long assignment. Today, Gavin looked worn out. The fact he was just now recognizing it made him feel awful. Luca began to worry that the wound might be infected.

Gavin walked up to the large wooden back door leading into the basement area of Helen's home. Gavin placed his pin next to the keypad, and the door clicked open.

Luca followed him in, too concerned about Gavin's health to take much notice of the room.

Gavin stood in the middle of the wide-open space. The décor was white and black, very structural looking. Both side walls were covered in monitors displaying different data searches. Four black desktop computers were on two tables on each side, a stark contrast to the white marble surfaces of the tables. Two plush white sofas were centered in the middle of the room. Gavin headed to the seating area, and Luca examined the room.

Luca studied the wall to the left side of the room. He allowed his eyes to adjust to the white words on the black background. Luca's heart hit his chest with the rhythm of the words and the substantial amount of text flying across the screens. The data moved too fast. He stood, unable to move. *Close your eyes, just close them!* Luca mentally screamed at himself.

Helen opened the doors to the control center. She observed Gavin for several long moments.

"Welcome home, Gavin; how are you?" she asked.

Gavin pulled his eyes from watching Luca and turned to Helen. As usual, she looked elegant in a cream-colored suit tailored to her thin frame. Helen's hair was still short, but now it was white, no longer blonde. However, those eyes had not changed; the vibrant emerald green stood out like two ponds on her pale skin. Gavin found he was still mesmerized by those eyes.

"Not as good as I'd like," Gavin admitted.

"You look like you have not slept in days," Helen said as she headed for the electric tea kettle on the sidebar. Then she noticed Luca.

"I finally get to meet Luca Medina in person!" she said, loud enough for him to hear.

But Luca was planted in that spot. He felt the air burning in his lungs, and he could not breathe. The information continued to scroll as his eyes darted from screen to screen. He could not look away, and his brain seemed to be trying to consume everything on the monitors. Beads of sweat trailed down his face.

Helen cocked her head slightly when Luca did not answer. She watched him standing there with his eyes darting rapidly. His face was damp. Then she realized.

"Gavin, hit the kill switch! Hurry!" Helen cried, shocking Gavin out of his own motionless state.

Gavin jumped up at the distress in Helen's voice. Pain ripped through his side, but he raced to the switch. Gavin watched as Helen quickly ran across the room, her tan heels barely audible as she sprinted to Luca. Gavin noticed Luca was still stationary but was otherwise unsure of what was happening.

Nearly hysterical as she raced to Luca, Helen called again, "Hit the switch!"

Finally, as she reached out to take Luca's shoulders to turn him around, he crumpled to the floor.

Gavin froze.

Chapter Forty-Two

Helen knelt and pried Luca's eyes—his pupils were dilated, and Helen hung her head, fearing the worst.

Gavin hit the kill switch on the wall, and every monitor went out. He raced to Helen and Luca.

"What happened?" Gavin asked breathlessly.

"I am hoping not, but I fear he may have suffered a stroke," Helen replied cautiously.

"What? How?" Gavin laid a hand over Luca's heart. "What happened to him? You saw something?"

"Did you know he had Hyperthymesia?" Helen asked.

"No! I would have noticed, I think," Gavin said, unsure, as he looked down at Luca. Gavin considered himself observant of the people around him. "Is that a memory disorder? The one that involves total recall?" Gavin asked.

"Yes, only sixty people in the world have a confirmed diagnosis of the condition," she said. "I am one of them."

Gavin looked at Helen with a bit of surprise. "Well, that makes sense, but Luca has not shown any signs of total recall, although he does have an excellent memory."

"He has more than an excellent memory," Helen said softly as she pushed the hair back off Luca's face. His dark lashes looked outlined in black liner, even with his eyes shut.

Helen stood, walked over to the phone, and hit the intercom button. "Clarence, would you come to the comms center?" If Luca needed to go to the hospital, Clarence would have to be the one to take him.

"Gavin, I will give him a few minutes to recover on his own. If he does not, he must go to a hospital before there is any permanent damage."

Gavin took a deep breath and contemplated what Helen was saying. How could he have missed such a condition? Luca was apparently better at hiding things than Gavin realized.

Luca started to moan slightly. Then, there was movement behind his eyelids. Both Helen and Gavin watched as signs of life drifted into the young man. Luca opened his eyes; the first image he saw was bright green eyes and soft white features on a pixie face. He thought he must be dead. *But if I'm in heaven, why does my head hurt so bad, and my throat feels like I've been eating rust?* He tried to focus his eyes, which seemed to have a haze over them. But they improved, and he soon noticed Gavin kneeling beside him. He thought to himself, *this woman with the fair features and those green eyes must be Helen.* He could hear voices but could not make out what they were saying.

"Luca, can you hear me?" Gavin repeated.

Clarence and Grace came through the door, and Helen motioned for them to stop. She did not want to overwhelm Luca. Both backed silently back out of the room.

"Luca, can you hear my voice? Blink if you can understand me," Helen said softly.

Luca blinked once and opened his mouth, but his throat was so dry that nothing came out. Gavin reached behind Luca and propped him against his chest, noting how red his face was. Luca drew a breath. He wanted water but was unsure he could swallow.

Helen stood and walked over to the table, opened the ice carafe, and shook a couple of pieces into a glass, which she carried over to Luca. Lightly, Helen picked out one of the cubes and rubbed it over Luca's lips. He opened his mouth and sucked in the ice. The cold soothing the heat felt good to him, so Luca let it sit on his tongue and slowly dissolve. Luca began to move, feeling he needed to get up, with the prickle of embarrassment. Luca sat up, refusing to allow Gavin to support his weight behind him. He did not need to be the reason Gavin aggravated his wound.

Luca looked at Helen. "I am so sorry," he said hoarsely.

"There is no need for an apology," she said kindly.

Luca looked at Gavin and barely shook his head. His head felt like it might explode if he moved too fast. "I did not mean to spoil the introductions, sir."

"I think you had a different idea for introductions," Gavin said, glad to hear something normal coming from him.

Luca rubbed his eyes and then his head. The pain was too intense to care what they thought, and all he could think was he needed to sleep.

"Can you get up?" Helen asked.

"I think so," Luca replied, pushing himself off the floor.

Helen was almost his height. She wrapped a thin arm around his waist, and Gavin took the other side.

"Thank you, I can walk," Luca said.

Helen backed off, but Gavin refused and helped him to the sofa. Luca sat down, leaned over, laid his head down, closed his eyes, and fell asleep, his feet remaining on the floor.

"Let's let him sleep it off. It seems he might have had a seizure," Helen remarked.

Gavin sat on the end of the sofa, watching Luca. He had never known Luca to be sick, and Luca hated sitting and doing nothing, so it was hard for Gavin to watch.

"Let's go upstairs. I will make us some tea, and we'll talk," Helen said, watching Gavin's face reveal his concern. "He can sleep here until the stress passes and give his brain time to recover."

Gavin reached down, pulled off Luca's shoes, tucked his legs up on the sofa, and left the room.

Upstairs in the kitchen, Helen started a teapot. Her kitchen was as refined as she was and bright white. Everything was white, from the clear bulbs in white lampshades that dangled over the breakfast bar to the sparkle of the white porcelain tiles on the floor to the two canisters on the counter. She pulled down white teacups from a cabinet.

"Will he be all right?" Gavin asked.

"I believe so, just as long as we keep the monitors down," she said. "I will speak with him about how deep his Hyperthymesia goes, or even if he's ever been diagnosed. Mine's atypical, and he may be as well, as he is high-functioning."

"What exactly do you mean?" Gavin asked.

The Sapphire Ghost

Helen waited for the kettle to heat and prepared the mushroom tea. It would help her and Gavin relax or at least help her calm down. Helen drew in several deep breaths while she prepared the tea.

"Most Hyperthymesia studies have shown that people with this condition remember every detail of every day of their lives. I can never forget any conversation or fact I read, although works of fiction do not stay with me. For some reason, my brain knows the difference. That is why I seclude myself; I can recall conversations I heard from a dozen individuals on a bus I rode when I was nine. All that overstimulation is too much; I must limit my contact with the world."

"And Luca, what did you notice in there?" Gavin asked. "I thought he was just in awe of the place."

Helen smiled, pouring hot water over the stainless-steel tea infuser. She dipped it twice and passed it over to Gavin. "This should settle your mind and help you sleep in a bit."

"Sleep, I cannot sleep!" Gavin protested.

Helen ignored the comment. "He was definitely in awe, but it appeared that something in him was trying to absorb all that information. I think he did not know how to stop it," Helen said, then asked, "he does your computer work, correct?"

"Yes, he works off a tablet most of the time."

"Interesting. So, maybe Luca can control it on his own, but here he became overwhelmed by the constant, multiple streams of information. It is nothing we cannot workaround. I am curious how much he remembers."

"If you have this same condition, how do you control it? You watch those monitors all the time."

"I do not actually watch them, and I have learned not to look at them, as it is too much unnecessary material. Each of those computers is doing a search, and when the search is complete, I read the printout," Helen replied.

Gavin sipped his tea, processing what Helen was saying. He remembered many years ago reading about a woman with the diagnosis. Gavin wondered what it meant for Luca. Gavin could always call Luca's father; he must know that Luca had this extraordinary ability. No, Luca would feel that was an invasion of privacy. Gavin needed to respect that boundary. He realized he already had his phone in his hand and closed it.

Even though Helen was a whisper of a woman, she could be hard as stone. None of that rational persona showed this afternoon as she raced to Luca in terror, and Gavin was unsure he had ever seen her so untethered. Now, standing in her kitchen, she was again poised and collected.

"Now, tell me, Gavin, what is the reason behind your visit?" Helen asked, trying to sound normal, and she had yet to get the hammering inside her chest under control. "I know it is not just for the swearing-in because you have avoided that for months."

"All of that seems less important now," Gavin said charily.

"Yes, I understand; that was rather eventful," Helen admitted. "That has to be the most substantial arrival by a visitor I have ever had."

"You never forget a conversation? Ever?" he asked. He wanted to understand this condition that Helen and Luca shared.

"Not ever. I still remember our very first."

"Wow. This worries me, and I have to know Luca will be all right."

"Gavin, you will not be good for anyone if you are stressed. You look completely worn out. What is going on?" Masked emotions still wavered in her voice.

Gavin sipped his tea some more. He decided he liked this tea even though he was unsure what was in it. "That obvious?" he asked, taking the steel ball out of the cup and setting it on the saucer.

"Like a scratch on a new car. What is it? Gavin, you have me concerned. Are you well? Do we need a second opinion?"

"No, no, Dr. Brody is quite adequate, dry but adequate," Gavin said, watching Helen make another cup of tea. "I am just not feeling like myself, and I'm unsure what it is."

Just then, a loud buzzer went off in the kitchen. "Holy mother of Jesus!" Helen exclaimed, exasperated.

Helen seemed to need the tea more than Gavin just at this moment. *This day was already too exciting for a woman who took refuge in the silence*, he thought.

The Sapphire Ghost

Hitting the speaker button on the phone, Helen spoke into it. "Yes, Grace?"

"Mother, will you be needing me again today?" Grace asked in her soothing, delicate voice.

"Grace, dear, would you mind sticking around for a bit longer? I am unsure, and it has been a little frantic."

"Yes, ma'am, I will be in my room," Grace replied.

"I will call you and let you know."

Gavin smiled at Helen being called "Mother." He knew how long she had waited to claim that title. Helen's husband had taken their two-year-old daughter and disappeared after the CIA recruited Helen. It took Helen twenty years to find Grace and bring her back to the United States from Brazil. Gavin had assisted in delivering the then twenty-two-year-old young woman to Helen. No one would ever know what happened to Grace's father. Grace was only ten years younger than him but did not look her age. Grace remained beautiful, just like her mother.

"Let us start again. What is going on with you?" Helen repeated, standing across from him at the island.

Gavin stirred his tea, watching the bits of brown floating in the hot water. "I am tired, very tired. But I cannot get enough sleep," Gavin confided. "Ever since Rusty left for the island, I have felt lost."

"I understand," Helen said. "Rusty had been with you for seventeen years."

"I can't get past the fact that he will soon be gone, and it has me thinking about my mortality and my legacy," Gavin said, taking a sip of the earthy-smelling tea and savoring the bittersweet tang of the mushroom.

Gavin looked through the kitchen window behind Helen. The wind had picked up, bringing with it crisper air. He was sure it was howling outside, but inside, it was calm. He watched tree branches bend and shift. The tempest threw leaves up from the ground like forced confetti. Yellow and orange, they swirled as the wind made them dance to a song no one could hear. This was the beginning of the dying of his fifty-fourth summer, he thought; soon, only skeletal remains of the trees would be the backdrop to this beautiful landscape.

"Gavin, are you still with me?" Helen asked, having gotten no response to her question.

Gavin shook his head. "What? Please excuse me; I think I drifted off."

"Yes, you most certainly did, and I insist you go to your room and rest. We will have this discussion later," Helen stated, her tone allowing no rebuttal. "I will keep an eye on Luca."

Gavin took a few more sips of the tea and left the kitchen. He wondered if she had put something in it.

Chapter Forty-Three

Luca woke to the silence of the control room. A dull thudding replaced his intense headache as his eyes adjusted to the dimmed lights.

Luca sat up, half expecting to see the fair woman, but he was alone. He stood and walked around to get the circulation back into his legs. All the computer monitors were dark.

He had not had a seizure in years. But with all that information that had buzzed through his head, he was not surprised—embarrassed but not surprised. All Luca wanted to do was find the car keys, drive down the mountain, and find a hotel until Gavin was through with his business here. Luca was unsure he wanted to face Helen after falling out the way he had. He shook his head as the heat rose in his cheeks.

He was starting toward the back door he had come through when he heard the main entrance to the house open. There she stood—and she was a remarkable image indeed, one he would not soon forget as she had been the first thing he saw when he woke. Then, Luca thought she was an angel and that he had made it into heaven after all. Now, he knew it was impossible after all he had done.

"Luca, are you leaving?" Helen asked before starting down the stairs and shutting the door behind her.

"No, ma'am, just stepping out for some air." His chest clenched with humiliation, and a wave of heat trickled back into his face.

Helen noted he was still slightly unsettled but was up, which was good. "May I join you?" she asked pleasantly.

"Yes, sure . . . I mean, yes, ma'am," Luca stammered.

Luca opened the back door for her. The night cut through his dress shirt, cooling the heat, and he stared off into the distant mountains, the shapes only visible thanks to the crescent moon. He was not sure what to say. *What should I say?* Helen remained quiet, waiting for Luca to speak.

"I am truly sorry; I'm not sure what happened." He finally broke his silence.

"Luca, you do not need to apologize to me." She gazed into his eyes.

Luca stared back into her deep emerald-green eyes. He saw an understanding there.

"I do believe you know what happened. I am nearly positive."

"I had a seizure. But it rarely happens anymore. After all, I could not drive with a medical record stating I have seizures."

"Luca, how long have you known you were different?" Helen asked.

"Different?" Luca asked, catching a glimpse of those eyes out of the corner of his own. And he knew she knew, and he admitted to something he'd never revealed to anyone. "I was seven."

"Only seven; that is awfully young." She contemplated this information.

"I was seven when the teacher asked the class to name as many states as they could remember, and I named all of them—and their capitals," Luca said, feeling somewhat lighter for saying it aloud.

"That must have been a treat for that teacher to have such a bright student in their class," Helen said.

"If only. The principal took me to the school counselor, and she began drilling me, and they thought I had a photographic memory."

"I am impressed that you could read so well as to be able to know the names of all the states. Words like Arkansas or Des Moines do not sound like light reading for a small child," Helen said. "And English is your second language, according to your files."

"Neither is Kissimmee or Patchogue," Luca said, trying to be casual. "Try those in a Colombian accent."

Luca turned to look at Helen, and she seemed genuinely curious. But what was she thinking?

"Luca, Hyperthymesia is so rare, and I find it absolutely intriguing to meet another one," Helen said, watching for his reaction.

"What?" The creases deepened between his brows.

The Sapphire Ghost

"Yes, Luca, I have atypical Hyperthymesia," she responded. "I do not have the most severe type, as I do not remember every hour of every day. And you? To what extent is yours?"

"Me, well . . ." he stammered. "I only remember what I read, but it's everything I read. Especially maps and detailed images, like blueprints." Luca sighed. "My father knew what that would mean if the government ever found out. He knew what they did to people in Colombia with 'special gifts." Luca added air quotes with his fingers. "I changed schools. I had been attending a Spanish-speaking school. My father put me in an English-speaking elementary school, and he instructed me to keep my mouth shut unless someone asked me a direct question. A habit I still carry today."

"Yes, he was very wise," Helen said, observing him. "Mine was not diagnosed until I went to work for the CIA. They looked at my test scores, saw I scored higher than anyone ever had, and began the diagnosis."

"I understand," Luca replied. "The fact that I could speak so many languages impressed the brass when I joined the Army. But they never questioned how I knew them, and I never disclosed that I could write them just as well. I passed the LSAT with nothing more than a few days with a study guide and decided to attend law school. Reading and testing I could do easily. In the end, I went into the Army as an officer and found my place and lost it." Exhaling in frustration, he continued. "I was lucky to be given this opportunity, and I can't imagine my life without it."

Helen knew that Luca, or Lucani Medina, immigrated to the United States when he was six, according to his immigration status. His father brought his two young children over seeking asylum, and Luca applied for citizenship after entering the army.

"Helen smiled. "Thank you for confiding in me."

"I wasn't sure I had a choice; I don't want to lose my position with Gavin, and I could not have you thinking I could have a seizure with him in the car." He was nervous. A hint of New Orleans and the Colombian accent began to drift out.

"You have nothing to worry about, your place is secure. I think you nearly gave him a heart attack," she replied, smiling again. "He is asleep now, and he needs the rest."

Luca nodded and felt the relief sweep through him. They stood quietly for a time, looking out onto the distant mountains.

Helen broke the silence. "I have a room ready for you if you would like to get comfortable and take a shower. It will be your permanent room here."

"I appreciate that," he said, walking back inside with her.

Chapter Forty-Four

August 28

Gavin awoke around 6:00, feeling more refreshed than he had in weeks. His side even felt much better. He lifted his T-shirt and noticed someone had changed the bandage during the night. A new bottle of antibiotics and a glass of water were on the bedside table. He read the label and swallowed two as directed. Gavin was not pleased to be touched without permission. But it was most probably Helen, and Helen did what Helen did. What did she put in that tea?

Gavin realized he was hungry and had not eaten the previous day. He needed to eat, he knew, with that medication now in his stomach. He showered and dressed and started down to the kitchen as a plain-faced Grace came from the formal living room. Her red hair was pulled up in a clumsy bun, and she was wearing tight workout clothes. He liked seeing her like this, and it reminded him of his last time with her.

"Good morning, Gavin. Did you sleep well?" she asked, smiling at him.

"Good morning, beautiful!" Gavin said.

"Oh stop, I do not have my face on yet," she retorted.

"And you are still beautiful without all the gloss."

"How is your wound this morning?"

He was not smiling any longer. Gavin's hand went to her arm. He gave her a quick jerk, pulling her against him. "Did you come into my room last night?" His voice deepened and was now barely above a whisper.

"Yes, I cleaned the stitches, applied some cream, and bandaged it back up. It looks infected, Gavin," she responded, surprised by his response. She looked down at his hand, grasping her arm.

"Do not ever do that again. Do not come to me when I am unconscious."

"Never, I will never do that again." She was not going to argue with the Ghost. His quick change and the hardness that now claimed his eyes revealed a man she would not choose to toy with at this moment.

Gavin and Grace entered the kitchen together, although Grace attempted to put some space between them.

Gavin stopped short at the entrance and observed Luca sitting at the breakfast bar, scooping up a forkful of eggs. A woman in a neatly pressed blue uniform stood at the stove. "Luca, you are looking much better this morning."

Gavin headed to the fridge to get a glass of juice. He had been here many times over the years. This was Gavin Garrison's place of rebirth. Grace noticed that Gavin's mood had shifted again. He was a confusing one. If only she could influence him as well as she seemed to do with many other men. Gavin seemed immune to her seductive charms. But Gavin was not any ordinary man; he was complex, sometimes soft, and other times he was most definitely not. She really liked the combination. He, however, seemed to have an interest in her in rare, brief moments. She grabbed a nutrition bar and water and left the kitchen for the gym.

"Yes, and I could say the same for you. sir, you are looking much more rested than yesterday," Luca said after swallowing.

"Yes, maybe it is the mountain air. But you and I are going to have a long conversation shortly."

"I expect so," Luca said, looking away from Gavin's piercing gray eyes. The red returned to his face.

The woman at the stove finally spoke. "Sir, Ms. Glass asked me to prepare breakfast for the two of you. What can I make for you? I am guessing you do not eat beef or pork meat since that young man appears to have cleared off a pound of bacon by himself, and I do have turkey sausage and bacon."

"Thank you. Surprise me," Gavin replied. "And you are?"

"Mrs. Ricci. I assist Ms. Glass from time to time."

"Very nice to meet you, Mrs. Ricci." He sat down beside Luca at the bar.

Turning to Luca, who was now delivering half a piece of bacon into his mouth, Gavin asked, "Would you like to take a drive after breakfast?" Gavin remembered that Luca would always deliver news he felt Gavin would not like in the car.

"That will be unnecessary, sir. I believe we can find a place to talk."

The Sapphire Ghost

After Gavin ate, he took their dishes to the sink. He tapped Luca on the shoulder to let him know it was time for that conversation. Gavin also intended to let Luca know the other reason for their visit.

Just then, Helen entered. "Gavin, will you please join me in the comms center?" Mrs. Ricci handed her a cup of fresh Earl Gray with a slice of lemon on the saucer. "Luca, you too, please."

Luca was unsure whether he was more relieved by the interruption or concerned that Helen had requested him in the control room. When Helen looked at him and smiled, Luca knew she was manipulating the situation. Luca felt a kindred spirit with Helen; she was far less frightening than he had anticipated. They followed Helen from the kitchen and down to the comm center, where they had come in yesterday.

"This only delays our conversation," Gavin said as they followed Helen into the control room.

"I understand, sir."

Luca walked in after Helen and saw that only one monitor was active. It showed people tied to posts who had been burned. Luca shifted his head and tried to make out the image to determine what he saw.

"Helen, do we need to rehash everything for the last twenty-one years?" Gavin asked, shaking his head. He hated looking over his work. "That was decades ago."

"Luca deserves to know your Ghost from the beginning, now that he is your first-in-command and soon-to-be my Warrior. It is time he knew the whole story of how the Orders began with you," Helen said, dismissing Gavin's protest. "And before he takes his Oath."

"Luca, sit at that station there," Helen said, pointing to the middle console. "You have some reading to do. Gavin, you and I also have some business to discuss, and I believe that is why you are here."

Luca went to the middle of the long white table. He clicked on the image and read its caption. It appeared to be old microfiche scanned onto a flash drive. Luca picked up the keyboard and mouse, moved to the front of the table, and sat on the floor, facing the monitor like a child with a new toy. He viewed the images on the screen and read about his boss's early work. Gavin

Garrison's first Dossier was of a man burned like a witch on top of a building. Eighteen more were tied to posts leading up to the compound where sixty teenage girls were rescued. Each one of the men on those posts had been burned alive. A whole-body shudder overtook him. The following image was of a young Garrison standing with several Latino-looking men, and Luca counted nine. Gavin Garrison's first team and how that had become the beginning of the Dark 9 army they had now. This photograph had to be the last image captured on camera of Gavin.

Helen watched the young man on the floor, clearly captivated by what he saw.

"Now, it is time for you to tell me why you are here," Helen said, leading Gavin to the sofas. "I know I requested you to come, but I also know you do not come home without other motivations." It had been this way since Helen had punished Gavin and the Emerald Ghost, Grady, for disobedience six years earlier. The extended seclusion in the cabins was why the Emerald Ghost had run off four years ago and Gavin had disappeared for three months. Still, Grady had never come home.

Gavin watched Luca as well, wishing Helen did not believe this was necessary. But, again, Helen did what Helen did, and she usually had a good reason.

Gavin sat on the sofa and crossed one leg on the other knee. "I have a couple of issues I think you could assist with. The first is an actress named Elaine Pratt, who was given an invitation to a fundraiser for a congressman I have acquainted myself with. The other is a guest staying in Dremmond at the small house.

I received a call from the same congressman regarding Herbert Enterprises. The company requested his help in releasing some shipping containers in Miami. He has reliable information that Elaine Pratt is acquainted with Duncan Bruscoe Jr., a major kingpin of the northeast coast. I want to know how he is tied into Herbert Enterprises. I feel sure that we can trace the connection," he said, matter of fact. "Elaine Pratt could be the most significant lead I have had on Herbert Enterprises in a long time. I feel she obtained the invitation because of her connection to the Bruscoe family. This could lead to his connection to King, or someone directly related to Herbert Enterprises."

"That will be easy enough. We might be able to get close enough to have Ms. Pratt's phone cloned," Helen said. "But I have some information already on Duncan Bruscoe, Jr. I can put together a file." Helen briefly looked off, thinking about the Bruscoe file.

"Two shipping containers should have hit the road last night. My source with the FBI has emailed copies of a shipping manifest that state that Camden Harbor Quest is the shipping agent." Gavin ran his fingers through his peppered gray hair, absently thinking he needed a haircut. "He has placed our trackers on those containers, and we will know where they end up."

"Is the source reliable?" Helen asked.

"Yes."

"When you get the information, let me know," Helen said. "Now, I need to talk to you about something. What about Dr. Brody? Has he accepted? Luca needs the help."

"We're unsure, but I think he will. Truth be told, I believe Dr. Brody is a bit nervous. I got the feeling he thought I killed Rusty." Gavin chuckled.

"Would you like me to give him a call?"

"No, let's give him more time. However, Luca has had all of this on his shoulders for two-and-a-half months, and he has handled it exceptionally well, especially the explosion in London and finishing the task there himself. Luca has not had a break in nearly three months. I want to give him some time to spend with his family. So, I do want Brody to decide soon. Luca took a quick liking to him, and he doesn't normally do that."

Helen watched Gavin; she knew him better than he knew himself. Luca was more than his team member. Helen kept these thoughts to herself. She looked over to Luca sitting on the floor like a boy. Luca was engrossed in the data and seemed to be going through it quickly. He would remember every detail.

Luca was indeed interested in the material he was reading and disturbed by Gavin's early work. He had not seen the cruelty in the last seven years as the second-in-command. At the same time, Luca was intently listening to the conversation going on behind him. He had dismissed Elaine Pratt, the actress; it was apparent Gavin had not. He made a mental note to check on the trackers to ensure they came online later today. Then, there was the fact that Gavin felt the need to give him time off. He was not ready to leave his duties again in the hands of Nate Brody—not yet. If Brody declined, Luca was not going to leave Gavin alone.

He decided to speak up. As Helen and Gavin hit a lull in their conversation, Luca said, "I am not going anywhere, sir."

"We will talk later, Luca," Gavin grumbled.

"You can talk, sir, but I'm still not going anywhere."

Gavin looked over at him and shook his head.

Helen examined Luca again. His posture relaxed, and his eyes watched the screen. He was completely immersed in all the information and activity around him. The fact that he took the initiative to tell Gavin *no* showed promise. Helen was impressed.

"I will work on getting the actress' phone cloned and put together a file on Duncan Bruscoe, Jr," Helen replied. "Was there something else you needed, Gavin? You mentioned a couple of things."

"I had an operation involving Bruscoe's father in 2000. Perhaps that family's operations run deeper than I originally thought."

"Duncan Bruscoe, yes, I remember—New York's Lower East Side. I believe you were hit by a car just after leaving a building in that op."

"Yes, broke three ribs. I healed fast. I was a lot younger then," he mused, the corners of his mouth creeping up at the memory.

Helen did not like where this was going. Gavin could be walking into a well-thought-out plan for retaliation. If, somehow, the Bruscoe crime syndicate was involved with the King and his operations, it could get extremely dangerous.

"What if I missed it all along? What if Duncan Bruscoe was King, and the reins were passed down?" Gavin wondered aloud.

"I will dig deeper into the family and their connections. What I have at the moment is prostitution, drugs, and guns," Helen paused, but Gavin said nothing, so she prodded. "Was there something else you wanted to discuss?"

The Sapphire Ghost

"Yes, but now it seems a bit silly," Gavin said, rolling his head to work out the kink in his neck.

"Go on," Helen encouraged.

"My retreat house at Dremmond. I have a neighbor on the beach, and her name is Henley Scott. I think I recognize the name, but I cannot figure out from where," he said.

Helen smiled knowingly. Gavin hated it when she did that. She assumed he was interested in the woman, but he was merely making sure he had never encountered her in a Ghostly way.

"No, Helen, it is nothing like that!" Gavin protested.

"No, it would never be," Helen smiled. "But you will be interested to know that I already have a file on Henley Scott."

"Why does that not surprise me," he said. It was not a question. "What do you know?"

"Not as much as I would like. However, I have introduced myself by, let us just say, dark chatrooms and alternate social media apps. She runs an adorable children's shelter called Haven Center." Helen watched for Gavin's reaction.

"Haven Center. Why does that sound familiar?" he asked, scratching his chin.

Helen stood, walked to the back of the control room, and punched in the code for the built-in cabinet on the wall. She retrieved a file. Gavin watched her, expecting the file to be gray. But it was brown, and brown was good, meaning Ms. Scott was not considered a target.

Helen handed the file to Gavin, who took it and flipped it open. Her picture, age, marital status, all the ordinary stuff. He flipped to the next page. Secondary bank accounts contained huge sums of money but were in various discreet business names. One stood out: Clover Leaf Reality. He read the synopsis of Haven Center and then realized that he had donated several million to the center. That was where he was directed to send those children five years ago, and that little girl's image came to his mind.

"Ms. Scott is in a bit of trouble," Helen said quietly, "and I am afraid it is because of me."

"How so?" he asked.

"I catfished her into going after a cargo container in Norfolk, and I did not think she would do it, especially once the FBI showed up." Helen smiled with a hint of confusion that said she was impressed by this woman.

"She browses the web looking for information on people who might have that sort of knowledge to share," Helen said. "She is remarkably crafty."

"You are watching her? Is she a possible future Ghost?" Gavin asked.

"I thought she was a possibility; however, I am unsure, as she has some secrets that have yet to be disclosed. There is something in her past that will not show itself. I sent her the info for Dremmond Beach because I wanted to get her away until I could figure out what to do."

"I guess that answers my question. Ms. Scott is not from a rogue organization sitting over there waiting to kill me." Gavin sighed gratefully. Then he looked again at Helen. "There is something you are not telling me."

"Gavin, by now, you should know there is always something I am not telling you. What would be the fun if I told you everything, and you did not have the opportunity to discover anything yourself? She could, however, be a good match for you."

"No, I'm not looking for that," Gavin declared.

"Maybe it is time to start," Helen said, placing a hand on Gavin's knee, "In any event, if you could get her out of the bind she is in, I would appreciate it."

"I'll see what I can do," Gavin replied, looking at Henley's photograph. She was an awkwardly attractive lady; her large dark eyes almost looked cartoonish.

Gavin looked again at Helen. She had never suggested that he look for a relationship. What was going on in that mind of hers? He thought of Grace.

"As far as your legacy goes," Helen said, eyeing Luca's direction, "Let us take a walk."

Gavin realized she did not want Luca to hear what came next, so he followed her into the garden. The trees rustled as the wind blew through their leaves and the air smelled of crisp apples and forest.

The Sapphire Ghost

"As I started to say before I interrupted myself," she began again, "your legacy, Gavin, I believe you have found that. Teach him. He is eager to learn."

Helen looked empathetically at Gavin; she had been concerned for a long time that Gavin Garrison's Ghost was growing tired. He was her first and the architect. His profile consisted of nearly two-hundred and fifty completed Dossiers, but Gavin had yet to seize the one he desired the most. It was impressive that he was still in the game after twenty-one years. Losing Rusty had indeed affected him; the loss of Rusty might even destroy him. Helen was unsure how much longer the Sapphire Ghost could continue. Helen thought she could give him something to look forward to by giving him an out he might be seeking.

"Luca, no, I do not believe . . ." Gavin trailed off.

He thought of Luca going out on his own in London, how he avoided any detection, and how he had been scared for him and proud at the same time. Luca was thirty-three, a year older than when Helen had recruited him, and Luca knew more. Gavin was unsure that Luca had the mental capacity to live a life like the one he protected. There was so much still unanswered about him.

Above all, the thought was a shock. It had never occurred to Gavin to pass the torch, and it would take time to digest.

"Luca has an amazing ability. Either you work with him, or I will," Helen stated. She had realized the future of what they built was at stake. She had initially planned to pass down the reins to Grace. However, after seventeen years, Grace was still not ready as far as Helen was concerned. Grace could not handle multiple situations simultaneously. Luca, however, did.

"Have you told Luca about the Oath?" Helen questioned.

"No, because I dread it," Gavin said.

"Why must you always be so difficult?"

"Because some fair-haired woman gave me permission twenty-one years ago."

"Well, let me say I learned my lesson."

"The only times I did not like Rusty was when you called him under the Code," Gavin said.

"If it were not necessary, it would not need to happen. If you would not behave like a child and have a meltdown each time your life was at risk, I would not need to override you. You are the reason for that Code, Gavin."

"What can I say? You created a monster!" But he knew she was right. "I'll tell him. When would you like to do this?" Honestly, he wasn't worried about Luca taking the Oath. The man was loyal to a fault. He was most worried about losing that loyalty for himself. Luca would then answer to Helen, which was the part that bothered him the most. With Rusty, they both worked for Helen; it had always been that way, and they had a wonderful friendship. However, it was different with Luca—it was built on another foundation.

"This evening, if that is all right with you." She needed to know that Luca would commit to her.

"Fine," Gavin grumped and headed back to the house. How would Luca react to being sworn to Arcadia and the Codes?

Chapter Forty-Five

Luca was placing the keyboard back on the table when Gavin came in and shook his head. "I had no idea," he said.

"I know you didn't, and I was young and angry," Gavin stated. He paused. "Luca, come sit with me for a minute. I have something to tell you, which is why we are here."

Luca sat and examined him, but Gavin looked away. He and Rusty had always had Luca's loyalty, and he hoped that wouldn't change.

Gavin thought about four years ago when he left the convent in San Francisco. After an operation ended in disaster. Gavin was working with the Emerald Ghost, Grady, on a target that Arcadia didn't approve. Luca had helped him get out but had kept that to himself for almost four years. Gavin had hesitated to trust Luca initially, but trust had grown and was deserved. Luca was always willing to do whatever Gavin requested without question. To this day, Luca had never spoken of getting Gavin clothes and transportation out of the convent. Rusty had tried to coerce Luca to admit it was him during the three months it had taken Gavin to recover. Gavin had not explicitly told Luca to keep quiet. He just had. When he was ready to return to work, Gavin called Luca again because he knew he would find a way to retrieve Gavin quietly and not give his refuge away. That was the very reason Gavin was afraid for Luca to take the oath. Luca's kind of loyalty was exceptionally rare, and more so, in his world. Even Rusty would have never allowed such a thing. Was it wrong to want that?

Now, Gavin would ask Luca to pledge his allegiance to Arcadia and Helen. Yes, it only applies in certain situations, but those would be important. Gavin felt he had an ally with Luca that he did not have even in Rusty. The peace in Greece, where Gavin took refuge, had relit his passion for life. It had allowed him a rare glimpse into what it was like to walk as a man. Because for that short period of time, he was more than a shadow, more than a ghost. Gavin had strolled through a market alone, stocked his own fridge, visited museums and galleries, and enjoyed the company of a beautiful woman who had no knowledge of who he was. For three months, Gavin was more than a shadow.

"Gavin, what's wrong?" Luca waited patiently, but his patience had begun to wear thin.

For one, Gavin never had to explain this to anyone else. Rusty had been new and accepted before they had a friendship. Explaining how Helen could take charge because of some bad decisions Gavin had made in the past made him feel childish. "There's something I've not told you about your role as the first-in-command. You are here to take an Oath to pledge your honor to protect me and become Arcadia's Warrior to a Seraphin Ghost."

"I don't need to take an oath to do that, but if it would make you feel better, I will," Luca said, sensing Gavin was holding something back because this wasn't news.

"No, your Oath will be made to Helen and Arcadia. This oath will take you out of my employment and give you to Helen. You will still serve as my FIC, but you will serve her as my Warrior. This oath gives you equal rights as me to the Sapphire Order, and it is a lifetime commitment. There's a list of codes, and you will unquestionably honor them. In certain situations, she can override me and anyone else within the Sapphire Order. You can be removed if you don't obey her orders during certain situations when the codes apply. And there can be other punishments."

Luca stood and paced the room. *I just met Helen, and now I'm being asked to swear an oath to obey her, to be loyal to her.* Helen was a stranger, even if they had found common ground. Loyalty was something far more precious. He ran his fingers through his hair, and anxiety coiled at his heart. This was most certainly news, and Rusty never mentioned any such Oath.

"Was Rusty sworn to Helen?" Luca eventually asked.

"Yes, from the beginning." Gavin watched Luca.

"May I read these Codes?" Luca asked.

Gavin stood and went to the glass case in the back of the room. Each Ghost had their own codes, subject to the individual. This book also contained his completed Dossiers. Gavin extracted his leather-bound book. He walked

The Sapphire Ghost

back, handed the book to Luca, left him, and retreated to the garden, where Helen waited.

"You have already told him?" Helen looked surprised at seeing Gavin so soon.

"Yes."

"And what did he say? He has been with you for a long time. Do you think he will?" Helen asked.

"He asked to see the Codes. So, I gave them to him, and I'll not persuade him one way or the other."

"I see. Luca may be unable to comply after all this; he is utterly devoted to you. Rusty was new. He needs to understand that I have the final word regarding your safety. You do not always have the best judgment with that, and I don't want to worry about your convincing him to go along with one of your independent operations. I nearly lost you the last time, and I did lose Grady."

"I trust that he will do what is best for this Order and me, as I always have," Gavin said thoughtfully and considerately. He knew he'd caused Helen a great deal of stress.

"Do you think he will want to speak with Rusty?"

"That'll be up to him. Let's give him some time. He'll find us when he has come to a decision." Gavin knew he sounded more confident than he felt. Gavin also knew that Helen would replace Luca if he could not swear to the Codes, most likely with Brody.

Luca sat on the sofa and began to read the Codes. There were not many.

***The Seraphim** is an order of persons - The Fire Beings of ancient lore cleansing the land of the wicked. Each seraph has vowed to become a protector for the highest cause. Upon joining, their life is extinguished, bringing forth a new person with no direct ties to power, riches, or laws. They commit to enriching the lives of the common persons by taking extrajudicial measures. Without the Ghost, there is no Order, and without the work of the Order, people suffer.*

The Sapphire Ghost Order—Gavin Garrison: 1989-present, leader.

On becoming Arcadia's Warrior to the seraph Ghost of the Sapphire Order, Gavin Garrison. Upon taking this oath, you will now serve Helen Glass. Protection of Arcadia and the Ghost is the highest obligation.

The Warrior, also known as the first in command, swears by the Code of the Warrior. This is the one by the side of the Ghost of the Sapphire Order who swears to uphold the following Codes without hesitation or question.

1. *From the point of taking the Oath, you must embrace all aspects of the Order. The Warrior acknowledges their role is secure and cannot be removed by the Ghost of the Order, only by Arcadia, death, or approved request. The Ghost cannot take the life of his Warrior except by permission of Arcadia. This oath does not give the Warrior authority to abuse his role or deny the Ghost's commands.*

2. *Warriors will not put anything, including their own life or a loved one, before the life and safety of the Ghost of the Order.*

3. *The Warrior could and should secure a wayward or out of control Ghost against his will if necessary. This could include subduing via bodily harm or drugging and returning them to Arcadia. Examples of loss of control might consist of hallucinations or other mental health issues. Warriors also have the authority to shelter in place with the Ghost if they feel this is the only way to secure the Ghost.*

4. *The Warrior are subject to harsh penalties if poor planning brings danger to their Ghost. Protection of the Ghost is the priority.*

5. *The Warrior must obey this oath entirely and without hesitation. This is the only Code that gives the Warrior permission to deny the commands of his Ghost. Should Arcadia, Helen Glass, feel that the Sapphire Ghost is compromised, and his life is in direct danger, she will issue a directive for the Warrior to transport the Ghost to Arcadia immediately. Warriors can be removed from the post for noncompliance. Branding or indefinite seclusion may also result.*

This Oath may be severed only upon a Warrior's death. Upon affixing signatures to this document, the life of the Warrior belongs to Arcadia, as does the life of the Ghost they serve.

The Sapphire Ghost

The Warrior swears to uphold this Code and, further, to acknowledge an addendum that may be issued. The Warrior must obey any instruction from Arcadia whenever the life of the Ghost of the Sapphire Order is in peril.

These are between the Warrior and the Ghost and may not be shared with other team members.

Sworn to the Sapphire Ghost on this date_____.

I pledge my life to the Seraph _____.

Addenda, Requirements, and training manual are attached and incorporated in this document.

Luca read over the Codes and other requirements for the warrior or first-in-command position. It was not as bad as he anticipated. The only difference Luca could see was that he would be Helen's warrior and Gavin's FIC. *Just semantics,* he thought. His signature would make little difference on the whole. His loyalty would remain with Gavin—his lifetime commitment was with the Sapphire Ghost.

Code 5 had been invoked a few times in Luca's memory because the authorities were too close, or Gavin had inadvertently drawn the wrong attention. Rusty had transported Gavin to Maine. It had not been pretty. Although Luca did not know what was happening at the time, he now understood. He realized so many of Gavin and Rusty's fights had come before leaving for Maine. The biggest one occurred when Gavin returned after disappearing for three months. Gavin and Rusty then disappeared to Maine for three weeks. Luca felt horrible for making Rusty worry—he had known where Gavin was, of course—and it had come close to making the big man crazy. Rusty and Helen had surmised the worst.

Luca placed the book back in the glass case. He would take the Oath but vowed his fidelity would remain with Gavin as it always had. Of course, if Gavin were in danger, Luca would do whatever was necessary to keep him protected, even if it meant getting him to Arcadia, with or without one of Gavin's notorious fits of anger.

Luca waited, wondering if Helen and Gavin would return to the house. He wondered if they waited on him. After thirty more minutes, Luca left to find Gavin because he was beginning to feel jumpy, and when that energy started, there was never ever a positive reaction.

Gavin and Helen entered the orchard when Gavin saw Luca leave the house. He began to stroll back toward the house with Helen at his side.

"You know, I am never the enemy, Gavin," Helen said as they walked.

"I know, Helen. It sometimes still bothers me that my life is not my own, and you can call a Code 5 at any time, and I feel like a child grounded by an overbearing parent," he said quietly.

"I really wish you did not feel that way. You are my best asset and know what you mean to me. Your stubbornness and temper tantrums are the reason I wrote that Code. You are not invincible, you know." Helen was nearly pleading, and she did not like overriding Gavin. "I respect you immensely."

"I realize that—when I am rational," Gavin said, smiling. "You gave me an incredible gift with this life. However, we have certainly had some bumpy times."

Chapter Forty-Six

Luca stood at the walkway's edge with his hands in his pockets, watching Helen and Gavin return to the house. Gavin noted that Luca seemed serious; his posture was tense.

"Well, Luca, what do you think?" Helen asked, a little breathless.

Luca looked over at Gavin and back at Helen.

"I'm ready," Luca said.

"All right, then! That is good news. We will hold your ceremony later this evening if that works for you and Gavin," Helen said, thinking this was too easy.

"How about we skip the fanfare?" Luca said, and he knelt on one knee.

"I swear to uphold all Codes directed by Arcadia. I give my Oath and my Honor to Arcadia to protect and serve the Sapphire Ghost until I'm unable to perform my duties or unto my death." Luca waited for an acknowledgment before he stood.

Gavin observed Luca, whose words conveyed the severe commitment that his features lacked. Gavin did not know whether to be merely surprised or scared at how calmly and quickly Luca made this decision. It had taken Rusty three days to agree to turn over his life. He knew Luca never decided something without knowing all the buts, whys, and what-ifs.

"I believe that will do," Helen said, motioning for Luca to rise. "Thank you. I was expecting resistance."

"The only difference from what I have already agreed to is Code 5," Luca stated. *And we will cross that bridge when it comes*, Luca thought to himself. Helen did not have to know everything. No one knew everything. A slight grin ticked up the side of his mouth.

Helen nodded in agreement. "Then I will prepare a page for your signature and get you a copy," Helen said.

"I have my copy," Luca said and tapped his head.

Helen smiled and understood and left them.

Luca looked over at Gavin and waited for him to say something.

"So, it is official. You are my handler," Gavin said quietly.

"And the world did not end because I chose to remain with you. Stepping aside did not seem to be a better option," Luca replied. "I could not risk her replacing me, and I do not think you would have wanted that. It was a Morton's Fork. Leaving you or one day facing your bad temper. As I said, I'm not going anywhere."

"You don't say much, but you make so much sense when you do speak!" Gavin smiled and clapped a hand on Luca's back.

"Sir, my commitment to you remains unaltered. You know you can count on me when you need me," Luca said.

Somehow, without mentioning San Francisco or Greece, he said nothing had changed. Not once in four years had Luca alluded to any turmoil when Rusty couldn't locate Gavin.

"Luca, you've never mentioned when you helped me disappear. What happened? Rusty suspected you at first," Gavin said.

"It's unimportant. It seemed to me you were suffocating and needed to breathe. You asked for my help. You were safe; that is all I needed to know. Rusty suspected, but he never knew for certain. He thought you found a way to pay off one of Dark 9, but nothing ever turned up," Luca said. "That's why Helen has not given you your own Dark 9 team again. You know as well as I do if Rusty knew it was me, I'd be dead."

Gavin looked thoughtful. "Yes, that's true. I knew that was why I lost my personal Dark 9, and Helen oversees those. How'd you do it all and leave no trail for Helen to follow?" Gavin asked.

Luca arched an eyebrow, winked, and gave Gavin a pat on the shoulder. "Some things are better left unknown." With that, he headed back inside.

Gavin smiled; maybe Luca's new moniker should be the Jester, abracadabra. He made a Ghost disappear. Yes, some things were best left unknown. Yet he knew the next Code 5 would be the test. He also realized he would never risk losing Luca as his Warrior and Helen assigning some stranger to him. He was fortunate to have two great men who had sworn to keep him safe, and he hoped he would not live to see a third.

Chapter Forty-Seven

August 30

It had been a long three days at the house in Detroit. Brody looked over all his work and realized he had not been this productive in a long time. Brody was tired but completely pleased, and his house was in order.

Helen Glass had sent him a package by courier two days earlier. It contained a file with information about Brody's role and whether he chose to take the job. She handwrote him a personal note of understanding that this was a big leap, and Helen had complete confidence in him. In reading the letter, he understood she expected him to take the position of Gavin Garrison's Second. The paperwork included instructions on how he would have to present to the world. Brody's image would have to be pristine, his home neat and orderly, not drawing any unnecessary attention. His finances would need to be planned and prepared so that his credit would not be questioned. In short, Brody's life would have to reflect everything Gavin's could not. He should appear normal if anyone ever grew suspicious of him or investigated his background. His employer would be Atlas Security, a private security firm. The papers stated his pay, which was impressive, thought Brody.

Now, he felt he could return to Dremmond prepared to give Garrison and Medina his answer. The house was immaculate, and even his neighbor visited to acknowledge it looked better. He was ready for his flight back to Florida.

Meanwhile, the tropical storm raged in the small Jamaican town. The winds angrily tore at the trees, and the water lapped at the side of the house from the high sea surge.

Rusty sat inside the house, watching the storm from the safety of his living room. Large blankets of water slapped against the house, causing the windows to rattle and the lights to flicker. He had never been in an island storm before and was grateful this was a small one. This was where he was born, but he grew up in Florida. Julianne lay asleep with her head in his lap while he absently rubbed her back. The little one slept in the chair. It had been almost four months since he had given up his place in the Order, and he missed it. He was, however, feeling much better. The pain rarely kept him awake at night; he was sure that Julianne was praying to some sacred *Santeria Spirit* to heal him. Rusty smiled at his love and the one who slept in the chair. Admittedly, though, his first love would always be the Order.

But now, Rusty was angry with Gavin. He was angry that Gavin had not mentioned the explosion and the injury when they spoke on the phone three days earlier. He found that out from Luca, who hadn't known Gavin had not shared the news. Rusty understood Gavin was trying to protect him—but that had always been *his* job, protecting the Ghost and lifelong friend, not the other way around. Listening to Luca's tale, he realized little could have been done to prevent the bombing. Still, Gavin should have told him.

It had been Gavin Garrison who plucked him from the manliest of all unravelings. In 1994, Rusty was the warden of one of the largest prisons in Florida, when in walked the man who had been in the headlines for nearly a year. His name was Donley Martin. At age thirty-one, Martin was convicted of one of the worst rape cases that Rusty had ever seen. The girl was only ten when he raped and tortured her nearly to death. The DA tried to get the death penalty, but the judge would not go for it, saying a murder had not been committed. Yet, in a way, there had been the murder of a young girl's soul from Rusty's community. And her body would never be what it once was. Every possible future she could have imagined for herself had been ripped away. The little girl would never be able to trust a man or become a mother. She eventually killed herself.

But there was that day when Donley Martin became his ward. The most hated man in the country came to be under Rusty's roof. Anger swelled inside him as the guards escorted Martin into the prison with that smug look on his face. Rusty knew he could wait for the prisoners to take care of him, but he did not. Instead, he asked the guards to look the other way on Martin's third night, and Rusty loosened his rage on the man. Rusty beat nearly every breath from Martin before the guards pulled him off. He would have killed him with his bare hands and lived with the consequences. There were consequences, of

The Sapphire Ghost

course. He was fired from his job of twelve years, the job he thought he would retire from with a fat state pension.

Then, out of nowhere, Gavin Garrison showed up at the lonely little bar, the one Rusty had become as much a part of as the stool he sat on each night since his wife had left him. Yes, one of Fate's fantastic plays.

Gavin Garrison just happened to be precisely where Rusty needed him to be, which began quite a story. Rusty shook his head at the memory of how a small white man compared to Rusty managed to offer him everything he never thought he wanted, but he did. Gavin happened, and he was the best bet Rusty had ever made. Gavin was his brother in every way that mattered, and their blood ran through each other's veins. Though Rusty was supposed to protect the Ghost, Gavin had saved Rusty's life more than once.

Rusty could admire the rage of the ocean, the anger in the winds. Feelings he felt all too often. After all they had done together!

Chapter Forty-Eight

September 1

Gavin allowed Luca to test his driving skills at descending the mountain, primarily because he wanted to have that one-on-one discussion with him finally. Luca gladly took the keys after he loaded the bags in the back. Gavin and Helen had been in discussions for a large chunk of the last two days.

Luca was no longer nervous. Especially after seeing all those electronic files and having so many secrets revealed to him. The main one was who the Ghost had been and the obituary for the man he once was, Gavriel Masterson. Gavin tucked his brown case behind his seat with the new files and sat up front with Luca. They started to make a steady descent. Clearing his throat, Gavin began to speak. Before he could, Luca cut in to relay what he had been working on that morning.

"The shipments have divided but seem to be headed in the same direction and might end up at the same location. I have already sent Dark 9 to follow the trucks."

"Thank you, Luca." Gavin cleared his throat again.

"I am sorry, sir. I never meant it to seem like I was hiding anything from you," Luca said. "And I never meant to scare you."

"You did scare me, but I am hurt that you felt you had to keep something like a medical condition from me. Had I known, I could have protected you from ever going through that," Gavin said.

"I understand you feel I kept a secret from you. But I have hidden that from everyone since I was a boy, and it's not something I think about. Honestly, it was not something you could have protected me from, because I've never had that happen before, and I've never been exposed to that much data at once," Luca said as he shifted the Range Rover into D2 to reduce the slipping on the gravel road. "If I thought it mattered, I would have told you. I learned to conceal it and use strategies so no one would know it seemed to be just a part of me for so long."

The Sapphire Ghost

"Maybe you do not understand how much I depend on you and value you as a person. Sometimes I am not good at telling people I care about them. The thought that you could have had a stroke! The thought of losing you and Rusty! That is too much," Gavin said warmly. "You should not feel like something like this would ever be a hindrance."

Luca listened as he drove. He knew Gavin cared about him. He would never intentionally cause Gavin to worry about him.

"Yes, sir. Again, I am sorry, and thank you," Luca said. "May I ask you a question?"

"Certainly, anything," Gavin replied.

"Why did you not question me when I returned from London?"

"I felt no need to. I know you always put the Order first, which includes me. I trust you."

Luca heard exactly what he needed to hear. After returning from London, he thought he felt it. Still, Luca wanted to hear Gavin say the words. Rusty had been Gavin's confidant for so long, and he was unsure he would ever reach that level of trust.

The terrain going back down the mountain wasn't bad. The SUV handled it efficiently, but it was slow going.

Roads were limited, in more ways than one, in this area. That was why Helen selected the location. In addition, her property butted the Canadian border, with a farm and its lovely farmhouse just on the other side. If Helen ever needed to flee, she had a clear path across the border to disappear.

"Do you know how to get back to Bingham?" Gavin asked.

"Yes."

"Will you explain the Hyperthymesia to me? I know you told Helen; would you explain it to me?"

"Actually, Helen told me more than I knew. I guess, according to her, I am atypical, as I don't recall everything. Thank goodness! But I do recall everything I read."

"All this time, I thought you were good at directions, but you memorize maps?" Gavin asked.

"Yes, and books, song lyrics, detailed drawings like plans or blueprints, anything on paper, a sign, a monitor. That is why I insist you give me a flash drive for the Glass files. If I am prepared, I can ignore unnecessary information, and I do not want everything in the file stuck in my head," Luca said.

"Interesting." Gavin lay back on the headrest and took it all in. "Okay, I have a question. How do you know your way back from the woods of northern Maine without a map?"

"Road signs, billboards, political signs in the yards . . . I am just reversing them," Luca replied.

"Now that is impressive," Gavin said and smiled. "What about the seizure? What are the chances that will happen again?"

"I cannot say for sure because that is only the third one in my life and the only one since adulthood," Luca said, looking hard for the slight right turn he knew was coming up.

"You have about forty more yards before your turn," Gavin said, noting Luca's attentiveness to the road. "So . . . you are all right?"

"Yes, I am good. However, Helen said I'm never allowed to come through her back door again."

"I am sure! You scared us both."

"She's really nice. Not what I expected, and I woke up thinking I had an angel kneeling over me." Luca spoke with awe.

Gavin laughed hard. "Yes, I had similar thoughts the first time I saw her."

"She is not, right?" Luca replied, completely serious.

"No, absolutely not."

Gavin had been thinking a lot about Luca the last couple of days. Luca's time in London and taking care of Bains, going undetected. Helen's observations and suggestions for him to train Luca. Luca was strong, he thought, but he had much buried inside him. Luca was too quietly contained, and Gavin wondered what lay dormant. Gavin wanted to know more about him. As a Second, under Rusty—Luca was excessively controlled. However, since Rusty's departure, things were starting to surface. Gavin was curious to know whether Luca would reveal more about himself.

Gavin thought a moment. "May I ask you another question?"

The Sapphire Ghost

"Yes, please, be specific."

Gavin turned to Luca and considered the most direct way to ask his question. "Why is your military file so black?"

"I was in an unsanctioned unit," Luca replied.

"What did you do in that unit?" Gavin asked.

"I just said it was unsanctioned, and I cannot tell you that." Luca thought a moment about the information he'd sworn never to disclose. However, there was no rule to say Gavin could not read it himself.

Luca glanced sideways at Gavin. "But I can give you an unredacted copy to read."

"You have an unredacted copy?" Gavin asked, surprised.

"Yes."

"Tell me, honestly, what do you think about the role of the Ghost?"

"I admire you and the role," Luca said.

"Don't tell me what you think I want to hear. I want to know what you really think," Gavin said, thinking about Helen's suggestion for Luca to succeed him.

Luca stepped on the brakes, and the SUV skidded about ten feet before stopping. The hard stop threw Gavin against the seatbelt, and he immediately reached for the bar at the top of his window.

Luca shifted into park. "Ask a question, and you will get an answer. But never again think I am answering you to appease you, sir. My answers will be truthful, and direct questions will receive equally direct answers."

Gavin saw an opening for the real question on his mind. "Have you ever resented me asking you to kill a person?"

"No."

"Even though I did not ask Rusty?" Gavin asked.

"No."

"Although it was not your responsibility. Did you ever wonder why?" Gavin asked.

"No," Luca replied again.

"The first time I asked was a test to see if you would. You did so without hesitation and did it quietly. I admired that in you, and you could have said no."

Luca did not respond, but he thought about what Gavin was saying.

"I know so little about you, and I need to know more," Gavin urged.

"I understand. Rusty explained it best. He said that my mind works like a computer. Ask a question and get an answer. I will teach you to be specific, sir."

"I will work on that," Gavin tried again. "Do I scare you?"

"Without question," Luca responded.

"Why?"

"Because I want to be just like you."

"That scares you?" Gavin asked, thinking the response was a half-truth.

Luca thought about the question. Gavin was everything he wanted to be. However, Luca was unsure if he had the confidence to pursue such an idea on this side of the line. However, if he were still the man he was prior to the injury in Iraq before he bottled that old demon away—he'd not hesitate.

"Yes," was the only response Luca could give.

Luca shifted into drive and continued down the mountain. Gavin tried to think of another question to get the information he wanted. Luca said he wanted to be like him, but it scared him. Something was buried deep in his new Warrior, and he wanted to know what it was. If Gavin were to ask Luca to take over for him one day, Gavin wanted to know he could handle the role. Gavin sighed. It might take baby steps to get there.

"What did you feel when you cut Steve Bains' throat?" Gavin asked, thinking of Luca's response that the Ghost was in control.

"Peace. Another devil could not walk around any longer," Luca replied.

Maybe Helen was correct about Luca, but he wanted to know what Luca hid behind that placid demeanor. They were quiet for nearly an hour as they turned and twisted their way back to civilization. Then, it occurred to Luca that there was something else he needed to tell Gavin. *This was not going to be pretty. Realmente malo.* Luca shook his head; Spanish took over when he was nervous. *English, Luca.*

"Sir, I have to tell you something which may upset you."

Gavin came out of his mental notes.

"Well, out with it," Gavin replied. There had been many surprises.

"I spoke to Rusty the night I fell out. I wanted some advice, which led to a discussion about London." Luca paused, letting the conclusion rest in the air.

Gavin shifted uncomfortably in his seat. He turned to Luca, and that crease between his brows was deep. "You told him I was injured?"

"Yes. I did not know you hadn't," Luca admitted.

Gavin brought his right hand to his face, covering his mouth with his index finger on his nose, and sat back in the seat. He sucked in a long deep breath. It was not Luca's fault. He knew Luca often spoke with Rusty, and he had not asked him not to tell. This was bound to happen.

"It's fine. I will deal with Rusty," Gavin finally said.

Luca was relieved. He supposed Rusty would be waiting on them when they returned to Dremmond because of his displeasure over this. *Maybe two pins north of angry would describe it better*, he thought.

"Take a week off after we are done in Washington, D.C., on Friday," Gavin announced.

"I'm not ready . . ." Luca began.

"That's an order. You and Brody will need to find somewhere else to be," Gavin said firmly.

"Both of us, sir?" Luca sounded confused.

"Do you think I am never to have any time alone?"

Luca arched his eyebrows and thought about the conversation between Gavin and Grace.

Chapter Forty-Nine

September 1

Brody arrived in Dremmond only to find the house vacant. He had been gone for three days. He was unsure when they would return from Maine, but he had thought it was today. He was anxious to see his patient. Maybe they were delayed? Brody pulled the phone from his pants pocket. Hanging his jacket on the hook by the entry, he glanced down where he placed the two stone lapel pins. Brody smiled with a bit of awe.

Noting Luca's sharp designer suit jacket hanging beside his, he ran his fingers over the material. Brody felt self-conscious about the suits he owned. He did not have a problem spending money but had not previously worn suits often enough to think of investing in nicer ones. For most of Brody's life, he had spent in a uniform, whether scrubs at hospitals, military fatigues, or the black uniform of Dark 9. He supposed he would have to invest in suits, his new uniform. Neither Garrison nor Medina bought off the rack at Men's Warehouse.

He dialed Luca's number, but the call went directly to voicemail. Brody waited and tried again and again it went to voicemail. "Mr. Medina, this is Brody. Just wondering how my patient is doing?" He hit "End" on the phone.

Brody looked out the balcony doors. He was unsure he had ever seen them closed during the day, and almost expected to see Gavin sitting there with a book in his hand and his reading glasses on his nose. He opened the doors wide and stepped out, taking in the gusts of wind picking up speed from an incoming storm.

Brody glanced over to the other house and saw the woman staying there, bringing in the patio furniture. He thought that might be a good idea since Tropical Storm Brenda would hit that night. Brody hoped Garrison and Luca would arrive before the rain and flood.

He stowed away the furniture under the balcony. Brody pulled the phone from his pocket to ensure he had not missed a call and prepared a salad for

The Sapphire Ghost

dinner and half a bottle of an unoaked chardonnay from the wine cabinet. The house was too quiet, so he went to put on some music since Gavin had quite the collection in the den. Finding an old, big band jazz record of Fletcher Henderson, he placed it on the turntable, and lifted the needle to the vinyl. It was so good it made his whole body tingle. Jazz was why he loved Chicago—the electricity of going to those jazz bars and listening to someone create such great tunes with all that brass. He turned up the volume and noticed another door for the first time.

It was barely visible against the thick wood-paneled wall. Brody turned the knob, and the door did not budge. However, this door lock was strange. The keyhole below the handle appeared to be a cross, with sharp tips on the top and bottom—*some specialty lock*. He wondered, not for the first time, about his new teammates. What made them tick? For the first time that Brody could remember, he was invested. He wanted to be a part of this team and earn Gavin's respect. Dr. Nate Brody had an aching desire to belong.

It was only half past six, and the house was cast in sunsetting colors washing across the water. Brody heard a car pull up and peered out the kitchen window and saw a dark sedan but did not see the driver. Taking his gun from his shoulder harness, he draped across a nearby chair and headed to the living room. Hearing keys in the door, Brody thought it might be Mr. Garrison and Mr. Medina, but the man he saw silhouetted in the doorframe was impossible to identify. The stranger was so broad he took up most of the door frame, with a large square head, thick neck, and dark skin. Brody cautiously brought up the gun. The man was as tall as himself but would make three of him in weight.

The stranger stood inside the dark house, his key clinking into the dish on the table. He looked at the light-skinned, thinner man standing in front of him with a gun. Rusty stood there for the briefest of moments.

"Don't get trigger-happy, boy," Rusty said, strolling by him. Rusty removed his sports jacket and hung it beside a dark jacket, noting the two stone pin. The corner of his mouth curled.

"You are?" Brody asked as the man walked past him to the decanter on the bar.

"Rusty."

Brody holstered his gun. "My apologies, sir."

"Don't apologize, son." Rusty took his drink to the big chair in the living room and sat as if that had always been his place.

Brody observed the lineman-sized man with a fascination. The way Rusty had called him *Boy*, his voice sounded like he ate rocks for breakfast and had chills running up the back of Brody's neck. Rusty appeared as warm and cuddly as rough-cut lumber. Brody recalled meeting him once before, but he had not seemed so intimidating.

Rusty studied the man. *Luca's new man.* Rusty wondered what kind of man Luca had chosen, who should make the team better, who could be trusted with Gavin's life.

But he was not there to interfere. Rusty was here to see Gavin and have a few words because, no matter how sick he was, Rusty deserved to know how his brother was doing.

"Where's Gavin?" Rusty asked.

"I don't know," Brody said. He was growing uncomfortable with Rusty's presence and his own lack of information. Because before Gavin and Luca left, he was not officially part of the Order.

"That sounds ominous."

"They were supposed to be back yesterday," Brody said, and he could almost feel the hairs on his chest disappearing because he felt like a small boy. Few people ever made him feel that way. "I've had no response to my calls."

"I see," Rusty said and examined the man. "You are?"

"Brody, Nate Brody, sir."

"You are the doctor. The one taking care of Gavin?" Rusty asked, although it was more of a statement.

"Yes."

"They left you behind and did not say where they were going? That's interesting. Hard to take care of a man from a distance." He arched an eyebrow and then sipped the brandy.

Brody was unsure if he should say anything more and suddenly felt extremely uncomfortable. This was Medina's mentor, someone Medina admired, Mr. Garrison's right hand for years. He was pretty impressive.

"Mr. Garrison has said you are ill. Do you mind me asking with what?"

"Lymphoma," Rusty said.

"Oh, dear. That's rough. Is there nothing to be done? I mean, I'm sure you've tried everything . . . ." Brody cut the question short at the glower Rusty gave him.

"Do I look like someone who would go out without a fight?" Rusty asked, amusing himself.

"Most certainly not, sir!" Brody replied, and gave up on small talk. His usual bedside manner wasn't working on this fellow. He hoped Mr. Garrison would be back soon.

They sat in deep, consuming silence for a long time. Brody decided it was too quiet, and he could hear every beat of his heart and maybe even the heartbeat of the fruit fly that kept buzzing around. However, the company of the fruit fly was more tolerable. Brody went to the den, turned on the record player, and laid the needle on the album. He let the sweet sound of jazz out into the quiet, and it felt like a shock wave.

Rusty smiled as Miles Davis's trumpet sounded through the room. *Well, that is promising*, he thought. Rusty sipped, laid back, and listened. Based on what Luca said on the phone, he knew where Gavin and Luca were and supposed they would return today.

If Luca told Gavin that he had spoken to Rusty about London, Rusty knew there would have been a few choice words. But he knew Gavin had to realize he was Luca's business, especially now because Rusty felt sure Luca would have sworn in. Luca was unaware that Gavin had not mentioned to Rusty about being injured, much less that Gavin had surgery. Luca confided in Rusty, feeling he had made a mistake and should have planned better. That wasn't possible because Luca was meticulous and cautious. Rusty had allowed Luca to direct Dark 9 for the last two years. However, it was different when you were doing it alone.

Luca decided on someone to work with him, which meant he trusted this man. Trust was not an easy thing to gain in doing what they did. From their first conversation, Rusty knew that Luca would devote his life to him and Gavin. Rusty never questioned Luca's commitment, and he hoped Luca would be able to say the same thing about Dr. Brody.

Rusty felt itchy with this man, something he could not put his finger on. And if Dr. Brody ever gave Luca reason to doubt him, that would be the end of the pleasant doctor because Luca liked to sneak off to Louisiana, and there were plenty of swamps.

Rusty had questioned Luca about Steve Bains and knew Luca had fallen over the edge. He knew that Luca's handle in the army was *Silent Knight*, and Rusty never saw anything that would earn such a moniker, but he did not doubt that it was earned.

Gavin's jet was not at the hangar when Rusty flew in, so when Gavin and Luca did arrive, they would see Rusty's plane, which would ruin the surprise. It would not be too much longer.

Chapter Fifty

September 1

Gavin looked over at Luca, sleeping in the chair beside him. Luca always fell asleep if he had to sit for long.

Luca mentioned that Brody had called while they were in Maine to ask about Gavin's health. They both believed he would be at the house waiting on them. They were confident Brody had decided to take the position, and Luca explained he felt secure in his selection and that there was more to Nate Brody than met the eye. Gavin was still unsure, but time would tell, just as it had with Luca, who had worked out perfectly.

Gavin thought about the prison warden of seventeen years ago. Rusty was big and mean, and Gavin had been ordered to find a bodyguard. Gavin had run off or evaded all those Helen chose to protect him. Gavin felt it was critical to make his own selection; he wanted to see into the person's soul.

Gavin remembered asking Rusty why he chose such a small guy as his backup, and Rusty had responded, "Do you know chihuahuas bite more people than pit bulls do?" Gavin had looked that up and confirmed it. Just as he needed to pick his first-in-command, it was equally important that his team members chose the people they would be dependent upon. That was a huge responsibility when placing your life into someone else's hands.

Gavin understood Dr. Brody would not be the only person waiting for him. He expected Rusty to be there. It would be good to see him; it had been a few weeks since he'd made it to Jamaica, and he missed the man.

Gavin nudged Luca. "We are landing."

Luca stretched and looked out the window. He could see the runway below, and their hangar lit up, awaiting their arrival. He noticed the shiny new plane sitting off to one side. Luca smiled because Rusty was in Dremmond. Rusty would have come to see Gavin, but he also looked forward to seeing him.

They landed back in Destin just before 8:00 p.m. Gavin observed that Marshal did not disembark after he and Luca stepped out, and he wondered if Marshal was all right. In fact, Marshal had not been his usual self when they took off—no dad jokes.

Luca observed more activity tonight than usual. Just off to the right of the tarmac, several hundred yards from the closest hangar, were several utility vehicles and men standing around in hardhats and orange vests. Luca took note and did not dismiss the feeling that something was wrong with a utility company working so late on a weeknight.

Luca retrieved the keys to the Mercedes, noting the blue sedan was missing. Quietly, Luca scanned the black Mercedes and studied the vehicle's weight. It was right on target with a full tank of gas. Luca watched the men in hard hats for several long minutes before pulling out of the hangar. Luca made a mental note to ask what was happening with the utility company the next day. Luca observed they were not doing anything but standing around.

It took only twenty minutes to get back to the gates of Dremmond. Luca punched in the passcode, and the gates slid open. He rode through the quiet, empty town with the perfect-looking storefronts shuttered for the night. Luca could tell there had been a storm because the water still stood deep in some parts of the road, splashing onto the car as they rode through. Then he turned onto the side street that led to the house. Luca saw two cars parked outside: a sporty little black rental and the early model sedan that stayed in the hangar. Rusty had carte blanche, he knew. Luca parked beside the Corvette and would have to speak to Brody about being more discreet.

Brody had put on his jacket because it was windy and took Gavin's chair on the balcony. He watched the water lap against the sand when he heard footsteps and saw Luca come into view.

Luca rounded the corner to the door and saw Brody sitting alone on the balcony. "Brody, good to see you. What are you doing out here?"

"Just thinking," Brody said and turned to look inside the house.

Then Gavin walked up behind Luca and smiled at Brody. "Brody, how are you?"

"I'm good, sir. How are you feeling?" Brody asked, noticing Garrison's movements were neither awkward nor pained.

"Better, feeling much better," Gavin said.

"That's good to hear." Brody saw Gavin's eyes fall on the bar on his lapel.

"I knew you would make the right decision. Welcome!" Gavin said kindly and backed into the house.

Luca looked at Brody, nodded, and walked in behind Gavin. Brody thought Garrison did look better and had given no indication of favoring his left side.

Gavin switched on the lamp on the table beside the bowl with the keys, and looked over at Rusty, sitting in his chair.

"It's good to see you, brother," Gavin said affectionately.

"Good to see you as well and see that you are all right," Rusty said, and stood to stroll over, placing his big hands on Gavin's shoulders. "It's not okay to not tell me things like this, and you know better!"

"I understand your concern, but my life was not in danger. You may ask the doctor here," Gavin said as Rusty pulled him in for a hug.

Brody stepped in beside Gavin. "Excuse me, gentlemen, but it has been four days since I have seen my patient, and he is coming with me." Brody motioned toward Gavin's bedroom. "After you, sir," he said without hesitation.

Luca nodded at Gavin and smiled. Gavin eyed Rusty and shrugged. "My doctor has spoken. I will see you in a few minutes."

Rusty observed Luca and the smile. *Brody has some nerve*, Rusty thought. Luca motioned to Rusty, implying he would refill his drink, and Rusty handed him the empty brandy glass. Luca went to the bar, refilled Rusty's glass, and filled another halfway with a single malt. Luca smiled again to himself and thought this felt like old times.

"I think I scare your new guy," Rusty said, taking his brandy.

"You scare a lot of people," Luca said with a sideways grin. "You're looking good."

"I feel pretty darn good," Rusty admitted. "How are you holding up? Did you enjoy your visit to Maine?"

"It was interesting. Helen showed me everything," Luca said.

"Everything?" Rusty questioned.

"Yes," Luca said. "And, yes, I have given my Oath so you can speak freely."

"Well, then you have the whole story. You understand it wasn't for me to tell," Rusty said.

"I understand." Luca sat on the sofa, and Rusty folded himself into the chair. "But someone could have warned me about the Oath. I was blindsided."

"I couldn't tell you; Gavin should've. How'd you feel about it?" Rusty asked.

"After the initial shock, I understood there was no choice. It wasn't like I would step aside," Luca said.

Rusty nodded with understanding. "Your new guy? Tell me about him."

"Brody . . . well . . ." Luca scratched his head. "I just saw something in him. He earned my trust when he followed through without question. I know Gavin can be dreadful when he is unwell, and he has a reputation for making people scatter and never look back. It says something about Brody because Gavin didn't run him off. Brody was still here when I returned. Gavin was unhappy, but with Brody's jolly bedside manner, he handled him—and that is a feat in itself." Luca ran a finger along the rim of his glass. "I read up on him and a few others while in London from the Dark 9 files. Brody has a great background, but I liked his personality. His colleagues noted his attention to detail and his power of persuasion. You know I'm not that good with people."

He missed this. Rusty had been his rock and had become his dearest friend. Unlike most people, he did not have a problem speaking to him. Rusty knew him, even the hidden parts. There is little reason to control what you say when someone knows you.

"I'll admit that I could not see what you could have possibly seen in the man at first. I think I understand now," Rusty replied. "I see he has a backbone."

"Rusty, you have a way with Gavin, and I am not sure I have any of those techniques. I need someone who can coerce him when needed," Luca said, smiling at Rusty. "You are irreplaceable, you know?"

The Sapphire Ghost

"I know, God broke the mold," Rusty said and raised his glass to Luca.

Luca set his glass on the table beside the sofa when he heard Gavin's footsteps coming back down the hall. "I'll give you some time to visit."

Luca stood, whispered something into Gavin's ear, and stopped Brody in the hallway.

"Pack an overnight bag. Let's go get drinks and celebrate!" Luca said to Brody and went to pack a bag himself. When his phone rang, he'd just changed into clean jeans and a black T-shirt.

"Yes."

"Luca, it is Helen."

Carefully holding the phone between his ear and shoulder, he placed clean, folded clothes into the bag he had just cleaned out. "Yes, ma'am, what can I do for you?" he asked as he tossed his toiletry bag into his overnight duffle.

"Do you remember seeing any numbers on those servers at Hollinger, Steve Bain's company? Serial numbers?" she asked.

"No, ma'am, but then again, I wasn't looking for any." He finished packing and zipped the bag.

"Okay. I am looking for something and cannot find the serial number for one of Hollinger's main servers, and I thought I could backtrack to the others if I could get into one." Helen sounded discouraged.

Luca held the phone as he walked back into the living room. "Would you mind holding on a moment, Helen?" Luca said and walked up to Gavin.

"Gavin, did you send that flash drive to Helen?"

"No, not yet. Why?" Gavin replied. He cocked his head, having heard Luca ask Helen to hold.

"Do you have that drive?" Luca asked, and Brody walked into the room with them.

"It is on my desk. Go and retrieve it."

Luca looked confused because he had been in Gavin's office just once when Rusty took him there before he left. Rusty nodded to Luca that it was all right.

"What is this about?" Gavin asked.

"Helen's looking for something on the Hollinger servers, and I'm not sure they survived. Maybe that's why she cannot get into them. But there will be something on that flash drive to help her."

"Go ahead and see if you can get her what she needs," Gavin said.

Luca turned his head. "Brody, I'll be a few minutes, then we'll take off."

"No problem," Brody said, looking back at Rusty and Garrison.

"Garrison is healing nicely, just in case you wanted to know. The rest of the stitches should come out next week," Brody said.

Rusty smiled and gave Brody a reassuring nod.

Luca walked out of the room and into the den where Brody stayed. He noticed how neat everything was, his bedding on one end of the couch. Luca had planned to give him the key to the bedroom, but with Rusty staying tonight, Luca decided to wait. Although he knew they had enough room to accommodate everyone, it was not the right time to put Brody in Rusty's old room.

Luca took the long narrow pin with the four square sapphires and pointed arrows on both ends from the pocket of his leather jacket. He removed the magnet from the back of the pin, revealing a thin cross, and placed that against the unpolished brass lock on the door of Gavin's office. The pin stuck, and he heard the lock tumble and click. Luca gently turned the knob and opened the door. To the right in the room was an old walnut desk with a white monitor, keyboard, and a closed desk calendar. Luca saw the flash drive beside the calendar.

He took the phone off mute. "Helen, are you still there?" Luca asked.

"I am here, Luca; what am I waiting for?"

"I have Steve Bain's computer files," he said, "but I also have more."

"How did you accomplish that?" she asked, surprised.

"Would you please open a backdoor to the computer I used while there? I'll need at least two minutes to complete the transfer," Luca said, ignoring her question.

"You want me to open my servers?" Helen asked. "I do not think that is wise."

The Sapphire Ghost

"It's only for a couple of minutes. The alternative would be to wait until we send the flash drive by courier. Your call."

Luca was already looking through the available memory on Gavin's computer and creating a block of space to send such a large file.

"Helen, something else," Luca said. "Something I will have to guide you through to find. Before I destroyed the servers at Hollinger, I put a virus in the network to kill any backup servers they might be using. But first, I made copies of everything they had on those servers."

This information grabbed Helen's attention. It might take weeks to comb through, but that would give her what she needed. This was a huge step toward discovering who Jack Byron King was and where he was located.

"All right, Luca, I will create a backdoor but closely monitor it. I will close it and wait on the courier if something looks off," she said.

Luca began to type in the algorithm for encrypting the file and started the upload.

Helen watched, and eventually, the remaining bits of the 240 GB of data slid into the partition and closed the backdoor.

"I have it," she announced.

"Good, now, follow me, please. Carefully. I will take you to a deep website." As Luca said it, he realized he could not do it from Gavin's computer; he needed his laptop. "Well, I cannot access that from this computer. Let me grab my laptop, and I will be right back." Luca laid the phone on the desk and hurried out of the room.

Luca did not acknowledge anyone on his way back through the house. Brody sat on the sofa, having a drink, where Luca had previously sat. Rusty seemed more amiable since Gavin returned. Brody watched Luca quickly dart through the room and dash back to the den within a few seconds. Brody concluded that Luca was using whatever room hid beside the den, and his curiosity was piqued. Brody kept his thoughts to himself, however. He was the new guy, and it would take time to build trust.

Chapter Fifty-One

Rusty observed the man sitting on the sofa beside him. He saw curiosity and a little confusion. Rusty was sure, knowing Luca as well as he did, that Luca had not explained in detail what Luca expected of Brody. Luca was often short on words.

Luca had been recruited as second-in-command. However, Luca immediately immersed himself in the details of the work and never really seemed like a second. He knew both Gavin and Rusty, as well as Rusty knew Gavin. He had taken on everything that they had asked of him. And due to going through rounds of chemo, Rusty had been able to give up some of the duties, trusting Luca. They shared the responsibilities rather than having clearly defined job descriptions—with one crucial exception: Rusty worked for Helen while Luca worked for Gavin.

Rusty cleared his throat and spoke to Brody. "Your job is to learn Luca, his moods, habits, and what he thinks the moment he thinks it. You need to know when he is off or not paying attention and be able to make up the difference. Luca's job is Gavin, ensuring the Ghost lives to fight another day. Learn Luca and study him like I will be giving you a test. And make sure you protect him, even from himself, if necessary. As the first-in-command, his whole purpose is to keep Gavin alive. That, now, is the only reason he breathes.

"Your purpose is to make sure he can do that. You need to know when to be backup or take up the slack and when you might need to pull him out completely. He has flashbacks to the war where he was wounded, and they have not interfered yet, but there is always that one time when they might. Keep an eye out. That is my advice to you, Dr. Brody."

Rusty continued. "He will be doing the same with you. Luca will get to know you and learn your expressions, tells, and weaknesses. Luca does not say a lot but when he does speak, you listen. He will have your back. He's not a man to easily anger, like me. He has dared to step me down and tell me to back off, and trust me, that's not easy. Do you think you can do that with Luca?"

Brody looked at the big man with his calm disposition. Rusty's advice was precisely what he knew Brody needed to hear. Brody knew it, too. He had asked Luca what his job was but did not get a clear answer, and here it was. Study Luca, be there if needed, and be a step ahead. That seemed simple.

"Yes, sir. I can do that." Brody gave Rusty a reassuring smile.

The relief on Brody's face told Gavin, who had been listening quietly, that Brody needed to hear what Rusty said. Gavin had never actually considered explaining his expectations of his team members—except for unquestioned loyalty.

The advice made Brody feel better about what he would have to do. Brody also thought that he probably had an easier job keeping an eye on Luca than Luca had, keeping an eye on Rusty. Brody was familiar with PTSD, so the fact that Luca had it was not concerning. He had faced combat vets often in his work. Brody knew how to handle those situations.

Ten minutes later, Luca relocked Gavin's office, returned to his room to get his jacket to cover his weapons, and headed to the living room. "Gavin, Rusty, we will leave you now and let you enjoy your time. I'm going to take Brody over to Destin for some beers. I'll have my cell if you need anything." He motioned to Brody that it was time to go. Luca was pleased that Brody owned casual clothing since he was always in a suit.

Brody unfolded himself from the sofa, where the warm room had made him a bit drowsy. He adjusted the gun, tucked into a soft holster inside the waistband of his dark jeans, and smoothed out the gray button-up with the sleeves turned up to mid-forearm.

"Luca, be back by 7:00 a.m., no later. We have work to do before Friday," Gavin called as they headed for the door.

"Yes, sir, before 7:00 a.m.," Luca confirmed.

Chapter Fifty-Two

Brody followed Luca around the house to the parked cars.

"How about we take the Corvette? You can drive," Brody said when Luca headed for the black S-Class Mercedes.

"We need to talk about that as well." Luca clicked the unlock button on his key fob.

"You have something against Corvettes?" Brody asked as he slid in.

"No, not at all. It is a beautiful car, but it draws attention. It would be best if you practiced being discreet," Luca said, trying not to sound like a scold.

"Your ninety-thousand-dollar car is not exactly understated," Brody pointed out, admiring the full-grain leather seats and extensive legroom.

"It is for this area. Lots of money around here. But it does not stick out," Luca explained. "A Corvette encourages you to take unnecessary risks, ones you do not need to be taking."

"Okay, I understand that sedans are safe and easily ignored." Brody saw Luca's point.

"How about we find a place with a good cheeseburger? I am dying for a cheeseburger." Then Luca remembered Brody was a vegetarian. "Oh, I'm sorry, you pick. Your diet is stricter than mine."

"You can get a cheeseburger. I'm guessing Mr. Garrison does not get to dine out often. I will find something I can eat, and you deserve to enjoy the few times you can go out," Brody acknowledged.

"It is indeed a rare event for Gavin to grace a restaurant. If we must be somewhere without a safe house, he will send one of us out to get something from a local restaurant," Luca told him. "Thank you for not being one of those people who pushes their lifestyle on others."

"I do it for my health. I have seen what some foods can do to the body. I do allow myself some chicken or fish from time to time, so I'm not a stickler," Brody replied. "Everyone can choose how they want to take care of themselves."

The Sapphire Ghost

"Yes, and at any moment, I could take a bullet—so I might as well eat what I want." Luca laughed.

"Touché!" Brody said. "What's happening on Friday?"

"Ending an op and sending one more back to hell," Luca said as he pulled out of the gates of Dremmond and into the ordinary world.

"Will I go along this time, or do I need to wait?" Brody asked.

"You'll be involved, but how much is up to Gavin," Luca said. "Be prepared to do whatever he asks of you. He may give you suggestions, but he won't give you directions because often we must come up with something on the fly." Luca headed to Highway 98 toward Destin.

"That's a lot like Dark 9. I enjoyed that part," Brody said and smiled.

Luca could see Brody's smile from the corner of his eye and noted how rare it was to see him show any emotion.

Then Luca noticed blue lights up ahead and watched the taillights ahead of him go red. He slowed and wondered if there was a wreck. People would be bobbleheading to see what was going on. Then he saw the three police cruisers with the lights bouncing off the night, about ten cars in front of him. Instantly, Luca reached for the gun under his belt, unclipped it, placed it into the center console, and did the same with his knife.

"Take your weapon off and put it inside here," Luca instructed.

Since he was wearing a casual button-up, Brody slid the 9 mm from under his shirt and placed it beside Luca's G19 and knife. Luca reached up and pulled the registration from over the headrest. Then he retrieved his private security card, a decoy license from Maryland, and a weapons permit under the same name and waited.

Brody hated license checks and wondered how this one would go. He watched Luca's calm preparation to address the officers; he appeared undaunted.

After ten minutes of waiting in line to be checked, an officer walked up to the Mercedes, shined his flashlight inside the car, and right into Luca's face. Luca hit the button to bring down the window just before the officer approached and placed his hands at ten and two on the steering wheel.

"Officer, I have a weapons permit," Luca said as he reached for the documents in his lap and handed them to the officer with his left hand.

The officer looked at the license, registration, and private security card, and then he directed his light at Brody in the passenger's seat.

"You fellows working down here?" the officer asked.

"Yes. Just dropped our charge at the airport and we're headed out to grab a bite to eat," Luca said calmly with his hands back on the steering wheel.

The officer directed his light to the empty backseat and the rest of the car. "We've got a tip; someone is bringing a load of drugs through here. Mind if we have the dogs go over your car?" the officer asked.

"Not at all. Do you want us to step out?" Luca asked politely, looking the tall white state trooper in the eyes.

"Do you have weapons on your person?"

"No, sir," Luca replied, "they are in the center console under the armrest beside me."

"Then stay in your car and open your doors and the trunk, please," the officer said, his hand still hovering on the hilt of his gun. Luca opened his door and hit the trunk latch, and Brody opened his door as well.

The officer with the dog opened the door behind Luca first. The large Belgian Shepherd sniffed Luca and the floorboard around his feet. Then, the dog handler guided the dog to the trunk where a single black attaché and the overnight bags lay. The dog sniffed. The officer brought the dog to the passenger's side and repeated the process.

"Thank you, Mr. Knox. You two have a good night." With that, the officer handed Luca back his documents.

"Not a problem. Y'all be safe," Luca replied, taking his cards and pulling ahead slowly. The officer with the dog crossed over to the other side. He seemed to stare into the windshield.

Chapter Fifty-Three

Thirty minutes later, Luca turned into the parking lot of a large brown brick hotel. The sign said *The Georgian*.

It would be just a couple blocks' walk to Harbor Docks, and his mouth watered in anticipation of the large cheeseburger with smoked gouda and bacon.

Brody followed Luca, who strolled casually down the side road beside the hotel. He admired the way Luca could be completely focused one minute and carefree the next. They walked up to a nice-looking seaside surf and turf restaurant within a few minutes. The restaurant did not look busy, and Luca's stomach growled loudly.

"I love this place; they have some great beers on tap," Luca said as he walked up to the door, holding it for Brody.

They took a table near the bar. It was September 1st, and most of the tourists were gone. The hostess told them Brittany would be their server. Luca sat down and closed his eyes and drank in the bar air. It felt good to be out in civilization. He knew Rusty was with Gavin so he could relax, maybe for the first time in months. Then, three tables over, he heard an obnoxious voice berating the waitress. Luca listened to the waitress explain that they did not have the customer's desired beer. Brody's interest was also drawn in that direction. Luca observed that Brody might jump up at any moment and was curious if he would do anything. The guy from the booth was big and bald, with tattoo sleeves on both arms. Luca watched Brody, and the corner of Luca's mouth crept up.

"Needing a fight tonight?" Luca asked, not figuring the quietly spoken man to provoke easily.

"Not really. It's just that I hate rude people," Brody said, wanting the man to make eye contact. It wasn't often, but sometimes his other side needed to make an appearance and plant his fists into someone a few times.

"Let her handle this. Servers deal with that kind of crap all the time. If he touches her, you can have him," Luca said, smiling when Brody looked at him.

"Hi, I'm Brittany; I'll be your waitress tonight." The tall girl was about twenty-five. "What can I get for you guys this evening?" She bestowed upon Brody a large smile.

Brody quickly ran his eyes over the menu, and Luca ordered without ever opening his after asking what was on tap.

"And you?" she asked, smiling at Brody.

"I believe I'll have the stir fry, please, Brittany," he said, giving the waitress a broad smile that had her blushing.

"Not a problem. I'll have your beers right out," Brittany stated and bounced away.

Luca looked at the other table and noticed the manager speaking with the tattooed man. "Looks like you will not be getting that fight after all," Luca said.

"Yeah, doesn't look like it," Brody said.

After they finished, Luca left money in the black foldover. "It's time we head to the hotel. I have rooms reserved. We have to be back early, and I will need you to stop by my room."

After returning to the car, they grabbed their belongings and headed into the hotel. It was well lit inside the large foyer and smelled of citrus. Luca greeted the man behind the counter, gave him his usual spiel, and handed over several hundred. The man's eyebrows arched. Luca accepted the keys and thanked the clerk. Their rooms would be across from each other.

It was just after 11:00, and Luca was not ready to turn in, as he had slept a couple hours on the plane. He invited Brody in, and Luca laid the attaché on the bed and motioned for him to open it. Brody hesitated, unsure what to expect, but stepped closer, clicked the latches, and raised the top. He nearly jumped back.

"What's this?" he asked, bewildered.

"Your starter kit. It comes with the job. For carrying out your duties. Two-hundred and fifty thousand dollars and two credit cards for when you absolutely have to use them. They're in Atlas Security's name. There's also a security ID card and two undetectable IDs. The journal contains a list of where to find additional assets if you are in a pinch and need to access extra cash," Luca said, sitting in the chair beside a writing desk. "There's also a list of dos and don'ts, along with things you need to become careful about. And a list of Gavin's preferences. Consult that when you are working with him without me. Finally, important phone numbers to sources and informants. I tried to include anything and everything I thought you might need to know. If there's something I missed, please ask me. I may not be great at training, but I'll do my best."

"That's a lot of money," Brody said, reaching to take one of the yellow-strapped bricks of twenties, thumbing through it, and returning it to the case.

"That might be used for just one job. It all depends on what you need to get done, be it paying off a manager to use her restaurant for a few hours or buying someone's personal vehicle because you cannot use the one you had. Everything has a price." He turned to his colleague. "Brody, what's yours?"

Brody tilted his head as if unsure if he heard him correctly. "What do you mean, what is mine?" He scowled.

"What is the price it would take for you to turn on Gavin Garrison?" Luca sat back, awaiting an answer to his question.

"There's no price. I would never take anything to turn in Mr. Garrison. I understand his cause, and it has become my own. I never considered that option when you asked me to take this position." Anger burned on his face.

"You better be sure because if someone finds out that you work with him, they will first try to pay you off, then torture you." Luca tucked his fist under his chin.

"I am completely sure. If you thought that I could be bought, why'd you ask me?" Brody slammed the case shut, throwing his hands in the air. His tone hissing in anger.

"I do not think you would, but I know in some circumstances that many would save their own lives if it were the only option." Luca added, "Look inside the upper pocket of the case, Brody."

Reluctantly, Brody reopened the case and felt inside the silk lining. His hand wrapped around a small prescription bottle, and he pulled it out. Opening the bottle, he shook two tiny capsules out into his hand. The capsules were midnight blue and about the size of a Tic Tac. He looked at Luca, who took a box of Tic Tacs from inside his breast pocket with only two blue capsules inside.

"If it comes down to a choice between keeping Gavin alive and you getting caught, one of the blue pills will render you to everyone as dead. We will find you and administer the antidote," Luca explained. "Two will kill you, so be careful," Luca said, tucking the Tic Tac box inside his jacket.

Brody redeposited the capsules into the bottle and tucked them inside the case, "What are they?"

"Snake venom, I believe; I've never asked. I will get you the breakdown if you want. We use quite a bit of lethal toxins."

Brody looked at Luca and nodded his head. He picked up the leather-bound journal and flipped it open. After a list of account numbers, he turned on and read over a list of Mr. Garrison's preferences in food, wine, scotch, and more, along with Mr. Garrison's expectations of his team members. Then, a part highlighted Gavin's fear of spiders—and keeping his room clear of projectiles because of night terrors.

"Study it. It will help you a lot," Luca said. "Mostly, though, keep your house in order and your nose clean, and when you can't do that, don't get caught. And then there is the small matter of your payment."

"Helen sent me my salary—" Brody started to correct Luca.

"No, Brody, that is only for keeping up appearances. Your payment is substantially more. The salary makes everything you do appear on the up-and-up. It is the standard two hundred a year, typical for a particularly good security firm. That money should stay local to your residence and be used as if you lived a normal life. Pay any bills, house payments, car payments, insurance, light bills, dinners out, etc. Make sure you throw in a couple of tanks of gas and buy groceries whether you need them or not. Have the bank send checks to your accountant, groundskeeper, and maid if you have those. Keep the account looking like you are legitimate. Do you understand?"

The Sapphire Ghost

"Yes, I believe so; appear to live normally," Brody said, removing his glasses.

"Appearances are everything because you will be anything but ordinary from now on. Gavin has no identity, so he depends on us to do things he cannot. Anything you need will be provided while on duty, which will be about eighty percent of the time, more or less. Being second in command is a lot less demanding and sometimes comes with long downtimes when you will not be privy to where you are.

"But I started to talk about your payment. It's another pot of money entirely. For the extra, you must become familiar with overseas banking regulations and open a couple of accounts, at least at first." Luca paused, watching the overload of information cloud Brody's face.

"You'll be given at least ten percent of the assets of any Dossier that is claimed. For example, my ten percent of Steve Bain's assets will be about twenty million once Helen liquidates his accounts. Unbelievable, huh? But the Order will not leave the targets or their families with anything made on human flesh. You can anonymously donate to causes you feel strongly about, maybe buy hospital supplies for storm-torn areas. I'll help you learn the process if you want," Luca explained as if it was as normal as sleeping. "Hey, I'm here for you. This is a lot to take in, and feel free to ask any questions once the shock has worn off."

"Twenty million, one job? That is a lot of money!" Brody exclaimed, wiping the sides of his face with both hands. He looked around the room and at the case but he never sat down. He almost wanted to laugh because he'd been certain Luca wasn't good at explaining things. When the number did reach his brain, a long, strangled laugh escaped.

"Bains's worth, so far, is two hundred million. It could be more as Helen keeps digging. You'll learn that the longer you are with this Order, the less money matters to you."

Brody grew lightheaded at everything Luca had thrown at him. Luca handed him the decanter, and he generously refilled his glass. He sat down, his mind muddled. Luca quietly waited for Brody to ask questions. But with the bewilderment on his face, he was unsure any had been able to form yet.

Brody finished his drink; he was uncertain it took the edge off. He rubbed the bridge of his nose and looked around for his glasses.

"Okay, then. It seems like I have some homework to do, and we have to be back by seven in the morning." Brody stood, picking up the case and his bag.

"Well before seven," Luca corrected. "Never, ever, walk in at the hour that Gavin requires. When he says seven, he is ready to work at that hour. It is not as daunting as you think; pay attention. You'll be fine," Luca said. "I have every confidence in you," Luca spoke the last in Russian.

"Thank you. I do not intend to disappoint you," Brody replied in perfect Russian.

Brody opened the door. He turned as if wanting to say something but decided against it and closed the door behind him. Walking across the hall, Brody let himself into his room. Brody did not bother to turn on the lights. He set everything down on one side of the bed, lay down fully clothed, and stared at the ceiling. People had always been intimidated by Brody, either because of his intelligence or medical degree. This was the first time he could remember being intimidated himself. It was evident that no member of his new team had ever felt that way. He could not imagine Luca being bothered by anyone; there was something almost unnatural in his calm. Yet at only 5'8 and a hundred and forty-five pounds, Brody could imagine Luca backing Rusty down.

Luca crawled up to lay against the bed's headboard and knew he had unloaded a ton of information on Brody all at once, but he felt it was better to yank the bandage off rather than tug and pull. He was not too proud to admit he needed the help and could not afford to hold anything back or leave too many expectations unchecked.

Brody would do well. Luca needed him with that chip on his shoulder fully intact. Luca knew the façade that Brody wore as a yoke would soon come in handy. Based on what he had heard at Helen's, the bottom was about to fall out, or so he hoped.

As for himself, he was thinking about what Gavin would do when he finally got to King. The one he had searched for from the beginning. Would Gavin retire also, and would Helen assign another Ghost, or would Luca be able to step up into that role? He had wondered about these things before, but it had never seemed within reach as it did at this moment.

Luca had one big obstacle that might keep him from reaching that goal: his family. Gavriel Masterson died twenty-two years ago by walking into the ocean; he was baptized as Gavin Garrison, the first Ghost. Luca knew if he wanted to reach that goal, he would have to be willing to leave his family.

It was 3:00 a.m., but Luca was still not tired. He thought about knocking on Brody's door and telling him they were going back to Dremmond, but he didn't. Luca knew Brody had left with a ton on his mind, and he would probably not have been asleep long. Luca could wait. He returned his gun to the holster and clipped the knife onto his belt. Luca left his room to walk in the night air and maybe find his way to the shore. It had been months since he did not feel like he needed to be on guard.

Chapter Fifty-Four

Luca headed down the hall to the stairs. No one seemed awake as he opened the door leading down. Gavin had a thing against elevators. Unless Gavin needed to take one, he would always take the stairs. This had become a habit of Luca's as well. Luca was making the first turn down the second set when he heard footsteps on the floor above. Luca stopped, the footsteps stopped, and a pounding began in his chest. He stood up against the wall, pulling and holding his gun, and waited for whoever it was to continue their descent, but he heard nothing. Luca thought about calling Brody and having him box them in, but it could be innocent. Luca tucked his gun and turned to head up to greet the person he had heard, and then he showed himself.

A white man, about thirty-five, was wearing an orange knit beanie, a green cleaning uniform, and black military boots. *No, this situation is not right,* he thought to himself. He looked at the man, and the man looked back at him. "Evening," Luca said.

The man dashed down the steps between them and ran directly at Luca, who dodged. Luca immediately snatched the knife from his belt just as the man attempted a swing, and then he recognized him. He was the officer with the dog. *What was going on? Gavin*! Luca steadied himself as the man tried to hit him again. Then Luca saw the knife in the man's right hand just before it came down. Luca moved in time, but it lodged in Luca's left arm. Then, the fellow pinned Luca up against the wall with the knife.

"My boss wants a meeting with your boss." He spoke with a strong Brooklyn accent.

Luca brought up his knee to the man's groin. He dropped the guy but nearly cried out as the man, still gripping the knife, pulled it down his arm and fell to the ground.

"Who is your boss so I can give my boss the message?" Luca asked through clenched teeth, staring down at him.

"You have no idea what you did when you killed Steve Bains. They'll find you and the entire Order and kill each of you." The man tried to gather himself, but Luca knelt on his chest, keeping him pinned to the floor.

Luca thought a lot about Bains's promise that the people he knew would find him.

Brody was getting out of the shower when he heard the door across the hall close. He looked out the peephole and saw Luca leave. *Watch him!* Rusty's words boomed in his head. He quickly pulled on a white T-shirt and a pair of jeans, slipped into his loafers, pocketed his gun, and headed out the door in under a minute.

Brody stepped quickly down the hall, which led to the stairs, wondering what Luca was doing at that hour. He opened the door leading down to the lobby and softly closed it behind him. Brody heard Luca's voice and a deeper one, and the other one seemed to be threatening Luca. Brody made quick steps down and saw Luca on the floor, kneeling on a man he held there. Luca's arm was bleeding profusely.

Luca glanced up at the sound of footsteps, thinking it might be this man's backup. He reached for his gun but then saw Brody. Luca exhaled with relief; he did not want to fire a weapon that would alert the desk clerk, who would call the police.

Brody examined the situation in front of him. He scrutinized the blood covering Luca's left arm, and Luca held a knife with the other to the man's cheek on the floor.

"Brody, take my key. Get our stuff, then get the car and bring it around to the side entrance. Do it fast." Luca fished in his pocket with a blood-soaked hand and managed to toss Brody the key to his room.

Brody quickly ran up the stairs to Luca's room. He grabbed Luca's untouched overnight bag from the bed and the keys to the car from the side table. Then Brody went across the hall, grabbed his bag and the briefcase, and ran down the other hall, which led to the second set of steps, taking two at a time until Brody landed on the ground level. He made a beeline to the side door locked to visitors during the night and threw it open. Brody placed a five-dollar bill between the locks so it would not engage. Quietly, Brody ran to the front of the parking lot and crammed himself into the car, not bothering to move the seat. He drove around to the side of the hotel. Running inside, he looked around for the clerk before taking the hallway to the other stairs. No one was in sight. When Brody got back to the door to the stairs, he opened it and saw that Luca had stuffed a sock into the man's mouth and bound him with the sleeves of the fellow's shirt. Brody looked at the enormous pool of blood on the floor.

"Help me get him to the car," Luca commanded.

Brody hauled the man to his feet and pulled him out into the lobby from the landing. He looked behind him to confirm that Luca was following. Luca tucked his arm up against his chest, allowing the blood to soak his shirt. Luca was observing and covering the lobby with his gun. Then they pushed through the side door where the car waited.

"Put him in the trunk," Luca instructed as he got behind the wheel. "Now find the janitor's closet, drench that blood with bleach, and wipe down the doorknobs."

Brody dumped the man in the trunk when Luca popped the latch. He then ran inside to the janitor's closet and grabbed two gallons of bleach. Brody dumped both bottles on the floor, diluting the vast pool of blood, and splashed it up the concrete walls. He quickly wiped away any fingerprints on both sides of the door and took the rest of the bleach, pouring it onto the spots Luca had left with his shoes.

Brody ran out to the car and turned to examine Luca's arm. Luca pressed the gas before Dr. Brody could ask about it, slamming Brody back in his seat. Luca hit the side streets at a speed that should not have been possible in such a short distance, ignoring the stop signs in between. Luca took two right turns, barely hitting the brakes, and headed to the center of Destin. Luca pulled into an abandoned parking lot of what could have been a grocery store. Luca was beginning to lose the feeling in his left hand, so he could not hold the wheel and get into the center console.

"What do you need? I'll get it for you," Brody said, looking at the long gash running down Luca's sinewy forearm to the wrist. He thought it might have sliced a wrist vein. If Luca died tonight, Brody was sure he would as well.

"There's a scanner in there. We need to sweep the car for a tracker. That man is the officer with the dog," Luca said, trying to move his fingers.

Brody retrieved the scanner, reached across Luca to hit the trunk switch, and jumped out. As Brody got to the trunk, the man threw his legs out.

"Oh no, you don't!" Brody gave the man a hard kick, slung his legs back into the car, and pulled out his Gucci bag.

Brody knelt and rummaged through the bag until he found another white T-shirt. He ripped it down the neck, pulled it into two pieces, tossed the bag back into the trunk, and closed it. He then went to the driver's side to care for Luca and get a better idea about Luca's arm. Brody opened the driver's side door, and Luca rested against the seat.

"Did you find the tracker?" Luca asked.

"I will try to stop the bleeding first," Brody said, spinning Luca around in the seat.

Luca did not protest as Brody gently took his arm and examined it. He thought it had missed the central vein. However, the knife had ripped through a few smaller ones, and the arm was pouring blood. Brody firmly wrapped Luca's arm and told him to keep it against his chest. Then Brody lifted him over the console and dropped him in the passenger's seat.

"Check the car! If it has a tracker, they will be here soon," Luca said, reaching to open the door.

"Stay here, Medina. I have this," Brody said.

Brody took the small probe from his pocket, flipped a switch, and a green light appeared. He first went to the back of the car, where the dog handler had spent the most time, and worked his way forward. A small square box with a red light was just under the driver's side bumper. Brody pulled it free and threw it into a storm drain, where it wobbled and fell over. Then Brody headed back to the car, pushed the button to move the seat back, got in, shifted into drive, and pulled out of the parking lot.

"I found the tracker, and it's in the storm drain." He looked over at Luca. "Where do you want me to go now?"

"Find another parking lot. We need to question that man and find out how they found us," Luca replied, reaching under the seat for a bottle of water.

"Why can we not take him back to the house?" Brody asked, thinking the Ghost would have ways of making him talk.

"No one, and I mean no one, goes to Dremmond! That is a sanctuary." Luca clipped each word.

Brody drove for a few minutes until he saw the construction site for a new hotel, where he pulled onto the uneven gravel behind the structure. Luca jumped out of the car and headed to the trunk with his left arm tucked against his chest. Brody met him there, jerked the man clear with one hand, and stood him up. Luca took note of the force Brody used.

"Who do you work for?" Brody asked.

"I'm sure you know. They will come for you, all of you. God cannot help the man who killed Steve Bains," he pronounced, along with a long line of other colorful words.

"Answer the question!" Luca pulled out his knife and, with the side of his blade, slid it down the man's arm, removing a thin section of skin.

The man yelled and kicked out at Luca and Brody, but Brody held him firm.

"Tell me who you are working for!" Luca ordered, noting the chilling grin on the man's face. "We found the tracker; no one's coming."

"Killing Bains has unleashed the wrath of the King! That is all you need to know."

"King! Where would I find him?" Luca asked, dragging the knife down and skinning the man's arm again.

The man gave a half-panted scream but began to laugh. "The King is the King; he is everywhere."

Luca looked at the man's face. A knowing look passed between them, and Luca shivered. King had found them. Luca drove the knife deep into the man's gut and twisted. This man was not going to speak without persuasion.

"How did you know where to find me?" Luca asked as he removed the knife.

The Sapphire Ghost

"It was much easier than you might think." He gave Luca a wicked smile as he fell.

Brody stood back as the cool-tempered Luca plunged the knife into the man's stomach. Brody let the man's arm go, and he dropped to the ground. Luca wiped the blade on the man's shirt. Then, he went through his pockets and discovered only a cell phone and key fob. The man continued to laugh like some evil villain until Luca shoved the knife straight into his esophagus, then there was a pinched gurgle and silence.

Brody examined what had been the white T-shirt on Luca's left arm, where blood was leaving a large red stain. He needed to get Luca out of here before he dripped blood everywhere. Taking Luca by his right arm, he forced him back to the car. Without hesitation, he shoved Luca into the seat and commanded, "Stay!"

Brody returned to the man, still gasping like a fish and holding his throat. Pulling the man to the front of the site, well away from where he and Luca had been standing, he removed nearly all his clothes, leaving him lying there in his underwear. Brody scanned the construction equipment, found a shovel, and brought it over, covering the blood and scraping it flat. Before picking up the clothes, Brody ensured the man was dead and removed Luca's knife. After throwing the clothes in the trunk, Brody pulled out of the construction lot and headed north to Highway 98.

Chapter Fifty-Five

It was only thirty-five minutes until Brody pulled the car in beside his black Corvette. This was a strange night, and Brody now understood Rusty's words more than ever. Each team member could have a target on their back, and each needed the others. Luca would have gone until he passed out because he did not know his limits, and Brody would have to know them for him.

Fog blanketed the night, nearly eliminating the street lamps, and the lights had no chance to fight through the haze. The road appeared haunted on the way to Dremmond. Long and eerie stretched-out forms lingered on the pavement before them. He glanced over to Luca, who seemed to be sleeping in the seat. The once tan leather appeared black in the dim light.

When Brody finally got Luca through the front door, he saw Rusty asleep in the oversized recliner in the living room. Luca, half being dragged and half walking, stepped inside. Luca was tired, and all he wanted to do was sleep.

"Stay awake," Brody whispered, trying to be quiet.

"What happened?!" Rusty's voice echoed through the house. The sound of the door had awakened him, and he was alarmed to see Brody half-dragging a stumbling Luca into the house. "Is he drunk?"

"A man attacked him, sir," Brody replied.

"What do you mean attacked him? Mugging, what? Be specific, son!" Rusty boomed.

"Calm down, Rusty, I'm fine. It's just a cut." Luca's words felt strange in his mouth, as if his tongue was too big.

"I'll not calm down! Get him to the kitchen, and let's take a look," Rusty ordered Brody.

"What is going on out here?" Gavin came down the hall wearing a black and blue robe.

"Good grief! Do y'all have to be so loud?" Luca said, rubbing his temple with his right hand.

The Sapphire Ghost

Gavin saw the blood on the floor, looked up at Luca, then down at his arm. Rusty, tired of the time it took Luca to walk to the kitchen, picked him up like a baby. He brought him into the kitchen and deposited him in a chair. Brody went to his room for his medical bag.

Gavin was a loud quiet, the kind that held all the questions he wanted to know but waited patiently to ask, floating thick in the air. Brody collected what he needed and went to the table.

"Since everyone is here, could someone bring me a drink?" Luca asked, the lights in the room shifting and dancing. He looked at Gavin. "I promised to be back before seven."

Gavin shook his head but waited.

Rusty went to get Luca a drink.

"No," Brody said firmly, peering at Rusty from the corner of his eye. He then injected Luca with pain medication.

Rusty stopped and ambled back into the room on the doctor's orders.

"It was King's people," Luca said, removing the curiosity that enveloped the room.

"What did they say, Luca?" Gavin asked in an eerie tone, which he used when reverting to Ghost.

"They are after the Order for killing Steve Bains," Luca said, no longer feeling much as Brody cleaned up his arm.

Gavin glared hard at Rusty and then Luca. This was a development. But at what cost? Gavin had not had a chance to tell Luca what Helen had called to tell him earlier that night. They had got this close to Luca! That made him rethink the bombs in London. *Were they meant for me? What is the connection?*

Rusty stood beside the breakfast bar, his arms crossed, watching Brody attempt to clean Luca's arm. Brody was trying to see what was damaged, but it was not going well.

"Will he need blood?" Rusty asked, his features furrowed in concern and deep lines engraved on his forehead.

"If you had a pint lying around, it probably wouldn't hurt. I have no way to tell how much he's lost." Brody continued searching for the cause of the blood loss to stop it.

"Take mine," Rusty said, sitting in another chair and extending his arm across the table.

"I cannot take your blood, Rusty! Number one, you have cancer. Number two, I don't know if it is a match." Brody looked sympathetically at the big man.

"It's a match. We all match, including yourself, it's a requirement." Rusty appeared hurt.

"B negative?" Brody said.

"Yes," Gavin replied, "it's for my benefit if I needed blood. Remember, I cannot go to a regular hospital. Luca gave me blood at the farm before you arrived. The bluestone you wore indicated you were my match."

"That's right." Brody saw that Luca had fallen asleep again and was not responding to his gentle insistence that he wake up. Brody took an FBTK from his bag, inserted one end into Luca's right arm, and rolled up his sleeves.

"You can take mine," Gavin said.

"No, sir, respectfully, I cannot." Brody inserted the needle in his own arm and opened the port. "He is my responsibility, and now that I know this little detail, it will make much quicker work of all of this."

The corners crept up on Rusty's mouth.

"Rusty, shake out the oats, please," Brody said, because he was using what was available, and the oats would absorb the blood and keep the table from becoming slick.

When Rusty did as ordered, Brody lay Luca's arm flat against the table, letting the oats soak the blood. He then took the headset from his bag and pulled it on, placing the microscope over his right eye.

"Rusty, could you help me, please?" Brody asked. "You could have warned me that he has no off switch."

Rusty came closer, awaiting instructions from the doctor. "I figured it would be easy to tell when the time came. Luca does not stop. He's a former

Green Beret. I never imagined something like this happening. When Luca has a mission, it's his mission until it's finished. There are no exceptions."

Gavin watched as Brody and Rusty worked. Rusty soaked the blood with a sterile gauze and oats while Brody clamped and repaired the damage. An hour later, Brody was stitching up Luca's arm. It was almost seven, and the coffee machine began to percolate.

"I'll get him to bed. I will tell you everything that happened when I get back." Brody picked up Luca and headed down the hall.

When he returned, he saw that Gavin had cleaned the counter and had a cup of coffee ready for him. Brody gave them the details of the night, from the traffic stop to hearing Luca leave his room to the construction site where they left the body.

"Luca had his phone, but I did not find it on him when I put him to bed. I know he took it, so he must have left it in the car," Brody shared with concern.

Gavin listened to every word, sipping coffee. He never interrupted, seeming to take in all the details. This did not happen just because of Steve Bains. Gavin had gathered that much from Helen; it was about Jack King. He tied into this. Luca's taking out Bains, and the Hollinger servers had put a massive dent in King's operation. Steve Bains seemed to be a much bigger fish than Gavin anticipated. They were sending a message, and that message was that they were close, and they were pissed.

Chapter Fifty-Six

September 2

Luca woke up at 10:00 a.m. with his arm killing him. He looked at the tight bandages and realized he had passed out during Brody's operation. The car was a mess, and he needed to get that cleaned before he scheduled a complete detail. Luca got up and took a quick shower, doing his best to keep the bandages dry. After fussing with clothing with one good hand, Luca headed to the kitchen, where he found a bottle of pills on the counter with a note: *If you are uncomfortable, take one of these, Brody*. Luca opened the bottle, shook one out, and went for the coffee.

He knew Gavin had big plans for them today; after all, the job was less than two days away. Luca took his coffee and the pill, went to the living room, and stepped onto the balcony. The sun was bright, and it was already hot. He looked over at the other house, now more than a little suspicious of the woman staying there, regardless of what Helen said about her. How had King's people known where they were? How had they known Luca would be going to Destin last night? It could not have been a coincidence. Much as he wished he didn't, he wondered if Brody, the newest member, was a factor.

Just then, Brody came around the side of the house with a bucket and a brush. "You're up! I didn't expect to see you until at least noon. How are you feeling?" Brody asked.

"Better, thank you," Luca said as easily as he could. If he had these suspicions, he knew Gavin would. "Where is Gavin?"

"He and Rusty are in the office, where they have been all morning," Brody said, heading into the house.

Luca took his coffee from the railing and swallowed the pain pill. He walked back to the den and knocked on the door.

"Gavin, may I come in?" Luca asked.

"Yes."

The Sapphire Ghost

Luca stepped inside, closing the door behind him. Rusty was sitting across the desk from Gavin, and they seemed to be in deep conversation.

"I didn't mean to interrupt," Luca said.

"You aren't interrupting anything. You belong here," Rusty said.

Gavin sat behind the desk with his fingers tented, his index fingers beating against each other. Luca moved to the only available seat and looked down at Gavin's neat handwritten list. He scanned the list quickly, then the laptop, tablet, and four phones.

"What is going on?" Luca asked, eyeing the gear.

"Helen asked to look at each electronic item in the house," Rusty said.

"Did she find anything?" Luca asked.

"No," Gavin responded.

Luca noticed that white light was lit on the phone and immediately thought Helen was listening. He pulled the chair closer, sat, and folded his arm against his chest.

"Do you have any thoughts, Luca?" Gavin asked.

"I have thought a lot about it. There would have been no way for anyone to know I was headed to Destin last night. No one could have known because I did not decide until I saw Brody," Luca said.

"Yes, we have come to that conclusion also. Seems random, but random is never random," Rusty commented.

"Luca, I believe it would be best if you sit out D.C. until we have a handle on what is going on," Gavin said. He leaned back in the chair, not expecting a dispute.

Luca clenched his fist on his right hand but felt the pain in his left arm as he went rigid. Closing his eyes, Luca watched white spots dance behind his lids. Right now, he did not need to respond. He wanted to wait for the energy assaulting him to diminish.

"Luca, it is for the best; Brody and I can help in D.C. It will give you some time to let your arm heal. Take a break; you have earned it." Rusty's voice was soothing, observing how tense Luca became. He understood it was unnatural for Luca to step aside when he had a mission, and Gavin's safety was his only mission. And Luca had always listened to Rusty.

"No! That is not going to happen!" Luca stood as his temper finally flared. "This is my responsibility, and I will take care of what needs to be done. Do not handle me, Rusty!" Luca growled in a dangerous warning to the big man, who started to stand at the assertive response from Luca.

"I would just be helping out, Luca." Rusty tried to find an even voice to address his friend.

"You may help. But understand," Luca continued, turning to Gavin and the open line on the phone. "Neither you nor Helen will shut me out of this. I told you I wasn't going anywhere!" Luca started toward the door.

"Where are you going?" Gavin demanded.

"To start on the list."

"But I have not given you the list."

Luca turned back, gave him a hot glare, and glanced at the notepad. Gavin looked down at the list and realized Luca had read it. Luca stormed out of the den, past the kitchen breakfast bar. He took the brown bottle of pills and threw them across the room. The small white oval tablets scattered on the floor as the bottle bounced off the wall. Brody jumped at the sound and spilled his coffee.

"Pack your bags. I'll be back for you in an hour. We have work to do," Luca spoke sharply, making Brody glance up at Rusty emerging from the den.

"Luca, wait, listen!" Rusty ordered. But Luca marched right out the door. Rusty ran toward the door. "Brody, help me stop him!"

Brody was unsure what was happening but immediately got up and ran after Rusty. Gavin followed them. Luca clicked the key fob on the black sedan and got in just as Rusty and Brody ran around the house. Luca slammed the car into reverse, backed out around the Corvette, and shifted into drive.

"Brody, get a set of keys. We need to follow him. They found him once; they can find him again." Rusty's words were harsh. Within seconds, Brody tossed the big guy the keys for the Corvette and crawled into the other side of the car. Rusty hit the start button, and the engine roared to life.

Luca did not bother to head toward the gates. He figured they might try to follow him. He was in no mood to be cajoled into doing something he did not feel was right, and he would not be considered a liability. This was his

The Sapphire Ghost

team; Gavin was his charge, and even if injured, he would protect him with his life, especially with King knocking on their backdoor. Luca turned right at the stop sign instead of going straight, then another right, and headed to the utility road the electric company used for emergencies. He passed the last of the six houses on the back street at well over fifty miles an hour—and his speed rose as he left the compound.

Rusty pulled up to the stop sign and went straight without entirely stopping. He headed for the gate, and Rusty did not see the black Mercedes near the still-closed gate. He looked to the right and left and came to a jerking stop.

"Where the hell did you go?" Rusty asked himself.

"What's going on?" Brody asked.

Rusty looked over at Brody as if he had forgotten he was in the car. "Gavin ordered Luca to step aside for D.C.," Rusty informed Brody.

"That didn't go well."

"No," Rusty huffed. "This behavior is unlike him."

Rusty punched in the code for the gates and waited long enough to get the car through. He took a right. If Luca had taken the service road, it would come out a couple of miles up. Rusty sped up. Rusty was unsure what he would do if he could cut Luca off, but he had to try. Rusty had never seen Luca refuse a direct order, and Rusty wanted to think about how to handle him. However, when Rusty got to the intersection, the dust from the unpaved road had yet to settle; Luca was gone. Rusty stopped and rubbed his forehead, looking at the morning traffic. Rusty took the right back onto the service road, and soon, the Corvette gave a bumpy jerk as the tires hit something besides pavement.

Brody thought that low-profile tires were never a good idea with these guys. It was not that they inspired unwarranted behaviors; they were just impractical. He felt every tiny rock on the road, and each one forced his head nearly to the headliner.

Luca sped through Destin, looking in his rearview mirror, but he saw nothing. He slowed to the speed limit. Once Luca determined that he was not being followed, he pulled over at the nearest pharmacy and ran in to purchase a sling. Luca needed to relax his arm and calm himself.

After making the calls to the scout team who'd be working in D.C., he went to a dealership to buy another vehicle. The Mercedes was being shipped to Galveston because it would compromise them. Finally, feeling calmer and more rational, it was time to have a reasonable conversation if Gavin was willing. Luca was now under contract with Arcadia, and this situation made everything mission critical. Nothing would happen to the Sapphire Ghost, not on Luca's watch.

Gavin, Rusty, and Brody waited at the house. Gavin paced restlessly, trying to understand the situation. Luca had never been unpredictable, and this behavior baffled him.

"Do you think he will be back today?" Gavin asked.

"I don't know. I guess it will depend on how much of that list Luca remembers," Rusty said.

"Rusty, he will remember all of it." Gavin gave Rusty a grave look. "Seems Luca left something out of your conversation while in Maine."

Rusty returned Gavin's look with a confused one but asked nothing.

"He told me to pack and said he would be back in an hour," Brody chimed in.

"An hour." Gavin looked at the clock on the wall. "It has been almost two, and he is never late. What if he's been caught?"

They heard a car pulling up to the back of the house. All three stood and waited. Neither Gavin nor Rusty knew what they would say when Luca strode inside. Gavin wanted to throw Luca to the floor and beat the petulance out of him. However, he also had to understand where this had come from. The attack may have something to do with this current mood.

Luca stepped through the door and tossed the two new fobs for the Range Rover into the bowl. He looked over at them. No one wanted to be the first to speak. "I bought a car," Luca said casually, heading into the kitchen for a much-needed coffee.

Rusty eyed Gavin, who shrugged. They followed Luca into the kitchen.

Luca laid a brown folder down on the counter. "I apologize for my mood earlier. But my viewpoint hasn't changed, and I am not standing down." Luca took a long drink of coffee, leaning up against the sink.

"Since when do you think you can give *me* orders?" Gavin asked. He waited for the backlash he had seen earlier. Luca had always been a myrmidon of merit; that is, until today. Maybe he was taking his new power under the Oath a little far?

"Since King sent someone to attack me last night to send you a message. You, sir, are *my* responsibility, and I'm not letting you out of my sight," Luca said. His mind was unbending unless Gavin wanted to fire him or shoot him, which he just remembered he couldn't do. Gavin would have to find a way to reconcile himself.

"That's not the way this works. I give directions, and you follow them," Gavin said, his voice becoming low and threatening. "I am sure you remember Code 1."

"*Your* protection is the Code, which is exactly how this will work. I never needed a flipping Oath to protect you. They attacked me twelve miles from here! Don't think you're getting your way. I can be where you can see me or be where you can't. Either way suits me fine." Luca had years of covert operations, and following and staying close to his charge wouldn't be a problem. He knew Gavin and Rusty well enough to predict their movements. The Silent Knight wasn't out of his system after all.

Rusty stood by, observing the exchange. The calm yet determined Luca was going toe-to-toe with Gavin Garrison's Ghost. He had a slight tingle of pride creep up his back; at this point, neither man was giving an inch. He remembered a comment in Luca's military record, 'Give Captain Medina an assignment, wind him up and let him go. It will be completed.'

On the other hand, Brody thought Luca was crazy.

"Talk to him, Rusty! He's being unreasonable," Gavin grumbled.

"Sorry, but I agree with him. I'm willing to bet that you will need to do something to put him out if you do not want him around," Rusty said. "Apparently, the arm is not enough," Rusty tried to hide his smile by biting his lips together.

For the first time, Rusty felt absolute faith that the Ghost would live on when Rusty was gone. It wasn't that he did not think Luca would protect

Gavin, but he had always been unsure that Luca could stand up to Gavin or his Ghost. The proof stood before him.

"You would never ask Rusty to abate his responsibilities under these circumstances; why would you think you could do that with me? Have you forgotten who trained me for the past seven years? I have followed through with everything you have ever asked, but I cannot comply with this. I'll do everything within my power to ensure you stay alive. That, *sir*, is *my* job." The sharp, commanding tone left no room for rebuttal; it is evident for the first time that Luca was in charge.

"That I have never questioned, Luca." Gavin hung his head; he knew he was beaten. He stood alone against two of the best men he could ever want by his side, and he would get nowhere with Luca's current resolve. Luca's battle stance, in-charge attitude, the former Green Beret, and Gavin's new Warrior had spoken for the first time.

"Fine, but Rusty will stay until we are done in D.C.," Gavin said. "I expect you to find your way back home and rest, Rusty. I have not seen you look this well in months. Be sure you keep it that way."

"Only if it is all right with the First in Command?" Rusty said, giving Luca an encouraging smile. He always knew Luca had it in him but was relieved to see it.

"Absolutely, sir," Luca replied. "Now, look in the folder. That man I killed last night had it in his car."

Chapter Fifty-Seven

September 2

Luca took Brody to the hangar so he could take the jet to D.C. Brody had a handful of orders—all the things he needed to have in place before Gavin's arrival on Friday. Luca instructed Marshal, the pilot, to drop Brody off and return to Destin.

Brody looked over the directives and the names of the Dark 9 who would be on the ground to help him. He also noticed the address and lockbox code for Luca's home in Georgetown.

After the jet landed in Baltimore, Brody retrieved the keys to the black Cadillac from a hook in the hangar. He placed his bag in the backseat and readjusted the seat before he could get himself inside. Brody punched the address for Georgetown into his phone and headed out of the jetport.

An hour later, Brody pulled up to a row of large, grayish-white, four-story townhomes. *This looks expensive*, Brody thought as he took his bag and headed up to the entrance on 30th Street NW. He punched the code on the lockbox hanging from the doorknob and removed the key. The door opened into a beautiful foyer that looked into a large open living area. The walls were an airy light gray, and all the window-coverings opened to allow the light into the rooms.

This was Luca's place, but it did not look like what Brody knew of the man. Brody walked through the living area and entered the extended kitchen on the right. The large, bright, white marble and eat-in kitchen seemed to flow into the garden. The back wall was floor-to-ceiling windows, interrupted only by a charming stained-glass door. He opened the fridge, which was stocked with various foods and fresh fruit. Brody took a green apple, rubbed it across his shirt, and walked out back into the garden, which he noticed was surrounded by fragrant gardenias behind a short brick wall enclosing the patio.

"Sir, you must be Dr. Brody." A voice came from the doorway.

Brody looked back to see a woman in her sixties, her white hair pulled neatly up in a bun, her eyes pale blue. She wore a tan smock with comfortable white shoes.

"I'm Iris, the housekeeper. I took the liberty of taking your bag to your room on the third floor, the bedroom to the left of the staircase. Is there anything else I can do for you before I leave?"

"Thank you, Iris; I have everything I need." Brody smiled at her.

"I have the house prepped for four: you, Mr. Medina, Mr. Marley, and Mr. Garrison," Iris said pleasantly.

Now Brody was surprised and a bit jealous. Luca had a maid in a house he did not live in, a genuinely lovely townhome, and she was familiar with his guests. It had to be a safe house, he thought. It was probably bought as a place to use when they happened to have business in D.C. or the area. It could not be Luca's; this house was worth a fortune, and Luca seemed consistently humble.

Brody decided to poke around a bit. He found the master bedroom on the lower level decorated in the same gray. There was a dark navy bedspread and white sheer curtains, Impressionism on the walls, and a beautifully restored Adamantine mantel clock on the light oak chest of drawers. Brody opened the walk-in closet and found it full of clothes: several suits, a line of dress shirts, and a shoe rack, all in Luca's size. There were extra blankets and pillows on a shelf in the back. He found the typical stuff in the drawers. The bathroom was two times bigger than it needed to be, with a huge soaking tub and a spacious shower. Beside the bed was a Bluetooth speaker and a handbook on clock repair. Two guns and a knife lay in the bedside table drawer. Maybe Luca did live here, at least as much as anyone in that position could live anywhere.

He walked upstairs and appreciated the winsome of the wall clocks that hung there. He wondered if Medina had restored each one. The second-floor landing boasted a large window between two bedrooms, and sunlight streamed into the foyer.

Brody inspected the rest of the home, but, as with the beach house, there was nothing to give him any more clues to Garrison or Medina. Then, he headed up to the next floor. Iris had said his room would be on the left. Brody opened the door. He saw a duvet in creams and royal blue, and open white sheers at the windows. Seeing his bag on a luggage rack beside the closet, Brody unpacked.

After eating a sandwich, he decided it was time to get organized and plan the rest of the day. He did not have time to waste, but the doorbell interrupted him.

Chapter Fifty-Eight

Meanwhile, in Dremmond. Luca sat on the balcony with Rusty and waited. Gavin locked himself in the office and had been there before Luca dropped Brody at the airport. Luca thought about the drawings with their names in the folder. That was terrifying. He and Rusty both hated this time when Gavin was better left alone. Gavin's mental state completely armed. He would pace relentlessly until whatever idea he was working on emerged.

Rusty's phone rang, and he looked down at the caller ID. It was Julianne; she was not going to be happy. Rusty was supposed to have been back that day, and he had failed to call to tell her he had extended his stay.

"I'll take this in my room," Rusty said, and he headed into the house.

Gavin paced his office but was not thinking of Friday or the folder. He was thinking of Luca. He grimaced and shook his head. The man had always been compliant and had always done exactly what he was told. This was his fault; Gavin's will led to the tension. The team belonged to Luca now, and Gavin left him out of the decision process. It all troubled Gavin. Luca was right to defend his position because he was ultimately responsible for this team. Gavin needed to acknowledge that Luca oversaw his safety. However, Luca was a lot like himself; he often failed to understand he had limits. If Luca did not take care of himself, that would put Gavin without anyone experienced— and that he could not afford. Gavin needed to get Luca out of tactical defense mode and talk with him. His face twisted at the thought that Luca had gotten angry. He had never seen him upset before. Maybe it was the pain? After all, Luca had had surgery in the kitchen that morning.

Mostly, though, Gavin was thinking about something else. King was close; he could feel it. Gavin also gave serious thought to what Helen said. For twenty-one years, the Ghost had been chasing a demon. Now Gavin felt death's breath on his skin—cool and icy. Gavin did not want to leave this world with regrets. He left the office and the house, finding Luca sitting alone on the balcony.

The Sapphire Ghost

"Luca, take a walk with me," Gavin said, heading down the short staircase to the sand below.

Luca grimaced as he was jolted back to the present, reacting to Gavin's request. His left arm was beginning to hurt. He knew there was damage and would have to see a surgeon, and Luca dreaded the idea. Luca rose to follow Gavin onto the beach. The winds were calm on this early fall day. The waters seemed to feel the unease in the air and lapped slow and soft upon the sand as if it didn't want to offend them.

As they walked, neither man spoke, and Luca felt smothered by the silent tension. Gavin thought about what to say and how to say it and wanted to ensure Luca understood.

"Luca, I want to apologize. It was wrong of me to demand you sit out this operation," Gavin said.

"Sir, respectfully, I believe there was wrong on both sides, and I should not have reacted the way I did, and I should have never displayed hostility. You always deserve my respect," Luca said, feeling uncomfortable but grateful that the air was clearing.

"And you deserve mine. Let us agree to speak first with each other. I commit to giving you ample opportunity to speak your piece and to hear you out. However, that does not mean I will always agree with you." Gavin thought about the report Helen had asked him to write on Luca's commitment to the Oath and Arcadia.

"I understand, and I appreciate that very much, sir," Luca replied.

"That said, I accept that you will be with me in D.C. However, I do want you to take some time off. You can determine how much, but I must insist," Gavin said. "I want you to see a physician about your arm."

"I plan to see a doctor tomorrow after we arrive, and I have connections with the local hospital," Luca answered, expanding on what he'd said earlier that day. "Gavin, I did not need the Oath to take your life seriously—and I respect the Codes, but I respect you more."

"That I know. Luca, you and I are more similar than different. When we commit, it's for life. We both would go until we drove ourselves into the ground. I finally learned the hard way that I couldn't do that. You don't have an off switch, which can be disastrous, and I cannot afford you not to be at your best. I need you sharp and aware. If you can't take care of yourself, you can't prevent me from being exposed," Gavin said. "Also, I feel you have abundantly proven yourself. Your commitment to me, to this cause, and Arcadia could not be stronger."

"Thank you, sir," Luca said, allowing Gavin's words to settle him. "I must make a request also. After this Dossier, I will come back here with you. I can stay in town if you need your privacy, and I don't have a problem with that. But I am uncomfortable leaving you in Florida. If you want to stay here, I will be close. However, I would prefer you to go someplace else, anyplace else. Last night, they were too close. I don't like that they got to me. That means they could get to you. They now have our names and descriptions."

Gavin shook his head, and he could not argue with anything Luca said. "I need to speak with the woman in that house," Gavin said, nodding at the smaller of the two houses. Helen has asked that I intervene and help her."

"Then I must insist, respectfully, on staying with you."

"Fine, but it will not be for working; get that arm checked out and do what you need to do in D.C. We will come back here and have some much-needed R&R. I'm afraid it might be our last for a while," Gavin sighed.

"I feel there is something you have not told me," Luca stated.

"Yes, after you and Brody left last night, Helen called with some news on the information you sent her. Steve Bains was a point man for Jack King's operation. When you burned up those servers with that virus, you destroyed hundreds, if not thousands, of videos. Taking out Bains was a critical hit to King's operation."

"They are too close for comfort," Luca responded, thinking of the previous night. And it had not yet been two weeks since London. "Have you been in contact with the prime minister?"

"Yes, I had a conversation with her two mornings ago. She resumed her duties after the news of Steve Bains' death, and she is still cautious and insists that Mr. Rango stay with her."

"Rango. He is a keeper," Luca said, stopping to watch two birds dive-bomb their way into the water.

"Luca, we may need to draw King's crew out. I want my hands on King and am ready to make my peace either way, but I know we are close."

"I understand it has been a long time coming, but please, let us do it safely and make sure you come to no harm," Luca said, not liking Gavin's state of mind.

Gavin contemplated his following words carefully. Choosing who to pass this legacy, this cause, and Gavin's reason for existing. Gavin had given two decades to take out the most corrupt, the truest of evil.

"I feel like I can see an end to this journey I began. I have something I would like to ask you, which is important," Gavin said, breaking the silence.

Upon hearing the severe and quiet tone, Luca stopped walking, "What is it?"

Gavin turned to Luca. "Would you consider becoming a Ghost? Become my heir and work beside me as my equal until I am finished here?"

Gavin knew it was a lot to ask. He knew what Luca would be giving up; not just his family, what was left of his independence, even his will, to become an asset and a guardian. Gavin wanted to put the thought out there and make Luca think about the idea. Gavin remembered that night in Georgia when an angelic-looking stranger walked out of the night looking like she had been sent by the deities. The night his life changed, the night he breathed in the celestial spirit of the Seraphim's fire.

Luca stared at the man before him—his dread about having a conversation over his outburst wholly dissolved. Elation and fear warred in Luca's mind, and the idea that Gavin asked him to accept the highest honor! And a dread that Gavin was preparing to die.

"I'm asking the question, and I don't expect your answer right now. Think about it, that's all," Gavin said quietly. "You are a good soldier and an even better man."

Chapter Fifty-Nine

Brody opened the door and looked down at what he thought was a girl standing on the stoop. She was short, with light brown skin and bottle-blonde, chin-length hair. She wore trendy glasses, a black jacket over a teal dress, and black wedge heels.

"May I help you?" Brody asked.

"Sir, you are Nate Brody, correct?" she asked.

"Yes, and you are?" Brody asked just as he saw the small blue square pendant on her necklace. "I am sorry, come inside."

"I am Camille, and I will assist you with anything you need regarding surveillance."

Brody watched the woman walk through the door, only chest high to himself. Camille pulled along a silver box with the blue Dark 9 team assignment portfolio. Camille wore a pendant that showed she was trusted, and that was all he needed to know. Brody watched her cross through the living area and turn to the left. Brody followed her through the house to a door he had not previously noticed. There was a thumbprint keypad to the right of the door. Brody stood there looking at the keypad.

"You going to open the door?" Camille asked.

"I'm not sure I can," Brody said reluctantly.

"How about you try?" she said, nodding to the scanner.

Brody approached the silver scanner and placed his thumb on the screen: one beep, two beeps, three beeps. The scanner went green, and the lock clicked open. Brody's face showed relief.

Camille reduced the handle on the case, picked it up, and headed down the stairs they found behind the door. The stairs opened into a large gym with several rings hanging from the large wooden beams, weights, parallel bars, a couple of punching bags, and a pommel horse. Camille passed all the equipment and turned right into another room with several computer systems and a

The Sapphire Ghost

large monitor on the wall. Camille began to set up the equipment from her case, plugging in cords and switching on the CPU.

"We have decided on Doctor Wasson's home for the event; it's secure and remote enough. The team is there now, installing cameras," Camille said. "That is, unless you have another site in mind?"

"No, that sounds fine," Brody replied, surprised at how quickly this team worked after noticing cameras come online on the wall monitor.

"You have not been around long, have you? A little green?" Camille asked, not looking up from testing the cameras.

He did not like her use of *green*. "Was on Dark 9 for six years, but I have just taken this assignment."

"Lucky."

Brody smiled. "How long have you been with Dark 9?"

"Twelve years," Camille replied as she spoke into the comm in her ear. "Team Leader here, all cameras are go, thank you."

"Wow, you don't look old enough to have been doing this for twelve years," Brody observed.

"I was recruited when I was fifteen." After more fiddling, she said, "I have to get back to the Capitol. If you need me, my number is on the desk."

Camille left Brody standing in the computer room with his hands in his pockets. He did not know what to make of the young woman who came and went quickly. She apparently worked at the Capitol. She was intelligent, beautiful, and direct. Brody wondered what the policy was on dating within the Order.

Brody headed upstairs and stared at the door that closed behind the woman. He wondered when she would return. Brody shook his head. He was responsible for one event and needed to get to work. He needed to create a distraction for the country club the next day. The instructions had been *no explosions and must last for at least thirty minutes*. He had an idea, but first, he needed to change.

Chapter Sixty

Gavin turned to walk the nearly two miles back to the house. Luca watched Gavin stroll away. If he did not make it, what did that mean? What was Gavin anticipating that he was not letting Luca in on? Luca would have to be extra vigilant.

Luca ignored the pain and turned to run in the opposite direction. He ran hard enough to lock the air from his lungs and push that ever-growing rage from his mind. Luca reached a narrow path leading away from the beach. Breathless, he bent to place his right hand on his knee and drew in several breaths. After a few moments, Luca stood up and looked at the derelict, wooden two-story structure. Its windows were permanently shuttered, and a large piece of plywood covered the front door. The broad, broken-down porch was unsafe. Luca scaled the dunes to the house and went to its side. He stopped in front of what appeared to be an old wooden door with three single glass panes at the top. Luca dug into his pocket and retrieved his pin. Luca tugged at the hinged piece of trim that exposed a lock. He then placed the pin to the lock, and the metal—not wooden—door slid into the wall.

Since they landed at the airport, something had been gnawing at his mind, and Luca wanted to learn more about those workers. The airport maintenance personnel had no knowledge that anyone was there working and had promised to investigate. Luca adjusted his eyes to the light and took in the room. He had rebuilt this space, allowing him to see everything happening in Dremmond. Gavin had joked that Luca was a secret voyeur.

Luca went to the wall and flipped the breaker that turned everything on, and soon a hum permeated the room. The house might look dilapidated, but inside was a techie's dream. The walls were the original thick panels that had once shined in a highly glossed mahogany, and he had reinforced the floors with wide wooden planks. With his adrenaline up, Luca went to the gym at the back of the house to dissipate some energy while everything came online.

The Sapphire Ghost

Luca stripped off his shirt and pants, exposing the ribbed stomach and lean muscular arms. Luca's body contained a near-zero fat ratio. In his underwear, Luca switched on the lights. The room came to life, revealing blue floormats and no ceiling, just exposed rafters. Two sets of rings hung from the high beams that ran diagonally across the twenty-foot space. Uneven bars were set to give space between the beams. A vault, parallel bars, and a pommel horse were on the floor. Carefully, Luca took his arm out of the sling and started stretching.

Luca drew in a breath and held it. He watched the cluster of lights behind his lids and waited to feel the pull, and Luca sunk enough into that inner place to take his mind off the pain. Gymnastics had a way of forcing you to work through the pain. He sat on the mats, spread his legs wide, and bowed forward at the hips until his chest rested on the floor. Sitting up, he then leaned left and right over each leg. An entire routine would be impossible because he was hurting. Luca did what he could to expend the anxiety, pushing its way out.

His dad had signed his sister up for gymnastics when they were young. Marissa was always less confident than her brother, so Luca volunteered to take classes with her in Bogota Colombia

Luca's mother was shot to death for being a political advisor of the Patriotic Union. Their family became a target. Luca's father fled with his six-year-old son and four-year-old daughter to the United States for political asylum. Once they settled in New Orleans, his father allowed Luca to register with a local gym and continue training. Luca excelled and participated in many competitions, both state and national. Nothing had channeled Luca's energy like gymnastics. Losing his mother in such a brutal way and getting used to another country, he needed a place to channel his pain.

Luca worked out his legs and did some crunches for over an hour. Then he grabbed a towel and returned to the hub to look at the cameras. He stood in the doorway, watching the six monitors displaying maps of Dremmond. However, the laptop monitor on the desk caught his attention. Scrawled across the screen was a single word - WARNING. Luca dropped the towel and went directly to the computer. His system tagged a bank account with an unusual deposit belonging to someone surprising. Luca returned to the gym, grabbed the phone from his pants pocket, and called Helen. She answered on the first ring.

He and Helen discussed the situation, and then he watched the video Helen had sent to his email, which showed the man in question shaking a stranger's hand and taking a briefcase from him. That man went to his car, which had been a gift instead of a bonus from Gavin last Christmas. Gavin knew of this man's gambling habits and had bailed him out multiple times but had seldom given him money. After everything Gavin had done for his family, this man had clearly betrayed them. Luca's skin burned with fury, and he could feel the heat rising through his body. There was no way to pull it back now.

"I need the Dark 9 teams here now, please," Luca said calmly into the phone. "Also, Helen, do not tell Gavin just yet. He has a lot on him with D.C. Friday, and I do not need him sidetracked." Luca was commanding.

"I understand, Luca, but Gavin deserves to know," Helen replied.

"He will, but not today."

"If that is what you think is best. But I believe Gavin can handle both. And how do you intend to get out of Dremmond without a pilot?" Helen asked. "Did you check the car before you left the airport?"

"I always do. I checked the sensors to ensure the car was not touched and checked the weight. And, before you ask, I disengaged the GPS when we bought the car," Luca informed her.

"I knew you would. Could they have tracked the car back to the house?"

"No, they added the tracker at the traffic stop, and Brody found it after that man attacked me. So, they have our descriptions from a folder I found in the man's car. With Rusty coming back, he might have assumed that I might take the night off, but that's all I can come up with."

"Be careful, Luca. I will have your teams there within two hours, and I am unsure how you will explain the excessive manpower to Gavin."

"Let me worry about that," Luca said. "Thank you, Helen. I will keep in touch."

Back at the beach house, Gavin was beginning to worry. Luca had been gone for three hours, and the sun was setting.

"Do you want me to go get him?" Rusty asked when Gavin began his relentless stalking.

"I can. I'm just unsure what to say," Gavin answered.

"Did you argue?" Rusty asked, thinking about the tension that had soaked the house that morning.

"No, we are good. I asked Luca a question, and I think it might have been too soon."

"I do better at speaking with him. Do you want to tell me, so I know what I am in for when I get to the shack?" Rusty headed to the door.

"I asked him if he wanted to be the Ghost once I am gone." Gavin went to turn on the kettle.

Rusty froze in place at Gavin's response, wrapping his head around those words. "That is a big question. What did he say?"

"Nothing, he just stood there." Gavin took down the teacup and a box of tea.

"I will go talk to him," Rusty said and walked out. He was a handler by nature. But this was different and unexpected. He was unsure how Luca would handle something like this. Heck, Rusty was uncertain he was comprehending such an idea himself.

Chapter Sixty-One

Luca examined the map and planned where to deploy the Dark 9 teams. He just needed to quietly contain Dremmond until this Dossier was complete because it was another link to the King. Luca worried that Gavin did not have much time to plan this one because of what happened last night and the trip to Maine.

Luca made an appointment to get X-rays the next day to see what needed to be repaired in his arm. Brody was a good doctor, but there was only so much anyone could do at a kitchen table. He wondered how Brody was doing in D.C. and if he had met Camille yet. He smiled at the thought of her.

Rusty drove the Range Rover and parked it, walking the last twenty yards down to the shack. Gavin hated its appearance, but Luca wanted it to look rundown. This was Luca's center of the world; from here, he could tap any agency and retrieve just about any information.

Rusty knocked on the side door. Luca answered, still in his underwear. His hair was a damp mess, but he was not sweating. A killer sat behind Luca's eyes, and it appeared to Rusty it would not take much for the rest of him to follow.

"Are you all right in here?" Rusty asked.

"Come in," Luca said and headed back to the hub.

Rusty noticed the notes on the whiteboard. Luca returned to the phone call in progress.

"I'm back. I will need the helicopter here tomorrow at 10:00 a.m. Great, I will have it. Yes, three passengers. You, too, and thank you." Luca laid down the phone.

"Rusty, have you come to check on me?" Luca looked up at the board.

"Yes, Gavin is troubled." Rusty walked over to see what was going on.

"I'm fine, and we are good," Luca said, preoccupied.

"You have Dark 9 coming? A lot of operatives," Rusty observed.

"Yes."

"Okay, out with it." Rusty grabbed Luca's shoulders and turned him around to face him. "I have never known you to overreact, but this looks like a grand overreaction."

"It's not. Rusty, Helen and I have evidence of the person who gave us away to the King." Luca stepped back, waiting for Rusty's reaction. "But I have convinced Helen not to say anything until after D.C."

"Who?" Rusty asked.

"I believe it best that you do not know." Luca searched Rusty's eyes. He did not want Rusty to feel like an outsider; before he retired, Luca would not have kept anything from him.

"Tell me, Luca. I can handle myself with Gavin. You know that." The lines on Rusty's forehead deepened.

Luca revealed the name and awaited Rusty's reaction. Rusty maintained his composure, but his eyes narrowed, where there was more than a hint of anger flickering. Rusty thought about this person and the information shared with him. At least they had never mentioned Dremmond; that was reserved for those only within the Order.

"I won't ask you if you are certain; I trust you know for a fact. But that's quite a shock. When do you plan on telling Gavin?" Rusty asked, wondering what Luca's plan was and how he intended to keep such a secret from the man no one could keep anything from.

"Once the D.C. operation is complete," Luca said.

"How do you intend to keep this from him? Luca, he will know you are hiding something. He always does," Rusty said. "Keeping something critical from him is a good way to tick him off, and I'm unsure you are ready to face that."

"I am good at keeping my mouth shut. Are you?" Luca asked, turning back to the board. "The extra security will arrive tonight. My mind is set, Rusty."

"What is your plan to explain using a helicopter instead of the jet?" Rusty could see so many problems in this situation, and he did not want Luca to put himself in a position to face down the Ghost. Gavin was easygoing and loved his team, but it was a different story when he felt deceived.

"I've got this; relax," Luca said.

Rusty was anything but relaxed. He looked at the semi-naked man who was sure to experience the wrath of a furious Ghost in less than a day. Gavin knew Luca well enough to have asked him to take his place. However, Luca managed to play a lot close to his chest.

"We need to head back. Get some clothes on; I have the car. I'll pour you a stiff drink when we return to the house." Rusty learned the hard way not to hide anything from Gavin, who always found out. Doing so yielded painful results.

Luca punched something into the computer and closed it, then went to the wall and powered them all down. Luca did have a plan. It was to remain quiet. Gavin had given him a good reason, saying he wanted to draw King out, but Gavin's mindset scared Luca. He knew Gavin trusted him, and using a helicopter after what had transpired the previous night would not be a big leap. It made sense; Luca was sure Gavin would see it that way. Luca also needed to contact Brody to ensure he was watching his six. Luca put his clothes on and followed Rusty up to the car. He knew Rusty worried about him and that if Gavin found out before Luca wanted him to, it could result in a horrendous episode, one he would prefer not to encounter. Gavin had never had a reason to be angry with him, and he didn't want to give him one.

Luca stepped through the door while Rusty lingered outside, considering whether to tell Gavin about this development. Rusty had learned early on that Gavin's temperament turned quickly. Rusty ran his fingertips over the scar on his left shoulder as a sixteen-year reminder never to push his weight around. Gavin wanted to know everything, and to keep anything from him never ended well, although Rusty had kept something from Gavin for four years.

Luca passed Gavin and went to his room. He returned a minute later when Rusty came through the door. Gavin observed Rusty and saw something there. Even though Rusty tried to keep his face expressionless, Gavin did not like what he read in his features. Rusty walked over and poured two whiskeys.

"Sir, would you mind joining us in your office?" Luca asked.

The Sapphire Ghost

Gavin stared at Rusty. "Certainly." Gavin turned, examining Luca's composure and body language, not liking what he read there either. This had nothing to do with the question he asked.

They walked into the office. Gavin took his seat, and Luca waited for Rusty to take the chair across the desk; then, Luca pulled up a chair to the middle.

"First off, sir, this is happening. No, I did not get your input, so if you are going to be upset, it should be with me, not Rusty. He has just learned about what I have planned. Please understand that I am suspicious of everything now and do not want anything to happen to you. I have already given you my suggestion to leave Dremmond, and you declined, so this is my only option." Luca paused.

"Get on with what you have to say, Luca." Gavin watched both men, especially the one who looked like a deer caught in headlights. Rusty's fingers lingered on his shoulder where Gavin had shot him almost sixteen years ago. Rusty always did this when he was anxious or knew Gavin would not like something he had to say. It was an awful thing to do, but he'd had few options for taming his Warrior's controlling disposition with Rusty's size and demeanor.

"Tonight, two teams are coming in to secure this compound." Luca opened his laptop, and a map appeared. Luca did not look directly at Gavin. "They will be stationed here and here," he said, pointing to certain houses on the map. There will be a sniper on overwatch twenty-four-seven." Luca showed Gavin where the shooter would be hiding. Luca became quiet and waited.

Gavin studied the diagram and thought about what Luca had planned. While Gavin thought it excessive, Luca was attacked and had not rested all day, and his mind was on high alert. Gavin tucked his two fingers under his chin and looked again at Rusty, who was beginning to relax. Gavin also knew Rusty would never have planned such insulation for this compound without consulting Gavin. Maybe that is why Rusty looked so nervous. Gavin was not yet convinced of the need.

"Go on," Gavin said calmly, feeling Luca would give away his real intentions if he could keep Luca talking.

"Okay, if you have no questions," Luca said. "I have a helicopter picking us up at ten in the morning near the shack, and it will take us to D.C." Luca stopped again and waited. He wanted to give Gavin plenty of time to absorb the plan and react now rather than later.

"Luca, do you feel all of this is necessary?" Gavin asked, observing Luca. He saw that Luca was cool and wholly committed.

"Yes, sir, I do. We can flush King out after the D.C. operation if that is what you wish, but we have a Dossier to take care of and not a lot of time. Sir, as you know, I am not a hundred percent right now. I would feel so much better if I knew other eyes were on this location, at least until you know who betrayed us." Luca had chosen his words carefully. He'd never lied to Gavin and did not plan to start now. "After we return, the security will stay in place, and Brody will stay in the tenth house, about a block away. You will get some privacy, and I feel like I can take those days off to recover. I will go see my family *one last time*," Luca finished.

Gavin stared at Luca, realizing what he'd said, and his chest gave a hard kick. Luca was ready to commit to whatever came next.

"All right. If this makes you more comfortable doing what you need to do, I will not block it," Gavin said with a small smile.

The lines in Rusty's forehead relaxed, and he exhaled. Luca said he had a plan, but Rusty did not expect him to play on Gavin's emotions. Luca was using the offer to accept the highest honor of the Order to convince Gavin to accept this plan. It appeared Gavin had bought it.

Luca stood, collected the laptop, and left the room. Rusty started to rise when Gavin used his hand and motioned him to stay put. Rusty imagined his heart leaping from his chest onto the desk, waiting for Gavin to put a stake through it.

"Rusty, is there more to this story?" Gavin asked, seeing the anxiety on the face he knew better than his own.

"Yes, some," Rusty admitted, observing Gavin's eyes, which said he wanted to know more.

"Tell me."

"Gavin, with the deepest respect, I cannot. You will need to discuss it with Luca," Rusty breathed.

"I am asking you," Gavin said.

"I can't," Rusty said, bracing himself for the fallout. Rusty knew he had the advantage as Gavin would not do anything to hurt his health. "Luca is your Warrior now."

"Do you trust what he is doing? Will it upset me?" Gavin asked.

"Yes, I trust he believes what he is doing is in the best interest of the Order and the current objective. Yes, I feel it will make you angry, and I warned him against keeping anything from you," Rusty admitted.

"All right." Gavin motioned dismissively at Rusty.

Rusty nodded to Gavin. He knew there was a slight chance that Gavin would let this play out how Luca wished.

Gavin sat back in the desk chair and linked his fingers behind his head. He reviewed Luca's words, looking for pieces in Luca's summation that did not make sense. Gavin closed his eyes, weighing each part of the information behind closed lids for a long time. He smiled; Luca knew. *'When you find out who betrayed us.'* Gavin was fully aware of Luca's careful words. When did Luca plan on letting him in on that bit of information? Did he have plans to take care of it himself? Surely, he would not be so foolish!

Chapter Sixty-Two

September 4

Brody stopped at the local Goodwill store and purchased some items to help him look the part. After paying for a leather jacket and an old pair of boots, he returned to the car.

Then Brody drove across the river, slowly watching the road signs and seeking a place where the bikers hung out.

Brody had driven many streets like this, especially in Detroit. Kids playing outside without supervision bothered him. If they went missing, there would be no massive search, and they would not make the evening news. Predators knew that.

Finding what appeared to be a former garage on a corner of a rough street, Brody examined the den. He parked the car beside several older Harleys and a couple of Indian motorcycles and shut off the engine. He placed his Sig 9 in the harness under the leather jacket. Then he removed the Breitling watch he wore, revealing the line of skulls wrapped around his wrist.

Cautiously, he approached the garage door, but he walked in, studying the men playing pool in the back. He summarized the disastrous space, looking for the alpha. Brody was the only black face in the converted garage. This should not take long. The shabby garage smelled of urine and smoke—and not just tobacco. The walls were covered in naked centerfolds and a variety of vulgar messages.

"You lost?" asked a man to the right sitting in a ratty old green chair. The owner of the voice was drinking a beer. A disturbingly skinny woman sat on the man's lap with shaggy blonde hair and tattoos covering her arms.

"You the boss around here?" Brody asked.

"Nope, that would be Beans over there." The man's words were long and suffering, but he nodded to the shorter, stout man by the pool table with a bald, tattooed head and a long, black, unkempt beard.

The Sapphire Ghost

Brody walked to the back; the room quieted. He could feel the eyes of the dozen or so men staring at him.

"You Beans?" Brody asked.

"Who in the love of a crack baby being used as a football are you?" said the man, who wore a black vest and tattered jeans.

"I have a proposition for you and your guys if you are open to one," Brody responded.

"And I've not had my daily dose of whoop-ass; how about I make that you?" Beans answered. The men laughed as Beans threw out his arms, inviting applause.

"I'd rather not, but if that is the only way to get you to listen, let's get this over with," Brody said.

"You some kind of sucker for punishment, boy?" Beans asked.

"Not exactly," Brody responded. "If I wanted to commit suicide, I would just climb up your ego and jump down to your IQ."

Beans looked at Brody's tall body, sizing him up. He threw a punch up toward Brody's left jaw without another word. Brody moved slightly to the right to avoid it, and the man swayed a bit, not connecting with his target. Beans swung again, this time an uppercut. Brody grabbed his arm with his left hand, revealing the skulls and crossbones on his wrist.

"Shit," said a man to his right in a black Metallica T-shirt, "He's Jaber."

The room became quiet as Beans stared at Brody's face and then down at the hand gripping his arm. He saw the line of death skulls.

"Anyone can get a tattoo," Beans said, jerking his arm, grasped firmly in Brody's long, dark fingers.

Brody's eyes bore into Beans, letting him see the discipline in them and that he would resort to the type of violence people feared of Jaber.

"Would I have walked into your piece of shit den if I did not have the experience to back myself up?" Brody snarled without any bedside manner.

"What do you want?" Beans finally asked. Brody released the hold on his wrist.

"I need about twenty riders tomorrow to stir up some noise. Country Club in Alexandria. You game?" Brody asked, now that he had the attention of the room. "If you're not interested—I'll find another group."

"What do we get?" Beans asked.

"I can have a Budweiser truck unload here tomorrow night," Brody said, pulling five hundred dollars from his pants pocket. "This will ensure you all have enough gas."

"Maybe. Tell me exactly what we would have to do," Beans said, eyeing the money.

"I need noise, lots of noise, for thirty minutes starting at exactly 1:00 p.m. I'm willing to bail any of you out of jail if it is only for disturbing the peace. You are on your own for anything other than that," Brody said, looking around the room he commanded.

"We get to play in a country club with a get-out-of-free jail card and free beer. What do you guys think of this deal?" Beans asked. A loud whoop erupted in the small den of smokey air.

"Looks like you got yourself a deal, Jaber, but how do we call you with any trouble?" Brody extracted the small gray card from his jeans back pocket with a single number written across one side, flicking it at Beans. "Call that number; you might want to clear some room for the beer."

Brody dropped the mothball-smelling jacket in the burn bin when he left the garage and got in the car. Looking over at the garage doors—*that had been unexpectedly easy.* He then stared at his wrist and thought about all the trouble his dad had gone through with him as a teen before Nate Brody Sr. got him straightened out and back on track for medical school. Brody brought out the Breitling watch and wrapped it around the tattoos to conceal them from the world. He kept them as a reminder of a vastly different time in his life—when everything was on the line.

Now he needed to get to a local hospital for heparin and phenobarbital. That would not be hard, and he had passed a hospital along the way.

Chapter Sixty-Three

The head of Dark 9 from the west coast, Samuels drove the SUV to the helicopter landing site at 10:00 a.m. Luca could feel Gavin's eyes on him, boring in. He understood that Gavin had suspicions. But after Gavin admitted he wanted to draw King's men out in the open, Luca could not risk that happening. A dread was building inside at the thought of what Gavin might do to him for withholding information. However, he swore to protect the Ghost—even when against his will. Luca felt this qualified. If he must bear the Ghost's wrath, he was prepared to accept it.

They ran to the helicopter once it landed. The prop wash stirred up the sand, and it felt like flakes of glass ripping at their faces. Gavin pushed Luca toward the back, leaving Rusty to sit up front with Robert, the pilot. He did not want Luca feeling too comfortable, and he did not want him planning anything else alone. Luca moved to the seat indicated after handing Rusty the cash envelope for the pilot. They strapped themselves in and put on the headsets. Robert signaled and took the chopper up.

"Gentlemen, I need to stop in Greensboro for fuel," Robert said once they hit altitude.

"Okay, that will be fine. We could probably stretch our legs for a bit," Luca replied.

Gavin tapped Rusty on the shoulder, put up two fingers, and motioned to his headset and back. Rusty, in turn, got Robert's attention and did the same. Robert hit the button, cutting communication between the front two headsets.

Luca looked down on the city of Destin, watching the congested highway grow smaller, and waited for the hammer to fall. Gavin had not spoken to him the rest of the previous night and had stayed locked away in his office. He assumed Gavin figured out that Luca knew the name of the person who betrayed the team and was keeping it secret. Gavin was almost psychic in reading people and information. He wondered if Gavin had spoken to Helen and if she revealed anything. A fight erupted in his stomach. He did not want to have this conversation where he could not escape if it became heated. Luca also did not want Gavin going into this Dossier in a mood worse than usual.

Gavin observed Luca's reluctance to look in his direction. He also watched him rubbing the palm of his left hand with his right thumb as if trying to get circulation to his hand, which looked swollen and blue, yet Luca had not complained. Gavin reached up, took off his sapphire pin, and turned to face Luca. To Gavin, it was essential to make a clear and specific statement.

"Take this," Gavin said and placed the pin in Luca's swollen palm.

Luca stared down at the blue square stone surrounded by diamonds. He picked it up with his good hand, looked at the two-carat dark blue sapphire, and turned to look at Gavin with confusion.

"What are you doing? I don't want this," he said and shoved it back at Gavin.

"Keep it. I get the impression you are overstepping your place, Luca. But for the moment, I'll give you that ability." Gavin wrapped Luca's fingers around the pin.

"No, sir, I will not," Luca said as Rusty turned to focus on the movement he'd caught in his periphery.

Rusty turned to the pilot and motioned for three headsets, pointing at his own.

"You know who gave our descriptions to King, and you plan to take care of that person yourself, do you not?" Gavin questioned.

Luca's hands began to shake with the pin wrapped in his fingers. "No!" Luca nearly shouted, surprising Gavin. "I know; however, I don't plan on doing any such thing."

"Then you won't have a problem telling me who the person is," Gavin said softly. "You do not have the authority to keep this from me. Your swearing-in with Helen only relates to her area, not mine. This is my area and *my* Order," the Ghost said.

"Gavin, I intend to tell you, but first, you need to focus on this operation. Your complete focus." Hot tears began to burn in Luca's eyes. The inflection of his voice changed. "You said you trusted me? You asked me if I wanted to serve as the Ghost when you were no longer around. I'd like you around for a long time to come because I am not at all ready to fill your role."

"The answer, Luca. I want to know the name, or I will not be responsible for my next actions!"

As Rusty listened to the exchange, he heard the emotion in Luca's voice, which had become thin and strained. Rusty knew the Ghost was now in charge, not Gavin, and he did not dare look back because he could not reveal he was listening.

Rusty had never thought about the world without the Ghost. Gavin offered the role to Luca, who would excel if he took it and if Gavin were around to guide him. Rusty concluded that Gavin mentioned something that had left Luca anxious about the offer the previous day. He could only see that Luca would place himself in this position because he feared something more alarming. In the last two days, Rusty had seen a different side to Luca. Rusty had never seen him angry until yesterday, and now he was on the edge of tears.

Gavin watched as Luca began to tremble. Gavin was questioning Luca's loyalty to Helen above his Order, or so it seemed. Luca turned away from Gavin and peered out the window, but he could see nothing because of the white circles dancing before his eyes.

"I'm waiting," the Ghost said sternly.

The screaking began in Luca's ears, and his body felt like he had been given a shot of adrenaline with his heart pounding to escape his chest. The headache began behind his eyes, erasing his vision even further with the consecutive blasts and rapid-fire sounds. *Sargent Doty pushed him into the hole and covered him as best he could as he tried to distract the men in pursuit. Luca lay in the hole, covered by two old car parts. It was just a four-by-four hole dug into the sand. His leg was bleeding and pooling into his left combat boot. Jerking his belt off, he wrapped it around his upper leg. Medina tried hard to stand, but his leg could not bear his weight. He needed help but did not know how long he would be trapped here with the sounds above. The blood loss was causing him to lose his thoughts, and Luca began to drift off. He sat and breathed in the disturbed dust, trapped in the dark, waiting to die.*

No, not this! Luca thought as the images appeared drenched in reds and oranges, burnt gunpowder, and the odors of hot sand overtook his senses.

Luca's skin became moist and grew cold. He unstrapped himself and lay across his knees, feeling like he would throw up.

Rusty peered over Luca's seat and saw he was in trouble. Rusty took a vomit bag from under the console where Robert had a stack and passed it to Luca. Gavin remained composed as he watched. *It might not be a bullet, but he would remember this just as well.* However unfortunate, each Ghost with a new Warrior often had to put them in their place. It was the nature of the beast.

Luca's hand was clammy and shaking as he took the bag from Rusty. Luca immediately vomited into it. Afterward, he sat back and willed himself to regain control, pushing the images out. He inhaled deeply, held it, and exhaled slowly as he had been taught, still feeling the ghost pains in his leg. Luca rubbed his scar.

Luca placed the headset back on and replaced the harness. He was still on the verge of needing to escape and fight his way out, and he could still hear the sounds of gunfire.

"I have nothing further to say to you." Luca dropped the pin in Gavin's lap.

Luca caught the pilot's attention in the mirror. He moved his still unsteady hand across his throat and pointed to his mouthpiece in a cutting motion. Robert cut his communication. Luca breathed in and out for several long minutes, bringing his heart rate back to normal. He could not deal with the Ghost right now, not while they were in the air, because it would not be safe for anyone on board.

Gavin didn't take his eyes off him, knowing if Luca did indeed need help, he would assist him. Gavin was not anticipating Luca to cut him off completely, and Gavin expected him to reveal the name.

They sat quietly for the remainder of the two-hour flight to Greensboro. Spotting the airport coffee shop, Rusty asked if they would like to go for a coffee while they waited. Gavin accepted and walked with Rusty. Luca debated renting a car for the rest of the trip. While his job was not to abandon Gavin, Luca did not like being around him right now. Instead, Luca went to the vending machine, bought a soda, and downed half the can. His stomach was still unsettled. In addition, his head and arm ached.

The Sapphire Ghost

Luca looked in the direction Rusty and Gavin had walked. After so many years, why had he become so upset over the last couple of days? He rarely angered, and when he did, he usually had an outlet. The fact that Gavin sent him into an episode so quickly in the air scared him. Gavin knew better and knew what could happen, but he did it anyway. Gavin was being careless and trying to prevent Luca from doing his job, and at the same time, had put everyone aboard that helicopter in danger. Luca needed to get himself under control before something terrible happened.

While Gavin walked with Rusty, he placed his pin back on his lapel.

"What was going on back there?" Rusty asked.

"Trying to teach Mr. Medina a lesson," Gavin said.

"Well, you got him pretty upset."

"Yes. I thought it would go differently." Gavin watched a helicopter take off.

"What do you mean? You did not intend to push him into a panic attack?" Rusty asked. "That could have been dangerous for all of us. You have never seen what he can do during one of those episodes."

"I came prepared." Gavin pulled a small syringe from his pocket and showed it to his friend. "Yes, I meant to push him, but I did not anticipate he would shut me out. I intended for him to share the information he is hiding from me. Rusty, I would not have allowed him to harm himself or anyone on board," Gavin said. "You have seen an episode?"

"Luca didn't give you the name?" Rusty asked, acting surprised. "Yes, I did, once, when you were away."

Gavin took in Rusty's words. "No, he took me to school."

"Care to elaborate?" Rusty asked.

"Let me just say his commitment to Arcadia is stronger than his covenant to me," Gavin replied honestly. "He loves me, that I have never questioned—just as I've never questioned you. But I don't believe shooting him would make him divulge anything more than what he intends to. Which tells me it will affect me greatly. Who is close enough to us to give our descriptions—who would do that?" Gavin asked, still hoping Rusty would reveal what he knew.

"I believe you are wrong, Gavin. He is pledged to you and has been since the beginning." Rusty spoke softly and ignored Gavin's question because this was no longer his command.

"I pushed him where he dreads to go, and he may not forgive me for that. I used his weakness against him. But I have the answer to Helen's question about where his loyalty now lies."

"Tell her whatever you wish, but his objective is to keep you alive. Speak to him as you, Gavin Garrison, not the Ghost. He is not a Dossier, and even if he were, you would not get any more information than he intends to give you. You must learn to trust him as you learned to trust me to have your best interest in mind," Rusty said.

"Sometimes, I tire of everyone else having my best interest in mind. You do know I have a mind of my own?"

Gavin took his tea from the young woman behind the counter and went to find a seat. Rusty had always been his confidant; he missed his advice. It was time to place Luca in that role. Gavin thought he had done that until today. Luca's amiable demeanor made Gavin think Luca would never purposefully defy him. Yet, Luca stood up to him twice in the last two days. On the other hand, Rusty always had that take-charge attitude Gavin came to embrace. Rusty always placed the Order above all else.

Gavin had to admit he might have added fuel to the fire with the conversation on the beach about calling all of King's men out into the open.

Gavin caught a glimpse of Luca walking in circles behind the refueling pumps. He could see that he upset Luca terribly, but he intended to have that name. Gavin thought about the sketches in the folder with their names and shook his head. Venom coursed through Gavin at the thought of a betrayal. Betraying Gavin was suicide.

Luca stopped circling, picked up a can, took it to the blue recycling bin, and threw it in. He hated all of this and, on some level, wished Helen had told Gavin first. That way, it would have been out of his hands. He saw the filling truck drive away from their helicopter. Luca breathed in a cleansing breath, finished his soda, and headed back.

The Sapphire Ghost

Luca donned a pair of sunglasses to hide what might be showing in his eyes and waited outside the helicopter for Gavin and Rusty. Luca could be a coward and get in the front and avoid any further altercations, but he was not made that way. If Gavin's Ghost wanted another shot at him, Gavin could have it, but Luca was mentally prepared to turn him off this time. Luca held the door open for Gavin when he got to the helicopter. Gavin got in and Luca climbed in beside him, to Gavin's surprise. Rusty sat again in the front, also somewhat surprised that Luca sat in the back. Gavin motioned for Rusty to have three comms on and intended to have a general conversation about the rest of the night.

Rusty and Gavin discussed the night and a meal. They spoke about going to the bookstore they both loved and getting Brody fitted with a decent suit. Luca sat silently, not listening to any of it. He felt his heartbeats pulsing in his sore arm. Exhausted, he fell asleep.

Chapter Sixty-Four

When they landed, Gavin nudged Luca and woke him. Luca pulled off his headset, unstrapped, and stepped out of the helicopter into the too-bright sun, holding the door for Gavin. The air smelled like dead hot air and river water from the Anacostia River. Luca yawned and stretched—peering over to what he could see of the monuments of the National Mall.

The three walked over to grab a cab. Gavin and Rusty got in, but Luca stood on the curb.

"I'm taking another one to the hospital," Luca announced.

"All right but let me know if you will be there long," replied Rusty.

"Will do." Luca smiled at Rusty wearily.

Luca turned to another cab as soon as they left. He followed Gavin's, and Luca watched the traffic for anything unusual. Luca took many precautions, but on the off-chance this particular someone knew that—he watched even more closely. Luca was being seen at the hospital only a few blocks away from the townhouse.

Gavin peered over his shoulder through the rear window. "Why is Luca taking a separate cab?"

"He said he is going straight to the hospital," Rusty said.

"I know his arm hurts; it is badly swollen."

"Yes, it looks rough, and he's drained," Rusty said. "He never asked Brody for more pain pills."

When they arrived at the townhouse, Iris greeted Gavin and Rusty at the door.

"Hello, Iris! It is good to see you again." Gavin planted a kiss on her cheek.

"Mr. Garrison," she answered sweetly.

Rusty hugged the woman. "How are you? And how is your son doing?"

"He's doing so much better since the transplant. We may get to keep him for a few more years," she said.

"That is so good to hear!" Rusty said. "Where is Dr. Brody?"

The Sapphire Ghost

"I am not sure, but he left a few hours ago. Might I ask where Mr. Medina is?" Iris inquired.

"He's gone to the hospital, and I don't know when he will arrive," Gavin replied.

"Oh no! I hope it is nothing serious!" Iris exclaimed.

"Nothing to worry about; he injured his arm and needs to have it looked at," Gavin reassured.

"Good. I rarely see him. Y'all work so hard," Iris said maternally. "I have a cold plate ready for you in the kitchen if you want something quick to eat. I'll prepare oyster stew and fried perch for dinner, which was Mr. Medina's request." Iris left them to relax.

Rusty took his bag up to his room. He took advantage of the few minutes alone to administer medicine for the pain he felt in his back. He opened his bag and took out a small black case with a vile of hydromorphone and a syringe. Rusty then rolled up his shirt sleeve, injected the medicine, and lay back on the bed. It had been a few weeks since he felt this bad. Julianne was not going to be pleased that Rusty was having symptoms again.

Nevertheless, he was happy to be here; this work was in his blood, even thicker than cancer. If he were going out soon, he might as well do it with all the vigor he could muster. Rusty picked up the phone to call home because he wanted to hear their voices.

Gavin also went to his room to relax before making himself a sandwich. He knew he needed to eat, but he was not feeling especially hungry after the first part of the helicopter ride. Luca had been respectful, but that was all. They would have to talk again.

Luca said he thought Gavin trusted him, and Gavin did utterly. But Gavin was also used to getting his way. The only other person who could do this to him was Helen; she had never told him everything. Gavin had been angry at Helen many times over her errors of omission. However, she was at a distance and could simply hang up the phone. Gavin took off his jacket and shoes and lay on the bed for a short nap.

An hour later, both Gavin and Rusty met up in the kitchen. Rusty was starving, and Gavin regained an appetite. Lemon pound cake sat on a glass platter on the counter. A fresh pot of coffee had just been brewed, and a tea kettle steamed. Rusty pulled the tray of meats and cheeses from the fridge. Gavin opened the bag of local artisan bread, which smelled amazing. *The smell of fresh bread is like a warm hug that you could eat,* he thought. Rusty made two sandwiches for himself and took a clump of grapes from a bowl on the counter. Gavin piled on the sliced turkey and Swiss cheese and added peppered chips to his plate. They sat at the long white table looking out onto the garden. Shortly, they heard footsteps coming down the hall, and they waited to see who it was.

Brody came into the kitchen and was startled by the sight of both Garrison and Rusty.

"Good afternoon!" Brody said.

"Good afternoon. How are things going up here?" Gavin asked pleasantly, taking another bite of the sandwich.

"Very well. I have completed the list Mr. Medina gave me," Brody said, smiling.

"That is good to hear," Gavin said after swallowing and noting he did not smell cigarettes. He then picked up the bottled water.

"Anything new on your end?" Brody asked.

"Nothing," Rusty said, finishing his first sandwich.

Brody got the feeling that something was up that they were not discussing.

Gavin and Rusty finished their meal, and Brody made a sandwich and brought it to the table.

"I am going to get fat if I stay here much longer. Iris made an amazing eggplant parmesan last night," Brody commented.

"Yes, she is a great lady. She has worked for Luca for about five years now. I did not understand why he kept a full-time housekeeper for the little he was here. But I believe he keeps her on to keep from losing her," Gavin said.

"Mr. Garrison, might I ask why Luca would own such an expensive house to never live in?" Brody questioned.

"Appearances. He looks good on paper. And you have to admit, this is quite an investment," Rusty interjected.

"Yes, it makes mine look dull," Brody said. "I'll have to step up my appearance."

"Not at all. Your family home is just fine, and it is who you are. This place serves two purposes: Luca's home and our local station since we often seem to be in D.C. Luca did not have a home when he came on board, and Helen arranged this for him," Gavin noted. "And Brody, please call me Gavin. You are part of the team now."

"Yes, sir. Mr. Garrison, sorry, *Gavin*. That might take some time." Brody smiled a broad smile.

"You have quit smoking," Gavin observed.

"Yes, I have," Brody said.

Brody sat with them in pleasant silence and ate. He wondered where Mr. Medina was, as neither of them mentioned him. After finishing his second sandwich, they reviewed the next day's plan. Their discussion was interrupted when they heard Iris greet Luca in the hallway.

Chapter Sixty-Five

Luca walked to the kitchen, where Iris said the others were eating. Luca's eyes were dull, but his arm no longer hurt. The attending physician gave him shots of morphine and cortisone. His head felt cloudy, and he intended to keep it that way. Luca observed them casually chatting. The room smelled of oyster stew simmering on the stove. Luca went to the wine rack, took down a bottle, and opened the cabinet for a glass. He walked past them and out to the garden without speaking to anyone. Gavin stood, followed him, and closed the garden door behind him.

"How long do you intend to avoid me?" Gavin asked.

"Unfortunately, it will not be long enough." Luca popped the cork on the bottle and poured himself a glass, and he downed the entire glass of wine like he was drinking water.

"Luca, stop. That is enough!" Gavin ordered.

"Nope, not nearly enough." He poured another glass and then sat in one of the rattan chairs.

"If you plan on staying out here with me, you might as well get yourself a glass," Luca noted wryly, the accent coming out.

"Very well," Gavin responded, then walked back to the house and grabbed another bottle and a glass from the cabinet.

"Are we invited to the party?" Brody asked.

"No," Rusty piped in before Gavin could say anything.

Gavin wandered to the grill where Luca kept the corkscrew and opened the second bottle. He set it on the table between the chairs with the first. He poured himself a glass from Luca's bottle and sat down.

"Do not say we need to talk." Luca was feeling the warmth of the wine.

"All right. That's fair. However, I expect you to tell me the name." Gavin sipped his wine.

Luca did not speak. And the silence was screaming, and Gavin could not stand Luca ignoring him. Luca sat there, finished his third glass, and reached for the second bottle for a refill. Gavin observed he was drinking to get drunk, which was something else Luca did not do. Gavin shook his head, unsure of where to go from here. Luca's thoughts drifted to the apartment in Destin. He wondered what the man was doing at this very moment. Luca closed his eyes and envisioned him watching a football game.

"What was the news at the hospital?" Gavin asked.

"I have a cut muscle, which they will repair with laser surgery tomorrow when we get back. Other than that, Dr. Brody did a fine job, and I should be as good as new in a week or so," Luca said.

"That is good news! Then everything will be back to normal," Gavin said.

"I am unsure anything will be *normal* again," Luca said, feeling bold from the wine. Luca was also out in the open and ready for Gavin's Ghost. But was Gavin ready for him?

"I need you to explain that statement," Gavin said, his eyebrows knitted, and concern written in his expression.

"Trust. You do not trust me. And if you don't, then I can't do my job. Protecting you is my only purpose. If you don't trust me, I can't do that," Luca said, not wanting to talk but somehow unable to stop himself.

"Luca, I trust you. I humiliated you, but I trust you," Gavin said, low and slow.

"Gavin, with all due respect, you did not humiliate me. You pushed me to a place you know I never want to go—a place I don't control. You put yourself, Rusty, and the pilot in danger. You were stupid!"

Luca sipped his fourth glass, and before Gavin could respond, Luca continued. "I understand I am currently omitting information, but you were awful. I just do not understand that, and I don't think you can explain it away!" Luca retorted. He swallowed the rest of the wine. "Stick to orders, those I understand. But don't pretend you care."

Without waiting for a response, Luca stood and headed back inside. He stopped long enough to open another bottle before taking the wine to his room and starting the shower. The fatigue was setting in, and the wine made his head light. Luca knew better than to stay in the garden, he was afraid of what would come out, but he was most afraid of *who* would come out. Luca was operating on a frayed leash, and it felt like it might break with the slightest tug. And he did not want to listen to anything else Gavin had to say. The conversation on the helicopter still felt raw, and the fact that Gavin pushed him to his breaking point bothered Luca; particularly that he was not better prepared and allowed that to happen.

Gavin finished his wine and returned to the house, thinking he needed something more potent. Brody observed them as they came inside. He noted that Luca was tenser than when he went out, even after consuming that wine. Gavin seemed more frustrated. Brody wondered what happened and thought, *for a man who I've been told never angered, there sure seems to be a lot of it in a short amount of time.*

Rusty rose to see Luca. He tapped on the door and asked if he could come in. Rusty did not hear any response and opened the door. He could hear the shower running, so he went to the chair by the window and sat.

This situation between Gavin and Luca cannot continue, he thought to himself. He would not be around much longer and could not leave seeing them at odds. The team members always had good relationships; even when they disagreed, relationships were put right after the discussion. Rusty felt down-hearted, and he knew Luca admired Gavin. Gavin went after him hard on the helicopter, knowing Luca was hurting. Luca walked back into the room in a towel around his waist within a few minutes.

"Rusty, please, not now. I'm beat, and between the morphine they gave me at the hospital and the wine, I will not be awake much longer."

Rusty heard the Hispanic accent. "Just listen, then, and sleep on it. Gavin knows he pushed you too hard. You earned a certain degree of respect by not caving. And, as bad as it was, know this: you passed your first test as the Warrior. That is something! You held your own and kept to your truth, which will make you a great Ghost one day. Do not hold onto this frustration. It will destroy everything you have built here, and I don't think you want that. You are the glue that holds everything together.

"Remember all the fights Gavin and I had over the years? Sometimes, he is difficult, but you learn to get past it and move on because this, what we do, is worth it. This experience is a lesson, and it will help you understand Gavin.

The Sapphire Ghost

"You and I can go where we like and do what we want in our downtime. The only world Gavin lives in is this one; the only one he has any control over is this one. And it is an exceptionally small world. For God's sake, he shot me for becoming overbearing, as he perceived it, the first year we were together. If I can get past that, you can forgive him and get past this."

Rusty had spoken with a warmth that was not customary. "You know you cannot walk away; you have committed your life."

"Rusty, I understand the Oath I took. Please don't patronize me. I may see things differently tomorrow. But right now, I am running on fumes. I need sleep." Luca's words began to slur as the wine and morphine took over. "I do love you both. All families have problems, right?" Luca pulled back the covers, dropped his towel, and fell into the bed.

Rusty left Luca's room because Luca was out when his head hit the pillow. Entering the living room, he found Gavin and Brody waiting—and so was Camille, Congressman Ashman's assistant and a member of Dark 9.

"Come here, girl, give me a hug!" Rusty lit up when he saw her.

"Rusty, I have missed that enormous face," she said as he wrapped her in a bear hug.

"Camille, you get prettier and prettier. And you have changed your hair. It looks nice."

Gavin studied Camille closely. Thoughts ran through his mind that he did not like. Camille had always been loyal, but Gavin wondered what conversations had occurred between Luca and Camille. Was she the one Luca was shielding? He shook his head. No, if she were, Luca would have told her to stay as far away as possible if, in fact, Luca was protecting her. But with Rusty knowing who this person was and his warm reaction to Camille, Rusty gave Gavin the answer he needed.

"I told her that Luca sustained an injury, and she would like to speak with him," Gavin said.

"I'm not sure how much talking he will be doing tonight. He has passed out, and they gave him morphine at the hospital, and then he came back and drank at least a bottle of wine," Rusty said.

"That's okay, thank you," Camille said. She walked down the hall, picked up the overnight bag she left by the stairs, and entered Luca's room.

Brody's eyebrows rose at the connection. Gavin watched Brody's reaction.

"Yes, she and Luca see each other when he is in town," Gavin said.

"I had just wondered if dating within the Order was permitted," Brody replied.

"What you do in your free time is your business. You are an adult, and I am not a babysitter. Luca is careful, as she's Congressman Ashman's assistant, and you must be equally careful. It may be the nation's capital, but it's a small town."

Chapter Sixty-Six

September 4

Brody was up and dressed by half-past six in the morning. It was to be his first Dossier, and he knew the take time was at 1:00 p.m.

Someone had already made coffee. Brody poured a cup and added sugar. He wondered who else was up because the house was still midnight quiet. He went to the living area and turned on the television to watch the news.

Luca got up earlier when he discovered Camille was in bed with him and made her coffee. He knew her alarm would go off at 6:00, and he planned on indulging in some alone time with her before that. Luca returned with a steaming cup with a touch of cream, just the way she liked it. Luca crossed to her side of the bed, set her mug on the nightstand, gently tugged the covers, and crawled behind her. Camille rolled over to snuggle up to his warmth.

"Good morning," she said into his chest.

"Good morning, lovely," Luca said, kissing her forehead.

Then she sat up, remembering what Gavin had said the night before. "I was told you're hurt. Are you okay?"

Luca sat up, silencing her with a kiss, and coaxed her back down. The way Luca kissed her made her completely pliable, and they enjoyed the early morning.

Camille was attracted to Luca the first time she met him, just after he started. However, he seemed uninterested in her because he rarely spoke. After buying this house, things changed. Luca noticed how she seemed to gravitate to him when the Order would come to town.

Rusty was the one who had brought her to the attention of the Ghost. Gavin paid for her Harvard education and gave her a sense of belonging. Luca was different; too quiet, giving her the feeling he held a deep, dark secret. She learned later that he was not secretive, just incredibly shy. She found that endearing. Plus, he never boxed her in. Given the work they performed, they had exactly what they needed.

After a shower where they enjoyed more of each other, Luca answered her concerns.

"I'll be fine, and it's nothing for you to worry about. Stay focused today; we need you." Luca dabbed her body dry with a towel.

"All right, but I wish you had called and warned me. I do not like finding this kind of stuff out second-hand," she complained as he moved the towel down her neck, taking small nibbles along the way.

Luca enjoyed the sounds she made when she was aroused and persuaded her to cry out softly as she curled her fingers in his wet hair. Luca firmly braced her body with both arms as she went limp.

"I have missed you," he said when he stood and kissed her again.

"And I have missed you," Camille said as she leaned against his chest.

Twenty minutes later, they were dressed and headed to the kitchen. They passed Brody watching the news.

"Morning, Brody. I hope you slept well," Luca said.

"I slept very well. How are you feeling this morning?" Brody asked, following them into the kitchen.

"I slept like the dead. The cortisone and the morphine did the trick." Luca poured himself a cup of black coffee.

The coffee was good, strong, and from Colombia. Iris ordered his coffee beans directly from a supplier there. He guessed she thought that, since he was Colombian, he would prefer the coffee. Luca so appreciated the gesture that he never told her that buying from a local coffee shop would do as well.

Brody watched Camille and Luca interact. If he had not seen her go into his room the night before, he would never have known they were together. Then he saw the affection.

"I'm going for a run," Luca said and kissed Camille.

Luca tugged the sling over his shoulder and headed for the door. For the first time in days, he stretched and found real energy. He set off on a five-mile loop. Luca headed out the door and down 30th Street NW toward Georgetown Waterfront Park. His mind was still unsettled from yesterday, but he was determined to clear things up. Gavin unleashed the Ghost on him and brought a fury to the surface that had already been threatening to crawl out. Luca's mind was clear, and the cars and houses he ran past were bright and distinct. The air smelled of car exhaust and the murky water from the Chesapeake and Ohio Canal. Luca ran until his mind was ready to face the consequences of what he had planned. It was now or never because he would not go through that with Gavin again. This may be the day he found out if there was a hell.

Gavin was the next to enter the kitchen. He arrived before 7:00, greeted everyone, turned on the stove for the tea kettle, and took down a cup and a box of Earl Gray. He was wearing a bespoke Milano gray suit.

"Brody, I am glad you are up. I have arranged for you to meet with our clothier here in D.C. I want you to choose half a dozen suits and get sized. Brandon will ship them when they are finished." Gavin fished a notepad from a drawer and wrote down the address. "He is expecting you at 8:00 a.m."

"Yes, sir, but I can buy my suits," Brody replied.

Gavin gave Brody the once-over, noting he wore a lackluster black suit that hung lifeless on his tall, thin form.

"Not like these. Brandon places a special micro-weave inside, similar to Kevlar but lighter and stronger. Leave it to the Germans to make such an amazing product. You are only here because there is less than a zero chance of you being shot, and I take your health and protection very seriously. If you want Armani, you will have to wait until we go to Italy. Brandon can place the material in those as well."

"Yes, sir," Brody said.

"Listen to him, son," Rusty piped in as he came into the kitchen dressed in an immaculate black Armani with a light pinstripe, a beautiful black and white tie, and a crisp, white shirt. "Consider these suits your best friends." He tugged back the jacket, showing the lining. "It does not mean you will not wear the vest when we are on assignment; just an added layer of protection."

Rusty went to pour the last cup of coffee from the pot and started another one. "Where is Luca this morning, Camille?"

"He went for a run; he will be back shortly," she said comfortably.

"How is he this morning?" Gavin asked.

Camille's eyebrows arched at the question. "He seems to be in a good mood." She tried to conceal a smile behind her coffee mug.

Gavin looked over at Rusty and shook his head. Brody felt the tension returning. He brought up the football and talked about the teams playing the coming weekend. Brody and Rusty debated who was the best quarterback in the league and seemed to enjoy the light banter. Gavin observed that Brody appeared less tense and had good humor about him. Gavin felt Brody was relaxing into his new role.

About thirty minutes later, Luca returned to the house. Luca had tied the black hoodie around his waist, and the white tank clung to him. He went directly to his room and shut the door.

Gavin poured water over a second teabag, cut another piece of lemon, and squeezed it into the steam. He waited to see what happened next. Gavin was not looking forward to the imminent cold shoulder, and he needed Luca today, and he needed him undistracted by their upset.

Luca exited his room and headed toward the voices in the kitchen. He stood in the entry and watched Camille and Rusty carry on. Then he looked in Gavin's direction and noted Gavin was staring directly at him.

"Good morning," Luca said pleasantly. He dressed in a jet-black Armani suit matching the curls on his collar.

"Good morning, Luca," Gavin said. "How are you feeling?"

"Much better, thank you," Luca said evenly.

Luca smiled at Gavin, walked to the coffee pot that had just finished brewing, and poured some into his mug. Luca was speaking to Gavin, and Rusty thought this was a start.

"Everything is in line for today; we just need to be on time. Brody has taken care of the distraction, and, I might add, it is a custom job." Luca spoke proudly and smiled at Brody. "Camille will handle the cameras, so we are in good hands there. Rusty will serve as overwatch on the street. Brody will be with me." Luca thought he had covered all the critical angles.

Now, this is the Luca I need today, the one in command, Gavin thought. Luca was professional and showed no hint of animosity.

"Oh, and Brody will go with me to the hospital when this is over, just in case I react to the anesthesia or need to find my way back home," Luca said over the brim of his cup.

Brody's expression turned hard. This was the first he had heard of this. Brody knew Luca had gone to the hospital to be checked but not that Luca was going back to have an anesthesia-required procedure. Brody nodded; he heard him.

Luca watched Brody's reaction and saw he did not waver. That was the response he wanted, and he needed Brody to learn to just do and not question, as that was how Gavin wanted things done.

Brody glanced at the clock and headed to the door. "I'm sorry, but I have to go. I have an appointment."

"Where is he going?" Luca asked.

"To the tailor," Gavin responded.

"That was a quick appointment, sir," Luca said.

"Yes, I called Brandon last night, and he agreed to size him this morning," Gavin responded.

"Sir, would you mind walking with me to the garden?" Luca asked, setting his mug on the counter and heading to the back of the kitchen. Gavin followed.

Luca stood in the back of the garden and leaned on the brick wall. He gazed at the neighboring house with pretty yellow flowers in pots on the covered porch. Although Luca had prepared himself, a dread built in his chest. If the Ghost decided to make another appearance, he might be committing professional suicide. However, just like Gavin, Luca had a point to make and intended to ensure Gavin heard him. He never wavered in his loyalty; if Gavin wanted to question that, there was only one reply.

Gavin wondered if Luca would reveal the name and return to peace. Gavin cleared his throat as he studied Luca's composure and concluded that was not what was on Luca's mind. Luca was presenting a commanding front with none of the reluctance from yesterday.

Luca spoke first; his back still turned to Gavin. "I need you to understand. London was a one-time event, and you were unwell, and I won't go behind your back to do anything that you should do yourself. And I want to be clear as glass when I say I no longer feel it to be in my best interest to take over your role as the Ghost.

"I do respect you, sir, and I have given you everything I have and only have one more thing to give. If I don't have your trust, you can take that as well," Luca said in a low and contrite tone, and he spoke low enough to force Gavin to listen rather than think.

When Luca turned around, he appeared to Gavin more like a politician than a security agent: his curls meticulously tamed, the rich black suit perfect, his hands clasped in front of him. But there was something different in his stance; a power, one of quiet intensity. Perhaps it was just a shadow from the clouds, but Gavin thought there was a sense of overcast on Luca's chiseled features.

"Luca, I do trust you. You would not be on this team if I didn't. I don't like secrets, though. However you dress them up. Even if you feel that keeping something from me is for my own good, that is hard for me. I became harsh, but I don't mistrust you. This information will be the last secret you keep from me. I gave Rusty only one, and this is yours."

"I'm not keeping a secret. I'll tell you as soon as we finish this today. It's delayed information. I don't keep secrets, sir." Even more quietly, he began. "Gavin, I have something to say, and I need you to listen carefully. I do not like conflict, and we will not do this again." Luca paused.

Gavin tilted his head to the side when he heard Luca's direct words, which sounded like a warning. He looked straight at the razor-sharp young man, and Gavin felt he was hearing the threatening tone Brody said he noticed that day in London.

"If my job is to be obedient beyond question, you have the wrong man. I refuse to watch you self-destruct, and I will not stay around to see that happen, but I will let the choice be yours. There is only one way to absolve me of my commitment to you and Arcadia." Luca's resolve was evident. "All you have to do is ask me once more, knowing you must take my life because Arcadia won't allow me to walk away. It can only be you, Gavin, because if I leave, you know no one will ever find me."

A chill crept up the back of Gavin's neck as he sat and looked hard at the darkness that enshrouded Luca. Although he always wanted to know everything, he wouldn't ask again when faced with what Luca expected of him in

The Sapphire Ghost

return. Gavin could see Luca was not posturing. He seemed ready to give him the name he wanted, but that would come with a sacrifice Gavin was unwilling to make. Luca was prepared to die today by Gavin's hand. Gavin had not seen this degree of total commitment from anyone, ever.

Luca stepped forward and placed his 9mm on the table before Gavin. "You own my life; you should own my death as well."

Rusty was watching from the windows. He froze. What was Luca doing? A fear hit his chest as the meaning dawned on him. He started to open the door.

Gavin watched as Luca slid the gun over the table and stepped back to the wall. Luca even placed a silencer on it. Gavin stared at the black gun and investigated a similar blackness in Luca's eyes, whom he cared for deeply. Gavin realized that what he had done backfired so severely that Luca no longer wanted to train to be the next Ghost. Instead, Luca was ready to die because he felt he had lost Gavin's trust. He had seriously misjudged Luca's commitment. It was not the clouds that created a shadow in Luca's features. Gavin belatedly recognized the difference in personalities.

"You see a distinction between secrets and withholding information, and maybe that is true," Gavin said and nodded to Luca.

"Gavin, I treasure you as if you had raised me. You gave me life when I was broken, and I did not think I had anything to offer the world. I would never betray you or willingly do anything to hurt you. If I had done as you asked, I would have placed you in harm's way. Can you not see that?" Luca asked compassionately.

"Yes, I believe I do," Gavin said. He stood, walked to Luca, and placed his hands on either side of Luca's face, then touched his forehead to his. "I see *you*, Luca."

Rusty stood by the door and watched the exchange outside. He finally breathed when Gavin approached Luca, and the gun remained on the table.

Chapter Sixty-Seven

Dossier 248

Dr. Wasson's lab conducted research on humans. Helen's fact sheet indicated he was currently studying an abortion shot. Most of his subjects were young girls he apparently impregnated himself. Helen had been unable to determine the number in the doctor's current study, but Gavin intended to find out today.

The large town car arrived at the country club at 12:40, and the lunch crowd was already inside. Luca and Brody exited the car and walked up the steps to await Dr. Wasson's arrival. Even with these cooler temperatures, the golf course was still lush. Several men were playing on the green across from the parking lot.

"Do you want to talk about it?" Rusty asked his friend.

"About what?"

"Do not be coy, Gavin; it does not suit you," Rusty replied.

"Luca asked me to choose between knowing the name and killing him. If I wanted to know today, he would have told me. But he expected me to relieve him of his duty to the Order permanently."

"Damn!" Rusty was shocked.

"Indeed," Gavin responded. "His dedication continues to surprise me. That boy would willingly hand over his life to me." He pondered the thought.

A blue Lexus sedan pulled into the parking lot five minutes later. Gavin looked down at the picture in his portfolio and recognized Mr. Galinsky as he stepped out of the driver's side of the car and buttoned his short blue wool jacket. Dr. Wasson got out of the other side in a brown blazer.

"He's headed your way," Gavin said as he placed a finger on the comm to open the microphone.

"I have eyes on them," Luca responded.

Brody returned to the car and got into the driver's seat. "Luca has asked that I bring the car around the back."

The Sapphire Ghost

Brody sat in the car, idle for the next five minutes. Luca followed the men inside the club. Then, they all heard the large mufflers of motorcycles begin to enter the clubhouse drive. Brody backed the car out and waited for them to get closer. The roar of the noisy bikes grew closer. The three golfers paused their game on the putting green to the left of the road. They shielded their eyes to watch a long stream of vulgar bikes ride into the private club. Brody pulled the car in front of the first bike and headed to the maintenance road around the restaurant's rear. He stopped by the back door. Brody turned off the car, stepped out, then opened the door for Gavin.

The bikers rumbled through, revving their engines and creating thunderous noise. At least forty bikes circled the clubhouse drive, and more were curling into the entrance.

"The patrons are heading to the windows," Luca said into the comm. "It is time to get Wasson out."

Gavin led Brody into the restaurant's back and through the kitchen to the dining room. Gavin locked in on Luca, studying the room near the hostess table. The tables were covered with lunch dishes that nervously trembled on white linen tablecloths, and chairs were cast about in every direction. Several customers had walked out to view the parade in astonishment. The sounds were deafening in the ordinarily quiet place. Luca noticed the two men on his left looking out the window. Luca gave Gavin a nod, and together, they approached Dr. Wasson and Mr. Galinsky, with Brody close behind.

"Brody, I need you beside me now," Luca said quietly into the mic. Within an instant, Brody was in position. Acknowledging that this situation was handled, Gavin strolled out and waited by the car. Luca was on his game and did not need a monitor.

"I will take the first one. Follow my lead and get the man in the blue jacket," Luca instructed Brody when he was close enough.

Luca took the knife from his belt, grabbed Dr. Wasson by the arm, and positioned the knife at his back. "Walk," Luca said sternly. Brody touched his gun to Galinsky's back and did the same. They led them out into the sun. Dr. Wasson appeared shocked but said nothing.

"The Ghost and I have a deal!" Mr. Galinsky kept pleading with Brody, but Brody said nothing.

"It is so good to meet you, Dr. Wasson. I have heard such horrible things about you," Gavin said sardonically as he stood with his hat clasped before him, the sun casting an iridescence across his tanned features.

"Who are you?" Dr. Wasson asked.

"I believe you already know, as I am sure you have received my package. Let us take a ride," the Ghost said. "Brody, get him in the car and give him the shot."

Brody shoved Dr. Wasson in beside Rusty. Next, he climbed in, sat across from Wasson, and took out the prepared syringe. "This may sting a little," Brody said as he pushed the tall, thin man back against the seat and inserted the needle into his neck. Brody got back out of the car, leaving the doctor with Rusty.

"Luca, I need to know how many have suffered from the doctor's current experiments," Gavin said to Luca. "Then take care of him."

Gavin stood outside the car, examining the surroundings before he opened the door. Brody stood beside the car and watched Luca take the short man by the arm and lead him away. Mr. Galinsky placed his free hand in his pocket, and Brody saw the small derringer he pulled out. Luca watched as the man brought out the rusted, stubby, double-shot pistol and pointed the old gun in Gavin's direction. Brody headed to Gavin, and he held out a hand for Brody to stay put.

Luca was more concerned the gun would explode than deliver a bullet to Gavin. He shoved Galinsky to the ground as it fired. Luca dove to the ground when he heard the shot and saw the backside of the gun explode in Galinsky's hand. Pieces of the weapon embedded themselves into Galinsky's hand and face. The man screamed in pain as Luca stood and jerked him back to his feet.

"Answer my question," Luca growled, watching blood stream down the man's head and pool into his left eye. Bits of his upper lip hung like blood-soaked slivers of beef, exposing his teeth. "How many subjects have been killed in Dr. Wasson's current research study?"

Mr. Galinsky reeled in agony and looked down at where he was now missing two fingers. Luca shook the man.

"One-hundred and eighteen," he managed to say through partial lips.

"Thank you," Luca said, stepping close enough to pierce his heart quickly.

Brody observed how Luca inserted the knife into Mr. Galinsky's chest and allowed him to fall quietly to the ground. In the deafening noise of the motorcycles, Galinsky's screams were never heard. Luca wiped off the blade on Galinsky's jacket, casually dusted himself off, and headed to the car.

Brody did not know what he expected, but he found Luca's demeanor eerie. Luca got into the car beside Gavin, and Brody returned to the driver's seat and drove toward the doctor's house, which was about an hour away.

"Camera's back on in five," Luca said to Camille via the comm.

"His last one was number one-eighteen, sir," Luca told Gavin when he closed the door.

"That's a lot more than I expected," Gavin added thoughtfully. "I did not think the gun would fire."

"I was afraid it would," Luca responded.

"That could have been much worse," Rusty noted.

"Yes, if it had been a larger caliber," Luca said, feeling where a piece of the gun's shrapnel had grazed the side of his face, leaving a thin red line. He wiped it away with the handkerchief.

Rusty looked over at the sleeping doctor lying back in the seat, his mouth wide open.

It took just forty-five minutes to get to Primrose Road. The house was a mid-century modern brick on a huge lot full of trees. The front yard was littered with an orange carpet of leaves. Brody drove directly under the carport and got out of the car. He went to the other side, lifted the unconscious man from the seat, and effortlessly draped the doctor over his right shoulder. Luca went to the side door, letting the others into the house. Rusty followed and looked around outside, then closed and locked the door.

"Camille, are you here?" Luca asked into his mic.

"Yes, Luca, I can see you. The setup is in the master bathroom, and it's through the den to the right," Camille said.

Brody heard the directions through his earwig and started through the den, which looked like it had not been updated since the eighties. Rusty stood by the back door to keep a lookout, simultaneously viewing the tablet showing the cameras' views with Camille. He did not mind stepping back and allowing Luca to run the team. Rusty enjoyed watching him direct and train Brody, much as he had with Luca. He was showing him, not telling him, which was the only real way to learn. Remarkably, Brody seemed like clay waiting to be molded and giving his full attention to every task.

"Luca, remind me to let Helen know I want this house," Gavin said into the comm.

"Why on earth would you want this place?" Rusty piped in.

"It has potential. Did you see the lot size? It is absurd for D.C.!" Gavin exclaimed.

"Yes, sir; I will remind you," Luca replied, holding back a laugh.

As the man stirred, Brody took him off his shoulder and placed him in the oversized tub, which had not seen a cleaning for some time. He removed Dr. Wasson's jacket and shirt as were his instructions. Gavin grabbed a wooden chair from the kitchen and followed Brody.

Gavin entered the generous bathroom and positioned the chair in front of the tub. He watched as the doctor emerged from sedation.

Dr. Wasson looked up and around, soon realizing he was in his bathroom. A tall, light-skinned black man was sitting on the corner of the tub, watching him. Brody took a small flashlight from his pocket and shined the light into the doctor's eyes.

"He's back, sir," Brody announced. Then he stepped around Gavin to the door.

"Welcome back, Dr. Wasson," Gavin said. "I hear you have been busy."

"And you are?" Dr. Wasson asked, rubbing at the injection site on his neck.

"The Ghost, and I'm here for information on your supplier," Gavin said.

"What supplier?" Dr. Wasson asked.

The Sapphire Ghost

"The girls you use for your experiments, of course. Brody, would you hand me the scalpels, please." He reached over his shoulder without looking to take the small paper-wrapped blades Brody placed in his open palm.

"How do you know about them?" Dr. Wasson asked.

"I know a lot about you and what you do in that place. I know you hide a lot in that lab of yours," Gavin said. "I heard you have killed one hundred and eighteen young girls currently."

"No one will miss them; they are disposable," the doctor replied arrogantly.

"No child is disposable. And you are a sick, dangerous man to have walking around in public, acting as if you hold some superior gene. What you do to those girls is unfathomable! So, I ask again, whom do you contact to get the children?" the Ghost asked as he tore the paper slowly away from one of the scalpels.

"I receive a text telling me two or three are available at a location, and I pick them up," Dr. Wasson said. "It is never from the same number."

Luca ran through the numbers on the doctor's phone. There were not many, and yes, the numbers were all different.

"It is true, sir. All the numbers are different, but they all have New York City area codes," Luca stated.

"We will play a game I like to call Live or Die. Which one happens is up to you." Gavin twirled the thin silver blade between his thumb and middle finger. "One-hundred and eighteen cuts by your hand, and I will let you go, or one-hundred and eighteen well-placed cuts that will most definitely cause a lot of pain and kill you by my hand. Which do you choose?" Gavin asked, thinking back to the choice that Luca had given him just that morning—which had not been a choice at all.

Dr. Wasson reached for the scalpel, and Gavin placed it in his hand. Dr. Wasson started with a slight slash across his stomach, and the blood began to stream. The large dose of Heparin blood thinner had taken effect. Gavin and Luca watched as the man inflicted another nine cuts across his abdomen.

"Only a hundred and eight more to go," Gavin said.

Dr. Wasson's hand shook so severely he could not place the blade against his skin again. He drew several deep breaths as he made two quick cuts. The

Ghost sat back in his chair, patiently watching the doctor draw out his death. The light-colored pants he wore were now soaked dark brown. The doctor trembled for a few minutes, holding the blade against his flesh, unable to move it again. His cuts were light, but the blood was dark red as it escaped each slice.

"Here, let me encourage you," Gavin said and stood.

"I can do this!" Dr. Wasson cried.

"Quickly, doctor, I do not have all day," Gavin said as he sat back down. He knew Wasson would not make it to the final cut, and he might not even survive the next twenty, as his skin was already turning a light shade of gray. The man was not the model of health; too skinny, showing every rib.

Dr. Wasson took the blade and tried to steady it in his right hand. He grew weak and felt the pain of each careful cut. The fear stampeded his chest as Wasson could not figure out why he was bleeding so badly. He counted off ten more cuts to his left arm and stopped, inhaling deeply several times. The bottom of the tub was running red, and his pants were no longer dry or light brown.

Gavin knew minor cuts were far more painful than deep ones because of the nerves that sit on the surface. He saw that given the way the doctor's hand was shaking, he would be unable to inflict many more into himself without dropping the scalpel.

"Take a break, doctor. Would you get the man some juice?" Gavin requested over his shoulder.

Brody left the room to see if Dr. Wasson had juice in the fridge, and he found a small bottle of grapefruit juice sitting beside a half-eaten bowl of what could have been soup. Indeed, this man did not have to squeeze his pennies, but he was a little miserly.

When Brody returned to the bathroom, he saw the doctor's head slumped onto his chest. The pool of blood he sat in was nearing a liter. He went over to the seemingly unconscious man and touched the left hand resting on the side of the tub. With icy cold fingers, Dr. Wasson suddenly grabbed Brody's hand boldly and attempted to jab Brody with the blade. Gavin watched as Brody grabbed the doctor's wrist, quickly twisting his other wrist out of the doctor's grip, then smoothly handed him the bottle of juice he still held. Luca watched but did not move. Brody struggled with the idea he was not supposed to save this man from a painful death but allow him to sit and suffer. It went against his medical code; however, this man was a malicious killer—of children, no less.

Dr. Wasson sat back in the tub, laid the scalpel on the side, and barely sipped at the bottle's contents.

"Let's start again. You only have seventy-eight more to go," Gavin said as Brody returned to the doorway.

"No. I'm done." The doctor slid the blade across his wrist. He decided that ending it now was the better of his two options, as neither would allow him to live.

"Well, that is anticlimactic," Gavin noted with irony.

"Go to hell," Dr. Wasson said as he felt the life leaving him.

"You'll beat me there," Gavin rebutted. He stood and leaned against the sink to wait until the doctor was past the point of rescue. After watching the blood leak down the drain for a moment, Gavin placed the gray envelope with the perfectly outlined information on the bathroom sink so the police would find the other girls and decommission the lab.

Luca watched Gavin and thought to himself, *this was not the worst I have seen.* But he knew worse was coming once Gavin knew who betrayed him.

Gavin seemed satisfied that death was on her way for the doctor and motioned to Luca that it was time to go. He could've had Brody stop the blood flow and continue the torture. Luca followed Gavin through the house. Gavin wondered when Luca intended to reveal the name, and he was hesitant to ask, but that name was why he had not taken a more prolonged approach with the doctor.

Luca took the folded paper from his pocket, handed it to Gavin, and strode out. He put on a pair of dark sunglasses before heading to the car where Brody and Rusty waited.

"Camille, the scene is ready to be sterilized, and the cameras removed. Thank you," Luca said into the comm, and he shut off the mic before she replied.

Chapter Sixty-Eight

Gavin stopped and gently opened the paper to reveal a single name. Luca had kept his word. As Gavin stepped out of the house, he examined Luca. Although sunglasses covered his eyes, Gavin could see Luca's expressionless countenance. They got in the car with Rusty and Brody.

Gavin was noticeably quiet on the way back to the townhouse. Luca nodded to Rusty, who looked questioningly and down at the paper Gavin still held. Rusty's eyebrows lifted in acknowledgment. He knew Rusty thought the same thing: betrayals are always worse than any Dossier.

Luca reflected on the conversation that morning and watched Gavin look out the window impassively. The good news was he had not shot him, but the bad news was he had revealed a buried part of himself.

"Rusty, the team in Dremmond has cleared your plane. Would you mind calling your pilot and asking her to bring it up here? We are still waiting on ours to clear inspection," Luca said, thinking now was as good a time as any to broach the subject of the jet.

"No, ask Marshal, please," Gavin said without looking at them. Finding out that it was Marshal was disturbing, and Gavin had always been good to him, even helping get his son, who was special needs, into a specialized school.

"Sir?" Luca questioned.

"Thanks to you, whoever he's working with thinks we are still in Dremmond, and they will have to scramble to get to D.C.," Gavin explained.

"I will have someone at the airport to watch the jet until we leave," Luca said.

"Fine," Gavin said.

Brody drove to the front of the townhouse, and Luca stepped out and opened Gavin's door for him.

"I need to get to the hospital and get this over with." Luca glanced down at his arm as Gavin stepped out of the car.

"Wait a few more minutes, please, and show me what you have on Marshal." Gavin's voice was disturbingly deep.

"I can do that," Luca said. He was relieved this was out but concerned about where Marshal's head would end up.

The last man disloyal to the Ghost was a bookkeeper named Wilson. Gavin had been fond of him until, while handling some assets, Wilson transferred funds into his own account. Wilson's head was found dangling from a flagpole in Little Havana.

Luca let everyone into the house. He went to his room to retrieve his laptop. Gavin and Brody waited for him in the kitchen. "Where is Rusty?" Luca asked as he set the computer up.

"He wasn't feeling well and went to lie down," Gavin said, motioning for Luca to start.

"Here is the video Helen sent me after discovering the deposit of money into an account in the Caymans in Marshal's wife's name." Luca played the video, which showed one of the construction workers meeting with Marshal the night they had arrived back in Dremmond.

Gavin watched the video intently. He saw the man with sandy blond hair and a light red mustache get into the car he'd bought for him. The corner of Gavin's mouth twitched, and those deep eleven forehead lines merged into a V. Luca paused the video.

Gavin sat back and closed his eyes, replaying the video behind them. *Luca had been right not to tell me before the Dossier.* Opening his eyes, Gavin studied Luca and instantly understood something else.

"Luca, you and Brody go get that procedure over with. We will talk when you return," Gavin said, dismissing them.

"Brody, thank you for doing such a great job on my arm. They need to repair a muscle," Luca stated, not wanting Brody to feel he had not done well.

"I did the best I could under the circumstances. I didn't realize you guys could go to a regular hospital," Brody said as they stepped outside, and Brody lifted his hand at an oncoming cab.

"I could go to a convent, but I have a real identity so that I can go anywhere I please. And that would be *we*, not *you guys*. Get used to it," Luca corrected him as the cab stopped.

"This Marshal person, is he special? Can you tell me about what is going on?" Brody asked once in the car.

"Sorry, Brody. I forgot you weren't here when I discovered the person who sold us out," Luca said. *How could I have been so distracted?* he thought to himself until he remembered the nightmare it had been to get here. "It was Marshal, our pilot. That is why I called you the day before we arrived and asked that you be extra careful and watch your back."

"That's not good! I can only imagine how Gavin would react to such deception." Brody rubbed the stubble on his chin.

"Indeed, you absolutely cannot imagine," Luca replied. "Just a word of advice: do not ever keep anything from Gavin because he doesn't take it well at all."

"Would that be what has been going on between you two?" Brody asked.

"Yes, that is part of it," Luca said and became quiet as they turned into the hospital.

Back at the townhouse, Gavin sat in the garden nursing a scotch. Refreshed, Rusty came out to join him. Gavin thought about the distance that seemed to have widened between himself and Luca. It had hurt when Luca said to issue orders but pretended not to care. He did care; he cared very much. Then, the one-sided conversation this morning when Luca had laid his life at his feet. What was he going to do to make it right?

"I'm assuming Luca and Brody have left for the hospital?" Rusty asked.

"Yes."

"You have that look again," Rusty observed. "What has happened now?"

"Rusty, how often have you seen Luca upset, much less angry?" Gavin asked.

"I'm not sure where you are going with this," Rusty said thoughtfully. This was not the discussion he expected, and he anticipated Gavin would want to speak about Marshal.

"He's angry, but it's not only with me," Gavin surmised.

"Elaborate."

"The first time he lost his cool was the morning he was stabbed. That's when everything went sideways. Today, he's been his usual self, but there seems to be a storm brewing in him. I can almost smell it. He is angry at himself for not paying enough attention and being unable to read what was happening. He is angry that King's men got to him. And it is all because of Marshal. Rusty, it has occurred to me that this is his first betrayal. Luca kept that information from me, not out of wanting me to focus on this morning's Dossier. But from a need for me to focus on Marshal—and give him my personal brand of attention," Gavin concluded.

"When you put it like that, it does make sense," Rusty responded. "He wants you to make Marshal pay."

"I think I'll let Luca have him. That will serve two purposes. One, it will give Luca the outlet I think he needs, and two, it will reconnect the trust he feels we have lost." Gavin sipped and then shook the ice in the glass.

"That is substantial, Gavin. I figured you would already have found a place to cut Marshal into pieces. Can you really give over control to Luca and feel satisfied? This is King we are talking about."

"Yes, I need to train my successor and rebuild that connection. He said he no longer wanted to be the Ghost, and I couldn't accept that because he was angry with me and how I treated him. Marshal didn't just betray me; he betrayed all of us, especially Luca, and I want to let him have this one. More importantly, he needs this," Gavin said.

Chapter Sixty-Nine

Luca and Brody returned to the townhouse a little before six. Gavin thought Luca looked in good spirits despite still appearing drowsy from the surgery. Gavin wondered if it were because Luca felt Gavin would deal with the object of his fury.

Several hours later, Iris prepared bacon cheeseburgers for Luca and Rusty and large salads with buttered French bread for Brody and Gavin.

Luca finished off his second burger and downed the rest of the beer.

"Luca, may we speak?" Gavin asked.

Luca looked at Gavin and gave him a sideways smile. *I've done quite enough talking to last a year*, he thought. "Yes, sir," Luca said with an exhaled breath.

"Sit; this is not something I believe I should keep from the team," Gavin said. Luca sat, now puzzled. "I have decided what I am going to do about Marshal."

"Okay." Luca's eyebrows rose because Gavin rarely relayed anything to the team this early.

"I'm going to do nothing." Gavin watched Luca's eyes and saw the bite of rage he expected. "You are."

"What?" Luca exclaimed.

"I'm leaving Marshal to you. As my successor and, as much as I would like to take out my anger on him, I think you deserve this more," Gavin said.

"Your successor? Sir, I believe . . ." Luca started.

"Yes, you're the future Ghost there is no question it's what you are meant for. I refuse to accept what you said in anger," Gavin said.

Brody watched the exchange. *Luca would be taking over for the Ghost!* That would mean he would be the one to ensure the Ghost remained invisible, and he did not have those skills! Brody's mind twisted at the thought. He had missed a few things.

Luca stood and paced back and forth between the table and the door. He was unsure what to think of this. *What was this exactly? Some kind of test?* Luca rubbed the back of his head. *Did I not just tell Gavin this morning that I would not be taking the role of Ghost?*

"I need to think," Luca declared and left the kitchen.

"That went rather well, don't you think?" Gavin smiled, looking at Rusty.

Brody found Luca sitting on the pommel horse in the basement an hour later. "Would you like to talk? I have been trained to listen and not offer advice," Brody said.

"Do you trust me, Brody?" Luca asked.

"Yes," Brody responded.

"Do you see me being a Ghost?"

"Yes and no. I mean, I know you are more than capable, but you do not seem to have a mean streak, which I think the job requires."

Luca's lips curled at Brody's observation, "Everyone has a dark side, Brody. I have learned that through the years, and mine is just not as apparent as Gavin's. Or as deeply entrenched," Luca said as he spun down from the pommel horse.

Luca gauged his arm, wondering if it would hold him. The doctors said he could resume normal activities in a few days.

"I would not recommend what you are contemplating," Brody said.

"You have not been around long enough to know what I am contemplating."

"I learn quickly," Brody replied. "Do not make me pull my doctor hat out again."

Luca walked in circles around the room. He really needed to release this pent-up energy but saw no way to do it without more damage.

"That man could have stabbed me just about anywhere," Luca grunted before executing a perfect one-handed summersault.

"Luca, may I ask you something serious?" Brody asked.

"Might as well. Serious seems to be in abundance these days." Luca walked over to the bench where Brody sat.

"I do not have the skills to keep you safe. Do you think I'm the best fit?"

"You're referring to the technical stuff, I am assuming?"

"Yes, it's always been a weakness," Brody replied.

"I have those skills in spades, and I will teach you what you need to know. If I wanted a techie, I would have found one. I need your level head and ability to see the whole picture, including the pieces that aren't there." Luca saw the panic in Brody's eyes. "I must have your total dedication if I am to go forward. I cannot risk any less. I would still choose you. Don't question yourself; I don't."

"You already have my commitment," Brody promised. "Rusty told me you were my job, which may be bigger than I expected. What do you plan to do?" Brody asked.

"I have no idea. I've never had to think about what to do because Gavin has always set the rules," Luca replied honestly. "In London, I was driven by forces outside myself and had a small window to get to Steve Bains. This man, well, it's different—I know him."

"That would make it more difficult but also easier. I mean, especially from someone you expect to trust," Brody commented.

Luca thought for a few minutes. He gazed at Brody, his comment on expected trust. *Yes, I chose well.*

"It would seem so. But I cannot focus on that until we are somewhere where Gavin is secure. He is always going to be my priority."

"I'll do whatever you need me to do. I hope you know that," Brody said.

"I do know, and Gavin has plans for you next week. From what I understand, it is an interesting assignment."

"Care to tell me what it is?" Brody asked.

"No, I will allow Gavin that pleasure," Luca said with a smile.

Chapter Seventy

Luca lay in his bed that night, tossing and turning. He wished Camille had been able to come by to distract him, but she had flown out for a function with Congressman Ashman.

Rusty had not seemed himself the last couple of days. Luca worried that what was going on between Gavin and himself troubled Rusty. Then he remembered the cancer and realized Rusty would never admit he was not feeling well.

Unable to sleep, Luca got out of bed. He pulled on a pair of pajama pants and went to the kitchen. He had a sweet tooth and went looking for Iris' lemon pound cake.

"Having a hard time sleeping?" Gavin watched Luca rummage through the fridge.

"Oh! You surprised me!" Luca stepped back and closed the door. He looked over to Gavin, sitting alone in the dark living room.

"That was not my intention," Gavin said.

"What's on your mind?" Luca asked, grabbing a bottled water off the counter.

"So many things."

Luca switched on the lamp beside the chair. "Want to talk?"

"I am concerned about Rusty. He was uncomfortable today; I could see it on his face. And he's been worried about us," Gavin said. He decided to ask the question directly. "Luca, will we be all right?"

"In time, I believe we will. I know Rusty has been concerned about our situation," Luca said and sat down, twisting the cap on and off his bottle. "I apologize, sir. I'm not sure what has been going on with me," he added.

"I owe you an apology. It was wrong to take you across that line, and it will not happen again." Gavin rested his chin on his hand. "But I see what is going on with you, and I think I understand."

"Really, want to clue me in?" Luca asked, half-smiling, trying to feel that familiar bond.

"Betrayal is a hard pill to swallow, and this is the first one for you here," Gavin said.

Luca did not respond; he leaned back in the chair and stared across the room. It was true: no one had ever really betrayed him. No one he knew would dare.

"I did mean what I said, Gavin. I would rather die than lose your trust," Luca said, clearing the thought about his directness with Gavin in the garden. "If I ever lost that, it would be worse than death."

"I don't believe you could lose my trust, and I could never take your life."

Gavin thought back to the man who stood before him the morning before. In his mind's eye, he saw Luca's steadfast nerves and the danger in his eyes. Luca had been protecting everything he loved by offering not to be around to see it destroyed. Gavin also recalled the dark tone in his voice and the quietly spoken words that had forced him to listen. That was how Luca had spoken each time Gavin had gotten belligerent in the past. Quietly, forcing Gavin's volume down. He saw himself in Luca. Deeply buried pain.

"This team, you, Rusty, and now Brody: you are my family, and I am at peace with that. There would be no team without you, and I know that also. I can't lose you, Gavin. I know we are losing Rusty, and my heart could not stand both," Luca said, waiting on a response from Gavin. "You remember how you felt when I collapsed in Maine?"

"I remember," Gavin limited his comment, wanting Luca to speak freely.

The wind was blowing now. A branch scraped across the back windows, and Luca jumped up. Gavin thought Luca seemed more wired than usual; he continued to observe and wait. Then again, he wasn't sure what he was waiting for; maybe something that would tell him where Luca's head was.

"When Helen asked you to become her first Ghost, what was your response?" Luca asked.

"I asked when I needed to die," Gavin answered.

"That easy?"

The Sapphire Ghost

"No, but it was easier than what I had been contemplating, which was dying. I found a purpose that night and reached out to claim it with everything I had. It allowed me to atone for the crimes I felt I'd been a part of and the ability to wipe them clean."

"I can't imagine you ever feeling vulnerable," Luca said. "Have you wiped your slate clean?"

"I've felt exposed every day, but I have made my peace that each day could be my last," Gavin said. "That slate will never be clean. In many ways, I've failed."

"Do you have any regrets? I mean, like having no life outside the Order?" Luca asked, recalling Rusty's words about how small Gavin's world was. He was ashamed to admit it, but Luca had never thought about it before but would consider it going forward.

"Not often. The Order has given me a full life. In fact, probably with more satisfaction than most people ever have," Gavin responded. "My life may be considered unusual by some, but I don't have their real-world problems. Politics, race, hate, and the hustle to go nowhere fast, I'm glad to be out of the rat race. People out there believe in social sorcery and ignore the true horrors they should fear. For me, there is only good and bad because my glasses have never been rose-colored."

Gavin paused and watched whatever Luca held back, ready to break him apart at invisible seams. He kept his voice soft as he continued. "There are few things I can't have. My needs are met. Yes, sometimes it gets claustrophobic. The worst part is seeing the condition of the children and the terrible things they have gone through. I never sleep peacefully. Even after all these years, I cannot accept that people can be so cruel and heartless."

Luca continued to pace frantically. He wanted to release this excess energy, but with his wounded arm, he could not. It was making him crazy. Usually, when he felt this momentum, he exerted it with exercise or focused on the tiny gears in a broken clock. Gavin waited, observing the unrest run through the man. Luca heard every word, and he realized he did want this.

"Come on. I'll make you a cup of tea." Gavin stood and walked into the kitchen.

Luca followed and could feel the electricity bouncing off the walls at him. Unfortunately, this had no place to go until his arm was healed. Luca was unsure how to keep himself tethered. He ran his hands through his hair, tugging at the longer strands.

"Here, try this," Gavin said, handing him a cup of hot tea.

"Thank you," Luca said, taking the teacup. "I feel a little lost."

"You are not lost; you are finally found. I believe it is time to accept what is inside you." Gavin sat across the table. "I told you yesterday that I see you."

Luca sat back and took in Gavin's words. The one man who could crush him also could make him feel strong. Gavin had seen, but not yet entirely.

"One person fuels this rage that you are feeling. It will have an outlet; accept that. You need to refocus all that energy on the subject that has brought what you had buried to the surface." Gavin had only seen a glimpse of Luca's future Ghost and was more than a little curious to see more.

"Marshal. I know him. So, as much as I hate him right now, I don't want to think about killing him," Luca confessed.

"Think about it this way, Luca; if you were to show such disloyalty to me, I would absolutely put a bullet in you as much as I love you."

"No, sir, something tells me it would not be that easy. If I were to betray you, I would not be shot. I'd end up skinned alive and hung from an oak tree covered in honey," Luca said.

Gavin laughed. "That is an idea I will have to put in the book! But I cannot say you are wrong. Luca, all I would need for you would be a small, cramped space," he said. "I also know you would never betray the Order or me."

"I think I'd prefer the skinning." Luca felt stones in his chest at the mention of being put in a small space. "Yes, I understand that, and I realize why it has to be done, and examples need to be made," he said, drumming his fingers on the table.

"Let me give you a harder example. If it had been Rusty to have put me in the hospital in London instead of Bains, would you still have done what you did?"

The Sapphire Ghost

"Not exactly," Luca said. "When you woke up, Rusty would be someplace waiting for you. But that's easy to say since I know Rusty would *never* turn on you."

"Damned straight, son!" Rusty said as he came into the kitchen. "Don't ever hesitate. We all know the risk and what the fee will be if we stumble across that line in the concrete." He had been listening to some of the conversation behind the wall.

"There is a reason Arcadia has been able to keep secret for so many years, and that is the complete loyalty of the Orders and those we trust. Without that loyalty, this ship would sink along with the rest of the world's good intentions," Gavin stated and glanced at Rusty to see if he could tell how he felt. Rusty's health was another concern.

"Luca, you do not have to fill my shoes. You do what comes naturally to you. I do not expect you to have my coarse tendencies because I feel strongly about an eye for an eye. You do the Ghost your way," Gavin concluded.

The wind made the kitchen windows crack and pop, and the branches gave off a haunting sound. Luca eyed Gavin, and a strange calm fell over his body. He tilted his head to one side, and his neck popped. Gavin noted how clear Luca's brown eyes had become as a renewed drive replaced the anxiety. Luca's restless momentum left. Luca's hands stopped drumming the table, and his shoulders relaxed. He looked from Rusty to Gavin with eyes they had not seen in a week. A spooky coolness could be felt in the kitchen. Yet he sat and stared off to somewhere else for a few minutes. Neither Gavin nor Rusty said a word, as if they felt someone else entered this space.

Luca smiled. "Thank you." And he stood and left the room.

Rusty waited for Luca's bedroom door to close. "Tell me you felt that?"

"Yes," Gavin replied.

"What just happened? It was like, well, I would feel dumb trying to explain it. Spooky, though," Rusty said.

"Luca's Ghost is about ready to make itself known," Gavin said, smiling. "All he needed was permission. This Luca is not afraid of me because I saw him yesterday."

"Well, it was weird," Rusty said and stood to pull a beer from the fridge. "I almost prefer the anxiety."

"Luca's been hiding from himself, but I saw what lies below the surface. The one who took over when he went after Steve Bains. Helen scolded Luca for going after Bains by himself, and he told her no one on earth would have been able to stop him. Helen was right to suggest I train him," Gavin said quietly. "But that might also have been the beginning of what we just saw. Whatever caused the genie to be released, Luca has been unable to return him to the bottle."

"I wasn't sure what you were doing when you said you asked Luca to become your heir. Care to tell me what you and Helen spoke about?" Rusty asked, finishing the beer. Rusty also thought his retirement might be another precursor to Luca's lack of control.

"First of all, Luca had a seizure in the comm center, which scared both of us. Then Helen suggested he had Hyperthymesia," Gavin said and looked at Rusty. "It's a memory condition, which Helen has. People with Hyperthymesia tend to remember everything, which can cause great suffering. However, neither Luca nor Helen has the full form of the disorder. In Luca's case, he never forgets what he reads. Ever," Gavin explained.

"That explains how he could always get us where we needed to be. Not to mention the times he quoted information he had read weeks earlier. And he always remembers everyone's phone number. How did we miss that?" Rusty asked.

"He did not want us to know. His father told him as a child to keep it secret. Helen was the first person he ever told, but that was only after being asked the question directly," Gavin said.

"Well, I'll be damned," Rusty said, scratching his head. "Do you think the condition could also help him remember body language?"

"What do you mean?" Gavin asked.

"Have you ever really observed him? How he studies everyone else? He can predict what someone is going to do beforehand. When he fights, he seems to know all their ticks or movements before they move," Rusty explained. "And with you, he can predict what you want from him before you

The Sapphire Ghost

ask. Like in the headmaster's house, he pulled the table away—you never asked."

"I guess; that's a type of reading. I wonder if he realizes he does that." Gavin decided he needed to pay closer attention.

"There's more?" Rusty coaxed.

"After you recruited him, I questioned your judgment. He seemed a little too tame. I was unsure he was cut out for this even though he had been a Green Beret. I asked Helen to get me his military file, and she couriered it. Rusty, eighty-five percent of his file is redacted. He has never mentioned what he did in the military to this day. I asked him when we were coming back from Arcadia, and he said he could not tell me but would give me an unredacted copy. Things got crazy, and he has not given it to me yet. I've never seen anything hinting at what would cause so much black in his file." Gavin stood and grabbed a bottle of water from the fridge.

"He's loyal. What's there to question about that?" Rusty asked.

"It wasn't that I ever questioned his loyalty. I never saw anyone hold their truths so close they became invisible. He can compartmentalize his life even better than I do. I've always found that fascinating, maybe because I hate secrets, and Luca has been a constant enigma." Gavin paused and took a few swallows. "Then yesterday, he said he didn't have secrets. But I know in fact he does."

"Have you ever bothered asking him?" Rusty asked and cocked a knowing eyebrow.

"No, not outright," Gavin admitted. "But he told me to ask him questions."

"You've got to learn how to ask the question to get more than a yes or no answer," Rusty said, smiling broadly. "He may not have secrets, but you must ask the questions. He is not the type to open up. That, again, has to do more with escaping Colombia at the age of six than being secretive. I know more or less what he did and what he is capable of. As for his family, besides you, his biggest fear is that they will find out who he truly is. They are perfectly happy, believing he rides around in a private jet taking care of a CEO with Axon Petroleum. Seven years, and you never asked him. I'm surprised."

"Who knew it would be that easy," Gavin said. "I've seen more of the side he keeps from the world in the last five days than in seven years. I knew there was something else in him, but I couldn't force it out in the open. I thought back to each time I had ordered him to kill a man. He did as he was told without the slightest hint of hostility or reservation. Then, he did what I never expected: he stood up to me."

"That was just stupid on his part. If he had caught you in one of your moods, that would have been the end of him," Rusty said.

"I saw the cold eyes that Bains must have stared into in the end, and I knew I was not just dealing with our Luca. I knew then he was ready to start the process. That switch had been flipped."

"Similar to you," Rusty suggested.

"Yes. My fear is he may not know that a Ghost has never retired. We all die."

"Oh, he knows. And it scares the hell out of him. He knows I am dying, and he can do nothing about it. So, he is trying to insulate you from any danger."

"I walk with death daily, and I feel her breath on my cheek each night. He needs to realize this is how it is," Gavin said quietly. "I have outlived every Ghost Helen has recruited, which is largely thanks to you and Luca. I trust my team, know my time is limited, and take none of it for granted." Gavin absently brushed the side of his cheek as if he felt a kiss.

"Yes, we are not promised tomorrow, and if I were to have my way, I would rather take a bullet than die a lingering death with cancer."

"Rusty, if you begin to suffer and request my help, I will not allow you to linger," Gavin said compassionately.

Rusty gave Gavin a smile of gratitude, but he would never ask his friend to take his life.

Chapter Seventy-One

Dim light filtered into the room from a smog-covered starless night. Luca stared at his reflection in the window. The affliction that had made him a dedicated soldier had resurfaced more times than he had cared for it to in the last week, and Gavin gave him permission to unleash that into the world. Luca could never be Gavin Garrison, that much he knew. But killing came easier to him than he cared to admit.

His innocence died when he was fourteen when he found what lived inside him. That evil delivered a gut-wrenching terror into his life. The day he took his first life. That image drifted into his head, and the heavy steel pipe felt right in his hand. Killing his sister's rapist had purged his feelings of helplessness. He realized there would be no sleeping tonight, so he went to the basement to temper that rage.

At half past five in the morning, Gavin slid out of bed. He had a feeling he could not shake, and he had slept fitfully once again. He showered and dressed in a polo and chinos. Gavin noticed Luca's bedroom door was open as he walked down the stairs. "Luca, are you in here?" Gavin asked, looking into the room. The bed was made, and everything was in neat order. After a moment, he went on to the kitchen.

Gavin made tea and went out in the garden. The cool air helped him clear his head of the dreams that always came.

The house was dark and quiet, with only the light hum of the AC unit in the background. It seemed everyone except Luca was still asleep. Another time, Gavin would have enjoyed the silence and the rarity of being alone, but something felt off. Maybe Luca slept in the basement. Gavin now understood why Luca put so much energy into his workouts. He chose hobbies that required complete concentration to keep himself boxed up. Gavin went down the stairs and heard dull sounds of repetitive thuds. Gavin peered around the corner before he stepped off the last step, watching Luca throwing knives at a board with a black and white diamond pattern. He was a little clumsy with his right hand, but he was hitting near the center of the diamonds. Luca was focused and controlled. Understanding Luca better now, Gavin knew he rarely needed total concentration this early. Gavin thought Luca was trying to regain control instead of embracing himself.

Gavin closed his eyes and drew a deep breath. The furnace inside him ignited. The idea that Luca was trying to pull that careful filter back up angered him. Gavin wanted to see the Luca he saw in the garden. Gavin walked over to him just as a silver shard of metal left his hand. Gavin reached out, taking Luca by the left arm, dragging him across the room, and nearly threw him onto the bench.

Luca landed hard, drew his arm to his chest, and looked up at the face of the Ghost but said nothing.

"Just tell me you are not ready. I will take care of Marshal. That is all you have to do. The assignment is simple; Luca, you, of all people, know how to follow orders," Gavin said, fury gleaming from his face.

Luca started to stand, and Gavin pushed him back down. The strength in Gavin's blow sent him against the wall. Luca balanced himself, gazed up at Gavin's face, and was unsure what he saw there. Luca closed his eyes and dug deep to manage what was wavering out of his control because he did not feel ready to go toe to toe with the Ghost.

"Stop that and look at me! You disappoint me, Luca. Why do you continue to put yourself in the box?" Gavin asked, and his voice was low and unpleasant.

"Sir, I am not in a box," Luca spoke softly.

Gavin grimaced at the sound of Luca's low, steady voice. Luca heard the beep on the keypad upstairs and waited to see who might have the pleasure of interrupting this moment.

"Stay upstairs!" Gavin demanded before he knew who was opening the door, and it immediately closed.

Luca glanced up at the stairs and back at Gavin, unsure what set him off. Luca ran through the conversation from earlier this morning.

Brody walked back into the kitchen, where Rusty poured coffee.

"I heard," Rusty said, giving him a concerned expression.

The Sapphire Ghost

"Is it always so hostile with those two?" Brody asked.

"No, it has never been this way. I'm not sure what to tell you other than I believe it's growing pains," Rusty said, wondering if he should try to intervene or let them get it out of their systems.

Luca grasped his arm, where Gavin grabbed him and caused a burning pain. Gavin knew precisely what he was doing, and Luca needed to figure it out so that he could counter this reaction. Gavin wanted something from him, and his mouth felt dry as crackers at the dread of what it was.

"Tell me what you want, and I'll do it," Luca said. "I will do *anything* you ask."

Gavin opened and closed his fist by his sides. He wanted to get Luca angry to find out more about what he stowed away. He wanted to really see Luca. Questioning Luca's loyalty, Gavin would not do again. Gavin walked to the wall and stared down at Luca's prized handcrafted knives, thin and deadly blades. Instead, Gavin selected a small but lethal throwing knife from the wall and felt the weight in his hand. Gavin flung the blade at the side of Luca's head, and it landed in the wall by Luca's right ear. Luca did not flinch. Gavin watched as he sat so still and did not seem to breathe. Gavin thought a direct attack might spin Luca out of control, and he was prepared for the response.

Luca felt the light draft as the blade hit the wall by his head. Fear crept into his heart because he felt the darkness sink into his soul, and then it opened the door.

"I know about your sister," Gavin stated.

Luca's gaze shifted from Gavin to the wall behind him. Everything around him grew bright and clear, and he focused on the area just behind Gavin. Luca held on to what was wavering of his restraint, which he felt could blow away by breathing too hard.

"Don't do this, Gavin," Luca said in a deliberate whisper that echoed off all the walls.

Luca started to stand again, and for a third time, Gavin put him back on that seat as if he were a schoolboy. He bit his lips in between his teeth. Luca knew what the Ghost wanted from him, and he felt its hot fingers curling inside his chest. He was determined to have the ability to look at Gavin from a standing position, and he started to stand again. Just as before, Gavin intended to push him down; without any effort, Luca moved Gavin's arm to the side and stood. Gavin stepped away and waited.

"You know about my sister?" Luca asked in a harsh breath.

"I do, and I know they found her attacker dead, but your father had been in the restaurant and had an alibi," Gavin replied, examining Luca, but not the Luca he knew.

"Then you know the only secret I have ever kept from anyone." Luca's words were haunted and cold, his eyes black, and his face carved stone.

"There you are. I have been waiting to meet you," Gavin said coolly as his eyes stared into the darkness of Luca's.

"You only need to ask, Gavin. I've never been in a box, just controlled chaos with a masterful illusion to cover the surface," Luca said and stepped toward Gavin. "I have done nothing but pretend to be something I'm not my whole life."

Gavin watched as Luca took two measured steps, and he lifted his eyebrows in a warning. He wondered if Luca would show any aggression toward him.

When Luca was within three feet of Gavin, he stopped and looked hard at the presence of the Ghost. He was the man he most admired in the world because Gavin danced between darkness and light.

"Gavin, what you want to see, I cannot begin to explain and barely control." Luca's face became damp, and his eyes icy. "I buried that part of myself sitting in that hole in Iraq, and it does not serve me to give in to it."

"Why?" Gavin asked quietly, allowing his Ghost to leave.

"Because I became arrogant and reckless, and it almost got me killed along with my unit," Luca said and turned his back on him and walked across to the knife Gavin threw into the wall. Luca tugged it free from the plaster, flipping it into the air. "This is as far as I feel comfortable going. Don't ask me to go further because I lack the courage to embrace that ferocity."

Gavin watched with interest when Luca returned the knife to its place. Gavin now realized how much precise control Luca demanded from every area of his life. Everything had a place, including his thoughtfully chosen words. Gavin listened intently to every word he spoke.

"You cannot divide yourself because it will tear you apart," Gavin said. "Drowning that part of you causes your anxiety—own it again. Make it belong to you. You would not make the same mistake again."

"Am I not enough, sir?"

"You are exactly enough to remain a Warrior. But you need to be whole to move to the next step." Gavin stepped forward and placed a hand on his shoulder. "What I was able to do to you on the helicopter should never happen again, not to a Ghost. You must be strong yet humble enough to know you are not invincible."

Luca backed away from Gavin's touch—the fear of the turmoil inside heated his body.

Then, as if in an afterthought, Luca went to the computers and took out a blue folder from the drawer. Luca stood at the desk and willed the heat down. Then he took the file to Gavin. "Then teach me."

Chapter Seventy-Two

September 13

Gavin studied Luca for another moment and accepted the file. Luca nodded for him to go. Taking the file upstairs, Gavin strolled into the kitchen and met a couple of anxious looks from Rusty and Brody.

"It's fine, nothing to worry about," Gavin said, taking a rare cup of black coffee, and going to the garden to read the file.

Inside the file he learned Marshal would be bringing the plane to Boston on Thursday under the guise that he was delivering two Dark 9 members to the location. Dark 9 would ensure nothing happened to the plane and watch and clone Marshal's phone.

The Sapphire Order would depart Boston to Destin on September 16th at 2:00 p.m. Gavin stopped reading when he reached the following few sentences. *Well, then, that is something,* and he smiled with approval.

Luca showered, dressed, and tried to get his curls under control. He needed to get a haircut, and since he had three more days in D.C., he would do just that. He chose a Kiton, brown, plaid, cashmere sports jacket over a black turtleneck with dark jeans. Luca needed to start looking the part at all times 'and do the Ghost your way' he reminded himself. Gavin would be a vigilant teacher, and that was what he was trying to do in the basement. Gavin always knew more than he let on.

However, Luca had not expected Gavin to learn about his sister. However, he was not surprised that Gavin came to that conclusion, even if it was a guess. Luca headed to the kitchen where Rusty and Brody were bonding over last night's football game. Rusty gave Luca a penetrating stare, and he smiled and nodded, saying that he was okay.

"I'm gonna take this outside," Luca said as he poured his coffee and left to join Gavin.

The Sapphire Ghost

Gavin looked up to find Luca looking stylish in the cashmere blazer. It was different than his usual white tees and jeans when they did not have to work.

"I'm a big enough man to admit when I am wrong. I am sorry, Luca," Gavin said sincerely, motioning to the folder.

"I don't need an apology," Luca said and sat on the edge of the chair, tapping his fingers together.

Brody watched the two outside. Whatever Gavin had worked up apparently worked itself out, and they were both still in one piece.

"Controlled chaos with a masterful illusion to cover the surface. I love the description as it is so appropriate," Gavin said, taking a sip of the bitter coffee. "I am impressed with your plan, but you didn't have to put it in writing."

"Would you have believed me if I hadn't?" Luca asked.

"Maybe not, but I'm concerned about this transition for you," Gavin said.

"I will handle the transition, and I'll still handle you, Gavin."

Gavin gave Luca a piercing glare at the word. He hated that word and everything it implied. Especially after yesterday morning, he sensed that Luca might be the only one who could really handle him.

"What happened the first time with the man who hurt your sister?" Gavin asked with more sensitivity.

"I couldn't explain it. When I saw my sister bloody and crying, something changed. My mind became completely silent; everything slowed, and something darker came to the surface. People talk about blacking out in anger. I don't blackout; for me, everything becomes pristine. My mind opens, and everything becomes possible. The clutter disappears, and I know exactly what I am doing," Luca admitted. "But that wasn't the only one. I also killed her husband when he put her in the hospital when she was pregnant with Carlos."

"Oh, well, I missed that one. I feel there is a pattern, and it has to do with protecting those you care for," Gavin surmised.

"Yes, like you," Luca responded.

"Bains sent you over the edge, but you handled it."

"I did, but I didn't fall too far, just enough to gain clarity. I was only fourteen the first time," Luca thought for a moment about how much to reveal,

"I thought I had a handle on it during the war. I was a great soldier, and I loved the army. That is until I was injured, and from then on, I lacked the confidence, so I kept it locked up." He was embarrassed to reveal he needed a minder, which had been Rusty.

"I feel I'm just getting to know you, Luca," Gavin said.

Luca studied Gavin for a moment. "No, you have known me all along, and you always knew something was off, something that did not align with what was on paper," Luca said. "I told you I have no secrets; all you ever have to do is ask."

"There's more?" Gavin asked.

"Yes," Luca confessed, stood to go inside, and nearly made it to the door.

"Someone hurt you as a boy."

Luca turned to Gavin, and an instant darkness claimed Luca's face, and then it was gone. He did not say anything, turning to go back inside.

Gavin sat in the cool morning air and thought about their morning conversations. He found the line not to cross, and one Luca was unwilling or unable to speak about. That storm went up like a shield, almost to protect Luca from the question. It did not matter; he felt he had the answer. The reason Luca devoted himself entirely to this cause. There was always a personal impetus.

Luca was willing to learn; from what Gavin heard, he would not be a difficult pupil. He was also speaking openly, which meant Gavin had gained access to a sacred part of his life, and he knew Rusty shared that. Gavin was certain the members of that club were small.

Luca had taken the file from the table before heading inside. He took a biscuit from the platter, cut its center, and placed a dab of jelly inside. Luca was ready to inform the team of what he had planned and waited for Gavin. Luca also had news on the shipping containers that had ended up in Maryland.

"I want you both to know everything is all right with Gavin and me, and I know it's difficult to understand, but we are both going through a learning curve. I won't say you'll not see some trouble in the future. But we have reached an understanding, and I believe that is a big step forward. I have agreed to become Gavin's legacy for some time, I hope, in the distant future.

My training began this morning." Luca finished, hoping to alleviate any distress that Gavin's outburst might have caused. He figured it was Brody because he was hanging back by the stove.

Luca took his biscuit to the table. The edginess was gone, and he felt at peace for the first time in a long time. If he fell, he trusted Gavin would pull him out.

"You all right?" Rusty asked, taking the seat next to Luca.

"I'm good," Luca said, reassuringly.

"Did he hurt you?" Rusty asked.

Luca gave Rusty a sideways grin. "No. I'm good, really good."

"All right," Rusty said. He knew if anyone could hurt Luca, it would be Gavin because Luca wouldn't stop him. His commitment to those Codes was unbreakable. "I'm glad you are finding your way."

"I know. It was Brody that opened the door."

"Yeah, you should have seen his face," Rusty said, a large grin engulfing him.

"Revelation; it's still written all over him. I'll talk to him. This is hard to get used to in the beginning. Now he's facing me going Ghost." Luca shook his head because he knew it was a giant leap not only for Nate Brody but also for himself.

Gavin saw Luca and Rusty talking and Brody standing by the stove, avoiding eye contact. It had been Brody to catch his wrath or at least his words. Luca finished his breakfast and waited for them to settle.

"Okay, we have a mission. The first step is to get back into Dremmond without incident. King has a lot of men on the ground, and unfortunately, two innocents have been shot for driving a black Mercedes. Dark 9 are currently holding four of their men, and how they will be taken care of will depend on Gavin. My target is Marshal. Helen is also working behind the scenes to get us safely back to Dremmond and wash any information away that would tie Atlas Securities to the hangar. I feel once we are inside the compound, we will be secure. Marshal is flying into Boston on Thursday to take us back to Destin. And as far as I know, Marshal does not have a clue we are onto him. There is a flash drive with videos from the airport where Dark 9 has been on overwatch for the past four days. We need to be ready for anything once we land.

"Brody, I have a list of weapons I will need you to get ready and ensure are loaded. Helen has secured us a second hangar in Ft. Walton Beach. But until I take care of Marshal, we will not be using the new one. If I missed anything, read the file. If you have questions or concerns, please see me. We have three days to prepare," Luca concluded. "Oh, and I almost forgot, and there are zero exceptions to this." Luca looked directly at Gavin.

"Zero!" Luca said again. He walked over and patted Rusty on the chest. "Those vests better be on your persons. If I find that you are not wearing them out of the house, you will be dealing with a side of me you have not seen."

Gavin felt scolded, and he laughed a little to himself. Rusty looked a little shocked at Luca's near threat. Brody stayed back and observed the men who were the Ghost and the one in training. Things were getting ready to take an interesting turn.

"Gavin, the two shipping containers have stopped in Maryland. I need to know what you want me to do?" Luca asked.

"We should probably ride out and look at the situation," Gavin stated. "I will also let Thomas Fagan know." He disliked that he kept those inside the containers on the road longer than needed, and Fagan would be ready to get those people out.

Luca nodded. "I'll get a team together."

"No need for a ride-through. Let us see what we are dealing with, and then you can set up a team," Gavin replied.

Iris came into the kitchen about that time, and Gavin looked at her with concern and over at Luca.

"Iris, I did not know you were working today." Gavin's eyes narrowed.

Iris set to work cleaning up the kitchen as if she did not hear Gavin, humming lightly to herself.

Luca pointed to his ears. "She has been instructed to keep her hearing aids turned off if we are all gathered. She can't hear a thing."

Chapter Seventy-Three

Gavin left Rusty behind to rest and made Luca aware that the Bruscoe Family oversaw the area. Before leaving, Gavin extracted all the information Helen had sent him on Bruscoe, compiled the evidence, and placed it in a large gray envelope. Unsure of why the idea hit him, he surprised himself. His hackles had been up since arriving in D.C., and he wanted Duncan Bruscoe Jr. before they left town. Gavin could make a plan, and take care of Bruscoe before going to Destin, or he could give Agent Simons a little something for ruining her big arrest in Nevada. Surely, with all the extra resources, they could get creative and get Bruscoe off the streets. Gavin mostly needed to know if Bruscoe was King. To get that information, Gavin would have to use his unique skills; torture. It was best to put Bruscoe on ice until he had more time.

"Thomas," Gavin said when Thomas Fagan answered.

"Yes, sir," Fagan replied.

"I know you're in D.C., and I need you to retrieve the precious cargo," Gavin stated.

"I was hoping you would call regarding that," Fagan replied.

"Yes, I have another question. Special Agent Simons, is she there with you?"

"She is in the building, but you don't have to worry about her. Simons' team is heading to Phoenix regarding a gray file," Fagan assured him.

"No, Thomas, that is not what this is about. Could you take her your phone, please?"

"I'm not sure this is a good idea," Fagan said.

"Just take her the phone and let me worry about what's a good idea."

Fagan left his office and went directly to the conference room where he last saw Simons. "Tonya, could you meet me in my office."

Impatience swept over her face as she followed Fagan. She needed to leave to get to the airport. "What's up, Thomas? You know I have a flight to catch."

Closing the door, Fagan cautiously handed her the phone. "Someone wants to speak with you."

She took Thomas's phone. "This is Special Agent Simons."

"Tonya Simons, this is the Ghost," Gavin said.

Simons became still, and the room lost all sound, "*The* Ghost."

"Yes, Special Agent Simons, I may have a gift for you in the next couple of days. You will have one shot - make it stick. Take a walk to the nearest coffee house to your location. I left a package with the shift manager. Follow the directions explicitly, and you will receive your prize. If not, you will receive another body," Gavin said. "I will give you one question. Make it a good one."

"Why do you do this?" Simons asked.

"You are getting ready to find out. This bequest proves that the legal system cannot do its job. There is justice, and then there is the illusion of justice. I, however, am an illusion, but I am justice," Gavin replied. "Tell you what, Tonya, I will make you a deal. You manage to keep the next one behind bars, and I will turn myself over to you. I will need your number when I have the location of your gift."

"You'll what? We had you in Las Vegas, didn't we?" Simons asked.

"You had your question. Follow directions, Tonya," Gavin said, ending the call.

"What was that about?" Fagan asked, amused by her expression "You're not going to Phoenix, are you?"

"I think he is giving me a gray file before they die. He has a package waiting for me." Simons looked at Thomas. "Does he always sound like that?"

"No, not always," Fagan lied. "Get your package. I will wait for you. It seems I am going after some kids."

"Interesting," Simons said, her eyes still wide, but she did not move. "He said if I can keep this person behind bars, he will turn himself into me."

"Well, that is motivation," Fagan said, and he thought *he might turn himself in . . . but holding him would be another story.*

Gavin, Luca, and Brody headed to the warehouse district in Baltimore. The road to the address where the containers ended up was busy, with freight trucks rolling in and out and the sounds of heavy diesel engines and forklifts beeping—pulsed against the metal-sided buildings. Gray stagnant air appeared to be locked in place.

Brody drove slowly, looking for building 1066. He found the building, and there were no trucks on the road. Luca looked around when Brody slowed further and counted seven armed men out front and two more sitting on the roof.

One truck with a yellow container was backed up to the dock. The men surrounding the building did not appear to be dockworkers because they wore military gear. Gavin glanced up and saw that the building was under video surveillance.

"I do not like this," Gavin stated.

"Yes, sir, we are being watched. Look at the building to the left. Reminds me of Fox Phantom," Luca replied.

Gavin peered at the building across the street. A man sat on the top with a rifle aimed at their car. "Get us out of here."

"I will, but let's not be so obvious," Brody said, considering the situation and the best way to have a reason to be there.

Brody slowed and stopped, examining a six-foot for rent sign, and put the car in park. When he stepped from the vehicle, he could feel the rifle move with him.

"What is he doing?" Gavin asked.

"Don't know," Luca replied, watching Brody.

Brody dialed the number on the sign and spoke loud enough in a Detroit accent to be heard. He began to ask the person questions about square footage, bays, and rent. Brody wanted whoever was watching to know he was not intimidated as he walked casually back and forth in front of the car.

A black Suburban drove up behind the car while Brody spoke to the real estate company. A broad-shouldered man approached Brody.

"Can I help you?" the man asked. "I own this property." His voice sounded like he gargled with hot ash and smoked six packs a day.

"Mike Anderson." Brody reached to shake the man's hand.

"Harlem Troft. It's a big space, and the security is free." Troft motioned to the top of the building across the street.

Gavin rolled the window down enough to listen.

"My employer is not interested in the size, just the location," Brody said. "Looking for a six-month lease and the real estate agent says the owner would have to approve a lease that short."

"What do you need the space for?"

"Privacy," Brody said dramatically.

"Three thousand a month," Troft replied.

Brody glanced back at the car and over at the roof with the rifleman. He rubbed the scruff on his chin and studied the building like he was considering his options.

"Twenty-five thousand upfront for the six months and no paperwork," Brody replied.

"Deal," Troft said and shook Brody's hand.

Brody went to the back of the Cadillac and took the cash from the trunk, and Luca caught his eye.

Brody handed Troft the money. "Tell your friend up there to aim that thing someplace else."

"Nice doing business with you, *Mr. Anderson*. Security is tight, and I'm sure you understand. I'll let my people know that the building is occupied," Troft replied. "No questions; you stay on your side."

Brody smiled, but a coldness remained in his eyes. "No questions."

Harlem Troft strolled past Gavin's window, but the tint was too dark to see inside.

Brody waited for the Suburban to pull around the car before opening his door. He got behind the wheel and drove to the building he rented.

"Might as well look around and see what we got for the money," Brody said, feeling like this was as good a place as any if he were going to be reprimanded.

"Quick thinking, Brody," Gavin said, sending a warning message to Fagan.

Luca smiled. Yes, that is exactly what he needed, and Brody was working into the team just fine.

Chapter Seventy-Four

Deputy Director of Special Operations Thomas Fagan gathered his team. After going over the envelope with Simons, she decided she would assist Fagan and send her team ahead of her to Phoenix.

"The call was a surprise," Simons said.

"I'm sure," Fagan said.

"You don't seem surprised." Simons headed to the elevator with him.

"Tonya, I'm rarely surprised by what he does anymore. The things he knows or how he gets things done. I'm not surprised the Ghost spoke with you, but I'll be surprised if you get the Ghost in custody. If he turns himself in, that'll surprise me," Fagan replied, knowing the Ghost left nothing to chance.

"Something tells me the same thing." The evidence in the envelope was against Duncan Bruscoe Jr's crime family. That operation had flown just out of reach for years. The evidence in the file was good but inadmissible due to how they obtained it.

"It could turn into a blood bath, so if you're coming, help me get the kids out safely," Fagan said.

"Agree, the kids first. But if the Ghost is onsite, I will not ignore him just because of this file," Simons said.

"I don't think he would expect you to," Fagan replied.

It was hot in the warehouse. The concrete floor looked polished, and a pile of wooden shipping crates sat off to the left. Large beams were across the ceiling to build a second floor if needed.

Gavin walked over to the crates and looked at the block letters on the side of the boxes. This will work nicely as a set-up for Dark 9 for what he was planning for Bruscoe. He stepped back quickly, hearing a rodent inside the crate.

"I'll work on getting a team in here. What about those containers?" Luca asked.

"I've called Thomas. They'll be here shortly, and I just let him know to come ready for a fight."

They heard the screech of a bay door opening, and Luca went for his gun. Footsteps echoed across the empty space. "The Ghost in the flesh," came a voice from the darkness.

Gavin looked across the wide-open space where the bay door had been left open. "Duncan Jr., you look just like your father," Gavin said when the man came into view. A second, much larger man stood beside him. Gavin was extremely surprised to see him in person.

Luca's eyes darted from the man to Gavin for a clue as to what to do.

"I was beginning to believe you were dead. I kept dangling the worms but never got a bite," the short man of just over thirty replied. "I made a promise to my father."

Luca went for his gun, but the more prominent man shot him in the chest, and Luca fell. Brody drew his weapon and fired. The big man moved before Brody pulled the trigger and sent Brody to the floor next to Luca. Gavin glanced down at the two who lay at his feet. Gavin forced himself to show no concern.

"Jimmy here really enjoys shooting people. Now it is just you and me," Bruscoe mocked. "I get a call whenever strangers appear when I have a delivery. You don't know how long I've waited for you to show up. Jimmy, take their weapons." Bruscoe stepped beside Gavin and took the pistol from behind his coat.

Gavin looked down at Luca and Brody again. A pool of blood formed by Brody's head and Luca lay face down, and neither appeared to be breathing. Gavin's heart thudded hard. He did not think he was being reckless, and he should have allowed Luca to get a team.

"No one else around, so what would you like to do? We could set up for a long conversation if you have a chessboard," Gavin said, thinking Simons might get a bigger prize than expected; *a dead Ghost.*

The Sapphire Ghost

"I do not intend for you to live that long, and I will watch you suffer just like you made my father suffer."

"I liked your father very much. Excellent businessman, but I warned him to stay away from flesh peddling. He was doing quite well in heroin," Gavin said and strolled across the warehouse to what looked to be an office. Gavin could feel Jimmy's gun at his back.

"Sometimes, you need to diversify to keep up. To be profitable you deliver what people demand; just good business." Bruscoe replied.

"It wasn't good business for your father, and it won't be good for you. It seems to shorten your life," Gavin said. "You make the videos also?"

"No, I don't produce them."

"Who makes the videos? Might as well tell me since you do not intend for me to leave," Gavin said and continued to lead the men away from his team.

"That's another part of the operation," Bruscoe replied.

Bruscoe followed Gavin into an office space. Gavin went through the desk drawers and found a bottle of whisky and a bag of Styrofoam cups on an old filing cabinet. Bruscoe left Jimmy by the door.

Gavin splashed the scotch into the Styrofoam cups and handed one to Bruscoe. "You look like your father with facial hair. To Duncan Bruscoe, Sr."

"You don't deserve to say his name. I was only twelve when I found him, choked to death, and I kept this." Bruscoe laid a chessman King piece on the desk.

Gavin recognized the chess piece from the set he shoved down Bruscoe Sr.'s throat. After Gavin confronted him about his name coming up in a Dossier. *The King, how appropriate.*

"Yes, I did. However, he started taking children away from their parents, children he sold into slavery."

"It's only business, and the business is good," Bruscoe replied, reaching over and tipping over the king. "Checkmate."

"I truly hope who you sold your soul to - gave you a fair price. You are a father, three daughters, correct?" Gavin asked, staring at the King piece.

Bruscoe held the .38 revolver on Gavin and sat in a tattered office chair across the desk. Gavin kicked a brown bowling bag to the side, sat on the desk's corner, and took a drink. He thought of his team members on the floor and the fact he had asked Luca not to call in Dark 9. Unsure of Luca's condition, Brody appeared to have been shot in the head. Gavin was alone, and knew death was close. Rusty was going to kill him all over again when he saw his friend again. No, Gavin did not feel confident he was long for this world. Briefly, Gavin wondered what he'd say to all the children on the other side, those whom Gavin knew would be waiting for him from his nightmares. It would be his eternal hell.

Luca woke on the floor and exhaled; the searing heat caught in his lungs. A pain shot straight through to his spine when Luca braced himself to stand. Unbuttoning his shirt and unzipping the vest, he scraped the slug from the material and rezipped the vest with great effort. Luca looked over at Brody, who lay very still. A throat-tightening fear crept through him. Luca felt for a pulse but could not find one and turned Brody over. Luca was relieved when he saw that the blood had come from Brody's fall. Feeling along Brody's vest to where the bullet was lodged, Luca unzipped the body armor. Luca struck Brody in the chest and did not get a response. Luca leaned in to see if Brody was breathing, giving him two quick breaths and doing compressions. Brody's body arched, and he sucked in air.

Luca quickly sat back. "Quiet, stay put," Luca instructed when Brody's eyes opened. The bullet hit Brody hard enough to stop his heart, and he would need a doctor. Luca shook free of his jacket and placed it under Brody's head. "Just lay here; I'll be back." All of Luca's military training came back all at once.

Luca studied the space and saw the man standing outside a room to the far right of the warehouse. He needed to get to Gavin. Luca removed his shoes and shinnied up a pipe to a beam across the warehouse.

Gavin finished his drink and studied the empty bottle. "You just going to talk, or do you have a plan? I'm sure you have dreamt of this day for years."

"I am just savoring the moment and having you all to myself. Do you realize what many would give for this opportunity? To have the infamous

Ghost alone. I'm waiting to see you pull one of your legendary vanishing acts." Bruscoe looked inside the Styrofoam cup and sat it on the desk.

"I can only assume," Gavin replied, looking bored. "Are you King?"

"King, that's cute," Bruscoe replied, "I prefer Ambassador."

Luca ran across the beam to the other end of the warehouse, where the big man stood outside the office. Crouching down, Luca tried to listen. He heard the voice of the man who came into the warehouse. *How could I have been so stupid?*

Gavin observed the man outside the door and the five-shot 38 revolver in Duncan Briscoe's right hand. Gavin thought about the chances of him getting that gun from the younger man before Bruscoe's associate shot him. Gavin glanced up and down quickly and began to rummage through drawers again to make noise. Gavin wanted Bruscoe's attention on him while keeping an eye on the man at the door.

The jake-brakes released on a large semi-truck, and the sound reverberated off the sides of the building. The clattering of a forklift dropping its load sounded like metal scraping metal.

"If you want to draw this out, be a good host. You should ask your friend out there to get us another bottle of scotch," Gavin said.

Bruscoe smiled and drew back the hammer on the gun. "I plan on using each of these bullets carefully. It won't be as quick as your associates out there. I promise you that."

Gavin rounded the desk, sitting again on the corner to face Bruscoe Jr. He watched Luca fall from the ceiling out of the corner of his eye, and Gavin felt Duncan Bruscoe Jr. was getting ready to meet the real Luca Medina.

Luca dropped from the beam during all the noise and landed just behind the burly-looking man with the gun. He made no sound when he landed on the concrete. Quietly, Luca crept up behind Jimmy, the man who shot him. Luca unsheathed his knife from his wrist. Luca peered in and saw Gavin sitting on the desk. Luca took the blade and quickly severed the man's spinal cord at the back of his skull. The man sank to the floor without a sound, and Luca retrieved Jimmy's gun. Gavin looked over when the big man fell, and

Luca was gone. Gavin sat still, wanting to keep Bruscoe's attention from the door.

"Have you chosen where you will shoot me first? I guess my favorite spot would be the feet. So many bones to break in such a small area," Gavin said.

"You are crazy, aren't you?" Bruscoe said with a half-snort chuckle and pulled at the collar of his shirt. The air inside the office was stifling.

"I have never really cared for the word crazy. I am principled if that is what you mean." Gavin watched Bruscoe and waited to see what was next. He promised Special Agent Simons a file. However, he did not think he would deliver today. Oh, Gavin wanted Bruscoe Jr., but would have to wait until the circus of a legal system let him go—the Ghost would be waiting, if he had to take up permanent residence in Baltimore until that happened.

Luca peered into the room when he killed the large man. Bruscoe looked to be Luca's age and was sitting against the wall with a handgun aimed at Gavin. Luca evaluated the room and silently moved to the window on the other side. The blind was broken and gave him just enough visual to aim. Luca stopped before pulling the trigger. The hammer was pulled back on the revolver, and Bruscoe's finger was firmly on the trigger. Luca needed a distraction. Slipping the gun into his belt, he found a small pipe, went back to the window, watched the man with the gun, and Luca tossed the pipe across the room.

Gavin heard a pipe hit the concrete and instantly stood. Bruscoe stood also and noticed his bodyguard lying outside of the door in a pool of blood. Gavin swung up with his fist connecting with Bruscoe's chin, and the gun went off. Gavin fought to get control of the weapon.

Luca heard the shot as it resonated through the warehouse. He could not see Gavin or Bruscoe from the hole in the blind. Luca stepped quietly to the door and saw Gavin holding the gun on Bruscoe.

"How is Brody?" Gavin asked, shaking out his right hand while holding the gun with his left.

"Alive," Luca replied softly.

"Get him and go to the car," Gavin ordered.

Bruscoe's lip was busted, and he was muttering curse words.

The Sapphire Ghost

Luca backed from the office, acknowledging Gavin had things under control. Luca went to Brody to help him to the car. The men across the street at the other warehouse were still there, and so were the men on the roof. Luca went to the large bay door and pulled at the cord to open it. Pulling the car inside the warehouse, Luca retrieved his shoes and jacket. Taking a box of powdered chlorine from the trunk, Luca shook it over the blood and picked up Brody's shell casing. He needed to safely retrieve Gavin and deal with whatever he planned for Bruscoe. Luca looked in at where Brody lay in the backseat.

Luca watched Gavin walk Duncan Bruscoe in his direction and was surprised Bruscoe was still alive.

"Pry that crate open," Gavin ordered. "Not exactly the presentation I wanted to give Agent Simons, but it will do."

Luca stared at Gavin with surprise but did as he asked, opening the trunk and taking out a tire iron. When he pried open the crate, he grabbed the rat by the tail before it escaped. "Does he need a friend?" Luca asked with a dark grin.

"Let's give him one; he will not be in there for long. Like I told your father, it's the wrong kind of business. Checkmate," Gavin said and threw in the chessman King.

Duncan Bruscoe refused to get inside, so Luca kicked his knee, pushed him inside with one hand, and dropped the rat. Gavin closed the lid, took the tire iron, and began to tap the nails back into place.

"I will find you again, old friend!" The lid muffled Bruscoe's yells.

"That is not going to hold," Luca stated.

"No, help me lift another crate," Gavin said, and with Luca's injured arm, it took a bit longer to maneuver it into place.

"I'm giving Bruscoe to the FBI, but I want everything the Bruscoes own to burn. That will be the most painful thing I can think of for him. I want him to live long enough to see how this affects his family. Get with Helen and have her dig up every business, house, office, or laundry mat they own or have an interest in and organize baptism by fire. Once Brody feels better, have him work with you. Given his experience with Dark 9, he might have some ideas," Gavin ordered, taking out his phone and typing in a message. *Simons, your gift came early, the same complex as the children.* Then he switched the phone off and pulled the sim card.

"Yes, sir," Luca responded when he got into the car.

"They're all associated with Camden Harbor Quest. I want to see it on the news before we leave for Dremmond," Gavin said, looking back at where Brody lay and taking the front seat.

"Call Helen and have her send a doctor to the house," Gavin said.

"I sent her a message."

The noise from the machinery stopped when the sound of sirens filled the air. Luca's chest constricted at the sound; this was too familiar.

Luca drove out the backside of the warehouse where Bruscoe came in. He rode past the other warehouses, observing no one was watching them. Everyone had scattered at the sounds of the sirens. A driver was backing up a truck with the second shipping container.

Luca took several left turns until he was close to the westside exit and further away from the sirens.

Chapter Seventy-Five

The FBI headed into the warehouse district and found several men waiting on them. Fagan drove the car onto the curb, jumped out, gun in hand, and sighted a man on the roof.

Simons' SUV pulled alongside Fagan's and was followed by two more with several MPD squad cars. Each agent and officer braced themselves behind the vehicles, and Simons took the megaphone and announced herself.

"FBI! Come down with your hands up; let's make this as painless as possible," Simons called.

One on the roof quickly dumped his ammunition onto the cars below and made a run for it while they sheltered from the shower of bullets.

"Keep the buses back. It's not safe," Fagan said on his radio. He looked over at the cargo containers—*those poor kids*. The side of the first container was riddled with bullets.

The men from the warehouse began to shoot at the officers and attempted to back into the warehouse. The police continued to fire. Simons saw an officer fall, and another pulled him behind a squad car.

"Keep clear of the trucks. There are kids in there," Fagan yelled into his HT.

One of the FBI agents fell and was pulled back to safety. The gunfire and the noise from the helicopter coming in overhead kept everyone disoriented. The storm of bullets on the metal buildings sounded like thunder. The air filled with the odor of gunpowder.

Fagan looked over at the containers, seeing the holes in the side. There was no way to get to them, and grenades were hurled through the air in his direction.

"Take cover!" Fagan yelled as he scrambled away.

Simons saw a grenade hit the ground just in front of her, and she ran to the back of a squad car. The blast blew her into a truck, and she lay on the ground, her arm twisted in an ugly way and her ears and nose bleeding.

"Simons, get up," Fagan yelled. "Officer down," he repeated for the third time.

The FBI's helicopter landed on the roof of an adjacent building. Several armed agents took position and helped deflect the firing on the agents and cops on the ground. In what seemed like hours, which were merely minutes, the firing stopped. The stench of gunpowder wafted heavily in the dead hot air.

Special Agent Simons shook off the disorientation and got to her feet, cradling her right arm. Fagan came up behind her.

"That looks awful," Fagan said. "Bring in the buses," he relayed into the HT.

Fagan watched the agents surround the containers and noted the bullet holes again. He feared what he would find behind the doors.

"I'll get you to an ambulance," Fagan offered.

"It's not going to happen. My present is here somewhere, and I mean to find him. Get me some aspirin," Simons barked, looking down at her twisted and discolored arm, which did not even look like an arm.

Simons took the bottle of aspirin from the SUV, bit off the cap, chewed half a dozen, and followed Fagan to the first shipping container.

Flashlights ready, Fagan's team prepared to open the container and inhaled before the doors opened. Fagan hopped up on the dock to be the first one inside. Another agent cut the locks and unhitched the doors, swinging them open. A horrid odor drifted out.

The ambulances gathered around the trucks, and Fagan's flashlight gleamed into the dark container. The smell was familiar and cloaked the interior with something rotten. At first sight, the container appeared empty, and Fagan stepped further in with Simons behind him. Then the light hit something moving in the rear, and they both showed their lights in that direction.

Huddled in the back corner were maybe eight or nine people. Fagan went nearer and knelt in front of a young woman. "You are safe," he assured her. "Do you speak English?"

"My name is Mandy; I'm from Ft. Lauderdale," she said hoarsely.

"Alright, Mandy, how about we get you out of here and to the hospital." Fagan held out his hand.

The Sapphire Ghost

Simons watched and looked at the others. They were only teenagers, and she began to help another one out of the back and handed her off to one of the awaiting paramedics. Then she tripped over something and looked down to find a boy.

"I've got one who's shot," Simons called and leaned over with the flashlight and saw that, no, the boy's wrist was ripped open. The piece of metal he used was still in his hand. Simons looked at his gray face and shook her head.

Simons left the trailer and breathed in deeply, her arm throbbing to the point of making her sick, and she knelt over the concrete and vomited. The smell clung to her like bar smoke. She watched the emergency personnel taking kids. The second container was open, and Fagan was already inside.

Fagan closed the door to the ambulance as they loaded the last victim. Twenty-nine from both containers and all but two were alive. Fagan called Ft. Lauderdale PD to have them send their list of missing persons. He would wait until each child was looked after and had a decent meal to question them. That was one of the hardest parts but also the most rewarding. These folks would get to go home.

Fagan watched Simons standing back by herself, and she looked like she might fall over. "You sure you don't want to be checked out?" Fagan asked.

"A medic gave me a sling, and as soon as I find what the Ghost left for me, I will go to the hospital," said Simons with determination as she gritted her teeth and fought the pain.

"All right, let's see what's inside," Fagan said, because Simons was not a woman to argue with.

The officers and the agents worked to clear the buildings surrounding the assault. The sirens stopped, but the lights still flashed on the squad cars. The clanging of metal and the sounds of machinery were silent. Officers barking orders and heavy boots and clicks of radios replaced the commotion.

Fagan took the third building, immediately smelled bleach, and examined the area. Two copper shells lay on the concrete, and a pool of bleached out blood. Then he saw a man on the floor across the building, and Fagan sent another agent over to check on him.

"Simons, I think I have something," Fagan relayed to the HT.

"On my way," Simons replied.

Fagan heard muffled yelling from the crates to his left. He observed the large square of missing dust on the floor where a crate had been.

"You find something?" Simons came in behind him. She spotted the pool on the floor and the signature bleach smell. "They were here, and it appears one of them was hurt."

"Man's deceased," the other agent said behind Simons.

"Yes, and there is someone in that crate. Although it does not have a bow, I think this is your present." Fagan motioned to the crate in question. "Help me get that one off."

Fagan and the other agent lifted the wooden box, and immediately, the top flew off the one beneath. They jumped back when a black rat hit the floor and scampered off. Duncan Bruscoe Jr. sat up and looked at them, with his lip busted, his right hand bloody from bite marks, and one on his chin.

Simons smiled and handed her cuffs to Fagan. "Would you help me out?"

Fagan helped Bruscoe from the crate, read his Miranda rights, and cuffed him. The moment he saw the agents, Bruscoe became silent.

Images of arresting the Ghost danced through Tonya Simons' head. *Now, that would make FBI history.*

Chapter Seventy-Six

Helen sent a doctor for Brody. The doctor ordered him to rest for a couple of days and stitched up his head. Luca sat in the corner of Brody's room, waiting for the doctor to leave.

"I'm fine," Brody said when Luca stayed.

"I know. I want to sit here for a few more minutes," Luca said quietly.

Brody observed Luca and noted he was tired. "You should go lie down. You were also hit and did not have the doctor look at you."

"You were dead," Luca said in a whisper, "*no heartbeat* dead."

"Lucky for me, you were there," Brody replied.

Luca stood and picked up his jacket. "Another painful lesson learned. I don't care if it is only a ride-through; we will have backup."

"Understood. Go rest. You look like hell," Brody said, taking the plate from the bedside table Gavin brought up.

"See you in the morning. If you need anything, call me, and I'll bring it up," Luca said and left him.

The next couple of days passed without incident. Rusty seemed a little more relaxed as Luca and Gavin's situation had become comfortable, and the animosity dissipated.

Gavin noticed how calm Luca was. The excess energy that would have torn the house down around them was gone. Gavin did not see the deep dive he expected when Luca realized Bruscoe held him at gunpoint. Gavin was impressed with Luca's restraint. He continued to watch for any indications that he struggled with his newfound freedom.

Luca sat alone in the computer room, exhausted, and rubbed his eyes. The screen in front of him had become a blur. He had been on the phone since they came back. Opening and closing his left hand, the fall caused his arm to hurt again, and he did not have time for the pain or the fatigue. Picking up the coffee, Luca inhaled the aroma and emptied the mug.

Camille came by the house after spending the day working with Congressman Ashman in Birmingham. She waited for him upstairs. Closing his eyes, Luca tried to shake her image from his head. The time would come to say goodbye.

Camille felt a change in Luca; he was always quiet but seemed to be speaking to her from a distance. She wanted to ask Rusty what was happening because Luca was not telling her something important.

Luca was floating through the days on autopilot because he was not there mentally. The lines blurred in his realities, and he was not feeling the comfort he usually had with Camille. Did she need to be involved with what Luca was evolving into? These questions and many more swam in his mind, and he avoided talking with her about her concerns.

His family was another mental debate about how he would have to let go. He knew Helen would never let him back in Louisiana once he turned from them himself. Luca had already arranged to take care of his family. Luca would miss his sister's graduation from Pharmacy school in the spring, and his niece's play in December. His father was not so much of a concern because he and Luca had a strained relationship since Luca ran off at eighteen. He would miss his sister the most because they were always close. Luca was under the mindset that he could continue to watch over her, even if it had to be from a distance. Luca promised to spend the day with Camille and went to get ready.

When Luca and Camille returned to the house later that evening, everyone except for Gavin was in the living area watching some reality show on the television. Two Dark 9 members had come to stay at the house to make Luca comfortable with everything happening in Destin. Luca kissed Camille on the head and told her he was going to the gym for a while.

"Rusty, may I speak with you privately?" Camille asked as soon as the door shut behind Luca.

"Sure, honey." Rusty got up from the sofa and walked with her into the kitchen.

The Sapphire Ghost

"What is going on with Luca?" Camille asked. "Something is off, and I mean more than usual." Her face was pinched as she looked at him for answers.

Rusty leaned back against the counter. He thought about what he could tell Camille and what would have to be left up to Luca.

"Camille, you know you are a big part of our hearts here and a huge chunk of mine, and I know Luca's. However, you are still on a need-to-know basis, and unless Luca decides to tell you, I can't," Rusty said gently.

"I feel something big is coming, and I see a change in Luca. He spent the day with me, but he was not present," Camille said, digging her black boot's right toe into the floor.

"I can't tell you what is going on. Unfortunately, you will have to get that from him." Rusty wrapped an arm around her shoulders.

Gavin was tucked away in his room, waiting for Helen to give him a callback. She was dealing with another situation when he returned her call earlier. He sat on his bed with the files laid out before him. According to the last update, Dark 9 captured five on the grounds around the airport in Destin. The King sent these men to find him, and most, from what he had gathered from the Dark 9 team leader, were mercenaries.

Duncan Bruscoe Jr. was still in custody. Gavin spoke with Thomas Fagan and found out that Simons was doing everything possible to keep him there. However, Judge Ronald Ware would be presiding over the arraignment on Thursday afternoon. Gavin knew the judge would not risk repercussions from the family. Bruscoe would walk out of the courthouse tomorrow afternoon a free man.

Gavin's satellite phone rang, and he picked it up.

"Gavin, I am sorry it has taken so long to reply. This has been a day for all of the Ghosts," Helen said when Gavin said hello.

"I understand you have a lot of balls in the air," Gavin said, flipping the folder over on the bed.

"You seem to have some real trouble in Destin. Luca has requested another team on the ground before you arrive tomorrow," she spoke.

"Yes, I'm sure he has. He has also been over the top here in D.C.," Gavin confirmed. "But I believe what we have prepared for will alleviate most of that situation."

"Yes, it is a big project, and I hope it ends this situation for good. I am quite surprised you turned King over to the FBI," she said. "Are you all right?"

"I want him to see his empire burn to the ground. He will have the opportunity to watch it crumble. I trust that with the legal system—I'll have another shot," Gavin replied. "I'm not a hundred percent confident that Bruscoe is King, and I think the operation is much larger. I could not get him to disclose who is responsible for the videos."

"I see. What can I do?" Helen asked.

"I need an address for Bruscoe's attorney. His name is Arna Froste, and I need to have him picked up. Do you think you can find him for me?" Gavin asked.

"I am searching right now. I am sure I can find Froste's information on these bank accounts. I will forward it to your email when I locate it. I will also try to find a phone number and give you a location," she replied as her fingers flew across the keyboard.

"Thank you, Helen. I understand I have been a lot of work for you lately. I apologize."

"I am happy to help. Luca is working so hard to keep everything together, and he still has not taken a break," Helen stated. "I hope Rusty is doing well."

"No, we will all have to take one as soon as this is over," he assured her. "Rusty will return to Jamaica when we get back."

"Okay, now that this is out of the way. Tell me, what else is going on? I hear there is some trouble among the ranks," she relayed.

"I wonder who you have been speaking with?" he mused, knowing it could only be Rusty. Luca was too private to initiate a personal conversation with Helen.

"Rusty called a couple days ago and said he just needed to talk. He was really concerned about some hostility between you and Luca."

The Sapphire Ghost

"I have done what you suggested and asked Luca to follow my path. There have been some growing pains, but we are getting through. Luca is a lot darker than I imagined but getting him to embrace that side of himself has been challenging," Gavin conveyed.

"When one walks within the center of the storm, he is always surrounded by the precariousness he avoids," Helen said quietly, but impressed Gavin had taken this step. "But you have come to an understanding?"

"Yes, I believe so. We are good, but I'm sure there may still be some turbulence ahead as Luca wraps his mind around this idea. I am here to guide him through it, just as you were for me. You need to be aware in case he comes to you for advice; he may feel uncomfortable asking me."

"I will make myself available to him in any way I can. Does this mean open doors, Gavin?"

"Everything available to me should be made available to him, and you should probably prepare the process to erase him. He plans on visiting his family once more when he feels it is safe to stash me away," Gavin said and laughed.

"All right, thank you for the heads up; I will begin with his school records. That will take some time," Helen said. "Will I need to transfer his assets?"

"I believe he will take care of that himself," Gavin said.

"You all be careful. This will be an experience; I have not had anyone to train their replacement. The Sapphire Order will remain intact, or do you think he will want his own Order?" she asked.

"I think he'll carry on in my Order as if I never left. He dislikes change," Gavin said.

"I have many more questions, but I think you two are still imagining how this will work, and I will give you time," Helen said.

"I don't plan on going out anytime soon, my dear."

"That is good. I am quite fond of you, Gavin."

Chapter Seventy-Seven

Luca removed his jacket and shirt and unbuttoned the top of his jeans. His arm felt so much better today, and he unwrapped the bandage and looked at the small line of stitches. He only felt slight discomfort. Luca looked at himself in the mirror and the dark purple bruise on his chest. Turning the stereo on and increasing the volume, Luca listened to the music. He stood and allowed the beat to fill him, cleared his mind, and pushed down the pain.

The burn would commence at midnight, and it had been a long three days of planning. Brody worked with the teams on timing devices so that they could spread out and work quickly. However, since the warehouse, Luca had been on edge. He felt the lump on his chest and the bruising around it. Luca needed to dull the light that had shrouded him since the warehouse. It took every ounce of restraint he had to hold back and allow Gavin to take care of Bruscoe.

Luca started with the parallel bars, tested his left arm, and could deal with the pain. He swung himself back and forth and let his body straighten out vertically, and he free-fell back down. He turned the music up when the song changed and turned to the pommel horse. Stretching first, Luca took the handles and pulled himself up to sit. He sat waiting for something with a better beat from the Bluetooth speakers.

Rusty could hear the music from upstairs and motioned Brody to join him in the gym. Brody looked at Rusty questionably.

"Gavin is upstairs; let's go watch. Trust me, Luca won't care if we are around," Rusty said, and opened the door where the music erupted into the living area. They walked down, closing the door behind them.

Brody followed Rusty to a bench on the side of the room, in full view of the equipment. There, Brody saw that Luca was sitting on the edge of the pommel horse with his back to them.

Luca swung out his body, grabbed the handle, laying one hand on the leather, and began to free swing his body. In one direction and then the other,

The Sapphire Ghost

Luca worked his hands across the piece of equipment. Efficiently, Luca worked his way across, and then the beat became much faster, and he began his routine. The continuous movement, the elegance as Luca moved from handstand back down to the rocking motion as he caught and released the grips. Rusty could tell it had been a long time because Luca was pouring himself into the moves. Luca swung up and around to the edge of the pommel horse and tossed himself down, landing steadily on his feet. Rusty noticed the bruise on his chest and wondered if he saw the doctor. However, he was grateful that Luca insisted they wear the extra layer. The suits were great to deflect a random shot but not at point-blank range. Rusty still felt they should not have walked into that warehouse alone. This was a hard and nearly deadly lesson for Luca to learn to be more insistent.

They sat quietly and watched Luca jump to reach the rings hanging from the ceiling. Luca drew himself up so that his body was rigid against the rings, and then he extended his arms, and every muscle gleamed under a thin layer of sweat. He then brought both his legs up over his chest, and as he started to fall backward, he held himself in midair with his legs stretched out over his chest.

"You ought to see him on the uneven bars." Rusty leaned into Brody's ear.

"Yes, he's strong. I hope he doesn't damage his arm again," Brody whispered, unable to look away from the rhythmic movements. "That bruise looks awful."

"I'm sure yours doesn't look any better," Rusty said as Gavin crept down to join them.

"No, and it feels much worse than it looks. I don't understand how he can do that," Brody said.

"Gymnastics is a sport that requires burying the pain. This isn't a sport for wimps," Rusty said. "When he could put weight back on his leg after he left the VA hospital, he worked out for eight hours a day."

Gavin came up quietly, listening to Rusty tell Brody about Luca. "Someone could have let me know."

Luca did a double backward flip and dismounted in a clumsy near fall. "Crud!" he said under his breath, jumped up, grabbed the rings, and began again. He forced himself higher but smoother as he flipped forward, then backward, and took time to hold himself horizontally as he adjusted his left hand on the ring. Brody studied that adjustment cautiously and watched for any trouble.

Luca began a forward set of flips that became a little faster. Then he swung out and landed, this time neatly on both feet with his arms stretched out to the sides. He loosened the jeans at his waist and ran across the mat, flipping and twisting himself into the air. The last long backflip landed him directly in front of his audience.

"Did you like the show?" Luca said, smiling, taking a towel from the shelf beside Gavin. He walked over to turn the speaker off.

"You knew we were here?" Brody asked, and Gavin gave him a sideways glance.

"I always know when I am being watched." Luca beamed. "I have to admit that felt good."

"You looked good; I am always amazed at your strength to be able to do that stuff," Rusty said.

"Thank you," Luca replied, running the towel over his hair.

"Luca, not to get off subject, but how do I get into that closet?" Brody said, pointing to the closet next to the computers.

"Come here," Luca said, admiring the dark navy suit and wondering how long it would be for Brody to feel comfortable dressing in jeans and T-shirts.

The tailor sent two over this afternoon that were finished. Luca reached to take the pin from Brody's lapel and motioned for Brody to follow him. Luca leaned in and showed Brody the thin cross beneath the magnet, placing it on the lock, and it clicked open.

"The only locks you do not have access to are the ones to Gavin's offices. Every other one like this, you can get inside with this pin," Luca said and returned the pin to Brody's collar.

"Thank you. You were gone all day, and I didn't know how to unlock it," Brody said.

"You could have asked Rusty or Gavin. They would have been happy to show you." Luca's expression was understanding. "I know you were

The Sapphire Ghost

intimidated the other morning, but you will have to let that situation pass because they will happen more often than you would like. If they are directed at you, I need to know you can take them and learn and move on."

"All right, I understand," Brody said, beginning to pull the requested cases from the storage room.

Luca said goodnight to everyone and started to leave. He anticipated Gavin wanting to speak again, so he lingered for a few moments to give him time to do so.

"Do you have a meeting place for tomorrow if we get Arna Froste?" Gavin asked.

"I am working on it," Luca replied, tossing the towel into a hamper.

Gavin patted him on the shoulder and moved over to Rusty. "Have you spoken to Luca since we returned?" Gavin asked Rusty.

"No, he has been preoccupied since you got back. However, he hasn't seemed like himself, and Camille asked me about what was going on," Rusty replied.

"He looks fine now. I hear we anticipate nearly a hundred fires tonight," Gavin stated.

"Yes, and the FBI has also been called into several locations where Dark 9 found children being held. I think something like eighty-eight children were discovered in various locations. I'm sure you heard they found a production studio in upstate New York where they have evidence of taping and a hard drive full of child pornography," Rusty relayed.

"I know. Fagan called to tell me they had the ones from the shipping containers. Between the two containers, they have rescued twenty-nine children and adults. Two were dead; one committed suicide and the other was asthmatic. I worried that I was risking their lives with the delay."

"Gavin, I am concerned about what happened at the warehouse. Tell me the truth, does Luca have the ability to tell you no?"

"Rusty, it was a fluke and odd fluke. I believe Luca can keep me safe," Gavin said, not wanting Rusty to worry over him. It was a strange combination of events, including Brody renting the warehouse.

"These two depend on you as much as you depend on them. Do not put their lives at risk because it feels safe. You all would be dead if they weren't wearing those vests!" Rusty dominantly replied, needing Gavin to understand the seriousness. *Or, God forbid, they'd been shot in the head.*

"I understand, and it will not happen again. I know how fortunate I am to have them. You have to know I would never do anything to bring any harm to Luca."

"I know, but please be careful; he looks up to you." Deep lines were engraved around Rusty's mouth.

Gavin acknowledged Rusty's words and remembered the bruise on Luca's chest as a reminder of that possibility.

Luca headed upstairs, where Camille waited. He watched her sitting quietly on his bed and knew *she* did want to talk. Luca owed her an explanation, but it would not be tonight. He walked over to where she sat on the bed, knelt, and laid his head on her leg.

"I know you can sense something is going on, and I understand you would like an answer. However, I can't give you one now," Luca said, looking up at her large, dark eyes.

"But you plan on telling me when you can?" she asked.

"I will tell you what I can when I can. I give you no promises that; it will be everything," Luca replied.

"I am used to not knowing everything, but I need something to help me understand where you were today," Camille said, running her fingers through his damp hair.

"We are expecting complications in the next couple of weeks, which will hinder my communications with you. Please know I am not avoiding you. Right now, I do not know how or if this situation will work to our advantage. Camille, as soon as I can, I will come to you, and we will have a long conversation about what is going on with me."

Camille stood and stepped into the bathroom and turned on the shower. She could wait, and she was used to it, and just knowing he would let her know something was enough because it had to be. That bruise on his chest scared her to death.

Luca stripped out of his shorts and joined her in the shower. He reached and pulled her close, because he needed her closeness. He gently kissed the sides of her face, and then he covered her mouth with his. Luca backed Camille up against the shower wall and lifted her to him, and she wrapped her legs around his waist. He buried himself within her, his possession of her filled with greed and a deep need to fall into the simpleness of this moment. The realness of wanting and being wanted. Luca held her firmly as she arched.

Camille enjoyed the way Luca took her. He could drown her senses in him, and he became everything in these moments. It was not just these intimate moments; it was the moments when it was just the two of them. The way he tended to her every thought, his quiet power that dissolved even the roughest day into the beautiful calm that spread around him. They only had these moments a few times a year, but she waited for them.

Camille felt his release, and she heard him moan, yet he held her there. Luca bent down, stole another kiss, nipped at her chin, and then gently let her slide through his arms until her feet touched the floor. Luca did not back away, though; he just stood there with the water pelting on his back and watching her. They could have had more than this in another life or another time. This was all he had to give, and he was unsure it was fair. If he became a Ghost, he would have far less of himself to offer her.

After the shower, they stood together and brushed their teeth, and then Camille took his hand and led him to bed. Camille knew she only had tonight.

Chapter Seventy-Eight

Luca was up most of the night. Gavin wanted Duncan Bruscoe Jr., and they would need his attorney to get to him. He was beginning to believe he was a jinx because almost everything he thought was perfectly prepared went wrong. Now, they had to extend their stay in D.C. because of planning the burn. There were many more places than anticipated, which also delayed things.

Luca knew that Special Agent Simons was still in town, but he hoped she would stay away with the hearing. Then, any of the Bruscoe Crime Family who might also be looking for retribution would be around someplace. With all the activity in Destin, Luca was on edge, and then there was keeping an eye on Rusty. Everything else, the collapse of what Luca held back, all that had to wait. Luca did not have time to deal with that rage, and it was only getting in the way.

Gavin received an email from Helen about where Arna Froste was staying. He and his wife checked into a hotel in downtown D.C. Duncan Bruscoe Jr.'s arraignment would be held in the morning, so it was time to get the attorney now.

When Gavin came down that morning, he found Brody standing in the kitchen reading the newspaper.

"Brody, how are you feeling?" Gavin asked, looking at the still swollen lump on his head with the stitches.

"I'm good," Brody replied, laying the paper down. The look on Gavin's face said he wanted his full attention.

"I need you to retrieve someone for me. You feel up to that?"

"Yes, sir." Brody was eager to prove himself.

Gavin set the photograph and address on the table. "Take who you need, but have him by 4:00 p.m. You must speak to Luca about where the meeting will occur."

"Yes, sir," Brody said, looking down at the face on the photograph and the squinted features and narrow eyes of the sixty-ish-year-old man. He immediately left the room.

Luca came in next, feeling apprehension drift through the house. He found Gavin in the garden with his morning tea.

"You look stressed. What can I do?" Luca asked.

"I am sending Brody to pick up Bruscoe's attorney. Duncan Bruscoe Jr. is being arraigned in the morning, and they will set bail," Gavin replied.

"All right, do you need anything from me?"

"No, you keep preparing for the burn. We will meet with Arna Froste this afternoon, and I'll need you then," Gavin replied.

Luca went inside, where Iris was starting breakfast. The kitchen smelled of vanilla and bacon, and he left to find Brody. Brody was at the computer in the basement. A map of downtown D.C. pulled up, and he was taking notes of the roads. Froste was staying in room 412 of the Marriot.

When Luca found Brody, he was checking the clip in his gun. Two plain-dressed Dark 9 members stood before him, and Brody dictated instructions. He saw Luca enter and smiled up at him.

"Do you need any help?" Luca asked.

"Not unless you want to tag along. I think I've got this," Brody assured.

"All right, I will see you at 4:00," Luca said. He came around behind Brody, opened a page on the computer, and printed off the location. "This is where you will take him. Keep your head down and eyes open." Luca started to leave.

"Luca, wait," Brody said and stood, his brows creased in.

Luca turned around and waited for Brody to meet him.

"If I fail, what are the consequences?"

"Don't fail, and you won't have to find out," Luca stated and went back upstairs.

At 9:00 am, Brody and the Dark 9 members stepped from the car and headed into the hotel. They wore black suits and looked like Secret Service if anyone was paying attention.

No one in the lobby gave them a second glance when they marched inside and headed back to the elevators. This was an unexpected visit, and the element of surprise would be useful. When they left the elevator on the fourth floor, Brody peered down the hall to find the stairway. Acknowledging the exit marked stairs, he turned right and headed to the room. One Dark 9 member stood beside the door, and the other took the other side. Brody rapped on the door. Brody heard footsteps, kept his head down, and waited to hear the locks.

"Who are you?" Froste asked from the other side.

"Mr. Bruscoe has sent me with a message about in the morning," Brody said.

"He has not told me," Froste called back.

"Mr. Bruscoe is afraid they have your phone tapped," Brody replied. "I would prefer to give you the message in person rather than standing out here in the hall," Brody said commandingly.

The chain moved, and the door opened a crack. Brody shoved the door with his shoulder and pushed Froste back, exposing the other two members. Froste held a 9mm in his hand. The member to Brody's right instantly reached out and twisted the gun from his grip.

"Let's take a ride," Brody said, glancing around the room, hearing the shower running. "The wife in there?"

"Yes, you do not have to hurt her," Froste bellowed.

"I've not come for her," Brody replied, taking him by the arm, "and I am not here to hurt you if you do nothing stupid. Let's go." The other members closed the door behind them and looked up and down the hall. "Do not say anything, not a word. If I hear a cough, the *not hurting you* idea is off."

Arna Froste looked at Brody and understood what he saw in his eyes. This man had been sent to retrieve him, but if other measures were needed, he would not hesitate to apply them.

"Who wants me?" Froste asked, and Brody glared at him.

"All clear," the member said.

They ignored the man's question. Brody and the first member guided Froste to the end of the hallway and took the stairs. They carefully kept their heads down from the cameras' views in the hallway. Black suits and military postures were not uncommon in this city.

They had Arna Froste at the meeting site by 10:30 am.

Brody looked over at the man zip tied to a chair in a dingy abandoned bar in Annapolis. The place was filthy, and the bar had been closed for years. He brought out his phone and called Gavin.

"He's ready for his meeting, sir."

"Thank you, Brody," Gavin said and smiled to himself. The man did not play around.

Gavin went to find Luca to tell him that they would be moving the meeting time up. Honestly, he had not expected Brody to retrieve the attorney so soon.

"Luca, plans have changed. Brody has Froste, and they are ready," Gavin stated.

Luca looked up from his notes and saw Gavin with a broad smile.

"That was fast," Luca replied.

"Yes, he did well."

Luca smiled. Brody had not disappointed him. "I'll call for a car. What else do you need?"

"One of Grace's cases," Gavin said. "Do you have one here?"

Luca thought about it. "Yes. It is in Rusty's room."

Luca opened his phone to make some calls. The earlier meeting time had thrown his plans off, but that could be remedied.

Gavin knocked on Rusty's door and asked him to mix a formula.

Rusty listened to Gavin's instructions and took the small black case from the bottom drawer of his dresser. He opened it to find that the green vial was empty, and that was the one he needed to give him a 48-hour window.

"Grace, it's Rusty. Do you have a minute?" Rusty asked when she answered her line.

"Yes, what can I do?" Grace replied.

"I am missing a critical dose of your toxins: the green Miasporin. Gavin wants a 48-hour window before death, and I have the blue, clear, and amber left. Will any of these work?"

The line was silent on the other end as Grace thought about what Rusty needed. "How will it be administered?" she asked.

"He's thinking coffee," Rusty replied, holding the empty vial.

"The blue is potent; even a small dose will only give you three hours. The amber will make him sick, the clear - now I think I have something. Let us give him the flu. Take one cc of amber and two of the clear; he will get sick, but it will take about 36 hours to kill him with the toxins from the clear. Twenty-four hours for him to hemorrhage and dehydration from the vomiting. Even if he ends up in the hospital, the testing will take too long to save him. All I can give you is maybe 36 hours with what you have," Grace replied.

"I'll take the 36 hours. We will be out of D.C. in twenty-four. Please send another case to Luca's condo so they have one available," Rusty said.

"Not a problem, I will have Helen send that out immediately." Grace watched her next target enter a high-rise office building in Chicago. "I have a new one and will send instructions."

"Thanks, Grace. I knew I could count on you," Rusty said.

"Anytime. I miss you."

"Miss you too, maybe I can see you and Helen before Christmas," Rusty replied, knowing he only had until Christmas.

Rusty tossed the phone and prepared the mixture in a small syringe. He left to tell Gavin. "All I can give you is 36 hours." Finding Gavin in the garden, he said, "We were missing the toxin you wanted."

"Just as long as Froste can still be in court for the bail hearing in the morning," Gavin replied.

"I believe we're good," Rusty replied. "Is Luca ready to leave?"

"Luca was working in his room when last I spoke to him. I wonder if he is all right; he has not said much since the warehouse," Gavin said.

"I'll get him," Rusty said.

Rusty knocked on Luca's door and entered before he heard him say anything. "You ready?"

"Yes, waiting on a car. It should be here any minute," Luca said, staring at the tablet.

The Sapphire Ghost

Rusty walked over and took the tablet from his hands. "What is going on? You are quieter than usual?"

Luca looked up. "I'm good."

"Clearly, you're not. You look tired, and you're not sleeping," Rusty stated.

"No, not a lot. But I will be fine, just a lot to do," Luca muttered.

"Luca, you have never been able to hide anything from me, don't try now."

"Just a lot going on, you know this, but I have to deal with it on my own. The work helps; staying busy keeps my mind occupied. This thing that Gavin has brought to light is clawing its way out." Luca stood to pace. "It is waiting for the opportunity to expose itself. The warehouse almost undid me. I don't think even you can hold my feet to the ground."

"I see. Have you spoken to Gavin? He is here for you, but you have to let him know how to help. If you are struggling with this, he is the only one who can," Rusty said. "I want you to speak to him before leaving. Honestly, I'm not excited to see that monster come out."

Luca only nodded because it would be useless to argue. Rusty left to get Gavin. Rusty always kept Luca in line. However, now, Gavin wanted to see Luca for what he really was.

"Gavin, I think you need to speak with Luca. He is struggling; maybe some of your words of wisdom will help," Rusty said, finding Gavin waiting in the foyer.

"All right." Gavin eyed him with concern and went to Luca's room.

Gavin opened the door and saw Luca waiting for him by the desk. "How can I help?"

"I don't know that you can," Luca replied.

"Speak to me, really speak to me. This is not a time to be silent," Gavin insisted.

Luca took a deep breath and sat on the edge of the bed. "What happened at the warehouse. It's surfaced, sitting right on the edge, and I feel like . . . this thing is going to choke me." He popped his knuckles. "I cannot pull it back. I'm locked in on Bruscoe, and until he is no longer a threat, it won't go away."

Gavin went over, pulled the desk chair before Luca, and sat. "Close your eyes and envision a storm around you," he said softly.

Luca looked at him, almost rolled his eyes, and groaned. "How will this help?"

"Try," Gavin encouraged.

Luca closed his eyes and imagined a dark storm swirling around him.

"See the storm, watch the clouds, inhale, and hold your breath," Gavin instructed. "When I tell you to release, exhale, and push the storm away. Each time it will move further away."

Luca breathed in at Gavin's instructions and exhaled, imagining the storm moving away. The tightness in his chest was getting lighter. After several minutes, he felt calmer.

Gavin watched him and the tenseness leaving his face. "You asked me to teach you. I'll do that, but you'll have to let me in," he said when Luca opened his eyes.

"Thank you," Luca said, feeling much more in control.

"Luca, I don't want Bruscoe dead; that would keep him from seeing the results of all our work. I will end him, but he will remain alive," Gavin said, studying Luca.

"Understood, sir. Do you want to tell me your plan now?" Luca asked.

Gavin began to give Luca the details of what he wanted with Duncan Bruscoe Jr. It was an intriguing idea.

Chapter Seventy-Nine

At 11:30 am, Rusty drove up to the location. Luca asked to be let out two blocks up the road to get the coffee. The morning was cool with a thin breeze, and the sun sat behind a stray cloud.

Gavin climbed out of the SUV and placed his fedora on his head, while Brody opened the front door for them and stood and waited on Luca.

"He'll be along in a few minutes," Rusty said.

Brody peered through the old newspapers covering the front door. He watched as a police patrol car went by. Brody saw Luca finally crossing the road with a four-cup holder of coffees. He thought it odd that Luca was not wearing a suit for once. Instead, he wore black pants and a cargo jacket. Luca was dressed more like a Dark 9 member.

"Thanks," Luca said, handing him the coffees and taking the one for Arna Froste.

Luca strolled over to the old bar and set the cup down for Rusty. This place still spoke of a bygone era of blind pigs covered with a disguised social club atmosphere. The walls were dark, and the bar would still clean up to a nice polish if tended well. Luca left Rusty with the coffee and went to investigate his surroundings.

Luca toured the interior, then opened the backdoor to find a red plumbing van parked outside.

Gavin stood with Rusty while they waited for Luca to return. It seemed to Gavin that Luca was more interested in the bar's layout than the situation at hand. Gavin wanted to say something, but Rusty shook his head.

"Let him be he's tuned in on something like a hunting dog. He will calm down when he finds what he is looking for," Rusty said.

Gavin nodded, taking the coffee back to where Brody and the other members waited with Froste.

"I will not be a bad host. Thought you could use a coffee, just sugar, I believe," Gavin said, setting the paper cup down in front of him. "Cut him loose."

Froste rubbed his wrist when the member cut the zip ties. "What can I do for you?"

"Finally, someone who does not tell me I have no idea who I am dealing with."

"Been around a while; either you are awfully dumb or terribly brilliant. Either way, it makes no difference," Froste advised.

"No, it does not." Gavin smiled. It's too bad Arna Froste worked for Bruscoe, or he might like him.

"Let's have it; what do you want? If it's Bruscoe, I can't help you." Froste picked up the coffee.

Gavin stood back and watched as he took a sip. "I want Bruscoe, and you will help me with that. I promise it would be in your best interest."

"Not going to happen. You have no idea who Bruscoe is tied in with, and I won't go against him." Froste looked thoughtfully at the man who stood before him. "You are that Ghost who managed to get him arrested."

"Yes."

Luca came back into the room and went to the front door. He peeled back a small section of newspaper, peering out. There wasn't anyone on the street, not a soul. He looked over where Gavin was speaking to Froste. Something was getting ready to go down, and Luca could feel the heaviness of gravity pushing him to the floor. Luca looked over at Rusty and shook his head.

Rusty's brows grew close, and his face shifted into a hard mask. Brody watched the exchange between the two and felt his senses heighten in alarm.

"What are you thinking?" Brody came over and asked.

"Maybe nothing but paranoia," Luca said. "Look out there and tell me what you think?"

Brody scrutinized the street and saw nothing—too much of nothing. The cars had disappeared, and the only ones remaining were their two. The shops across the street had no lights, and it felt like a storm had shut down the road.

"Yes," Brody said softly.

The Sapphire Ghost

Luca fixed his gaze on Rusty and tilted his head for him to get closer to Gavin. The ticking of a bomb had started in Rusty's mind.

"Sir, we might want to take this someplace else," Rusty said.

"Don't overreact, Rusty. I can deal with one doing that, but not two," Gavin bellowed.

"No, sir. I do not believe it's an overreaction. Something is wrong," Rusty said.

Arna Froste's eyes met the Ghost's. "Neither of us is getting out of here. Bruscoe has an army, and they are the worst of the worst."

"Fox Phantom," Gavin assumed.

"Yes. If they tailed me, then we're all dead. Bruscoe will not risk me saying anything," Froste said helplessly. "It will finally be over."

Gavin studied Froste, and the man looked like a sad dog on a chain to Gavin. He took the coffee from the table. "You are loyal to him?"

"I'm afraid of 'im," Froste said. "He will not hesitate to kill me, my wife, children, and their children."

Luca sat and rubbed his temples. He took several slow, deep breaths and listened to everything going on. The distant blare of a ship horn, the sound of a freight truck, and the ticking of his watch. The room smelled of dust and mildew and Froste's aftershave. He continued to listen and become one with the air around him and could almost taste the colors of the energy in the room. Luca heard a click from the backdoor.

"Luca, Luca . . . !" Rusty shouted when Luca lifted his head.

"What is it?" Luca spoke into his mic. "Team two, are you in place? I am sending them in."

As if not hearing what Rusty said, Luca went over to Gavin. "You keeping him?"

"I think so," Gavin said, and his hackles immediately rose at the dark expression on Luca's face.

"Let's go." Luca lifted the man from the chair like a doll and led them to the back storage room.

"Brody, grab the other side," Luca commanded. They moved the large storage shelf from the wall, exposing a short door, and Luca pried it open with his knife and revealed an old wooden ladder leading down. "Get in." Luca pushed Arna Froste through the space and motioned for Brody to follow, then Gavin and Rusty.

Luca stepped back when Rusty climbed into the hole and started down. "Tell him I am sorry for this."

"Where are you going?" Rusty called when Luca started to close the door at the top.

"Out the front," Luca said, closing the door. He struggled but managed to get the shelf back in place. He hurried from the storage room, closing the door behind him.

Luca's nerves jumped when the back door hit the interior wall as he headed to the front of the building. He opened the front door and stepped out; it was eerily quiet—and Luca could imagine the music from an old western just before a shootout.

Chapter Eighty

Brody stepped on a bag at the bottom of the steps and picked it up before Gavin climbed down. Gavin stood still in the dark and waited for Rusty to get off the ladder. Brody fished out three flashlights from the bag and handed them off. "Team one, stay with Luca if you can hear me." Brody ordered into the mic. Nothing came over the earpiece.

"Where is Luca?" Gavin asked Rusty.

"He said he was going out the front," Rusty said, looking over at Brody with a concerned expression at hearing no response from the team.

"What did he hear or see that had him panicked?" Gavin asked, turning on his flashlight. "Where are we?"

Brody led them down the old tunnel and shivered at the sight of all the spider webs. *This was not going to be good.* Rusty surveyed the old wooden boxes that used to contain bootlegged liquor. Gavin was going to have a meltdown of epic proportions.

Gavin showed his light around and came to a dead stop. His feet would not move.

"Gavin, look at me. Let's get out of here," Rusty said. "Do I need to cover your eyes?"

Gavin swallowed hard and handed his flashlight to Rusty, taking a handkerchief and covering his mouth.

Arna Froste stood in the dark, waiting for the door to open. He felt like his chest would turn outward, but he would never be safe if he ran.

"Brody, lead the way. I have him; keep that man upfront," Rusty warned.

Brody followed the instructions and led them down the tunnel. The air was heavy, and the dust was making him cough. The tiny particles of too dry earth shifted in the beams of the light.

Luca walked out the front door, took a grenade from his pocket, and pulled the pin. He tossed it under the Lincoln and jogged down the street. Two men came out of the alley and began pursuit. The Lincoln blew up, and then there was one. Luca led him away from the building and took a left onto another alley. The man in pursuit caught up quickly. Luca bounced off the brick wall and onto a dumpster, grabbing ahold of a pipe and heaved himself onto a fire escape.

The guy fired, and Luca felt the bullet pass his face as he flung himself onto the roof. Luca heard the man jump on the dumpster and listen to the scrape of the fire escape. He stood and looked down at where the man was getting his hand onto the fire escape railing. Luca ran to the other side of the roof and jumped onto the next one, hearing more bullets coming from below. A dark Jeep was riding along the buildings following him, and he jumped again. The fellow behind him landed on the second building. Luca flung himself off the building and landed on a car below, and rolled off onto the pavement. The car alarm went off. Hurriedly getting to his feet, he felt a splintering pain in his leg. The Jeep came around just as Luca rolled off the car's roof and ran in the opposite direction. He cleared the storefronts and took a narrow passageway, too small for a vehicle. The Jeep stopped at the end, and several men got out.

Luca headed to the alley's end and sprinted toward the graveyard by the church. He was hoping the gravestones would provide some cover. The men were catching up, and Luca turned to fire, and they fired back. Grimacing through the shooting pain in his leg, he had no choice but to push through, even though the entire left side of his body was straining. He would have to come up with another idea. Going for cover at the church was not an option.

Brody saw lights flickering up ahead and pulled his gun.

"Sapphire," a Dark 9 member called.

"Yes, we have him," Brody replied, relieved.

"Mr. Medina called ahead for us to retrieve you," the member said, standing with three other Dark 9. "The first team is not responding."

"I know. Do you know where Mr. Medina went?" Brody asked.

"No, sir." The member said, "He was supposed to head to the church if he got away."

Rusty's brows knitted, and his lips twitched. "If he got away, he planned this?"

The Sapphire Ghost

"Yes, this morning. Medina had three teams, and I have asked the third team to find the first and Mr. Medina," the member replied. "He had three contingencies. A van waiting by the back door, the tunnel, and through the building next door where another team would have picked you up," the member relayed.

Gavin stepped in front of Rusty. The idea that Luca was endanger overrode Gavin's fear of something crawling on him. "Find him!"

"Yes, sir," the member replied.

They followed the Dark 9 members out of the tunnel into the lower parking lot of a bank, where a car waited.

When Luca ran onto the bridge, the Jeep was right behind him, and another followed. The automatic fire rang out, cars screeched to a stop, and horns blared.

"Stop, you are surrounded," the gunman yelled at Luca.

Luca stopped, put his hands behind his head, and turned to face the man. He was at the end of his physical limits and struggling to come up with an exit strategy that would keep him alive.

"You are surrounded, nowhere to go. Now we need Arna Froste back, dead or alive, it makes no difference," the gunman said.

Luca kept his hands behind his head while they trained their weapons on him. He saw the green dots on his chest. "I don't have him."

"But you know where he and that Ghost are, and you're gonna tell us." The gunman replied and started walking toward Luca. "Or this will be a painful experience."

"I would not do that if I were you." Luca gave him a grim smile.

The skinny bearded fellow continued toward Luca with the semi-automatic trained on his chest.

Luca pulled the pins, held the spoons, waited and tossed two grenades, and leaped for the side of the bridge. He jumped, the grenades went off, and the blast's energy forced him further out over the Potomac.

Gavin, Rusty, and Arna Frost, who Rusty blindfolded, sat in the back of an SUV while Brody rode up front with the Dark 9 member.

"I'll take y'all back; everyone else is going to Servera Park. They have a report of gunmen on the bridge," the member said.

"Take us to the park," Gavin ordered.

"I'm sorry, sir. Mr. Medina was specific and said you were to be taken directly back to the house. No ifs, and, or buts," he replied.

"Rusty, make him take me to the bridge," Gavin insisted and knew he had no pull with Dark 9. They were the FIC's command.

"Gavin, I'm no longer the FIC, and Luca gave him orders. I cannot override them, not even if I wanted to," Rusty said. "Believe me, I want to know that he is okay."

They reluctantly got out at the house, and the Dark 9 member followed them inside.

"You don't have to stay," Gavin said.

He looked at the Sapphire Ghost apologetically. "Yes, sir, I do."

"He covered everything in a short amount of time," Rusty said.

"No repeats of the bombing, arrest, or warehouse," Brody replied.

"You knew?" Gavin asked accusingly.

"He told me about the three teams. I know that those situations bother him. What do you want me to do with him?" Brody asked, nudging Froste.

"Find him a room and ensure he has no means of communication," Rusty ordered.

Gavin went to the bar and poured two drinks. "He planned for any conceivable possibility, even the crazy ones. What gave him the idea that things would go wrong?"

"London, Las Vegas, the warehouse. He had a backup to his backup," Rusty said, taking the glass of scotch from Gavin. "So, I can only assume he planned to get himself out safely."

"Yes, the last few months were complicated, and it was all about learning, and it did not take long for him to remedy the situation. I agree; if he had three plans to get me out, he had a plan for himself. Have we heard what happened to the Dark 9 onsite?"

"They have not been found, and the Fortress thinks they've been taken for information on you," Brody said, hearing the conversation.

The Sapphire Ghost

"We will take care of their families," Gavin said. "Brody, call Helen and find out if the first team was ever at this house?"

"Yes, sir," Brody replied as he took out his phone.

"Where would Luca go if he could not get back here? Where should they look for him?" asked Gavin.

Rusty shook his head and looked at the team member standing by the door. He had a look of worry scrunching his face.

"What is it, kid?" Rusty asked.

"Mr. Medina went into the river under heavy gunfire," he said, listening to the information in his earpiece.

Chapter Eighty-One

Braxton Fox stood with a man from his army out of sight of the local PD. Fox watched through the monocular, looking for any movement in the water. The man they chased onto the bridge took a swan dive into the river. They needed that man to get the attorney back. Arna Froste held too much information on the business practices to allow him to escape. Dead or alive, that is what Byron King told him. Get the attorney back.

He rubbed at the rough, scarred skin on his face. Most of his face had been reconstructed after the Ghost had torched a building with him still inside. He lost six of his men that day. Fox, however, was not easy to kill, because it wasn't easy to kill the devil. Fox hunted the Ghost for ten years, and Garrison was in the city. He would tie that loose end up soon, and it was well earned. The man who had dove into the river would talk as soon as he could locate him. Fox adjusted the eye patch over his right eye. The Ghost almost burned Fox alive, and he intended to return the favor.

A rough-looking fellow of thirty came up. "Haven't found anything yet. FBI is still on the bridge. The crew at the abandoned bar are still combing the area. We have three of their men being held back at the house."

"I will speak to them this evening, but I don't think they will know much; just footmen. The man who jumped off the bridge is who I want," Fox said, his voice breaking in and out.

"Do you know with certainty that the Ghost is here and not back in Destin?" the rough man asked.

"No, not with certainty, just a gut feeling. King's in Destin and the scouts are working overtime." Fox coughed and cleared his throat. "Find a boat and take it downriver. Find him."

"On it," the rough man said, pulling a cigarette from behind his ear.

Fox was unsure of the organization's depth but knew it was big. He did not care. Braxton Fox had no stake in the game other than the kill, which would gain him a mint because the Ghost had a fifty-million-dollar bounty on his head. Fox's army was the most ruthless group of individuals on the planet, and most were already presumed dead.

Whoever held Arna Froste in that bar had escaped out of a tunnel leftover from prohibition. When his soldiers found their way to the end, they were gone.

Chapter Eighty-Two

Luca held onto the pier just below the bridge. He heard sirens above, and someone was barking orders into the handheld. He heard a familiar voice just overhead. Tonya Simons was standing on the bridge.

Luca climbed up and onto the girder with the last bit of his energy and lay below the bridge. He could see the uniformed men on the embankment who had pursued him. Their uniforms were green like the Army, but their stances were more informal. Mercenaries, no doubt working for Fox Phantom.

Luca lay on the beam below the bridge, sputtering, trying not to cough, but his breathing instincts were stronger. So, he timed his coughing fits with the squawks of the sirens. His left leg throbbed. It did not hurt often, but it hurt now. Dropping onto the car was bad but falling into the water had caused such pain that it almost drowned him. He planned for almost any problem they might encounter except water, and his phone was wet. Luca could see no way off this bridge any time soon.

Luca thought back to the walk to the abandoned bar. The road was a little too clear. The area was too quiet, and the stores were left unopened. They followed Brody, and he was unsure how. Brody was incredibly observant. A tracker, maybe, but that made no sense because the man appeared to have been taken even before he was fully dressed; he wore no jacket, tie, or belt. Dark 9 would have scanned him for any internal chips. Could a member of Dark 9 have been compromised? Luca thought back to the Dark 9 members in his house that morning with Brody, and nothing about them raised any alarms. Luca needed to rest and clear his head to see the solution he knew was there. However, all he wanted to know was if his team was safe.

Luca would have to decide on one of two things. He could lay here until the police above and the army below left, or he could crawl back down and swim with the pain in his leg upstream from everyone, get out, and find a phone. Adjusting to the small space and moving his leg, he bit his lip to muffle

The Sapphire Ghost

a scream. That answered that question; he was stuck, and for the moment, somewhat safe.

Moments later, Brody returned to Gavin with the phone. "She wants to speak with you."

Gavin shook his head. "Yes, Helen."

"Gavin, you had Brody call me when it should have been you," Helen scolded.

"Yes, Helen, because I don't want to hear it," Gavin replied.

"I have sent more scouts to the bridge and some to ride the river. No, the members who have been taken have not been to the house, and I feel it would be in your best interest to move," Helen demanded.

"We need to be here when Luca makes it back," Gavin said.

"You have Arna Froste in that house. What were you thinking?" she asked.

"He's an unwilling participant. His wife was also picked up and held at Dr. Wasson's former home. Brody will allow them to stay at his house in Detroit when we get them out. I must get to Bruscoe, but I do not have time to plan anything else."

"Gavin, you know what I am thinking. You need to be careful and consider what you have already planned. *Do not* force my hand," Helen said.

"I know exactly what you are thinking. Why do you think I am still here?" Gavin replied. Helen was on the verge of forcing him to go home, even without Luca.

"Stay inside the lines, Gavin; I will not warn you again," Helen said and hung up.

Gavin handed the phone back to Brody. "I cannot leave, or everything will be compromised, including Destin." Although Luca may not be around to take him in, dozens of Dark 9 were in D.C.

Rusty acknowledged him with a nod. He may be retired, but if needed, he would do as Helen requested, and they both knew this because of his Oath.

Brody took his phone. "I am going to make a sandwich."

Brody crept upstairs, changed, and headed down. The member stood like a sentinel at the front door, and he knew others were outside. Gavin and Rusty went downstairs to look for Luca's plans, and Brody slipped out the back and over the brick garden wall.

Luca nearly fell off the girdle when he dozed off. He caught himself, his leg hit against the beam, and he almost screamed. The men on the ground were gone, but there was still a lot of activity on the bridge above him.

Brody went to the valet parking lockbox of a restaurant two blocks down from the townhouse and fished for a set of keys. Slowly and staying under the cameras, Brody clicked the key fob for a Chrysler. He heard the beeping and ran up the deck and found the car. Getting in behind the wheel, Brody thought, *where would Luca go*? As he drove out of the parking deck, he began to get inside Luca's head. He would not do anything that was expected; that Brody was sure of, but what would not be expected? He could have left the water immediately and headed to town, but those men would have followed him. Dark 9 had been looking for him for the last two hours without results.

Brody feared the worst; either he had been captured, shot, or drowned. If he were Luca, he would stay closer than either the police or the others would have anticipated. He would have stayed right under their noses. Brody smiled to himself; that is precisely what Brody would do—staying in the brush, under a high embankment, or even lying low beside a boat.

Gavin came upstairs to find something for him and Rusty to eat. Rusty needed to eat to keep his strength up, and today's extra stress worried him. Nothing was disturbed in the kitchen. The guard stood by the door, and Brody was nowhere in sight.

"Brody," he called and headed up to the rooms. Arna Froste was sitting quietly, but Brody's room was empty.

Gavin opened the door to the basement and called Rusty upstairs. "Brody's gone."

"Oh," Rusty said, "guess he took it upon himself to find Luca. I did tell him Luca was his job, and unless Helen told him directly to stay put, I would have done the same thing."

"Helen is on the verge of shutting us down. If Luca is all right, he will find his way home."

"And if he's *not* all right?" Rusty asked.

"I must believe if he took such great care to manifest three plans for my safety, he had his own plan," Gavin stated. "He has a lot more going on than I have given him credit for. He is a full-on soldier if he has sunk back into that hidden place. And he knows that Bruscoe is responsible for this. It will be another Steve Bains."

"He told you he would never do that again, and you're not injured," Rusty said.

"I know what he told me. Luca also knows what I wanted, and if he feels I personally cannot accomplish that, he might try," Gavin said.

"You're curious what he is capable of?" Rusty asked.

"I'm interested to see what lives inside him, yes, but not to his harm," Gavin said. "He's done things, bad things, things he does not want to discuss. Yes, I want to know because I want to understand how to help him face himself without loathing himself."

Brody drove around where the police were still directing traffic on the other side of the bridge. Parking the stolen car out of sight, Brody examined the parking lot before stepping out. Taking the duffle bag from the back seat and walking down to the sidewalk's edge to get to the water. He observed those who stood around talking on phones, jogging, or tending to children. Brody did not see any military-looking folks in the area. Taking cover behind some trees, he removed the rifle scope from the duffle and studied the river, paying attention to the brush, tall grasses, and then the pillars under the bridge and scanning the edges for anything that should not be there. Brody knelt and closely explored the entire area. There was no sign of Luca. The fire trucks were leaving the bridge, and he looked up to see how many officers remained. Then he thought he saw movement. He sighted in on the bridge girder and studied it carefully. "I see you." A black-clad form, stretched out on the metal, hidden from sight by the overhang.

Brody took off his watch and used it to glint light toward Luca's direction. The light danced off the side of the steel beam.

Luca lay still, hearing the trucks rumbling overhead. The water was twenty feet below him. He saw a reflection in the water and thought a boat was coming and pulled himself up more tightly on the beam. Then he saw it again, and it appeared to be flickering in Morse Code. He watched the flickering lights, trying to decipher the message. The message was **BRODY**. Luca sighed in relief that his team got out, and Brody found him. The lights were coming from the left side of the bridge, and crawling across would be slow and painful. Luca gritted his teeth before dropping down and nearly let go when pain slammed into his right shoulder and arm. He hand-walked himself across the bottom. Luca tried to push down the discomfort and swung himself along the bottom of the beam, his right hand weakening with each tug. However, the only place he could go when he reached the other side was in the water. Hitting the water again wasn't something he needed. His body already protesting each move, the cold, wet clothing causing him to tremble. His fingers were numb, and the lower half of his body weighed too much.

Brody watched Luca drop and start pulling himself along the bottom of the bridge, and he ran back to the car. He would have to get closer. Pulling the car out on the road, Brody found a turnaround gravel area near the edge of the bridge. He took the long overcoat out of the bag and a ball cap to the water's edge. Brody slid down the bank to hide and wait. Luca was over halfway across but seemed to be taking his time. He was favoring his right arm. Luca's left hand held on, his fingers slipping, but his right arm would not follow. Luca's hand lost strength, and he fell.

Brody dove into the water and swam out to help him. When Luca surfaced, Brody was already there. He reached out and pulled him close, Luca's back to Brody's front, then swam back under the bridge's cover.

"I've got you." Brody got Luca out of the water, draped the long coat over him, and helped him to the car, and they were back on the road. Brody hoped no one was paying attention to them. "Where're you hurt?"

"My leg mostly, but my shoulder is throbbing. Maybe I dislocated it when I fell on the car," Luca's voice was slight and wavered between chattering teeth.

"Did you get shot in the leg?"

"No, it's the old injury; I aggravated it when I hit the water. It'll be fine," Luca replied groggily.

"We'll get you back to the house and check you out. Why'd you not come with us into the tunnels?" Brody asked.

"They needed a target, and I needed to draw them away," Luca said.

"That makes no sense. You could've taken to the tunnels, and they would have never known."

"If I had, they would have known exactly where you went and followed. Also, they wouldn't have been distracted and would have gotten to you all before you reached the end," Luca said, rubbing his arms because he was freezing. "Blowing up the car bought you all a few minutes." Luca felt the wound under the vest. "We have a problem."

Brody looked over, "What?"

"I've been shot," Luca said, staring at his hand. Blood on his fingers.

"Relax, I'll find a place to stop and check you out. Trust me."

"I don't feel so well," Luca said, his head slumping forward.

Panic hit Brody when he saw him pass out. He took out his phone.

"Helen, I need a safe place; please, I am driving south on Rowe Boulevard."

"What's wrong?"

"I found Luca. He's been shot, and I don't have a safe place to pull over and check him out. He just passed out," Brody relayed.

"Give me a minute," Helen said and logged in to find someplace they could use.

"Call Rusty for me and let him know what's happening, and that I have Luca. I will get back to the house soon."

"I will," she said. "I have you an address, and I am sending it to your phone."

Brody reached over, taking Luca's wrist and searching for a pulse. His hand was cold. "Thank you."

"Brody, if he needs more than you can do, let me know immediately. I will start on transport just in case," Helen said.

"I will," Brody hit end, opened the message to retrieve the address, and let it go to maps.

Brody followed directions into a residential area and a small house with a for-sale sign. He drove under the carport and went to the door, breaking the window to unlock it, then retrieved Luca. Once inside, he laid him on the kitchen floor. He began to tug at the jacket and vest, "Wake up!" he said, tapping on Luca's cheeks.

Brody got no response. The jacket was wet and hard to get off. He felt over Luca's front and did not feel anything. He turned Luca over and saw the bloodstain on the back of his shirt. Brody worked the vest off and unclipped the knife from Luca's belt, cutting the shirt so he could see the damage. There wasn't an exit wound. Brody's phone rang in his pocket, but he ignored it, knowing it would be Rusty wanting information.

The bullet came in under the vest. The flesh was open just beneath Luca's left shoulder blade, and he would need to get the slug out. Brody ran back out to the car and grabbed his bag.

Brody turned on the lights, knelt beside Luca, wiped down the area, and took out his tools. Brody felt around the wound and thought he felt it in the muscle. Using the forceps, he dug in, clamped on, pulled it out, and applied bandages. Luca was fortunate that it had not gone too far, and it did not cause too much damage. This did not explain why Luca passed out. Looking at the seepage from the wound, the vest had given pressure to the injury. Brody took his pulse, which was extremely low, as was his heart rate. Then he examined him again. He was puzzled at finding no other wounds. Luca's skin was cold but not overly so.

"Luca, wake up." Brody tapped at the side of his face.

Luca grimaced and opened his eyes. "Where are we?"

"We are safe, and I extracted the bullet," Brody said, relieved.

"I need to get back. I need to see Gavin," Luca grumbled, sitting up.

"You need to rest. I think you are exhausted. You passed out on me," Brody said.

"I'm sorry, but I'm fine," Luca said. Pain hit his leg, and his jaw tightened.

"I am taking you back, and you are going to rest. Do not make me get Rusty involved," Brody threatened.

"Keep your mouth shut!" Luca said in no uncertain terms.

"No, either you rest, or I will make sure you do. Don't try me on this," Brody said.

Luca heard the promise in Brody's tone and backed off. If he could handle Gavin, he could clearly handle him.

"Fine, Dr. Brody, I'll rest. But don't worry them about this. Please, Rusty doesn't need the stress."

"I know, and as long as we understand each other, I won't," Brody spoke with an authority he usually did not use.

Brody dug the phone out of his pocket, hit the number, and handed it to Luca. "They're worried. I think it would be best if they heard your voice."

"Hi, Rusty," Luca said.

"You're okay? Helen called to tell us that Brody had found you, and he was going someplace safe to remove a bullet," Rusty said.

"I'm good and patched up. I am a little tired, and we are headed back," Luca said, looking at Brody. "Nothing a little rest won't solve. You know I don't stay down for long."

"I know, son, we will see you both soon," Rusty said, smiling at Gavin.

"You know I already have two overbearing dads; I don't need a third," Luca said, while limping out the door. "I guess you've already called for a cleaner?"

"Yes," Brody said and smiled. "Consider me a protective older brother."

Finding a parking lot out of the way, Brody called a team member and asked for a pickup because he was driving a stolen car. Within ten minutes, Brody and a Dark 9 member exchanged vehicles. Brody then rode around the block twice before settling on a parking space.

"You all right?" Luca asked.

"Yes, just being careful. I can't shake the feeling I am being watched. I cannot figure out how they found us this morning. No one followed me, and I was extremely aware of everything around me," Brody said and turned to Luca. "I didn't miss anything. We scanned him before we left the hotel, and he didn't have an embedded chip or anything. Froste is in that house, and it scares me."

"I know. I lay under that bridge for over three hours, thinking about things. Somehow, they followed you or had Froste tracked. I don't know unless it is something high-tech we are not aware of yet. I cannot believe that because we usually have those things before the military does."

"We checked everything, even threw away his glasses," Brody said.

"I know you were careful; maybe a drone followed you. The same drone would not have been able to follow Froste back here because it would not have had sight while you all were going through the tunnels," Luca said.

"Could be. Anyway, you are going in to eat and to bed," Brody said while opening the car door.

"Yes, boss," Luca said. "May I at least take a shower?"

"I would hope so; you smell." Brody laughed.

Chapter Eighty-Three

The Dark 9 member opened the door when they stepped up to the front of the house. "Good to see you, Mr. Medina," he said. "They are waiting for you."

Luca hobbled in and stripped out of the long coat. His chest was bare, and he went to the kitchen.

"Good to see you." Gavin hugged him, and Luca flinched. "You had me worried."

"I'm sorry, couldn't be avoided. You are safe, and that's all that matters," Luca replied.

Rusty approached Luca and looked him over. He walked around him and saw the bandage on his upper back. "How bad?" he asked Brody.

"Muscle," Brody replied, and they acknowledged that Brody was in doctor mode. This is where Brody took control, and Gavin knew this well.

"Iris has made a chicken pot pie, and I'm sure you are hungry," Gavin said.

"I'm starving, but I have been in the river and need a shower. I'll be back in twenty." Luca smiled and left.

Rusty watched him limp off. "What's he not telling us?"

"Somehow, he hurt his leg, the left one, when he dove into the river. He says he will be fine," Brody said. "I would feel better with some X-rays."

"See what you can set up," Gavin stated.

"Yes, sir," Brody said and also went to take a quick shower.

Luca stood in the shower and rubbed the jagged scar on his leg. It had been years since he hurt like this. It would never be normal, and he put a lot of stress on it. This might mean another visit to Ecuador and he would speak to Gavin about that in the morning. Right now, he wanted to keep Brody off his back.

He dressed, took care of his newest injury, and headed out for a big plate of chicken pie.

"You look much better," Gavin said when he returned.

"Sir, I am fine. Nothing I cannot deal with," Luca replied.

"I know. Let me know if I can do anything," Gavin said.

"Okay, you can call Ecuador and get me an appointment after Destin. I think it might be time for more injections," Luca admitted.

"I can do that. Can you wait that long?" Gavin asked.

Luca smiled. "Yes, it's been seven years. The doctor said it would need to be redone by eight. Just a little reminder, that's all."

"All right," Gavin said, relieved Luca was opening up.

Luca took the plate Brody handed him. The pot pie warmed him more than the shower. After he ate, he intended to go and lay down and obey Dr. Brody's orders. Right now, Gavin and Rusty appeared calmer, and Luca wanted to keep it that way.

"I think I need to lie down for a while. I'm tired," Luca said, taking the plate to the sink and nodding at Brody.

Brody gave Luca a knowing half-smile. "I will check in with you this evening."

Gavin stood to follow Luca to the bedroom. "May we speak in private?"

Luca waited for Gavin to go into his room. He had no idea what Gavin needed to say that he would not say in front of Rusty.

"Today, how did you know?" Gavin asked.

"I didn't. I've felt like a jinx lately and wanted to be ready for anything."

"You knew something when you walked into that place this morning. You were in a mood," Gavin said.

"Yes. There was no traffic, and the shops were closed. Something was off," Luca said.

"You drifted over," Gavin asked, not seeing anything from earlier.

"No, I sank into the clarity. There's a difference. The clarity enhances my senses. Drifting overtakes me," Luca explained.

"How far?" Gavin asked.

"No further than what I normally use. I didn't drift over Gavin, and I remained myself," he said. "I don't need that."

"I thought you might go after Bruscoe."

"I told you I would not do that again," Luca replied. "You still don't trust me!"

The Sapphire Ghost

Gavin held up a hand. "That's not what I'm saying. I don't have another plan, and I have Froste sitting upstairs," Gavin said.

"What are you saying?" Luca was getting an idea.

"You know what I want, and I cannot make that happen right now. Helen is on the verge of taking over the Sapphire Order, and if I step one foot out of line before Destin, she will call a Code 5." Gavin stared Luca directly in the eyes. "I want Duncan Bruscoe Jr. disabled before we leave."

"No problem if that is what you want," Luca acknowledged, "but if I don't rest, Dr. Brody will disable me."

Gavin smiled knowingly and left the room.

Gavin asked him to take care of Duncan Bruscoe because Gavin could not and remain free. He would find a way to disable the man at the courthouse. If Bruscoe made it into a car and got away, Bruscoe would go into hiding. That gave Luca until the next day to formulate a plan to ensure Gavin's wishes.

Brody came in later to check on the bullet wound and give him something for the pain in his leg. Luca gratefully accepted the pain pills.

"Thank you. I appreciate you finding me," Luca said.

"No problem. You would do the same for me," Brody replied, leaving the room.

Luca rolled over to sleep. It had been a long day, and with what Gavin was asking, he did not sleep that afternoon. His leg hurt, keeping his mind off his shoulder. The bullet wound was not bad at this point. But he needed to rest the leg for whatever came tomorrow.

Helen was close to shutting the Sapphire Order down and calling Luca to bring the Ghost home. Luca had never been directed to do this and did not like the idea. Especially now that they had so much on the line, he needed to call Helen and see how close she was.

"Luca, how are you feeling?" Helen asked.

"I'm well," Luca said.

"Brody said it was not bad but required a few stitches."

"Yes, another one for the collection," Luca said. "Gavin remained safe; he was never in danger."

359

"I know, Rusty spoke to me. You took many precautions. I appreciate your attention and know it was well earned after your troubles. Your planning today is the only reason you are still in D.C."

"Gavin alluded to as much. He is under house arrest then?" Luca asked, relieved Helen did not seem to be wanting to enact the Code.

"He should stay where he is until you go to Destin. I know he wants Bruscoe, but that must wait until another time. Gavin has enough trouble going on. You, the burn, and his plan for Destin. I am sending someone to retrieve Froste in the morning." Helen paused. "Luca, I do not want to lay waste to his plans in Destin, but he has bitten off more than he can chew. Do you understand?"

"Yes, ma'am. He will stay here under guard," Luca replied.

"Ensure it happens."

"Trust me, he understands and is fully aware of the cost."

"I hope you are correct. Gavin thinks Bruscoe is the King or in his kingdom. Do not let Gavin get away from you. I know how he is when he is intent on something," she stated.

"You have my word," Luca said.

"Thank you, and I hope you feel better in the morning," Helen said.

Helen felt a little bad that almost every time he had been responsible for ensuring his Ghost was safe since Rusty retired, something went wrong. At least he was learning how to prepare better. Although Gavin took his instructions well this afternoon, he seemed to be distracted by Luca's progress into a Ghost more than his work.

Chapter Eighty-Four

Luca woke around 4:00 a.m., with about all the laying around he could stand. He limped into the kitchen to make coffee and start on his preparations. Taking his coffee downstairs, he booted the computer and looked up the penal codes for the District of Colombia.

Gavin and Brody met in the kitchen several hours later while Iris prepared breakfast. Brody wanted to ask Gavin questions about what Luca was doing today but could not in front of Iris. Gavin sat quietly, watching Brody out of the corner of his eye.

"Speak your piece," Gavin said.

Brody looked over at Iris. "Not here." Brody followed Gavin into the garden. "What is Luca going to do today?"

Gavin smiled at Brody; he was gaining his nerve, and his devotion to their Order was building.

"He's going to take care of Bruscoe Jr. today," Gavin stated.

"You understand that this concerns me. He took a bullet yesterday, and his leg is hurting him. He's going to collapse from exhaustion!"

"Brody, I appreciate your concern, and if I did not feel him capable, I would not have enlisted his help," Gavin said. "This is a good experience for you."

"Would you advise him to take me? I want to be close, in case he needs me?"

"Why don't you insist? You're his backup, and sometimes you need to exhibit some control. If you plan on handling a Ghost." Gavin turned it around on him.

"He listens to you better than me," Brody argued.

"You wouldn't be on this team if he didn't trust you. You have his trust and his ear; speak to him. I've learned to."

Brody eyed Gavin, but he was not budging on the topic. "I'll find him; he was not in his room."

Gavin sucked in a breath; it was possible; Luca had already left. The possibility did scare him. Luca liked to work alone, which would have to change.

"Check the basement," Gavin said.

Brody gave a short nod and went to find Luca. He headed to the basement and found Luca at his desk. Still in his nightclothes, which told Brody Luca had gotten up early. The coffee was still untouched in the cup.

"Luca," Brody said.

Luca looked up as if not realizing what time it was. "What are you doing up at this hour?"

"It's 6:30," Brody said.

"Oh, well - I lost track of time. I need to get dressed." Luca stood and stretched. He flinched with the tenderness in his back.

"Are you in pain?" Brody asked.

"Not really, just a little uncomfortable," Luca said, looking down at the cold cup of coffee. "I am hungry."

Luca stepped around Brody, who did not appear to want to move.

"Luca, I'm going with you, so plan for two," Brody stated.

Luca continued upstairs without acknowledging him or his request. He went to change before heading to the kitchen. A navy suit and a red tie would be appropriate for the courthouse and would not draw attention. He tamed his hair and trimmed his face, leaving a little scruff. He needed to borrow a pair of glasses from Gavin.

What is the plan, Luca?' Rusty asked after Luca sat with his breakfast.

"I am going to the courthouse. Maybe I can convince Bruscoe; that Froste sent me in his place," Luca said.

"You're going to act like an attorney?" Brody nearly choked.

"No, Brody, I'm not acting as an attorney. Rusty, would you get Froste for me?"

Rusty left to go upstairs and fetch Arna Froste.

"You *are* an attorney?" Brody asked; his brows rose an inch over his eyes.

Luca scooped up a forkful of hash browns but did not answer.

Gavin sat watching with amusement. Brody was slowly learning so many things. This team was very diverse.

The Sapphire Ghost

"I need to get with Froste." Luca stood to leave. "Brody, get dressed."

Brody looked to Gavin for answers. "Is he a lawyer? When did he have time to go to law school?"

"New York University," Gavin said with a playful smile.

Brody shook his head, thinking. *What else do I not know? I thought he joined the military out of school.*

"He graduated from Loyola University at eighteen and left home. His father wanted him to attend culinary school and thought Luca joined the Army when he left. That is all I know. He doesn't talk about that time in his life." Gavin studied Brody. "He is taking you with him. Did you insist on that?"

"I told him to plan for two," Brody replied. "I did not think he would."

Gavin nodded with approval.

Brody excused himself to change. He wanted to sit in on the meeting with Froste.

Luca and Froste were in the living room with Gavin. Brody acknowledged the tension and Froste's unwillingness to speak.

"Mr. Froste, I will do everything I can to keep you and your wife safely tucked away until Bruscoe is no longer a threat. Please understand that I can do things to you that would make a trip to hell look like ice skating in the park," Gavin said.

"You must understand also, Froste replied. This is not just Bruscoe; the hierarchy runs too high for you to protect me. They will come for me, and they will *kill* me. The things I know, the players involved, will send the most perverse hunting dog they have."

Gavin sat back, examining Froste, who appeared to be a timid bird.

Luca relaxed back onto the sofa. He adjusted the eyeglasses. Arna Froste was not scared. He was something else. Something he could not put his finger on. The thin man had teeth too big for his mouth, his eyes glistened with tears that never fell, and his skin was smooth even though he was in his sixties.

"What did you do before Bruscoe picked you up?" Luca asked.

"I handled his divorce," Froste replied.

Luca smiled and nodded. Gavin looked at Luca's expression and remembered seeing the same face yesterday in the bar. Luca stood, took the jacket from the chair, and left the room. Gavin followed him out.

"You think you know something?" Gavin asked.

"Yes, Duncan Bruscoe Jr. has never been divorced and has been married to his college sweetheart for eight years. That man is lying. Do not send him to Detroit. Send him to the Fortress," Luca said, thinking Froste might be trying to find the compound.

"I know and feel that this man's ties run deeper than he wants to tell. I'm going to work on him for that information later."

"All the way to the top, wherever that ends," Luca said. "First chance he gets, he will call someone, and they will strike us."

Gavin had already reached the same conclusion: Arna Froste was more than an attorney, and the threat of having Froste in the house was too high.

"Let us keep him where we can see him until we leave. I will decide what to do then," Gavin stated. He knew what he needed to do. Froste saw each of them, and if there was a chance of him getting away, that was something Gavin wouldn't risk. Not even for all the information Froste held in his head. The thought was disappointing.

"All right, I guess I need to finish getting ready. I have a big day," Luca said and slipped down to the basement.

Luca examined the wall of knives, each perfectly balanced, and none could be bought in a store. He handled several, picking them up and feeling the cold steel in his hands. Brody came down to see what Luca wanted him to do. Brody watched Luca, who appeared like a surgeon trying to decide on the best instrument. Luca opened the small drawer below the table and took out a tray.

"You do not have to stay in the background," Luca said.

"You cannot get a knife into the courthouse."

Luca smiled, picking up a small, scary black triangle with a hole in the handle to hold inside his hand. The knife was only two inches long, and he slid it back into the case and placed it in his pocket.

The Sapphire Ghost

"One day, you'll learn the word *cannot* doesn't apply to me." Luca returned to the desk. "I need you to stay near but not too close. Keep me in sight and watch the bodyguards in the courthouse today. If I get close enough, it'll be over in seconds. Have a car waiting."

"You're a lawyer. I still can't believe it," Brody said.

"I passed the NYC bar and never intended to practice law. I just finish what I start." He glanced over at him. "I hate liars, and that is all the law is, twisting the truth to suit whoever's purpose. I thought about medical school, but I hate blood." Luca paused and corrected himself. "Well, um, I don't want to be rummaging around in someone's body."

Brody noted the limp when Luca moved. "You hate blood, yet your weapon of choice is, well . . . very up close and personal."

Luca picked up one of the Appalachian knives handmade by a blacksmith. Their thin edges are sharp enough to cut a man in half. He walked over to Brody.

"Take it." Luca handed him the knife. "I can draw this across the front of you and be two blocks away before your guts spill. It makes no noise, and the victim does not feel a thing when used correctly. It's not personal or bloody, it's quiet and efficient. No one screams, there is no risk of a stray round, and nothing is left behind. There are cruder forms of blades, those big, nasty ones that tear at the skin, but I don't own any of those."

Brody held the knife, which lay quite nicely in his hand. Its edge was as sharp as a surgical scalpel. He went over and put it back on the table.

"That one." Brody nodded to the one in Luca's pocket, "What kind is that?" Brody asked.

"It's a self-defense knife for ladies walking alone at night, held easily in the palm and double-edged. Deadly, short, and mean, a lot like the women in my life." Luca extracted it from the sheath, placed it on his middle finger facing his palm, and then closed his hand. A look crossed his eyes, and he went back to the table. He clamped the knife down in a vice and took a round file, and he gently ran the file over the neck.

"That is what you intend to kill him with; it looks like there will be a lot of blood." Brody nodded to the knife.

"No, Brody, Bruscoe isn't going to die. At least, that is not what Gavin wants. He wants Bruscoe to see the destruction of his dynasty," Luca said and closed the drawer and cleared the mess. "Time to go."

"So, what're you going to do?" Brody asked, slowly following him up the stairs. This didn't feel right. Luca wasn't a hundred percent.

"Still unsure, I'll know when the time comes," Luca stated.

Gavin overheard them. He was surprised to hear that Luca did not have a plan.

"Gavin, this is suicide!" Brody exclaimed.

When Luca heard the comment, he stopped and turned to them. He said nothing and waited for Gavin to speak. Brody was growing bolder, addressing Gavin in this way.

"I trust Luca, and if he says he can get this done for me, he will," Gavin said.

That was all the motivation Luca needed, and he headed into his room to get his bag. Removing his shirt, Luca taped the small blade to the underside of his upper arm.

Chapter Eighty-Five

Luca stood in line, waiting to go through the courthouse's metal detector. He held the leather satchel under his arm and shifted uncomfortably. Brody offered him a pain pill before they left, but Luca declined, needing to be focused. He watched the line proceed. The metal detector beeped as he passed through. He came back, taking off his belt.

Luca didn't show emotion or hesitation at the metal detector. "I have metal pins in my right arm and left leg from a skiing accident."

The officer looked unconvinced and held out the wand. Luca limped to the side and raised his arms. The man scanned him, and it beeped over his arm and left leg. The officer patted him down, not finding anything.

"Sorry for the inconvenience," the officer said.

Luca nodded, pushing the glasses up.

Brody passed through the detector and stepped quickly, trying to catch up to Luca, who had ducked into the men's room. When he exited the restroom, Special Agent Tonya Simons walked past him, and Luca brushed against her.

Luca saw Duncan Bruscoe Jr. with two prominent men. Bruscoe scanned the area as if waiting for someone, and Luca stayed several feet away and waited for an opportunity. The hall was growing crowded, with groups jostling each other. Bruscoe headed to the trash can, dropping his coffee cup inside.

Luca stepped forward and bumped into him hard enough to knock Bruscoe off balance. He reached out to grab Bruscoe's arm and apologized while he braced him on his upper back. Seeing one of the bodyguards headed toward him, he found Brody in the crowd and motioned to him. Brody called the driver.

Luca left the courthouse, avoiding eye contact with anyone; he limped along, blending into the crowd. Once outside, he inspected the road for their ride, stopped, and waited for Brody to catch up. Alarms began wailing from the courthouse. Brody took Luca by the arm and led him to the awaiting SUV.

When Luca and Brody returned to the house, it was only 11:15 a.m. Luca went directly to his room to change. He listened to his messages. Rusty's plane arrived last night, and they had eyes on Marshal. Luca quickly showered and dressed in athletic pants and a T-shirt, then bagged his clothing from earlier for disposal.

Stepping over to the guard at the door, he said, "Get rid of these, please."

The guard nodded and left.

Luca gave Rusty a nod of his chin. "Just in case, call Helen and have her place you and me on a flight from anywhere last night."

"Something went wrong?" Rusty asked.

"No, it went too smoothly, which means I want to prepare for trouble," Luca stated. "Will not hurt either way."

Rusty took out his phone to call Helen.

"Do you need something for the leg?" Brody asked.

"Yeah, please," Luca said, exhaustion sitting heavy in his voice.

"Well, how did it go?" Gavin asked, surprised to see him so soon.

Luca smiled. "As you wished. He will never walk again, but he can see perfectly fine."

"Oh, Brody did not see anything," Gavin said.

"If he had, then many others would have as well. Wait for it." Luca handed him a phone. "Special Agent Simons should be calling shortly."

Rusty returned from the kitchen. "I have started chili."

"I haven't had your chili in forever, but I also haven't had heartburn in about as long." Luca grinned.

"Put hairs on your chest. I'm making it with turkey so that Brody can eat. Since he said he'll eat chicken and turkey."

"I prefer to keep my chest hairless." Luca continued grinning.

At the courthouse, Special Agent Simons heard the alarms go off and headed back to where a crowd was forming.

"What is going on?" Simons asked.

"Got an ambulance coming, Mr. Bruscoe can't move," said a man in a light suit.

The Sapphire Ghost

Simons stepped forward. Bruscoe was drooling like he suffered a stroke. "Can you speak?" Simons asked.

Briscoe's tongue moved in and out, and he mumbled something.

Simons' face became tight. The Ghost warned her. She looked around the hallway, and Simons felt something in her pocket and pulled out a flip phone. She grimaced, and her lips all but disappeared. *The Ghost is here.*

Simons passed the paramedics on the way out of the courthouse. She found a quiet spot and opened the phone to the only number entered.

"You said if I could keep him held," Simons bit out, but no one said anything.

"Special Agent Simons, nice to hear from you," Gavin said.

"Are you still here?" Simons asked, looking around to see who was on the phone.

"I never was. I'm a Ghost." Gavin replied calmly. "You know very well that you could not keep Bruscoe. I'm only helping. Now, he cannot get too far. It will give you time to build a real case."

"Where are you?" Simons asked.

"I am everywhere. Go home, drink a double shot of that scotch you keep for special occasions, and count this as a win. Get some rest, Special Agent Simons; you will need it."

"Wait, what do you mean?" Simons said, and the call ended.

Gavin took the SIM card out and dropped it in his tea. "She'll pull the video footage."

"Yes," Rusty said, looking over at Luca.

"The camera caught a Hispanic man helping Bruscoe when he decided he could no longer stand. That is all it'll show. There is nothing left behind. When they move him from the gurney to a hospital bed, they will discover the blood and the knife in his back," Luca said.

"Would the handle not have given that away?" Brody asked.

Luca sighed and shook his head. "You saw me file the handle when we were downstairs. I snapped it off; it wouldn't be noticeable with his dark suit."

"You make my head hurt," Brody said. "You think too fast."

Rusty came up, put a hand on Brody's shoulder, and chortled. "Feeling like a part of the team yet?"

"Yes, from zero to a hundred in 3.3 seconds," Brody said.

Luca poured himself an iced tea. "If you guys don't mind, I'm heading into a nose-dive. I'm going to sleep for a few hours. It has been a hectic week."

"Luca, I have called a carpet cleaner. Froste is leaving the house in thirty minutes," Gavin said.

Luca acknowledged that Gavin took care of Froste, "All right. Were you able to get anything out of him beforehand?"

"No, unfortunately. He wasn't going to talk. Froste had a pacemaker, and it shorted out," Gavin stated.

"Brody, get me up if anything needs attention. Otherwise, let me sleep. I'll be up for the final preparations for tonight," Luca said.

"No problem," Brody said, thinking he did have an off switch.

Brody and Gavin were watching Headline News at 3:00 p.m. The top story was the attack at the courthouse. The reporters were standing in front of the courthouse, which was still surrounded by police cars.

Brody jumped up, startled by the loud knock on the door. The kind of knock that only the police mastered. The guard came into the room.

"Black SUV," he said, peering around the curtain.

Gavin stood, and Rusty came into the room from the kitchen. The whole house smelled spicey, and Brody went to wake Luca.

"Luca, get up." Brody said, disturbing Luca out of a deep sleep.

Luca sat up and saw the panic on Brody's face.

"What?" Luca asked, jumping into jeans and pulling on a sweatshirt.

"FBI," Brody said.

Luca took only a second for the information to hit him: "Get Gavin, the guard, and get to the house next door. There is a cat planter by the back door; the key is under it. Wait until I call." Luca walked out barefoot and observed the others gathered in the living room.

"Go with Brody, please," Luca instructed Gavin.

Rusty waited for them to get through the doors to the garden. "You ready?"

The Sapphire Ghost

The heavy pounding hit the door again. Luca mussed his hair. Looking around a moment, Luca took his ID and gun from the entry table drawer. Then Luca answered the door.

Special Agent Simons stood there along with her partner, Special Agent Wyatt.

"Can I help you?" Luca asked groggily.

"You Lucani Medina?" Simons asked. "Special Agent Simons and Special Agent Wyatt," she said, flashing her badge.

"Yes, what can I help the FBI with today?" Luca looked half asleep.

"We had a tip that a man matching the description of an attacker at the courthouse today was spotted here. May we ask you some questions?" Simons asked, looking behind Luca into the townhouse.

"Attack? Come in, as I'm sure your list is long if it is a thirty-ish Hispanic male." Luca stepped back from the door, running his hand through the mop of black curls.

"Yes, a little long," Simons agreed.

When they came inside, Simons turned her head to the gun and glanced back at her partner. Luca watched them eye the weapon, and he stepped over and tucked it inside the drawer. Rusty came out of the kitchen and glanced at each agent. His presence was daunting, and Simons even had to look up at the large man.

"What can we help the FBI with?" Rusty boomed.

"Just a few questions. Are you aware there was an attack at the courthouse this morning?" Simons asked.

Simons looked from Medina to the large man. Medina appeared to have just stumbled out of bed.

"Rusty Marley." Rusty reached over to shake Simons' hand. "No, we only flew in last night."

Simons eyed Rusty, dressed in a golf shirt and slacks.

"What do you do?" Simons asked.

"Private security," Rusty replied.

"Come in and have a seat," Luca said, rubbing his clean-shaven face and leading them from the foyer.

Simons and Wyatt took seats, and Luca stood back by the kitchen.

Simons studied Medina and thought she recognized him. She thought back to the man coming out of the men's room at the courthouse. She rarely forgot a face. He was not wearing glasses, and his face was shaved clean. Simons watched him for the limp and saw no indications.

"What firm?" Simons asked.

"Atlas Securities," Rusty replied.

"You been to the courthouse today?" Simons asked Luca.

"No, I left this morning to pick up a few groceries," Luca replied.

Luca did not like the way Simons kept looking at him. He wondered if she recognized him from the courthouse.

"How long will you be in town?" Simons asked.

"Leave tomorrow to meet our charge in New York City," Luca stated.

Simons observed the clean and well-kept space. "Must pay good."

"Better than the government," Luca admitted, hoping they did not want to look around. He was unsure if Froste was gone.

"Do you mind if we look around? I'd like to check you off my list," Simons said. I can wait on a warrant, but it would hold you up."

Luca looked at Rusty.

"Have a look around," Rusty said.

Simons and Wyatt stood to walk back to the bedroom they had passed with the bed still unmade. She peeked inside and did not see anything unusual. Simons turned on the light in the closet, looking for the navy suit. There were many suits and garment bags, and she shifted through them. Two navy suits hung still neatly pressed straight from the cleaners. A gray suit and a Kevlar vest lay across a bench in the closet. There was nothing to indicate they had not arrived last night. They inspected upstairs, and everything was neat. Several rooms contained clothing. She assumed that Mr. Medina and his partners stayed here. Simons found nothing that indicated anything other than what they said they were. Back downstairs, she indicated the door at the back of the living room, and Luca came forward and punched in the code. Luca walked downstairs with her.

The Sapphire Ghost

Luca stepped over and pulled the mirror, blocking the door for the weapons. Simons looked around the gym: the equipment and the wall with the throwing knives. Duncan Bruscoe's spine was severed with a small blade. She looked at the knives on the wall.

"Nice collection," Simons said. "Could you do a demonstration?"

"I wish I could." Luca pulled up the sleeve to his left arm, showing the stitches. "I had an accident," Luca said.

Simons observed the lighter skin on his right wrist, where he usually wore a watch. Medina was left-handed, and the man in the videos was right-handed.

"That looks like more than an accident," Simons stated.

"Hazards of the job," Luca said.

Simons indicated to her cast arm. "I understand." She smiled.

"Who were you protecting?" Simons asked.

"I can't say," Luca said. "That's why they call it private security."

"I could get a warrant," Simons replied.

Luca stepped toward her. "You could, but you would need your passport and permission from the Swedish Government to apply that warrant."

Simons stepped back. The shadows crossing the man's face gave her chills. She felt that Mr. Medina was not someone to mess with, nor was the big man upstairs.

"*Private* security that is what it means," Luca stated. "We not only protect lives, we protect their privacy, and I'm not at liberty to disclose that information."

Simons pulled out her phone, "Do you have any knives like this?"

Luca took the phone and studied the picture on the screen. Scratching the side of his face, he said, "I have an unhealthy obsession with knives, probably somewhere in here." He motioned to the wall and the knives on the table. "Take a look, I don't mind." Luca untied the ones on the back of the table and rolled them open. Then he opened the drawer.

Simons stepped over and looked through the knives. The ones on the table were beautiful. The drawer held another tray with smaller collectible-looking ones. There were small daggers with embellished handles and narrow Damascus steel-looking ones.

Luca still held Simons' phone and, while he had it, decided to look through her contacts. "Appears to be intimate, small blade. Where is the handle?"

"It was personal. The attacker broke it off," Simons said, picking up a silver knife with an ornate handle and something Latin engraved on the surface.

Luca smiled. "I'll give you a good price if you want it."

"No, it is beautiful. You've been collecting for a while," Simons said.

"Yes, I have been almost everywhere. That one came from a market in Italy," Luca said.

Simons closed the drawer because she saw nothing resembling the one found in Briscoe's back. She looked at the diamond board and saw that nearly every diamond's center was notched out.

"How often do you get back home?" Simons asked.

Luca looked like he was thinking. "About every six weeks. This is only a stopover."

Simons nodded to him. "We'll check the flight manifest, and I think we can mark you off the list."

Luca followed her upstairs, eyeing Rusty, and the other agent.

"Glad we could help," Luca said, walking them to the door.

When the door closed, and they saw that the SUV had driven off, they both went to the table, took out scanners, and scanned the house. Neither said a word. When they were satisfied, Rusty called Brody to come back. Brody, Gavin, and the Dark 9 guard returned.

"Everything all right?" Gavin asked.

"I matched the suspect's description they are looking for from the courthouse," Luca said.

"Yeah, I get an itch from that one," Rusty said with a bite of hostility. "She'll be back."

"I have a knife with her prints if she becomes a problem," Luca stated, his voice void of any emotion. "And all her contacts and numbers. She handed me her phone to look at a photo of the knife."

Gavin examined Luca at that response. He seemed tired and was irritable.

The Sapphire Ghost

"Go back to bed, and we will get you up in a few more hours," Brody said.

Luca nodded and left. He ran his hand up his back to where he had been shot. Physically and emotionally, he was done. They still had the burn to commence tonight and fly back to Destin tomorrow. Luca sank into a deep sleep.

Chapter Eighty-Six

The news was on the television, where the cameras were trained on fires in the warehouse district of Baltimore. The frame switched and showed several other fires that erupted overnight in other areas of Maryland. The reporter came on the air, and the cameras panned out, revealing a massive fire behind her in downtown New York City. The fire trucks' lights paled compared to the raging fire behind them. According to the news anchors, the world was on fire. Smoke blocked the sun, and ash fell like snow.

Gavin came downstairs, and Brody and Dark 9 were set up in the living area, working on the weapons and watching the news. Gavin stopped to watch the screen, and the world seemed on fire. The reporter claimed that several other fire departments and the National Guard were helping with the fires in Maryland and several in D.C.

The Sapphire Order started congregating in the kitchen, where Iris had prepared an early breakfast for their big day. Brody felt great in his dark gray Canali suit with a light blue shirt and a blue Foulard tie. Rusty was in his preferred Armani in a blue double-breasted pinstriped wool, silk blend, and red silk tie. Gavin walked in wearing a Tom Ford three-piece in charcoal with a purple pin dot tie. Luca and Camille came in a few moments later, and he wore a gray Zegna suit with a box check and a black Zegna shirt with a silver tie. Camille wore an Armani short teal dress and a black embellished jacket.

Camille studied the men in the room: Rusty, whose presence was so dominant and foreboding, and Gavin, the picture of elegance and refined taste. Brody, the newest member, looked much better in a gray suit that fit and made him look like he belonged in a Calvin Klein ad. Then Luca, his quiet and polished restraint with just a hint of mischief.

They were dressed and ready for what was ahead, but no one spoke. The air felt like broken glass, sharp and waiting to be stepped on.

Gavin watched Luca kiss Camille goodbye, and he stayed behind with his coffee while she let herself out. Luca's features were tight, and his eyes were

The Sapphire Ghost

tense. Luca strolled over to where Gavin stood by the window in the living area.

"Do you have a plan for the men on the ground?" Luca asked casually.

"Well, you know, I do."

"Do you care if I ask you to take care of them first?" Luca asked.

"Luca . . ." Gavin's voice grew stern.

Luca smiled. "It's not what you are thinking. I just thought it would be something horrific. I would make Marshal watch and think he was getting away with what he had done with a slap on the wrist. Don't worry; I already have what I need, complete. Have a little faith, sir," Luca said, giving him a confident smile.

"Okay, I will put on my show to entertain Marshal," Gavin said, thinking he might add him to the line if Luca faltered. "You are all set then?"

"Yes, Samuels is working on it; he has my specifications."

"Do me a favor, Luca," Gavin said quietly.

"Anything."

"Watch Rusty; he is not a hundred percent, and I am worried about him," Gavin said.

"I planned to," Luca replied, feeling well-rested and eager to finish this. Then he could deal with his leg.

Luca raised his voice, and everyone stopped. "We all know the plans, but we know that plans can go south. Stay vigilant and aware because I'm certain there will be dozens of Fox Phantoms on the ground," Luca stated. "If we have taken out King, we should know by day's end."

Rusty met Luca and Gavin when they left to go to the garden. "Sounds like this could turn into a blood bath."

"I am ready if it does. Helen has sent more scouts to Destin, who are watching for anything or anyone out of place at the airport. They will be bringing in the captives in a couple of hours."

"Well, you seem to be back to normal," Rusty said.

"Yes, I am feeling great and ready," Luca replied. "How are you, honestly?" Luca asked.

"I'm well; tired, but I'm okay. I might not be when I get back because Julianne will kill me herself," Rusty said with a half-laugh.

"No, she will not. She adores you," Gavin said.

A couple of Dark 9 members came through the kitchen and motioned Luca to step back inside.

"Sir, we have the equipment loaded into the SUVs. We will return your car to the hangar when we return from dropping you off in Boston. Let me know if there is anything else you need before we leave," Akim said in a strong Russian accent. "Lev and I are here for whatever you need."

"Thank you," Gavin said to the brothers in Russian and shook both their hands. The brothers nodded their heads at Gavin and backed out of the room. The brothers were on Gavin's Order's team before he disappeared, and Helen had yet to assign him Dark 9 of his own.

The silence was deafening as they all seemed to be watching the clocks, the many clocks.

When they arrived at the jetport, Marshal greeted them. "I did not expect to see you all here," Marshal said in surprise.

"I expect not." Luca smiled and patted the man on the shoulder as he passed to get on the jet.

Luca stepped through the door and into a small interior. Two more black-clad Dark 9 members stood at attention when he entered.

"Stand down," Luca said and motioned with his hand to sit. "That is unless you need to go out and stretch your legs?"

"Honestly, I could use a stretch, but we are under strict orders not to leave the plane," said one of them.

"Good, we could use an extra hand getting the equipment on here," Luca said, jutting his thumb to give the man a reason to get out.

Rusty's plane was not uncomfortable, and the seating was ample. It was just smaller than the one with the sofa and recliners. There was no way to avoid being next to one of the five other people. Their plane had plenty of weapons, but Rusty's did not.

Luca felt the nerves start in the pit of his stomach, and he pushed them down, not wanting to repeat the helicopter ride or relive the Ghost in the basement. Luca would feel better when this was over. However, he could feel that energy growing through him with that same momentum that Gavin had grown to recognize in the last few days. Luca was always like this before something big; the anticipation and the waiting of the unknowns. Gavin would have to come to terms with the fact that he had an abundance in reserve. Most of the time, it had nothing to do with what he wanted or did not want. This, however, was something Luca really wanted to do, and after seeing Marshal, he was unsure his patience would hold. Luca went to the door, started taking the cases as the team handed them up, and stashed them away. He also noted that Rusty was keeping an eye on their future ex-pilot.

"Find out if one of these guys can fly this plane if I can't wait until the end of this flight," Luca said when Brody came close. Brody looked seriously at Luca and thought about going commercial as he ducked his head to walk through the door.

"Okay, I will but keep your cool. You have this," Brody said as Gavin came inside.

Gavin looked at Luca with concern because he had heard what Brody said. Luca smiled and went inside while Gavin walked past Luca and directly to Brody.

"What did he ask you to do?" Gavin asked, looking up at Brody.

Brody glanced over at Luca. His eyes looked like two pale green marbles behind his glasses. Luca caught Brody glaring in his direction and Gavin standing in front of him. *What now?*

"Gavin, I asked . . . ." Luca stopped short at Gavin's confrontational expression.

"I asked Brody what you said, and I realize I could have asked you myself," Gavin stated.

"Never hesitate and reply honestly," Luca said, stepping away as he had more to do than worry about Gavin's impromptu intimidation.

"He asked me to see if either of the two Dark 9's were pilots," Brody said evenly.

"I ask, you answer; Luca cannot do that for you," Gavin stated and found a seat in the front. He did not care what Luca said, all he wanted to know was that Brody would tell him regardless of whether he thought he should.

"Well, Luca might just throw Marshal from the plane. Would that not be exciting," Gavin said when Brody sat across from him.

"No, not at all, neither Dark 9 can fly this plane," Brody said.

"Well, that is a shame," Gavin said.

"But I can, sir. I attended flight school and have nearly 200 hours under my belt, but I do not have my license," Brody said.

"You can fly it, but can you land it?" Gavin asked.

"Yes, sir, I can," Brody said.

"Good to know," Gavin said.

Luca finished putting the cases away and walked with Rusty to the front of the plane.

"Brody, what did you find out?" Luca asked in front of Gavin.

"No, neither one can fly." As Marshal stepped through the cockpit, Brody stopped speaking. "If needed, I can."

"Well, that is a talent you have failed to tell us about," Rusty said.

"I have flown for years but never got my pilot's license," Brody explained.

Luca took several deep breaths as the jet rumbled down the long, narrow tarmac. He wanted to end this and get it over with badly. He did not like the planning and waiting that Gavin was notorious for. It was just too nefarious and took too long for Luca's patience. He was more of an over-and-done kind of person or, at least, his future Ghost was.

Gavin watched Luca as his right foot constantly tapped, concentrating on his breathing. That restlessness seemed relentless in the last two weeks, and it did not seem to matter how many conversations Gavin had with him. That energy was not going anywhere until Luca disbursed it in one way or the other.

Marshal took the plane into the air, set the controls, and unstrapped to walk to the back. He needed to keep up appearances, and he did not think Mr. G. had any clue that he was the one who was approached to give them up.

Marshal thought he was clever in having the money sent in his wife's name, and if this group were keeping tabs on him, his name would not come up. However, Mr. G. was no dummy and would notice if he acted differently.

"What do you call cheese that isn't yours?" Marshal asked in his dearest dad's voice.

"Don't know," Gavin said with a smile.

"Nacho cheese," Marshal said and laughed. Then they all laughed at one of his awful dad jokes. It would be the last one they would hear.

"Marshal, may I have a word with you, please?" Luca asked and stood and clapped a hand on the man's shoulder.

"Sure, not a problem, Mr. Medina," Marshal replied, still reeling in the joke.

"I'm not sure if you are aware, but something is happening in Destin. Have you heard of anything strange?" Luca asked Marshal when he guided the man away from the group.

"No, can't say that I have been paying too much attention; it's football season," Marshal replied with a rehearsed line.

Gavin sat in his seat and watched the exchange between the young Luca and the pilot. He waited for the cabin door to be thrown open and see Marshal take a spontaneous flight. Luca had a mean streak when it came to those he loved. Gavin observed Luca when he seemed pacified by whatever Marshal said, as Luca smiled easily and remained calm.

"Thank you, I just needed to check. Someone divulged some sensitive information to someone outside our organization," Luca said.

"No, you would be the first to know if I heard anything of the sort," Marshal replied innocently.

Luca strolled up and sat beside Gavin, and Marshal attempted to talk football with Rusty. Rusty was having no part in the attempt as he feigned being tired. Brody, however, stepped up and spoke about this weekend's games and carried on with Marshal about the topic. Brody set the man's mind at ease with relaxed body language and a simple conversation. Luca watched Brody and thought this was precisely the style of person he needed. Brody had that ease and ability to see from point A to point B, knowing the ending of the story but not letting it show. Brody had a deceptive quality that he was unsure that Gavin would appreciate. Marshal left the conversation, returned to the cockpit, and closed the door.

"So, did you get what you wanted? Will we need the good doctor here to fly?" Gavin asked Luca.

"No, he skirted the questions as if he had rehearsed for days," Luca replied. "I thought if he would fess up or break down, I would give him an easy out, but there is no way that will happen," Luca said with a fierce determination. Everyone grew quiet, contemplating what was to come.

Chapter Eighty-Seven

Police cars, beaming blue and white, blocked the airport entrance, and one of the Dark 9 members gave Gavin a reassuring nod.

The hangar doors were closed, and Marshal taxied the plane to the space for the extra plane and stopped. He intended this to be his final flight with his employer, and he expected to be on some tropical island with his mistress next weekend.

When the plane came to a stop, the hangar doors began to open, and one by one, the four men and one woman were brought out and forced to kneel in front of the building on the sun-bleached concrete. Marshal paused at the sight of the exit, and Luca placed a hand on his shoulder to urge him forward. Brody came out next, with Gavin between him and Rusty, and then the two extra guards stood to take up the rear.

The usual buzz of the comings and goings of small aircraft was dead, and the entire space felt like it belonged somewhere haunted and devoid of life.

Gavin came down the stairs and watched as Luca marched Marshal to the line of people who were gagged, bound, and kneeling outside the hangar under armed guards.

Luca nearly dragged Marshal, his legs stiffening with each step. He could hear the drumming in his chest in his ears.

"It wasn't me, I swear, Mr. Medina, you have to believe me." Marshal pleaded as he approached the group of five on their knees.

"I know exactly who it was, and I have the money trail to prove it and a beautiful video of you taking a briefcase. I want you to understand what you have done and see the penalties for those actions," Luca said as he eyed the future corpses.

Luca marched Marshal up to the end of the line and kneed him in the back of the legs. This brought Marshal down to kneeling beside a rough-looking redheaded man in his early thirties.

Samuels stood, examining the situation from the hangar. He was the lead Dark 9 over the Fortress on the West Coast, and Wright requested that he fly out and help the Sapphire Order, because of the specialized devices the Order wanted. Samuels wasn't a large man, standing just under six feet tall, with a lean, scrappy frame and a bald head. Samuels walked out of the hangar and handed Luca a device, and Luca placed the remote in his pocket. Luca knew this team would not speak another word until Gavin finished with whatever he had in store for this group.

"I am the one you have all been sent here to find," Gavin said, standing in front of the group as he took out a pair of sunglasses to deflect the sun's glare. "Take a long look because it will be your last. But I have a question for you, and the one who answers it first will get a bullet in the head instead of what I have in store for the rest of you. Trust me—you'll want that," Gavin stated as he looked through the wallets and identifications collected from the people kneeling.

"Take their gags off. There is no one to hear anything out here," Gavin said, and a young woman in black came and pulled down each person's gag.

"Who hired you?" he asked.

Gavin marched the line with long, smooth strides like a drill sergeant. Two men were crying and babbling something that sounded more like baby chatter, and the woman spoke first in a crystal-clear voice.

"It was on the deep web. A call out for whoever could capture you and/or any teammate would receive twenty-five thousand dollars," she said, looking at Gavin without fear.

"Really! Only twenty-five thousand. I would have paid you that just for showing up," Gavin said and went to stand in front of the light-skinned young woman. She was in her late twenties, with her hair braided down the back of her head, in a black tank top, with Semper Fi and a dragon tattoo on her wrist. You chose the wrong team, young lady. What is your name?" Gavin asked.

"Treena."

"Are you prepared to die, Treena?" Gavin asked.

"Not really, but if that is my fate, I'll face it," Treena said, her chin up in defiance.

The Sapphire Ghost

"Your fate; that is a statement. Why did you come out here from Texas?" Gavin asked, holding her ID in his hand.

"My ex-husband took my son when I deployed, and I wanted to get him back," she said, with unwavering clarity.

"Your son," Gavin said, looking down on the young woman with a hint of compassion. "Take her inside. I want to speak to her later."

Gavin went to the car parked beside the hangar and took two large rolls of copper laid on the hood, and slowly, he began to unwind the first one. The Ghost went to the first man and wound it four times around his neck as he protested. Gavin continued down the line after the first guy resembled an Egyptian god. However, the third fellow, the one with all the cursing, stood and went after Gavin. Brody went for his gun, and Luca placed a hand on his arm and shook his head. Gavin stepped aside as the man bulled his head toward him, avoiding being rammed. Again, he wailed as he ran at Gavin as if going after the red cape of the Matador. Gavin walked up behind the man while regaining his balance, placed a firm hand on his neck, and moved him back over to his spot. "Good try," Gavin said, motioning for a member to stand behind him. Gavin finished the roll off on the man. He then twisted the end of the first roll of copper to the second and continued to the end of the line. He studied Marshal, tempted to finish off the roll on him.

"You can enjoy the show and know you caused this interruption in their lives," Gavin said as he knelt to wrap the last bit of copper line to an exposed extension cable from the hangar. "You will serve as a message for your new boss, and be sure to relay it for me, would you?" he asked the line of men.

Marshal seemed dazed as he sat there still as stone and his face white as a napkin. Gavin stepped back, reached inside his pocket, and withdrew a bottle of peppermint oil. He sprinkled it on a handkerchief and passed it across to Rusty, who did the same and passed it down. Luca was the last in line, and he placed the bottle in his pocket. Brody had copied the others and stood still observing Gavin. Yes, he was as cruel as the rumors. Samuels approached Gavin with a small box with a switch to turn on the breaker for the electricity. Gavin took the controller and listening to the remaining men as they begged, except for the one who cursed and threatened even yet. But each man here made a choice, and they would send a message back to anyone left in King's operation. Kingdoms crumble when the wages are slight. He watched the woman who stood inside the doorway to the hangar between armed guards and paused to really look at her. Her sin was wanting her son back, but this had not been the way to make that happen. Gavin liked her spirit and her composure, and she had not begged. She just wanted a quick death, but first, she would watch the alternative.

Gavin placed the handkerchief beneath his nose and flipped the switch. It seemed for the longest of seconds that nothing would happen, and then the first in line began to scream, then his throat began to smoke. The smell of burning flesh hit the air when the first man cried out. The current struck the second and then the third with all the cursing as he sizzled, his mouth twitched, and blood poured from his nose and ears. The electricity ran down the line as each man who knelt before the Ghost lit up with enough voltage to light the entire airport. By the time the current returned to the beginning, the first man's head had burned up and fallen to the ground at Brody's feet. The liquid from the last two men's faces resembled umber; a sick brown, greenish color as their throats were charcoal black. Brody felt his stomach lurch, and a vile taste filled his mouth.

The stench hung airless as if trapped in a bubble, and the only sound was the electrical current. It cracked and sizzled, and not even a bird dared to squawk. Gavin switched the button off and handed the control button over to Samuels, who disconnected it from the cord.

"What about her?" Samuels asked, motioning to the woman who stood rigid between the armed men.

"Take her to a holding site until I decide how we might best use her," Gavin said. "Find out what you can about her."

"Yes, sir," Samuels said.

Luca walked over to Marshal, took him by the arm, and pulled him to his feet. He then started walking over to the silver car parked on the left side of the building.

"Brody, do you think you can back that plane up, please," Luca shouted over his shoulder.

The Sapphire Ghost

Brody moved the plane, and Gavin walked over to the hangar away from the crispy corpses sitting in a line of black dust. He breathed deeply and watched closely as Luca marched Marshal to his car. Gavin shook his head; it was a beautiful car and had been a gift from him to Marshal.

Marshal's phone rang, and so did the phone of one of the Dark 9 members from the plane. Luca dug the phone from Marshal's pants pocket, hit answer, and placed it to Marshal's ear.

"He wants to speak to you," Marshal said to Luca.

Luca motioned for Gavin before placing the phone on speaker.

"You want to speak with me?" Luca said into the phone.

"You took one of mine, Mr. Medina. And I am sitting in D.C. awaiting the attorneys to get Duncan Bruscoe's bail. You are attempting to burn my world to the ground. Let me be truly clear. I will take you all down with me. Figure out which team member you'd rather lose first." A frigid voice came over the phone. "Let the Ghost know."

Luca's body became tense at the sound of his name.

"Message received," Luca said and waited to see if Gavin wanted to say anything.

"You have found me. What do you want to do?" Gavin said gravely into the phone.

"I already warned you about this endless pursuit. Now you will see what I am capable of." King hung up the phone.

Luca forcefully took Marshal by the arm and strode to the side of his car. He opened the door and shoved the man inside.

"Betrayal is never your best option," Luca said with an expression of deep malice.

He allowed Marshal to shut the door, but the car doors locked as soon as he turned on the ignition. Luca extracted the remote from his pocket, which ignited the fuel line in the engine, and pushed the button.

The smoke began to swirl through the vents in the car, coming out from under the hood like small phantom spirits escaping into the light. Luca watched the smoke creep like a sleepy ghost into the car. Marshal fought with the door as he tried to get out. The flames began a torturous crawl from the floorboards and up the windshield. Marshal curled up on the sports car seat like a life raft, but there was no water. Luca observed Marshal's skin blister, starting with his lips that puffed up three times their size, and more prominent blisters enveloped his eyes as the fire slithered up to meet him in the seat.

Luca did not seem to notice the flames were too close. He listened to the man inside the car scream. The air was soaked with cries so loud that the air ran away as if trying to hide from the bitterness of death. The stark black smoke and orange-amber flames erupted into the beautiful blue sky.

Gavin watched the coldness on Luca's face. The sheer evil formed on his features behind the smoke made him appear an utterly different soul. Luca's Ghost was here and present, and his sharp features behind the gray smoke were vaguely familiar. He did not move from watching Marshal burn. Gavin moved to Luca as the flames engulfed the car to drag him back.

He took Luca by the arm, led him back to the team, and motioned to one of the men in uniform to put the car out. Rusty flanked Luca and walked with them to one of the black SUVs parked on the other side of the hangar. Gavin pushed Luca into the back seat and got in beside him. Rusty came around to the other side after looking into the hatch for a water bottle because Luca was hot to the touch.

"Luca, are you all right?" Gavin asked as Rusty took the cap off the water.

"He knew my name; he knew I was there that night with Bains," Luca said coarsely.

"We will sanitize everything, and Samuels will take you to the meeting point for the second car," one of the Dark 9 members said when he walked up to Gavin's open door.

"Yes, thank you," Gavin said, still looking at the wrathful young man.

"Yes, he knew your name. Now that Marshal has given him our descriptions, he knows all of our names. Luca, you took the jet back from London, and Marshal knew you were there. This person did not see you. King figured it out from Marshal. You did not miss anything." Gavin spoke slowly and steadily, waiting for Luca to regain some semblance of himself.

"King is going to kill one of you," Luca said as Brody opened the front passenger's door of the SUV and got in just as Samuels placed the SUV into drive.

Luca sat between Gavin and Rusty, feeling pinned in and needing air. The road ahead was beginning to come into focus as the blaze of the fire left his vision. Samuels took the back roads and several other side streets, watching his rearview mirror. The other SUV followed. Samuel pulled back onto the main road and headed to a large hotel in the center of town with a parking garage and drove in and took a ticket. They went two levels up and parked. The drivers then instructed the Sapphire Order to transfer into another car.

Chapter Eighty-Eight

It took Samuels an hour before he was convinced that they were not being followed. He headed to Dremmond and the service road several miles up from the end of the compound. Another member would be waiting for them.

Gavin, Brody, Rusty, and Luca walked into the house after 6:00 p.m. The air smelled fresh, and they knew the caretaker had been there. Luca left the group and went directly to the shower to wash off the smell of smoke and burnt flesh. That seemed to be the only thing he could smell.

The satellite phone rang when Rusty placed his and Gavin's bags on a chair. Gavin took the phone to his office, saw the satellite number, and needed to send Helen a quick report from today's activities.

"Yes, Helen, how are you?" Gavin asked.

"How is the team?"

"We are all safe at the moment. A man who I believe to be a part of King's operation called while we were at the airport and threatened Luca with an eye for an eye," Gavin stated.

"Well, you have around-the-clock security, and Dark 9 has locked down the compound," Helen relayed.

"I observed, but I don't think it makes Luca feel any better," Gavin said.

"Speaking of Luca, how was his first Dossier?" she asked.

"Intense, and I think the call from King heightened his mood, and it became *very* personal," Gavin replied.

"We have a problem, Gavin," Helen spoke calmly, knowing this could send Gavin into one of his tempers.

"There's more?" Gavin asked, rotating his head on his shoulders, wishing he had poured a whisky before taking the call.

"Lucani Santiago Medina, AKA Luca Medina, has no paper trail prior to his joining the Army in 1994. He obtained his United States citizenship in 1996. However, no one has that name in any school system in Louisiana." Helen spoke quietly.

The Sapphire Ghost

"I see. How did we not know this until now?" Gavin asked.

"We only gathered his military records, which seemed substantial," Helen replied.

"All right, I will see what I can find out," Gavin said. "We are all quite tired and will only be here about three days before heading to Galveston."

"That is a smart move. I will have Grace meet you there before you leave to get Brody started on the assignment," Helen responded. "I am sure there is a perfectly good explanation for Luca's missing information."

"I'm sure," Gavin replied and hung up the phone.

He turned the chair to face the window staring out through the clump of trees that separated his house from the smaller one. He thought about what Helen said about Luca. Before getting upset, he heard Luca's words from that early morning in the basement in Georgetown, *all you ever have to do is ask*, and Gavin resolved to do just that.

Luca exited his room in baggy sweats and a white tee shirt. The team would be hungry, and if the community were on lockdown, he was concerned they had not stocked the fridge. Upon inspection of the refrigerator, he was unsurprised to find it full of meats and vegetables, so he decided to go out and start the grill.

Gavin came out of his office as Luca lit the grill on the balcony. Gavin looked around and found that it was only he and Luca. Gavin walked out to address this current revelation from Helen before he thought too long about it. Gavin stepped out just as Luca came in and blocked his path.

"Yes, sir, what is it?" Luca asked, noting the perplexed expression. He was dog-tired and didn't have the energy to get into it with Gavin.

Gavin observed Luca's eyes had yet to regain their normal light, grimacing. *Keep reminding him*, Gavin thought. Remembering Luca's expression as he watched Marshal burn to death.

"Luca, what's your legal name?" Gavin decided to be direct.

Luca ran his fingers through his wet curls and smiled. "My birth name is Lucani Santiago Medina, sir."

"That does not seem to be the case before you joined the Army," Gavin said, arching an eyebrow.

"The name given to me by my father upon entry to this country with immigration was Lucani Silva Montes," Luca said in a Colombian accent.

Luca did not wait for Gavin to digest this information. He walked past him to the cove in the living room, took down a painting of a shipwreck off the wall, and opened the safe.

Luca retrieved a small black box from the back and held it out to Gavin. Gavin took it and found a flash drive.

"That should take care of any further questions you may have. My identity, family, and the unredacted copy of the military file I promised," Luca said.

Gavin turned it over in his fingers, "You knew this would come up?"

"I didn't think it would take this long, but you never questioned me about anything, so I believed it was unimportant. There is one of those flash drives in each of your safes, and the password is the date we met. I always wanted the information available to you if you found or saw something questionable. I added the military file after we spoke. I didn't want to feel like I was hiding anything, even if I felt it insignificant," Luca stated, leaving him to go season the veggie burgers.

Gavin headed to his office, passing his room where he had told Brody he could stay until Rusty left. Gavin would sleep on the bed in his office. He powered up his computer, inserted the flash drive, and entered the date 06062007 for the password. Gavin opened the *Journal* file, revealing a thirty-two-page explanation of Luca's finding that Carlos Juan Montes was not his biological father. He also found out Suzanna Santiago Medina-Montes, his mother, was gunned down when he was six.

The journal revealed Luca's unrest as a teen, when he had trouble with the local authorities and searched for information on his relatives in Colombia. He finally found his mother's sister, who assisted him in obtaining his original vital statistics and sent him a copy. Luca spoke of his father's resistance to Luca joining the Army and explained why he used his original birth certificate when he entered the Army to protect his father's name. Luca divided his life years ago.

The Sapphire Ghost

Gavin sat back after reading the first twelve detailed pages. This file contained everything he had ever questioned about the young man who had said so little, and it had been here waiting for him all along. He read over some pages in the military file. Luca Medina was more decorated than he had initially read. What Gavin found on the pages explained some of what he had seen in Luca during the last couple of weeks. Gavin realized Luca had a long way to go before he reconnected himself. Gavin closed the laptop, deciding he did not need to read anymore. Taking out a blue zippered bag beneath the desk, he placed the flash drive inside. He would send it with the courier so that Helen would have everything she needed.

Brody sat in Gavin's room and thought about the mood today. The images of the men who were electrocuted in front of him, were burned deep in his mind. He looked at the uncovered tattoos on his wrist. Brody was unsure that sending that message was the best course of action. Although, who was he to say what would work in this war against the world's children.

The smell of seasoned burgers cooking over charcoal filled the air when Gavin walked out on the balcony to find Luca. The others had yet to come out of their rooms. The sun was beginning to set, and he saw Luca standing by the water. Gavin took two glasses, poured whisky in both, and joined him.

"Thought you could use a drink," Gavin stated as he came close enough to be heard over the waves, which appeared restless.

"Thank you. I appreciate that." Luca smiled and took the glass. "Did you find everything you were looking for?" Luca asked, ready to fill in any gaps he might have left out.

"I didn't read it all, and I don't believe I will," Gavin said, seeing Luca's features still hollow. "How far have you fallen?"

"Maybe halfway. I will not fall completely, even if it means I will stay where I am. Gavin, detaching myself completely," Luca said, trailed off, and watched the water come in inches from his feet. "On the battlefields, detaching and ignoring what made me human was easier. This is the real world, and I would rather see the faces. Sir, if I fall that far, I will not see you, and you may be unable to reach me until I exhaust myself."

"Halfway, that is where you are comfortable. Observing you, I was sure you had hit your climax," Gavin said and took a drink. He felt the gentle bite and thought of what Luca was saying.

Gavin had watched him, the pure incineration of Marshal and Luca's characteristics. A heavy, dark fog wrapped Luca in a spooky embrace. Halfway, that was a good indication of how far Luca could go. The thought was terrifying.

"Tell me how. If you hit your climax, how do I reach you?" Gavin asked.

Luca turned to him. "Gavin, listen carefully." His voice quaked with a caustic tone. "There will be no reaching me. You'll need to knock me out, shoot me. Until the object I tune in to is no longer a threat, I . . . won't . . . stop. Do you understand?"

"Yes, I'm listening. It is time to pull yourself back and let the storm pass by you. Let it go," Gavin coaxed.

They stood there, and Luca focused on the steady sloshing of the water and felt harmony in the ocean's music. Marshal was dead, and his fury was released.

"How do you do it, sir?" Luca asked, "I mean, how do you ever trust anyone?"

"If I never trusted anyone, I would truly live a lonely life," Gavin said. He took a long drink, winced, and welcomed the heat as it hit his throat. "Trust is earned, and sometimes those I give it to disappoint me, but that is part of the process."

"I feel I should've seen something," Luca confessed.

"Luca, look out there and look closely and tell me what you see," Gavin said.

Luca peered out over the purplish waters with creamy pinks and yellows on the horizon of the setting sun.

"I see beauty," Luca replied, trying to decipher the colors mingling together.

"We fail to see that the elements are as emotional as human nature, but they always withdraw from their tantrums and subside like a child would being content with a lollipop," Gavin stated as he looked out onto the sea.

"It is by God's design. We are meant to feel inadequate in contrast to the obsessive beauty and the devastating misery that only nature can bring. Only man would feel compelled to try his hand at a paltry replication. However, that has never stopped the artist or the monstrous hearts from trying. We can't predict human behavior any more than we can predict the elements."

Gavin stood quietly and inhaled the salty, cool evening air. A couple of pelicans called above as they circled, looking for crabs. Luca kicked at the sand with his bare foot.

"I think I understand," Luca finally said. "Storms come, and they go, and we pick up the trash and watch as the air clears, and the world sits up to take on another day. We try again."

"Good summation," Gavin remarked. "And I will continue to remind you to walk through the storm, and you must learn to let go of the debris."

"Thank you," Luca said, then asked, "What if I *am* the storm I run from?"

"We will take one day at a time," Gavin said.

The two stood out and finished their drinks before they heard Rusty call from the balcony. "Hey guys, did someone forget the burgers?"

"No, I will be right up," Luca yelled back. He headed to the house and noticed the woman next door sitting on her deck.

The rest of the evening, they filled with good food and drinks and played poker. Gavin schooled the two younger men, but Rusty won more of Gavin's money.

Chapter Eighty-Nine

The next day, Rusty and Brody went to stay at the number ten house on the street behind the beach house. Gavin wanted to invite Ms. Scott for a meal and have a heart-to-heart. He knew why she had run here; that is the only reason anyone ever came to Dremmond.

Gavin wore a casual light blue golf shirt and a tan pair of slacks. He had seen Henley Scott in her regular perch on the sand and decided now was as good a time as any. Luca had already started seasoning the scallops and shrimp. Gavin wandered down the beach toward her.

Hopelessly lost in her novel, Henley was oblivious to the shadow walking up. Gavin stood beside the beach chair when he blocked her light, and she looked up.

Henley examined this tallish man, maybe fifty, standing over her without a reflection of surprise. He was handsome in a very refined way.

Gavin knelt by her side in an attempt not to scare her by looming over her.

"Hello, Miss, my name is Gavin. I am your neighbor just up there." He pointed to the blue house. "I thought I would introduce myself."

"Oh, hi. It's a pleasure to meet you. I'm Henley." She laid her book on the towel beside her and shook his hand.

Gavin looked her over casually. She wore a pink tank top and a pair of green shorts. A trail of tiny heart tattoos just over her heart led down to the top. Henley was small, maybe a hundred pounds, and her heart-shaped face was inviting with soft features from what he could see because she was wearing oversized sunglasses.

"Would you mind sharing what you are reading?" Gavin sat on the towel beside her chair, interested.

Taking off his sunglasses, he revealed beautiful steel gray eyes the color of distant mountains, she thought. His head tilted to see the title of the book.

"*The Book Thief by* . . ."

The Sapphire Ghost

"By Markus Zusak," he finished for her. "I enjoyed that one as well. It is an interesting story, and the author's descriptions of death are evocative. Let me know what you think when you finish. I love to talk books," Gavin said.

"This is my second time; I didn't bring any books with me, so I picked up a few at the bookstore in town," Henley said as she twisted a gold band on her right middle finger.

Being near her made him uncomfortable, and he did not understand why. Her easygoing manner of speaking seemed natural, unlike that of a stranger.

Henley liked the sound of his voice, low and gravelly, as if death was coaxing her. There was something dangerous hiding behind those smoky eyes.

"Would you like to walk on the beach, maybe have wine with me?" Gavin asked.

"Why not?" she asked.

Gavin examined her, and there was zero trepidation.

Henley stood and picked up her book and the near-empty wine bottle and glass, which Gavin took from her hands and carried. They headed to her house, and she went up while he waited on the landing. Henley freshened up, washed her face, and changed clothes. Grabbing a straw bag, she placed her pistol inside. Henley was not scared, but she had drunk over half a bottle of wine and may not be having the best judgment. It would be nice to have some company, but Gavin did not give her the serial killer vibe. However, there was a vibe and curiosity that made her want to learn more.

There was something about this man—something dark, something sensual. Gavin had the appearance of power and coolness from affluence, with an air that people did what he said. Henley did a second check in the mirror, and she headed out the door, leaving several lights on inside the house.

The temperature was comfortable in the mid-September evening. When she came down, Gavin was waiting for her at the foot of the steps.

Henley had the poise of someone raised in wealth, except her easy-going speech did not sound pretentious. Her clothing said very little about her lifestyle.

They walked for what seemed like only minutes, lost in conversation on their travels and art. He said he was a professor, but Henley did not believe him. Gavin's demeanor did not resonate with someone who dealt with fools.

Gavin liked the way she spoke like a dreamy whisper. Henley's energy gave a delectable pattern to her stories. She talked about her time in Spain and about the museums.

Getting close to his house, he said, "Would you like to come up for wine? A co-worker is staying with me, but I promise you will be safe."

"I would like that. I'm not worried about my safety as much as I am yours," Henley said, and her smile gave a challenge.

"Interesting, care to elaborate?" he asked.

"No." Again, her face lit up with a knowing inflection.

Luca was sitting on the balcony when they came up. "Luca, I want you to meet Henley Scott, our current neighbor."

"Ms. Scott, a pleasure to meet you." Luca held out his hand.

"Can I offer you a drink?" Luca asked.

Henley eyed the glass on the table, the bottle of Bordeaux, and a large tray of food. "Whatever you are having will be fine."

Luca went inside to fetch two more glasses and another bottle, bringing them out on the porch.

"I'll take mine inside. Enjoy your evening," Luca said, leaving them to speak alone.

"You too, nice to meet you, Luca," Henley said.

The next afternoon, Gavin again went next door. Their evening had been pleasant, which should be enough to let Henley know he was safe, at least for her. It was time to address the situation that Helen had asked him to intervene in, and Henley met him at the door before he could knock.

"With all these windows, it's hard to sneak up on someone," she said, her smile bright.

"Yes, exactly." He returned her smile.

"Would you like coffee? I made a fresh pot," Henley asked.

"That sounds great," Gavin replied.

"What do you like in your coffee?" she asked.

The Sapphire Ghost

"Whisky," Gavin replied because he needed to speak with her and wanted to be gentle.

"I have that," Henley said and went to the cabinet to retrieve a bottle of Irish Whiskey she had bought a week ago.

"What are you doing here, Henley?" Gavin asked her in a gravelly tone.

"I'm unsure what you mean; holiday as you are," Henley replied, seemingly skeptical of the question and turning the ring, taking comfort in the smoothness.

"I'm certain you are not because nice ladies like yourself do not holiday alone. Are you running from someone? Maybe I can help," he said with too much tenderness.

"Well . . . if I answer your question, you must answer mine," Henley said, not wanting to disclose anything to him she did not have to. She was enjoying the ambiguity they both shared.

"Seems fair," Gavin said.

"I have some problems, and they are of my own making. There's a certain agency breathing down on me, and I have not figured out how I'll handle the situation," Henley confessed and waited for Gavin's response.

"FBI? Do you know the agent's name?" Gavin asked quietly, but his eyes said he knew more.

"Thomas Fagan," Henley said with a questioning look that yelled *how do you know?*

Gavin's eyebrows rose at the name. The very man he had recruited and had a long-standing relationship working with rescuing children from several ports.

"Your shelter, what's the name?" Gavin asked, wondering if she would be honest.

"Haven Center in Kentucky," she replied, puzzled. How did you know I ran a shelter?" Her curiosity derailed, and her skepticism barreled forward.

Gavin looked at her and motioned with his hand to give him a moment, then walked out of the house, closing the door behind him. Taking out the phone and dialing a familiar number, Thomas answered on the second ring.

"Thomas," Gavin said when Fagan answered.

"Sir, what can I do for you?" Thomas Fagan asked, feeling his stomach flip as it always did when the Ghost called him.

"First, thank you for assisting in Maryland," Gavin said.

"I hope you know you can count on me, even if the situation seems different," Fagan replied.

"Yes, Thomas. Thank you. I need information on another matter. You are investigating Haven Center," he said rather than asking. "Tell me why?" Gavin was not questioning Helen, only confirming.

"The Director, a woman by the name of Henley Scott, took a shipping container full of children out from under our noses," Fagan replied, wondering where this was going.

"I will get back to you," Gavin said, hit the end button, and walked back into the house. "Henley, would you mind if I visited Haven Center?" Gavin asked, observing her with pent-up nerves on full display; she reminded him of Luca.

"Why would you want to do that?" Henley asked, sure it was time to find another place to hide.

"Covenant Holdings," Gavin said and waited for her reaction.

"You're a donor," Henley tripped over the words as she managed to get them out of her mouth.

"Yes, Henley, and something more," Gavin said, "Do you still want to ask your question now?"

Henley examined his unyielding features and daring look in those pools of gray. She wanted to ask him many questions, but the suggestion in his eyes said she had better not.

"Yes and no. I believe you've already answered my question."

"I am curious." Gavin's face took on a kindness again.

"You and Luca are not professors."

"No," he said, relieved.

"Henley, go home to the Center. Next Wednesday, I'll visit, and I would appreciate a tour—a real tour. Then, the Deputy Director of Special Operations Thomas Fagan will join us after I have viewed the place," Gavin instructed.

The Sapphire Ghost

"Wait, what?" Henley said, her brows knitted together.

"Please understand I'll not put you in any danger. Let me resolve this for you, but I have to do it my way," Gavin stated.

Henley went to sit in the yellow chair and stared at Gavin, shaking her head. She had been around influential people in her world, some pretty scary ones. But Gavin Garrison was in a league of his own, and he dominated his world, and if he could not, he would break it like a colt.

Luca quietly sat on the balcony. Although he knew security was all around, he kept an eye on Gavin and had Brody watch Rusty. That voice still resonated in his mind, *'Which do you want to lose first?'* King had asked. Luca could not comprehend losing any of them, but his gut told him, King would fulfill his promise soon.

Grace would be here tomorrow, and then they would take Rusty to the airport to fly out. At least Rusty would be safe. Grace would go over her and Brody's mission in Los Angeles, and then it would be back to just him and Gavin. The Ghost and the one in training, and he hoped he still had many years of training. His allegiance to this Order was profound.

Chapter Ninety

September 27

Grace stepped off the light gray Learjet with a black snake painted across the body. Luca, Rusty, Brody, and Gavin watched Grace saunter toward them. Luca mainly wanted to see Brody's reaction, and if it were anything like his own the first time he saw Grace, this would be hilarious. Brody sees himself as somewhat of a lady's man.

Gavin stood beside the car; his hands clasped in front of him. Luca and Brody watched as the redhead advanced in their direction. Grace wore a short white leather jacket, a low-cut red blouse, and black pencil pants with her signature four-inch black Christian Louboutin's. The way she walked made men want to stop and gawk because she was not the skinny kind of girl. She had full-on curves in all the right places. Brody put on a pair of sunglasses to view the beautiful woman. Her lips were full and red without the slightest hint of a smile, and her hips were round. In those heels, Grace looked tall.

A moment later, Gavin saw Clarence coming off the plane with a box with a black covering, and he shuttered.

"Gavin, you look delectable," Grace said when she bypassed the others and headed straight to him.

"You do as well, my dear," Gavin stated as he kissed her cheek.

"Rusty, you are looking well." Grace glanced at him, silently watching Clarence bring the box toward the SUV.

"I am, and you are as lovely as ever," Rusty said, grazing her cheek.

"Luca, how are you?" Grace acknowledged him.

"I'm good, Grace, and I'll take Joy from here," Luca said and smiled at Grace, took the box by the top handle, and placed it in the hatch of the black SUV.

"And you must be Brody," Grace cooed as she looked him over.

"Yes, ma'am," Brody replied and immediately regretted it as he watched her face grow tense at the word "ma'am."

"Just Grace, please," she said softly.

Luca tapped Brody on the shoulder, letting him know it was time to leave.

"Damn," Brody said when he got inside and shut the door.

"Yes, she is something," Luca agreed. "And she is your new partner."

"You're kidding me?" Brody exclaimed.

"Hands off, she and Gavin have a thing."

Brody loosened his tie.

"I had a similar reaction the first time I laid eyes on her. She is exquisite and cunning," Luca said admiringly.

After lunch, Grace wanted to examine Brody because she needed to figure out what part he could play.

"Brody dear, would you mind stepping out into the light?" Grace purred in a slow, appealing tone.

Gavin, Rusty, and Luca also stepped out on the balcony and took seats to watch the show. Brody stood buttoning his jacket before turning around and heading out the door at the redheads' request.

"Do not look so tense; I don't bite . . . hard," she said, winking at him. She was trying to set the poor guy at ease.

Brody smiled nervously and stepped out to what seemed to be a viewing party.

"Yes, Grace," he managed to say.

"Take off the jacket. Let me see what I have to work with. You can't go to LA in a suit, at least not like this," Grace stated.

Brody hesitated, turned to Luca with a strange expression, and slowly shook from the jacket. Brody smiled sheepishly. Grace looked him up and down, ignoring what was making Brody uncomfortable. The other three could feel the heat radiating from him when they saw what he was trying to hide behind the jacket. Rusty had to cover his mouth with his hand. Grace walked around the lean man of six feet two inches and ran a hand up his back.

"Take your shirt off, please," she requested, and Brody unbuttoned his shirt.

"I am beginning to feel what it must be like for a racehorse being sold," Brody complained.

"You are not being sold, Brody; I just need to know how to dress you before getting to LA. The style is slightly different, and we must look like we belong. So, consider me your personal stylist," Grace said.

Brody's chest was bare with a cut stomach and muscular arms he hid beneath his clothing. Grace reached over to take off his watch, and he pulled back his arm. "The watch stays on."

Grace eyed him. "Let us see, Brody. It can't be that bad."

Brody unstrapped his watch and peered over at Gavin, then Luca. He felt like he was being put on display and did not care for it. He took the watch off and stuck it in his pocket.

"I see," Grace said, studying over the line of shadowed skulls wrapped around his left wrist. "I believe I have a Harry Winston that will cover that," Grace stated without judgment.

Rusty looked at the tattoo and recognized it immediately from his days working at the prison. It was a Jaber gang tattoo. The good doctor had a regretful past, but he was sure Helen was aware. Gavin looked over the tattoo and said nothing. He was aware of the Jaber connection and appreciated that small detail. Gavin thought back to all the motorcycles parading through the country club. He was certain this tattoo had something to do with getting them to assist.

"I think I can work with this: good form, athletic, and trim. Do you run?" Grace asked.

"Yes," Brody said.

Grace took off his glasses, noticing the translucent green without the small spectacles, and handing them back with a nod.

"Good, that is how we will meet Elaine Pratt first." Grace smiled one of her dazzling smiles and stepped away from Brody. "I will get to work on a wardrobe. You brush up on the local lingo." She took the shirt from the teak table and handed it back.

"Not a problem. Who's Elaine Pratt?" Brody asked.

"You need to keep him informed of what is going on, Luca," Grace scolded.

"I will do better," Luca replied. "I will fill you in on the woman," Luca said to Brody.

"You still believe this will work?" Gavin asked Grace.

The Sapphire Ghost

"I don't see why not—we have tracked her movements for weeks and have a good idea of where to—bump into her," Grace said, giving Gavin a soft smile.

Grace sat across from Gavin and told the group about what they had planned so far, mentioning that most of it would have to come as they got close to Ms. Pratt. Gavin did not doubt that Grace would blend in with Hollywood, but he was unclear if Brody could. Brody was a bit stiff and had difficulty relaxing, as far as he could tell.

"Okay, I think you have covered the bases. We will be headed to Galveston tomorrow, but today we need to take Rusty to the airport in Ft. Walton to get back home," Gavin said and looked at Rusty, who did not seem to be in a hurry.

"Yes, I told Julianne I'd be back tonight. I have to show up this time," Rusty said.

Luca placed Rusty's bags in the Range Rover and waited outside while Gavin, Grace, and Rusty said their goodbyes. This would be a long couple of weeks, and Gavin may not get to see Rusty again before Christmas.

Chapter Ninety-One

Luca took the wheel and followed the other black SUV out of the compound carrying Brody and Grace. Gavin and Rusty sat behind Luca, talking. Luca tucked his gun between the seats and was ready if something went wrong. The SUV ahead of him was also full of weapons and carried two additional Dark 9.

Luca intended to ensure that Rusty's flight made it out without a problem, even though Gavin still considered the staffing excessive. However, he went along, knowing if Luca was making Helen feel comfortable, he was safe to stay out in the world. They pulled into the airport and drove past several large hangars until they found number fifty-four, and the SUV pulled up to the front. A young woman of maybe twenty-five with dark curly hair greeted Rusty.

"Uncle Rusty, I wondered when you would call me; Auntie is having a fit." Her dark face lit up as Rusty got out of the vehicle.

"I'm sorry it took me so long, darling," Rusty said to Danica, his niece and pilot.

"Danica, how have you been?" Gavin asked as he followed Rusty out of the car.

"I'm terrific, been staying in the city just waiting for my uncle," she said. "My, you are beautiful," Danica told Grace when she walked up beside Gavin.

"Thank you, and you are gorgeous yourself," Grace said pleasantly and honestly.

Rusty said his goodbyes and made Luca promise to keep him apprised of anything happening. Luca agreed, even though Rusty knew he would only tell him what Gavin permitted. Rusty placed an arm around Danica's shoulders, and they headed to the plane and boarded.

They watched as it taxied to the runway, and they returned to the SUV when the plane's wheels left the ground. This time, Brody sat with him upfront while Grace and Gavin conversed in the rear. Luca drove away from the

The Sapphire Ghost

hangar ahead of the other SUV and dodged a fuel truck that pulled out in front of him when the ground shook, and a ripple of energy hit the vehicle.

Quickly, Luca placed the vehicle in park and got out, looking up at the sky with a pair of blazing orbs and black smoke, which was where Rusty's plane should be. Gavin slowly stepped out and stared into the massive blaze stuck to the blue canvas. The high-pitched scream was caught in his ears from the blast. With his hat clutched in his hands, Gavin stood there in a trance as pieces of wreckage fell over the water. Luca could feel his heart melt in his chest, and the words of King came roaring back. Luca bit into his lip, gazing in utter disbelief. Brody lingered by the passenger's door, his ears ringing, and maybe bleeding. This moment felt unmoving, otherworldly. The massive ball of fire seemed to pause as if suspended in time.

Grace tried to find her balance as she stumbled out and walked up beside Gavin. Her head hurt, and she found the bruise with her fingers. She must have hit the window. She looked at the black ball of horrible smoke and the shock on Gavin's face. She needed to get them out of there because this was definitely a sign that King's men were watching the area.

"I'll get a search team here, but we need to go, Gavin," Grace said, taking him by the arm and attempting to pull him back to the vehicle.

Finding that place inside himself where he conditioned himself to do and not think, Luca walked over to Gavin, took him by the arm, and guided him back to the SUV.

"Get in. We have to go," Luca ordered.

Gavin could not take his eyes off the sky as the plane littered the porcelain blue with fiery rubble. Luca placed his hand on Gavin's head and returned him to the vehicle. Grace got in on the other side, and Brody returned to the passenger's seat. Luca took off from the airport without looking back to see if the other SUV followed.

"Do we have a pilot?" Luca spoke into the phone as he drove. "Yes, go to the house, pack for us, and meet us here in an hour. We have to go," Luca relayed to Samuels.

Luca drove around aimlessly until he received a return call.

"Yes, have him meet us at the hangar. Have them lock down the house and get out of there," Luca said urgently.

"Where do you plan on going?" Helen asked, trying to find space to ask what had him in such a state. Luca morphed into an order-giving commander.

"Galveston," Luca replied. "They blew up Rusty's plane," Luca finally said.

"Oh, no, Luca," Helen replied.

"Yes, they took one of us just as King promised," Luca said, and the heat was rising.

"I am calling in a helicopter; do not return to the airport. They will have it locked down," Helen said, thinking past this information. "I will take care of everything."

"That is probably best. Grace's plane is there also," Luca replied.

"Grace can go with you. We will get the planes to Galveston when they are safe."

Helen was impressed with Luca's composure despite what he had just witnessed. She was more concerned about Gavin and what this would do to him.

"Is Gavin all right?" Helen asked, wanting to speak with him.

"It's Helen. Speak to her, Gavin," Luca said as he passed the phone back to Grace.

"Gavin, tell me you are all right," Helen said when Grace placed the phone to Gavin's ear.

Gavin could not hear anything around him. The world seemed to be going by in a fictional slow motion. He knew the SUV was moving but could not see the scenery outside the window. The world went hollow, and he felt trapped by the image of the flames scorched against the blue sky. Rusty would never reach his beloved Julianne, and she just lost Rusty and her niece Danica. How was he supposed to explain this to her? The pain inside his chest broke into his ribs, and he thought his heart would burst.

Luca heard another ring and looked in the center console. The face on Marshal's phone lit up, and Luca picked up but said nothing.

"You're Next!" King said.

About the Author

EM Templin lives in a small town, cradled in the North Carolina mountains, with her husband and son; her career spans working with vulnerable populations, from children to seniors. She is a Guilford College alumnus, where she obtained a degree in legal studies. She loves to hike and spend as much time at a beach as possible and is in pursuit of dreaming like a child again. Writing and studying people has always been an obsession; she wrote about anything and everything. That was until empty nester syndrome set in when she decided to take her stories seriously while envisioning the what ifs of how the world should be. Collecting case studies and armed with a deep understanding of the people around her, she decided to write stories the average human chooses to ignore and twist a tale into a world she wishes existed. So, EM invites you into worlds of flawed characters who make large impacts.

Upcoming New Release!

EM TEMPLIN

THE SAPPHIRE GHOST REPRISAL
The Seriphin Ghosts
Book II

The Sapphire Order comes to terms with the loss of their dear friend. Gavin's determination pushes him towards reprisal, to end King—permanently. At any cost, and maybe his own life. Then things change, when a secret Rusty kept from Gavin emerges and throws Gavin's world into a tailspin.

Luca finds himself battling with his personal demons and when Gavin pushes Luca beyond his limits those demons emerge. Will Luca's loss of control end his Ghost before he has a chance? Will Brody be able to save Luca and his family when they find King is lying in wait when Luca goes home to say goodbye?

**For more information
visit: www.SpeakingVolumes.us**

Now Available!

JODY WEINER

RAISE YOUR OTHER RIGHT HAND
The Krafters: Partner In Time
Book I

For more information visit: <u>SpeakingVolumes.us</u>

Now Available!

NICK GREENBERG

THE CULINARY CAPER
By Cook or By Crook
Book One

For more information
visit: SpeakingVolumes.us

www.ingramcontent.com/pod-product-compliance
Lightning Source LLC
LaVergne TN
LVHW091614070526
838199LV00044B/797